CITIZENS AND SOLDIERS

The narrator does not restrict himself to merely delivering facts and dates. He is ever ready to pass judgement, to present his observations with irony, to sharpen them into satire.

Klaus Hofmann,
Modern Languages Review 2008

ALFRED DÖBLIN

CITIZENS AND SOLDIERS

The Missing First Volume of
November 1918: A German Revolution

Translated by C.D. Godwin

GALILEO PUBLISHERS, CAMBRIDGE

Published by
Galileo Publishers
16 Woodlands Road, Great Shelford
Cambridge CB22 5LW

www.galileopublishing.co.uk

Distributed in the USA by SCB Distributors
& in Australia by Peribo Pty Ltd

First Edition

ISBN: 9781915530561
Bürger und Soldaten 1918 first published in 1939 by
the Bermann-Fischer Verlag, Stockholm /
Querido Verlag, Amsterdam

Currently published by S Fischer Verlag,
Frankfurt am Main, 2008

This translation and introduction
© C D Godwin 2024

All rights reserved. This book is sold subject to the
condition that it shall not, by way of trade or otherwise,
be lent, resold, hired out or otherwise circulated in
any form of binding or cover other than that in
which it is published and without a similar condition
including this condition being imposedon
the subsequent purchaser.

Printed in the EU

CONTENTS

Introduction 7

Part One

Sunday 10th November 1918	19
Monday 11th November	46
Tuesday the 12th	84
Wednesday the 13th	117
Strassburg	151
Departure	174
On the train	182
The Pastor and the Widow	188
The Wilhelmshaven sailors	198
Of death and love	207
The Chief Medical Officer	228
They scattered like fallen leaves	238

Part Two

Shattering defeat	245
Floored	252
Hilde	262
Seaman Thomas	268
Strays swarm like flies	277
Greetings, home sweet home!	289
Funerals for the revolution's fallen	300
Bluebottles and corpse-robbers	315
Maurice Barrès	333
The last German days of Strassburg	339
Sprucing up, and disappearing	352
Snippets from the daily news, Berlin	363

Marshal Foch	373
The Forester watches the French march in	382
The Procurator seeks his son	391
Frau Anny Scharrel	397
Of deep and dangerous Germany	413
Strassburg, I must leave thee	430
ADDENDA	437

A Returnee
Maurice Barrès
Murky goings-on in Cologne
The Pharmacist
The Pastor
Anny Scharrel

NOTES	468

Introduction

Here, for the first time in English, is the first volume of *November 1918: A German Revolution*, Alfred Döblin's mammoth fictional recreation of the two fateful months between the Kaiser's abdication and the murders of Rosa Luxemburg and Karl Liebknecht. The English translation by John E Woods, published in 1983 by the now-defunct Fromm International and available only in the used-book market, not only omitted this first volume entirely, but also cut some 57,000 words from the subsequent volumes. Several of those cuts are restored here.

November 1918: the missing first volume

Towards the end of 1937, having just completed his South American trilogy *The Land without Death*, Döblin embarked on a new project, one much closer to home. As a military doctor in Alsace he had witnessed firsthand the chaotic scenes in Haguenau and Strasbourg following the Kaiser's abdication and the Armistice, and had written about them for the Fischer periodical *Die neue Rundschau*.

He and his family (now with three small children) left Alsace on 14 November 1918 with his hospital's staff and patients, reaching Berlin several days later. In March 1919 he witnessed the savage repression of the uprising in Lichtenberg, the eastern Berlin district where he had settled; his sister Meta, who lived nearby, was killed by grenade shrapnel as she fetched milk for her children. In his essay "On Cannibalism" he vents his anger on both the ineptitude of the insurgents and the callousness of the Social Democrat Minister of War, Noske.

Citizens and Soldiers presents a vivid panorama of fictional and historical individuals, scenes and events over a period of two weeks in November 1918. It appeared in

Amsterdam and Stockholm in October 1939, shortly after Britain and France declared war on Germany. So it had little chance to circulate, and only two reviews are known, both in exile periodicals. (See below for excerpts.)

When Döblin (a French citizen since 1936) returned to Germany in November 1945 as an officer in the Public Education Directorate of the French Occupation Authority in Baden, his main role was to censor German publications. he also planned to found a new cultural magazine – *Das goldene Tor* (The Golden Gate) was launched in October 1946 – and to explore republication of at least some of his own works: a new edition of *Wang Lun* appeared in 1946, and the first *Amazonas* volume in 1947.

In November 1947, after meeting representatives of the Karl Alber Verlag about their intention to publish *November 1918*, Döblin wrote to the publisher:

> I myself discovered at this meeting that ... the Censor (not I, in this case) had meanwhile rejected the first volume as not opportune for the French Zone. It is beside the point that I consider this rejection as unjustified and unfounded, of course the motive is political, they don't want to stir things up in Alsace. Anyway, as I had predicted, the first volume is out of the question for the French Zone.

The remaining three volumes (*A People Betrayed*; *The Troops Return*; *Karl and Rosa*) appeared in West Germany successively in autumn 1948, spring 1949 and spring 1950. This truncated postwar edition was the basis for the Woods translation in the 1980s. (Woods seems never to have seen the first volume: on page 34 of *A People Betrayed* the Apothecary says he returned from Strassburg "by train", instead of by buggy as recounted here in Chapter 1.) In

Germany the missing first volume was first re-published in 1961 (four years after Döblin's death) by the East German firm Rütten & Loening in a 4-volume hardback edition of *November 1918*. In West Germany, dtv produced a 4-volume paperback boxed set in 1962 (reprinted 1978 and 1995); and in 2008 Fischer issued *November 1918* as four separate titles in hardback – very attractive, but with disappointingly little introductory apparatus – and in paperback in 2013.

November 1918: composition

In summer 1937 Döblin came to know a French Germanist, Robert Minder. They became close friends, and Minder a staunch advocate of Döblin's works up to the 1980s – when he was sued by Döblin's son Claude for revealing sensitive family secrets; he died before the case came to court.

The two men made a trip together in Alsace in May 1938, to refresh Döblin's memories of the First World War and its chaotic ending. The manuscript of *Citizens and Soldiers* was completed in January 1939. In March, excerpts began to appear in the exile weekly *Die Zukunft* (The Future).

By May 1940 – a week after the German assault on France and the Low Countries began – the MS of the middle volume was complete. After the evacuation on 10 June of the French Ministry of Information, where he had worked on counter-propaganda since October 1939, Döblin entrusted the MS to Minder as he began a desperate and exhausting trek across the middle of France to meet up again with his wife and youngest son, including a tragi-comic incident where they missed each other by one day heading in opposite directions through the same little town. At some point he retrieved the 600 page MS from Minder, and hauled it all the way from Marseilles across Spain and Portugal to Lisbon, and then across the USA to Los Angeles.

By September 1941 this MS had been typed up, and Döblin revised and enlarged it to the extent that it had to be printed as two volumes in a four-volume "trilogy" (not a novel, he insisted, but a "work of narrative"). The final part, *Karl and Rosa*, was completed in February 1943, after both Alfred and his wife Erna had suffered serious illnesses; they were also in dire financial straits. The complete typescript of the latter three volumes was completed by September 1943, thanks to the loan of a steno-typist from the European Film Fund.

The place of *November 1918* in Döblin's oeuvre

The First World War never left Döblin. His last novel untouched by the War was *Wadzeks Kampf mit der Dampfturbine* (Wadzek's Struggle with the Steam Turbine), written between August and December 1914 but not published until mid-1918. His choice, in mid-1916, of the Thirty Years War for his next big project (*Wallenstein*) was an attempt to grapple with the meaning of the recent War: not just the politics, but the demonic forces lurking in the human psyche. (There were demons already in the *Wang Lun* novel. Carl Jung was at this time working his way towards understanding the same dark forces that he would later elaborate as the Collective Unconscious and The Shadow.)

The several essays Döblin published in 1919-20 under the pseudonym Linke Poot ("Left Paw") are not merely reportage: they attempt to expose the roots of a profound social and spiritual malaise. The dystopian epic *Mountains Oceans Giants* (1924) points seven centuries ahead to a world where 20th century trends continue to a dreadful culmination; the Urals War is the First World War redux. In the 1927 verse epic *Manas*, the hero's obsession with discovering the roots of sorrow and death lie in his wartime revelation: "This man I have just killed is – me!" The South American trilogy (1937-38) traces five hundred years of Europe's 'civilising' encounters with native populations; the subtext throughout is "the Nazis did not come from nowhere". And Döblin's last big novel, *Hamlet: Tales of a Long Night* (written 1948, published 1957 in East Germany) continues the themes (guilt, demonic bad faith, a meaning to life beyond the everyday) explored so thoroughly in *November 1918*.

November 1918: reception

Only two reviews of the 1939 edition have been found. In the exile periodical *Mass und Wert* 3 (1939/40), A M Frey noted the implications of the indefinite article in the title: "We speak of THE French Revolution, but A German ...", hence Döblin is investigating and describing "a deviant kind of revolution, an attempt, an insufficiency, a dubious endeavour ... a failed experiment."

This first volume shows why that is so:

> ...the 'respectable' behaviour, the self-righteous cluelessness of the Soldiers Councils, ... the devastatingly unfounded trust in their good cause, ... the cunning pretence of their opponents to yield while they gathered strength for the future...

Frey notes how the city of Strasbourg forms the spatial centre of the novel, this capital of the Reichsland Elsaß-Lothringen (Alsace-Lorraine),

> which never received the courtesy of being an equal member state of the federal empire, rather a quasi-colonial appendage ... never more than halfway German... Döblin's gift for encapsulating while spreading out, his overview into the small which in a magical way serves to illuminate the big and the whole, his observation and appreciation of the apparently incidental, his seemingly cool recording of a thousand banalities – all at once this multiplicity comes together to the reader's inner eye as a magnificent picture pregnant with meaning ...

Hermann Kesten, in the final (1940) issue of the Paris-based periodical *Das neue Tage-Buch*, wrote:

> With Döblin it is not only people who figure in the narrative, but also ghosts that sometimes appear in a naturalistic framing ... blood corpuscles and bacteria play an active role. Nature and History are not thereby anthropomorphised, rather they act biologically and biographically... This novel is a magnificent epic picture-book, where scenes of individuals are the cue for mass scenes, where individual fates are drawn out from the fates of masses ... The author shows events from many sides and the perspectives of many people ... Invalids and madmen, presidents and generals, workers and intellectuals, citizens and soldiers, all equally significant in an epical rank-ordering that has nothing to do with social and intellectual gradations, all equal in the eyes of poetic justice: bacteria and Herr Ludendorff.
> Döblin paints a sad picture of Germany's condition in 1918: the general weariness and dissolution, businesslike ideals and little religion, more obedience than a sense of what is decent, confused junior officers, moral neglect, and an absence of political goals. He shows revolutionaries with no plan or idea,

malicious or stupid citizens, glib leaders, smoke with no flame ...

The complete editions from the 1960s on seem to have attracted little critical attention until the 2008 Fischer hardbacks. Jan Süselbeck, in an essay at https://literaturkritik.de in November 2008 wrote:

> And so we have in many narrative retrospectives an emotionalising tableau of war experiences 1914-18, which put deeply in the shade the comparatively one-dimensional works of Ernst Jünger or even Erich Maria Remarque, which have shaped our concept of literary representations of the First World War up to the present day. Many doctoral dissertations, many conferences and collections of papers will be needed to come anywhere close to doing justice to Döblin's novel.

And Eberhard Rathgeb, in the *FAZ* on 23 November 2008:

> The best book on the revolution comes from the writer Alfred Döblin. It is called *November 1918*, and was written in exile. The novel is a singularity, and not just within German literature. In a grand manner he composes facts, fictions, events, experiences, history, philosophy, politics, poetry, diagnoses and drama, life-world and forms of life. It's the blue pool into which anyone should dive who would like to find out how it feels, revolution, history, and yourself in the midst of it. You can learn much from this book. Above all the reader learns in these 2000 pages [of the four volumes] what it means to discharge your duties as a historical person. In the German Revolution of 1918-19 no one gets anywhere just by reading the newspaper and chewing bread rolls.

Citizens and Soldiers

Passages cut from the Woods translation

The major cut in the Woods translation was an entire novella-length storyline featuring the failing writer Erwin Stauffer, who is introduced briefly towards the end of *Citizens and Soldiers*. Although interesting as a fictionalised (and rather burlesque) reflection of Döblin's own life, this is tangential to the main storylines of the novel, and so is not included in the present volume.

Other cut passages feature characters developed to some extent in *Citizens and Soldiers*, whose appearance in the subsequent volumes would have required tiresome backfilling. These are appended to the present translation.

One cut, a recap of American history from the *Mayflower* to Woodrow Wilson, has not been restored.

C D Godwin
Stroud, UK
Summer 2024

Part One

SUNDAY 10ᵀᴴ NOVEMBER 1918

She glanced with a slight turn of the head back into the room. The husband was sitting in his place at the table, crutches to the side, little cap on the bald head, newspaper spread in front of him. He was polishing his steel-rimmed glasses and assessing the grey morning light entering through the window from the yard.

"You can light the lamp." He: "It'll do."

She pulled the door shut behind her.

The rain had stopped, but the yard was full of puddles. In the entry by the wall where it was pitch dark, she hoisted her skirts, felt about with a foot and slipped into heavy pointed clogs. She clattered off.

The man scraped out his short briar pipe, sniffed at a tin tea caddy, and spread a few pinches of tobacco onto the newspaper. He snipped thick stalks off one by one, pulled apart a few big leaves. Then he tamped it all firmly into the pipe, topped it off with dust shaken from the paper. Then he lit up. After a few puffs he took the pipe from his mouth with his left hand and spoke out loud into the small grey room, as he did every morning once his wife had left. "So. It's the tenth of November," and puffed away contentedly. The paper was from the eighth, the parson in the front house had recently become less regular passing it on. The man set to work, arms spread, studying family news, furniture sales, reports from fruit and vegetable markets. "Small russets two-fifty. Oh, that's dear," took a few deep puffs, looked at the window, frowned, his wife was probably just now crossing in front of the water-tower, it'll be a swamp, they ought to pave it, but who's got money for that in wartime. He read on about apple varieties.

The wife was indeed just now crossing in front of the

water-tower. She had the brown family umbrella clamped under one arm, with the same arm she clutched tight to her chest the big black shawl she had pulled over her grey head and shoulders. Only one eye could peep out through the gap. In her right hand was a wooden pail with a wide wooden shovel. She approached the scaffolding at the exit from the open space, for years now there'd been no building work, ravens had taken possession of the poles, from here they flew out over the woods and the road leading to the barracks. She brushed the shawl fringe back from her face to see if the ravens were still on the scaffolding. And having looked and seen nothing she quickened her pace, for that was a sign they were already up and doing.

The long low school building at the crossroads housed recruits. The big gate to the schoolyard was closed. There were shouts, loud male voices. The woman, who had just stepped off the pavement in front of the school, heard the shouting. She frowned disapproval, but kept moving, she had to look lively. There the ravens are already, covering the whole roadway by the school, pecking and cawing, grey starlings flapped among them, and they were all intent on their pickings as if it was a field of barley. It was horse droppings, she needed them for her vegetable garden. The woman, still annoyed at the young soldiers, badly raised brats with their yelling, had already slid the umbrella into her left hand, a gust of wind made the shawl billow, the knot at her chest came loose, but the old woman ignored it. She set about the ravens with the umbrella, they flapped at her with furious caws, they knew the old girl. Sparrows flew up in a cloud and settled on the gutters of the school roof, waiting and scolding. Down in the roadway the old woman fastened the shawl at her chest as wind tugged at her clothes, she set the umbrella down on the kerb, the bucket beside her. She cursed the gang of ravens for scattering the dung all over the roadway, cursed their unmannerly way of stuffing themselves, then set about filling her pail. The ravens kept a respectful distance. When she'd finished shovelling and climbed awkwardly to her feet, those little thieving sparrows were already among the fat ravens, pecking and making a din. She jammed the shovel into the pail and retrieved the umbrella.

Approaching the sentry box by the wide schoolhouse with her full pail, she was nonplussed. She looked around. She meant to give the pail to the sentry for safe keeping, same as every morning, until midday when she came back from work. The lad wasn't there. Inside they were carrying on with their incessant shouting behind the closed gate, it was uproar. The old woman, pail in her hand, had a mind to knock and tell them to quieten down. She stood glaring, held the umbrella high. Then made nervous by the yelling, she turned about and stomped off in annoyance. To vent her anger she marched cursing through the swarm of birds. She turned into long quiet Barracks Road.

Every morning at this corner the blind artillery captain waited. He had risen just as early as her to take an unvarying walk of several blocks. He knew exactly how many paces from one corner to the next, with a precisely maintained length of pace he set off at seven sharp, the slender walking cane in his right hand preceding him like an antenna, he'd give the woman his house key, she'd go up to make his coffee before heading to the military hospital. There was no traffic on the straight road, the old woman struggled forward under her shawl into the gale. She kept brushing back the fringe to orient herself. The road was flooded across its full width.

There the captain was, tall and stiff as always in a black winter coat, brim of his black slouch hat bent up to show to the light his very pale narrow face, the lifted chin and the sharp folds at his throat. His head was tilted left, he had hearing only on the left, the same prematurely exploding shell on the firing ground that cost him his eyes had also destroyed the hearing in his right ear. In the town they said the captain was a bad man, his battery hated him, the men fired too soon on purpose to hurt him. The white eyeballs flickered restlessly. He heard the woman in her clogs and called in a military tone: "Frau Hegen."

She clomped up, bade him good morning, and felt as usual for the left hand that held the key. But he kept hold of it.

"Do you have time this afternoon?"

"This afternoon? Why?"

"You must tell me if you have time."

He was always stubborn, but she was too: "Seems you don't want your coffee today. Give me the key." He would not give it.

"If you don't have time this afternoon, I must look elsewhere." The old woman glared at him, everyone's behaving stupid today, she's been helping the captain out for eleven years already.

"I have to pack," the captain declared when she made no reply.

She pondered: "What time should I come?"

"Two o'clock."

"Good." Now he gave her the key, and as always they parted without a word, he towards the water tower, she to his apartment to drop off her pail and make his coffee.

The schoolyard gates opened, shouts filled the street, people were gathering on the opposite side. Young soldiers among them, unarmed, formed up, some were smoking cigarettes. At the front were several with rifles. Noisy, out of step, they set off down flooded School Road into the little town, which was still sleeping. Behind them trucks and cars came out of the yard, filled with shouting singing soldiers waving caps and red ribbons, some bearded reservists as well. They swept off in the other direction down the long road to the airfield.

*

In the military hospital by the airfield, an airman lay in a private room in the Surgical Station. The slate at the head of the bed read, in Latin: abdominal gunshot. The wide eyes were dull. The tall nurse in white, as she rattled the dressings trolley from his bedside away to the window, leaned down to him: "Feeling better today, lieutenant?" He tried to smile, and she shrank back. There were deep folds around his mouth, the nose was thin, the face had a grey-blue sheen. His voice was slow and slurred: "Thank … you … nurse." His head moved side to side, his fingers played. "You want a drink, lieutenant? Are you thirsty? I'll bring you something." Oh God.

She hurried to the big hall, the Station nurse was recording temperatures on a chart. They whispered. The Station nurse, cold: "Well, good luck finding a doctor." She shrugged, continued writing. Then she left the pen lying on the chart and looked directly at the younger nurse: "But why do you need a doctor for that one? Just wheel your trolley into the room with a big smile. He already had the priest last night."

The dressing-nurse's eyes widened. The older one: "Anyway, where is your trolley?"

"Still in his room."

"I'm nearly done here, just three more beds. Then we'll deal with the empyema over there, he really needs it. The other beds are moaning about the stink."

The nurse hurried away. The older one frowned again

at a thermometer: "You still haven't brought it down, Kunz."

In the private room it was just a day like every other. Ever since the room was there and opened its windows, every morning started grey, bright, brighter. The sun shone in around eleven when the trees across the yard shortened their shadows. Then the sun slipped away, the brightness lasted another hour while the room's occupant breathed and suffered, it grew dark, darker, night came. Now one man lay there in bed, fading. There was the dressings trolley, when the nurse tiptoed back in – by the window next to the bed, looking out calm, friendly, full of hope from its white-clothed glass surface. In the basins and trays lay shiny sterilised knives, pincers, scissors, clamps, sewing things; tall glass jars stuffed tight with swabs. Below were plaster-shears and bandages, uncovered. Thus did the nice dressings trolley bide by the window, metal glinting. It had swung in on white legs with little red rubber casters. The tall blonde nurse stood between the bed and the trolley, to hide it. It was necessary for the nurse to stay here, she wouldn't run away, death was calling to her.

Not much had happened to the young man. He was observer on a reconnaissance flight, the machine gun of an enemy plane was playing in the area, one bullet, as it flew on its hundred-kilometre journey, landed up in his body. A second earlier, before he straightened himself in his seat, it would have found empty air. Now the leaden round zipped through the young man's belt, jacket, trousers meeting no resistance, nor did the soft skin, untouched as yet by any lover, offer a defence. The bullet embedded itself as smoothly as if it belonged there. It grew from the world into this soft body like the root of a plant into soft soil. Along its path it encountered the mirror-smooth peritoneum, and made a little tear. The long slender intestines were in motion, but didn't shrink back when the bullet came, it was too fast, cut a path through tasting as it went the thin porridge still there from breakfast; the bullet carried none away. It traversed the gut. This enormous vessel undulated mightily, in it blood from the heart pulsed and beat, the bullet nipped, planted itself in bone behind, a vertebra, and stuck there. Meanwhile, along with the man in which it sat and the airplane, it was much farther off from the little gun that had spat it out. When they landed they unstrapped the man and did lots of things to him of which he had no awareness. The bullet was extracted from its hiding place, every tear located and closed. The little surgeon, always ready for a joke, looked up as he rolled the bullet between two fingers, his hands tucked into pale tan gloves: "So whose turn is it today?" Two assistant nurses called out one after the other: "Me." The doctor, still burrowing away deep in the body (he had dropped the bullet into a discharge basin) growled: "So, we'll have to draw lots again." One of them sighed: "Oh, I always lose." The surgeon adjusted his head mirror, murmured behind the gauze mask: "You're not the only loser." The war lost, we're lost, this man here lost, so wash up, wash the peritoneum, saline infusion, maybe he'll pull through.

The tall blonde nurse in the private room stood stolidly by the dressings trolley, hands at her back. She'd seen enough dying in the east, in Romania, and in the west. But still happening, now when it's all over, still happening. She pulled herself together, touched the damp trembling hand on the blanket, and held it. In case someone should suddenly come in, she pressed a finger to the pulse (but there was no pulse to count); she held the patient's hand in both of hers, he never stopped staring at the window. She didn't know what she was doing, holding his hand so long, pouring impetuous emotion into her hands. What can I do, she thought, she feared, she wanted to share her breath with him. The war's over, it's all finished now. He looked up at the ceiling. She let go the hand, the emotion was too much for her. You won't die, I'll hold on to you, you mustn't, what's your name, on the slate she read: Richard, come, Richard, hold tight, she squeezed his hand, the patient became aware, his eyes flicked to her.

Just then the door opened with a bang, a big red-cheeked young man in striped linen hospital pyjamas rushed in, his right shoulder was thickly padded under the jacket, without pausing he belted out: "Richard, hot news, they're here, sailors. Everything with legs is running away." The nurse had turned around at once, the patient's hand still in hers as if she was taking his pulse. The visitor was at the bed frame, he stared at the patient whose wide eyes were still fixed on the nurse. He let go the frame, clapped a hand to his mouth, said "Oh, oh." The nurse: "Please don't shake the bed." He ran out. She too left, on tiptoe, pushing the trolley.

The patient faded alone. Delicate tiny flora carried by the bullet from the air and from the jacket into his body proliferated inside him. They draped a sinister pall over the guts, dulling their sheen. Grey specks sank into niches around the intestines, which were still pulsating, rising, falling. The fungi strayed into the man's veins and let the warm stream of blood carry them merrily along, how blissful they felt in this sweet sap, so different from life in cold air, on cloth. Like an orchestra awaiting the conductor's signal, they set themselves in whirling motion. And now the human was a great hollow vault through which their music echoed. He lay limp, sweating.

Vines creep over the walls of the vault, they dangle into the space, it's a jungle and these are the Tropics, monkeys clamber, monsters with wizened necks, they crawl from the swamp, colibris flit with curved beaks, plants present their blooms, shoot out narrow red tongues. Now there's organ music, and sombre cassocked men descend the scales, they drag long trains behind them, they preach and exhort, it's a long dark song.

The grey daylight outside brightens. Hours lurch by. A day has set itself in motion, 10th November, Sunday. Little sunbeams slither across the bed.

Nurses come, support the airman's head, hold wine to his lips. His face (whose face) grows ever longer. His lips fall open — not he opening his mouth. They call out. They call to him.

But he's been swallowed by the jungle.

*

The room next door. It belonged to First Lieutenant Becker and young Lieutenant Maus, the red-cheeked man who burst into the airman's room.

Maus opened and closed the door slowly when he came back in. Becker regarded him from his lounger by the window. He waited until Maus had slipped past the little table that stood at the foot of their two beds. When Maus said nothing, Becker turned his head brusquely back to the window and asked in a businesslike tone: "What news?"

Maus, staring distraught at the table: "Richard's done for."

Becker: "So?" and again regarded the bare branches outside. Then he told Maus: "Sit down." Without thinking, Maus sat on the chair by the table. "You're sitting on the papers," Becker observed. Maus, head propped on elbows, made no reply. "You're sitting on the papers, Maus," Becker repeated. Trumpet sounds drifted in from the garden, deep, slow, someone checking his instrument. Maus spoke softly: ""It's all over with Richard now."

"I hear you, my son," Becker answered coolly. "War's a perilous business."

Maus: "We played cards just yesterday. I bought cards in town, specially for him."

"Quite so," Becker remarked. When Maus lifted his gaze to the window, Becker's eyes were glaring angrily at him. Becker's fine narrow fleshless face, parchment-white, was crooked, but he said nothing.

Then, very calmly, Becker said: "Have you been out, seen what's going on? What's happening with this rebellion?"

"I'll put on my coat. I'll go to the Internal Station."

"You do that."

From the door, Maus saw his friend reclining there motionless, frowning. It occurred to him that Becker had been horribly ill so long, he should have avoided mentioning death. As if to excuse himself, Maus called uncertainly from the door: "I'll be back shortly. Maybe I'll bump into the Chief Medic."

*

In the hospital garden, a trumpet sounded beneath black trees. It started a tune, then found a note pleasing and blew long and released it only after a while, then swung into a melody. The trumpet stopped. The man playing it, a tall thin figure, capless, in a grey army greatcoat over hospital pyjamas, took the trumpet from his lips and leaned against the tree, very slowly. Something brown, a little creature, showed itself by the fence, there were gaps at the bottom; it slipped into the garden, a little wild rabbit, it searched for food by the rubbish bins outside the main building. Where can I find a stone, lots of branches lying, maybe a thick one will do the trick. He squatted, felt over the ground for a cudgel.

At that moment something splashed and spattered against the fence and a laugh came from a window, the rabbit hup! out through the hole, it was soaked, the trumpeter climbed to his feet, readied his trumpet, began to blow again: "Know'st thou the land where the lemon trees bloom."

The Chief Medical Officer stepped long-legged through the main door, field-grey uniform with cap, no sabre, a tall amiable fellow, thin. He had a slight limp, people thought it a war wound, but it was tight boots and corns that made his life a misery. He was anyway a hypochondriac, they'd sent him to the rear because of his heart, arteriosclerosis. He'd spotted the wild rabbit just as it vanished into the woods. His concern now was where and how it had escaped from the hospital grounds. As he investigated along the fence line, a window crashed open above. He looked up, recognised the orderly, waved to him to open wider. "Where did it go through, Kralik?" The orderly: "More to the side, Chief, sir. They always come through there." A big gap. The Chief stood in silence, looking, the fresh air did him good, the wards were all overheated. He waved, and walked with forced steadiness back along the fence into the admin building.

His room lay to the right of the stairs, looking onto the street. He placed cap and gloves on the desk, freed himself laboriously from his greatcoat, and wiped his brow groaning. He rang the bell. Almost at once Kralik was there, eager for orders, a peasant type in paramedic garb, short with a brown bristly moustache. The elderly Chief Medic had already sat down and stretched his legs out to him. Without a word Kralik, squatting down, pulled up the trouser legs, tugged the boots off, the socks, and carefully rubbed the feet one after the other as they rested on his knee.

"They're softer already, Chief, sir."

"You think?"

"Always put bran in the bath."

"It's the boots, Kralik."

"Yes, the boots." The orderly fetched a pair of wide yellow army boots from the filing cabinet and helped the officer into them.

"Believe me, Kralik, the cobbler who made these was a true master. A Polack he was, on the Eastern Front." The thought came to his mind: where I picked up my heart problem; and at the same time the calming assurance: maybe I don't even have a heart problem, they just imagine it.

"Everyone on duty, Kralik?"

"Actually yes, Chief, sir." The man grinned: "Only the two new nurses from the town, they've stayed home, it's safer for them."

When the man left, the Chief made a note of the barometer reading on his desk calendar, read the room temperature and noted that too. Then in the left hand corner of the calendar, where sunrise and sunset were shown, he drew a little circle and a double-pointed arrow. This meant generally good health, and twice stabbing heart pains. He made no note about his feet. As always he then looked to the wall on his left, where notices were affixed with drawing pins: appeals for War Loans, pithy slogans:

> No fretting or frowns, The foe's hour is past!
> Till victory sounds, We'll stick to our last!

> *Subscribe to the Ninth!*

Another beside it:

> **For Germany's Freedom**!
>
> Envy and lust for conquest impel our enemies east and west to fall upon a rising Germany. In the east we shattered the Iron Ring and in the west we are successfully foiling the enemy flood. However heated the battle may become, our compensating righteousness shall give us strength to break even this surge! Germany's bounties for Germany's blood!

The Chief read this word for word every morning, it gave him strength. Next he made his desk nice and tidy before summoning the paramedic corporal to report, conjuring in advance some comforting fantasies: actually I've already come through, heart's not a problem, war's over, at least they'll give me my pension, I'll extend the orchard beside our little house, maybe acquire a neighbouring plot. He reached for the gardening catalogues he kept concealed under files.

Another truck full of howling soldiers rattled past, heading for the airfield.

What's going on? They should leave us in peace, not get up to mischief. Even these fellows! He opened the window. It's overheated in here as well.

When a knock came and he uttered a gruff "Enter", it was the fat staff surgeon from Offenbach, eye specialist, who delivered the educational lectures. The flustered Chief shifted uneasily in the chair: "Take a seat, my friend. You'll allow me to keep the window open." The staff surgeon sat down.

"Ah," the Chief murmured, "I forgot to thank you

for the wonderful lecture you gave in the barracks. Congratulations. You no doubt noticed how the men enjoyed it. Land must be distributed. We need space. A good idea. You know, even the ancient Romans provided land to their veterans."

The staff surgeon from Offenbach, flattered, inclined his head. He had a paper in his hand: "These are the topics I've drawn up for the next course, in accordance with the guidelines. If you are not too busy, sir …"

"Show me."

"It's the course ending 12th December. Because of all the holidays in the following period, from 12th December to 11th January, I haven't sketched anything out yet."

"Good, good, my friend. Very diligent. The appointment suits you, I'd already noticed. But that's not why you've come? Well. We must keep up morale." He scratched his head and mumbled: "Have you actually been out in the streets, my friend? What do you think of it?"

The staff surgeon bowed, beaming.

"Come, what's your opinion?"

"Very cordial, Chief, sir, highly honoured."

The Chief: "What?"

The Offenbacher blushed, made shy little bows: "I've not yet given it my attention."

"You may speak freely when I ask you."

"Most flattering, Chief, sir." The staff surgeon beamed with pride: "I'm sure the matter will be speedily settled, troops from Strassburg will be here by noon."

The Chief's eyes widened: "From Strassburg? Who told you that?"

"I believe Strassburg, or from the front. They're sure to come from somewhere."

The Chief frowned at him: "Strassburg. It'll be no different than here."

"Yes, sir."

"And from the front. You can wait a long time for that. They've more to do than round up reservists and recruits."

"Yes, sir."

The Chief Medical Officer pulled out a handkerchief and gave his nose a good blow. "Have you been in the observation hall? What's new?"

"Ten new flu cases. Two fatalities, one about to die."

When the Chief was alone, his thoughts strayed to the gardening catalogues. But as his left hand felt under the pile of files, his right reached for the telephone, he lifted it from the cradle: "My residence, Albert. – Darling? It's me. What have you made for lunch?" At the other end a youngish pretty woman twittered, chubby, lively: "I was about to call. Our phone line has a problem. I tried and tried but couldn't get through."

"My call came through at once."

"Maybe it's the storm."

"Yes, dreadful, isn't it. Well then, better let me deal with it. The butcher's?"

"All of them, there's nothing in the house. I gave your lad his errands, he took the money and he's not back, it's been two hours already. How can I start cooking. And today's your salt-free day!"

"My God, what shall we make."

"Don't worry, dear. It'll be ready in half an hour, cauliflower doesn't need much."

"I'll send a man out right away. You say the lad went off two hours ago, with the money? That's outrageous."

"The barracks won't answer. Should I go over there?"

"No, please don't. Keep indoors. Let no one in."

"But why so anxious, dear?"

He wrote down the fruit and vegetables dictated by his wife, rang for Kralik, who picked up at once, and asked

Citizens and Soldiers

for the artillery barracks.

Reply: "They're not answering."

"Try again. Tell them I'm on the line and want to speak to Colonel Zinn."

After a pause: "The artillery barracks is not answering." He flung the receiver down. He stood in a fury, agitators, ringleaders, hang up, run off with the money. He shouted into the speaker: "Paramedic corporal to me!"

There was no greeting when the corporal entered. He helped the Chief into his white overgown. Nurses ran down the stairs ahead of him, the Chief didn't see them, he stormed ahead neither seeing nor hearing, ignored the Station's scheduling doctor, through the first ward in the Internal Station. Down a side corridor lined on both sides with mild flu cases lumbered a figure with a bandaged shoulder. The Chief's face brightened: "Lieutenant Maus, in the Internal Section?"

"Beg your pardon, Chief."

"No need, I'll be there shortly."

"We were curious, Becker and I, about these ..." fingers wiggled "goings on in town."

"Ah, you know something?"

"No, I just thought the Chief might."

"Not a thing. Just ..." he pondered "the artillery barracks is not answering."

"On the phone?"

"Yes." Suddenly they were no longer Chief Medic and patient but two officers. When Maus said nothing, the Chief swept on his way.

A few paces on he stood facing his corporal and looked as if he might eat him whole: "Any disorder here? Are they running away too?" The corporal looked left and right, the senior nurse made herself scarce, the corporal whispered: "The people in this Station know nothing yet, Chief, they're too sick. But downstairs, Infections and Surgical."

The Chief was speechless: "What's up with Infections? The germ carriers?"

"All absconded without a second thought. Almost the whole Station's gone."

"And you tell me only now?"

"Sir. Report's on your desk, Chief, sir. I begged leave to report in your room, Chief, sir."

"And?"

"You didn't hear me out, sir, you left the room."

The Chief goggled at him, you put your life in play, they conspire against you, bandits, it's my salt-free day (just don't get agitated, hurts the heart). The corporal: If he lets fly at me, I'll roar too.

The tall blonde nurse had just finished her last dressing in the main surgical ward and was about to wheel the trolley back to the operating theatre when a door banged. Mother Hegen was at work in the corridor, behind her two orderlies were manoeuvring the airman's bed out of the private room. They wheeled it into the little room by the entrance, where cadavers awaited collection.

In the operating theatre, door closing behind her (it was empty) Nurse Hilde stood by the wall. The white tiles cooled her back. She moved away from the wall, inspected herself in the wide square mirror over the surgeons' big washbasin, she was wearing a white flat mob cap, pale blonde hair hung down past her ears, she flicked it back.

Not a glance at the pale grey full face, slack now, at the empty eyes. How used up you are with your twenty-four years. The war. Only now, at the very end, did it hit her.

Slowly she slipped back out of the operating theatre to the big ward, where the torn remnants of war lay tossing and turning. She sat at the huge central table, patient

Citizens and Soldiers

records in front of her, thermometers and ointment jars, and stared into space. The day was still windy, but sunny now. She slipped glumly into the kitchen, chopped ice for icepacks, and filled two. She hung these by a string on the two brain-shock cases and placed a hand towel over their heads. There'd be no visits today.

★

Frau Hegen had finished in the corridor. She knocked at the first private room on the left; the two gentlemen, Becker and Maus, paused their conversation and moved their feet aside. Maus sat on the little table and urged her to hurry. She knocked at the room next door. No answer coming, she opened the door. The room was empty, medicine bottles on the table, temperature chart, playing cards, glasses, crumpled handkerchief, all a mess. Window wide open. No bed, no patient. She began to scrub. Then she fetched a fresh bucket of water and started on the cadaver room.

Two beds stood tightly side by side covered in white sheets, the frames where charts and hand towels usually hung loomed like flagpoles. She worked around the beds as best she could. Her son was long gone, twenty years ago, near Saarbrücken, mining accident. Young people now die in war or in hospital. She scrubbed under the beds. She began a conversation with the two bodies: "Don't get up, it's all right, we manage like this with all of them, my mother's been gone a long time, and the grandparents." Suddenly she spoke to her son, he'd come home on a visit: "What do they cook in Saarbrücken? Mutton? You and your mutton, your dad likes it too, I have to cut it up small for him, he's got no teeth. What else he does? Not much. Sits in his room and smokes. Doesn't smoke too much, bad for the teeth, but his are all stumps."

She saw Albert, a little boy, down in the corner, a child's whip in his little hand, a spinning top between the little knees.

She scrubbed, banging against the bed legs.

★

When young soldiers with red bands on their left arms appeared outside the hospital just as she was going down the admin building stairs past the porter, he signalled urgently to her: "Take care, Mother Hegen, better come in here with me." Unruffled she turned the door handle, a big gust of wind, she closed it behind her, men squeezed past to press the bell. Shouting, calls, two of the men had rifles at their backs, stock uppermost, they made way for her, she tightened the shawl knot at her chest and clattered across the road, climbed over the ditch. She had a rabbit trap in the woods.

★

The young soldiers stood on the steps of the admin building and demanded the Chief Medical Officer. He had to be fetched from Infections. With two of the men, accompanied by his paramedic corporal, he went through the wards. The two presented themselves as the Soldiers' Council of the garrison. During the whole visit the Chief never once dared look directly at his corporal or the nurses. He forgot all about his heart and his boots. He was numb, couldn't feel his body. He showed the soldiers whatever they wanted, his voice automatic, apathetic. They thought he was feigning deafness, but really he couldn't hear. The sky was falling. To every remark from the soldiers he replied, "As you like." Every time they entered a ward (they avoided the rooms of the dying) the older of the two soldiers called out: "We're the Soldiers' Council of the garrison. Anyone have anything to report?" Which brought deathly silence, here and there grins and titters and glances at the Chief Medic and the corporal.

The soldiers asked the nurses about food. They flushed, looked helplessly at the Chief.

In the Internal Station a door was locked. "What's this?" The corporal: "Isolation room." – "Open it." It was a roomy cell with bed and chair, the high window was barred. "It's a prison cell! What's wrong with him?" The Chief, as the prisoner turned his back on them in a corner: "Observation. A deserter. Trial pending in Strassburg."

"Call him." The corporal turned the prisoner around, a strapping figure: "Walter, visit." A soldier-councillor: "We're the Soldiers' Council of the garrison. What's the matter with you?"

The man had smeared cheeks and forehead black, and drawn weird circles around his eyes. He stared mulishly at the floor. "Doesn't he understand?" The corporal, when the Chief cast a wild look in his direction, took the liberty of repeating the question. Now the prisoner seemed to understand. His face acquired movement, his forehead tightened in fear. He couldn't make his voice work, for weeks he'd not uttered a word. The soldier stepped closer, clapped him on the shoulder: "Soldiers' Council of the garrison. Understand? Where are you from?"

"Kaiserslautern."

"See here. It's revolution. The war's over." The besmeared man looked from one to the other. The corporal shook himself and stepped up to the prisoner: "It's true. The war's over." The prisoner sniffed. The corporal nodded at him. The prisoner brought his face close and said: "You're a swine." The corporal grinned: "He always says that to me." The two soldiers grabbed the prisoner's arms: "Come along, old chap, no trouble now." They dragged him out through the door, he struggled, shouted: "Help! Murder!"

"Shut the damn door!" the soldier-councillor shouted in a fury.

The Chief stood indifferent in the corridor. The soldier roared: "You tell him!"

"What?" the Chief huffed.

"War's over, he doesn't understand." The older soldier growled: "It's revolution." The man, like a cornered animal with his back pressed against the cell door, shouted, "Filth, swine!" It echoed through the wards. Patients gathered in the corridor.

"What is it you want?" the older of the soldiers cried.

"Shithead!" the prisoner replied and went for his throat. The corporal grabbed him from behind. "Back in the cell," the assaulted soldier snorted.

The Chief complaisantly smoothed his white gown. Slowly he regained composure, drew himself to his full height. For the first time he gestured to the corporal, who promptly presented himself at his side, notebook at the ready.

*

Around the same time – long past midday, the salt-free menu awaited the Chief in vain – around this early afternoon hour when day after day clouds gathered and a steady rain set in that flooded the roads, in a villa across the fields from the military hospital, in the ground floor lobby, a man and a woman hugged.

He wore an officer's uniform, epaulettes torn from the shoulders, the cap on his head lacked a cockade, he stood in tall yellow leather spats.

"Come in, Hans, come, please, no, there's no one here, you're shivering, just look at you."

"Your parents aren't in, Hanna, really? You won't betray me."

"I betray you, Hans, my God."

"Sorry. I've been lurking all morning in the stables at the barracks, they've pulled out now, I shall stay here. Can you find space for me? I don't want to mess up your living room."

"You can, Hans. There, cap's off. Take off your coat. I demand it. I've waited for you all day."

"You won't betray me, Hanna."

A pleasant quiet room, gaslight burning, bunch of roses in a tall glass vase on the round velvet-covered table, it was warm, a big black grandfather clock ticked. She wept on his neck. She was slim, older than he, dressed all in black. He whispered: "If you would do me a favour, Hanna. Your father has green leggings. I need civilian."

"I'll fetch them."

"I can't stay long, Hanna, I shot two of them. They're after me." She kept hugging him, saw now his grubby unshaven face, picked a straw from his hair: "You shot them."

"They knocked the colonel to the ground with sticks. He'd punched their leader in the face for insolence."

"And you?"

"There were five of them on the colonel. When he fell down I fired. Two were hit. The others ran off. I escaped through the window."

"You must stay here!"

"Your parents?"

"I'll take you to the maid's room."

They crossed the carpeted lounge, the young lady

leading, he turned: "My things." Then down a passage, through the kitchen, up the back stairs, door on the right with a key in the lock. She opened, it was a narrow room with a window overlooking fields, a bed, a chair, bare creaking floorboards, paraffin lamp on the table. She closed the door behind her: "Leave the key in. Close the shutters, then they won't see the light."

"Doesn't the maid come up here?"

"We don't have one."

She pushed the window up, closed the shutters, they were in darkness. She gave him a long hug. He whispered: "Forgive me, Hanna, for causing you so much trouble."

She felt how he trembled, knew he wasn't thinking of her at all. "Now sit on the bed. You can change later. I'll bring some of father's clothes. First you should eat."

She was gone. When she reappeared with a tray, since she couldn't see he pulled her in by the arm, took the tray. "When will your parents be back?"

"Maybe not till evening. They're together in town."

"Ah, the locals, the French Committee."

She lit the candles she had brought. He helped her unload the tray. "Thank you. You're a local too. You'll be staying."

"I am yours, Hans, and will always be."

"I won't draw you into our calamity. Be glad you can stay here. It's going to be a madhouse with us."

She sat on the bed: "Eat now."

"You'll have some?"

"Yes." When they had finished and the glasses stood empty, he was full and no longer trembling. He sat slack-shouldered: "I'll set off once it's dark."

"As you like. Stay for the afternoon." She snuffed the candles. Her black dress rustled to the floor. She wept as they lay twined: "You'll forget me."

"You have my address in Berlin."
"And then."
"I'll fetch you."
"Can't I come with you right away?"
"They're looking for me, Hanna."

In the silent villa, in the bedroom, tears, surrender, bliss, despair. Hanna opened the shutters, it was dark, rain pouring down. The front door closed. She was quickly downstairs. Her parents were arguing loudly, they were back from the reception committee for the French that had formed around the mayor. At the supper table the daughter yawned, her mother suggested she go to bed. It was still pouring. A window was open so they could listen for shooting in the town. But all was quiet. They ate and drank without speaking.

The daughter studied her father, he was bigger than Hans, but the sizes would do. After half an hour she got to her feet.

Towards ten she let the officer out by the back door. She whispered: "There's a little gate, you only need to push." He set off quickly under the opened umbrella.

In the meantime she had visited the druggist in town, her former fiancé. At first he'd just stood there in the back room of the pharmacy in his black leather apron, the room smelled acrid-sweet. She knew this back room well. Then he invited her to sit, she explained again from the stool what she had in mind. Now his eyes lifted from the table's lino covering. She pushed back her rain hood, lowered her head, and wept. He needed several minutes to master himself and agree. The officer should come over at once, he'd take him to Strassburg in the morning, in the shop's buggy.

At the front door, before she pulled her hood back up, she planted a kiss on the cheek of the serious little man, who seemed stunned.

SUNDAY 10TH NOVEMBER 1918

★

When the prisoner, a manservant from Kaiserslautern, had been left alone in his cell for a couple of hours and no one brought him food, he began to hammer on the door. The nearby ward heard, but let him rage. His behaviour towards the Soldiers Council men had ruined it for him. Finally during the afternoon they fetched a paramedic, who together with a companion opened the cell. The filthy man in the corner had lifted his bed on end, and from behind his hillock emitted thoroughly exhausted cries: "Grub! Grub!" He looked hideous, stank horribly. The two paramedics first opened the corridor window to air the cell. The man kept roaring from behind his barricade. Then one said calmly, "Ziweck, why are you still acting up. You really don't have to, now." He kept shouting. They caught hold of him by going around each side of the bed, and with the aid of two patients dragged him into the corridor, a mad procession, shoved him at an opened window that looked onto the yard and the barracks. The Surgical and Infection wings had hoisted red flags, two child's pennants poked out from the Operating wing. They pointed to them; he kept his eyes tight shut.

They felt he was no longer so tense. They could let go. He stood by himself. His face was apprehensive, he glanced mistrustfully from one to the other. A patient shouted: "Bring him a newspaper." They held it out, fingers pointed to news, proclamations. He read greedily, stood all by himself.

As if struck by lightning he lay on the floor. He jerked and foamed. The paramedics bent over him, sprinkled water: "He's still not all there." They emptied a whole cold bucket over him, flooding the corridor; the man clambered shivering to his feet. They led him to an empty bed, he slept till evening. Then he played sulkily at cards with the others, smoking.

★

In darkness Frau Hegen, soaked to the skin despite the umbrella, clomped past the water-tower, through the yard, and shook off her clogs in the entry. She was surprised to hear voices in her apartment. The Pastor's deep tones. She lugged the pail behind the little house, under the projecting eaves of a shed, dragged a heavy wooden lid over it. She left the opened umbrella in the entrance lobby, and with the big shawl over her arm creaked open the door to the apartment; all was quiet in there.

The gas flame in the frosted glass chimney hanging from the ceiling gave a weak ruddy glow. From the chair behind the table a big strong male figure stood up, the full healthy face smiled at the woman in amiable discomposure, the gentleman in his thick brown fleece jacket offered his big hand across the table and said softly, in a tone of practised gravity:"Here you find me, my dear Frau Hegen, a guest in your apartment. I was keeping your husband company." The woman looked around for her husband, he was sitting in the dark on the edge of the bed, waving a crutch: "We've been waiting for you, woman. What's the news out there."

The woman told the Pastor: "My hands are wet."

"Yes, the storm," and he sat down. The husband: "Pastor thinks the weather's just right for this commotion. People keep to the house."

"What commotion?" she asked, hanging her shawl over a stool by the iron stove. The husband behind her: "Pastor wants to know what's going on in town."

"My dear Frau Hegen, we were worried about you,

SUNDAY 10TH NOVEMBER 1918

you're back so late. I presume you didn't have to force your way through? Are they still blocking the main road?"

The woman mumbled, warming her hands: "What's going on, what's going on."

"Come on, woman, out with it."

They're all mad, no sentry by the schoolhouse this morning, now Pastor plonks hisself down here this evening.

No, main road's same as always, she's been helping the blind captain pack up.

"Aha," said the Pastor with a nod to the husband.

A long silence. "Well then, I won't disturb you any further."

The old woman opened the door for him. The husband at once hobbled on his crutches back to his chair: "He's been sat here all afternoon. Scared they're coming for him." She: "Don't you start." She felt in her skirt, a three Mark and a five Mark.

*

On his way back through the yard, the Pastor threw into the rain-tub two scraps of paper he'd found by chance in his jacket pocket: an old envelope, and a crumpled tissue from a cake. They lay in the tub for four days with the other rubbish, until the woman emptied it onto the midden behind the building. There the old envelope ended up, with its inscription in the hand of the Pastor's son announcing his imminent arrival back from Poland on leave; and the tissue paper along with cabbage stalks, cinders, crumpled tins. It all formed a slowly growing mound. The tissue paper disintegrated in the wet, trickled into the ground with the rain. The Pastor's son's writing was soon washed out, the envelope lay more months in the midden while the Pastor was already long since in

Hessen, in his home town, awaiting a new living. At that time his furniture was still in the front house, he was suing for delivery. In July a migrant family of rats came past the house, there were lots of potato and fruit peelings, they even ate scraps of leather (the lame husband felt stronger in summer, and was back at his cobbling) and so it was that the envelope too, addressed from Grodno to the Pastor, was devoured by young rats.

MONDAY, 11ᵀᴴ NOVEMBER

The sky was dark the whole night. An invisible moon cast a magical glow from its hiding place onto the few clouds that dragged heavily past. As day dawned, just like the previous day a sharp icy wind set in, the sky was swept clear, it was white-grey when the town awoke. Now and then sounds of gunfire. The morning grew bright, radiant. People strolled down streets as if on holiday. Groups gathered in the market square, at the station, outside the emporium on the high street. They were in a happy mood, brought children along. The war's definitely over.

The druggist had set off very early for Strassburg, to fetch diphtheria serum. He exchanged not a word with the officer huddled beside him on the narrow buggy, the pony trotted briskly, no one stopped them, outside Strassburg he confirmed his identity and that of his "assistant". At Broglie Square the officer indicated he wanted to get down. Still seated they exchanged stiff bows, the officer jumped down, the pony was ready to go, the buggy went on its sprightly way.

★

MONDAY, 11TH NOVEMBER

Lieutenant von Heiberg wandered the streets of Strassburg.

Heart-stopping sight of slovenly troops. Yesterday's dreadful scenes all over again. He was blind to the untroubled life of the ancient city now slowly starting its daily round, shops opening, trams winding through the narrow streets. He had to read the notices plastered on buildings, always the same thing, he read them word for word in five different places and couldn't work it out: "The Kaiser and King has resolved to abdicate his throne." Ten words, the sentence swallowed every thought he might have. What the despatch went on to say made its way only vaguely into him, the conclusion was clearer: "Printed by M. Dumont Schauberg, Strassburg in Elsass, 10 pf. per sheet."

He plodded on through the inner town, pushed across the little bridge behind St Thomas Place, and was striding along Finkweiler Quay when a hand clapped on his shoulder from behind, made him jump. He turned, and there was an older soldier with a big friendly grin but a shocking face: the entire right side horribly swollen, blue-red under the eye, the eye itself visible only as a slanting line, the rest concealed under the swelling. But the man was laughing with the left side– somewhat stiffly to be sure – as well as with the hideous right. He held a hand out to Heiberg, who'd jumped so snappily just now, and in a good old Berlin accent said: "Mornin'." Heiberg sniffed at the drunk, held out a hand, which the fellow squeezed in both paws. Leering into Heiberg's morning-after face, the man wheezed: "No cause to panic, Heiberg. I'll not harm ye. Don't know me, eh, with my face? Bottrowski, Neukölln, 2nd Company."

And heaved a great laugh and kept hold of the hand. "In Strassburg! Down by the waterside! Man, you'd never dream we'd meet up again like this, and I'm nothin'

47

and you're nothin'." And he gave his former company commander a big hug.

All Heiberg could do was take the arm of his subordinate from the Arras Front and allow himself to be led along the narrow quay until a rivermen's tavern slowed Bottrowski's pace. He peered in, they went down the steps. The few men sitting there soon made themselves scarce. As they sat down in the farthest corner of the cellar, Bottrowski nudged him: "They 'opped it 'cos of us, locals, don't want to besmirch theirselves with us." And he explained to his former company commander, who was helpless against the man's insolent familiarity: "Got in a fight, three chums an' me, yesterday. Fellow said an Elsasser knows more about bringin' up kids than what a Berliner does. 'Cos we're not refined enough, nor religious enough. I challenged 'im to prove it. He copped out. So there's the three of us as had been in hospital, and we had our tankards and then took on the 'ole table and fought like the Devil."

After a few gulps of coffee he suddenly grew serious: "What d'you think of this shambles, eh? Man, we set our sights too high, there's revenge comin'. Back home on leave I always said they oughter cut the highfalutin' words, the other lot still have it in 'em."

Heiberg: "What's the quickest way to Berlin?"

The soldier shook his head vigorously: "Back home, what for? You think I'll let 'em drive us out? That lot, not by a long shot. I have no desire for the mess back home. You might. Air's too thick in Berlin, let me tell you, specially for officers."

When they'd finished their drinks in silence, Bottrowski launched into a whispered account of events in town. He was attached to a convalescent company. "Last Thursday they all let fly here in town. Revolution, you think? Not on your nelly! Against us! Against Germans. So we stayed indoors and started thinking it over serious-like and what to do if it keeps up like this. They didn't dare try it on with us, only with civilians and businesses. Then over in Kehl they set up a Soldiers' Council, and on the ninth we had one too. And then the Elsassers was all chicken." He gave the lieutenant a squeeze, no one's going to take him off me: "Bet you're glad we sorted out that gang, those base-wallahs and so on." And the man leaned gravely back on his stool: "The slaughtering's over now, me old mate. You lot made the war, we're making peace. Ten-shun! We will make it. True as I'm a ceiling painter."

Heiberg understood none of it, he remembered the posters outside, the Kaiser and King has resolved to abdicate his throne.

"Saturday the ninth, we was all out in the streets. Sergeant Rebholz, a tiptop young lad, was running the show. Telephoned all the regiments, they must set up Soldiers' Councils, all went like clockwork. Only the 15th and 19th Pioneers kicked up a fuss. Then around ten, us lot to the Town Hall, to Peirotes, he's the new mayor here, socialist. He had to set up a Workers' Council. And all of us in a grand procession with red flags up front, him in a car, off to Kleber Place."

Heiberg ordered kirsch for them both, my last cash, I was ashamed to tell Hanna.

"And then the police, we sacked 'em all. And then patrols into the jails." Bottrowski placed both hard hands on the table, a strong heavy-cheeked man, the drunkenness had dissipated. Gravely, without rancour, he briefed his former superior: "I was there at three places with my shooter. The warders said there was common criminals among them, thieves, grievous bodily harm. So I says, now there's amnesty. Every king has the right on his birthday to set people free. We have the same right. And they'd better shut their gob. Not a mouse left in the place. And we took away all the secret papers up there by the police. They'd make a bitter morsel for lots of 'em hereabouts."

Heiberg, sitting small beside his former private, thought: maybe it's a happy chance, maybe I can place myself under his protection, and he steered the talk to officers: "What did you do with your officers, Bottrowski?" Big serious male eyes stared steadily back at him: "Except for epaulettes and swords, we made no demands. They had to leave. Disappear. Totally. You were a good chap, some others too, they knew, or they learned, what it is to be a man. But all in all, my advice is, make yourself like the air, so no one can see you."

This was too much for Heiberg. It was rising up in him again, dreadfully. He glanced around. He forced himself to ask: "But why?"

The man in the army greatcoat didn't move, his face didn't change, his calm expression remained steady. He stared straight ahead at the wall-shelf with the three small metal jugs: "It's good you talk like that. Others don't. They infiltrate among us and act false. We'll make it hot for 'em soon enough. You lot lost the war and ruined the people. Just look on, or come over to us. You lot better keep your gobs shut now. That's the safest thing you can do. Or else we'll have to change our minds. You asked why, Heiberg. 'Cos you're young, and know nothing. When I ask my daughter, she's twelve, why don't we eat meat and why don't we send Mum off to the country in summer when she needs it, she laughs in my face: Dad, you must be crazy! She thinks it's just the way things are. Us housepainters and whitewashers kept quiet when war broke out, 'cos that's all we could do, and off we went, put our lives on the line, and a lot of us trade union men fell, or they run about now crooked and bent and won't never climb a ladder again. But now the war's over and you've lost it all. You lot, Heiberg. 'Cos it's a part of you just as much as my daughter is a part of me, and now we can make it different and it will be different." He turned his unshaven face to Heiberg. He showed no ill will, just determination, earnestness.

Rage sat in Heiberg's bones. The soldier added jovially: "Well, I won't eat you!" He produced a cigar, inspected it lovingly. "Sorry, can't offer you one. Someone give it me."

"What did you do with your officers?" Heiberg was recovered enough to dare pose the question again. Bottrowski glanced to the cellar steps; two soldiers had just come down and taken seats in the front room. "Elsassers," Bottrowski growled once he had lit the cigar; "Keep your voice down, I don't know 'em. The officers? Clattered away like a clog room. We only gave 'em a little push, like giving a little puff at this table here, and they all fell over. Lots have run away. The commanders and the chief of staff are still around, far as we know. We give 'em till this morning to say if they'll put themselves under us and join in. I'll be goin' to the meeting. You can come."

"I can't come," Heiberg breathed. Bottrowski laughed: "We don't eat anyone, there's already half a dozen officers in the Soldiers' Council."

"Where is it?"

"On a ways, still down by the water, that posh area by the palace."

He stood up, Heiberg had to go along. They wound their way through the town. Heiberg kept looking about, how to escape the fellow. "Come on," the executioner cajoled, "come on, Heiberg. You still haven't told me how our company's doing." I must slip away, thought Heiberg. Then a military truck flying red flags rolled up from the commercial zone in the south, it stopped right in front of them, a head poked out and yelled, "Bottrowski!"

Now it was all up with Heiberg, he tried to slip away but his companion put an arm around him as they lowered the tailboard: "He's a lieutenant from my company, he's coming along." And greeted by hallos and vigorous handshakes, pulled aboard with a jaunty swing, Heiberg was forced into the truck, the tailboard was banged shut and fastened. They rattled towards the Palace of Justice.

★

The newspapers brought back from Strassburg by the druggist were the first editions of the day; railway traffic was suffering major delays. When he came to a stop a small crowd gathered around the buggy, some neighbours had heard of his early business in Strassburg. The young owner of the pharmacy, a lanky beanpole, hurried out to collect the little medicine bag, and was vexed to learn that the two musical instrument shops the druggist had searched out to buy violin strings were still closed. Then the little man on the buggy opened his raincoat and pulled out a sheaf of newspapers. The pharmacist tried to hurry back indoors with them, but was hemmed in. Amid the throng he opened one of the papers, despite his resistance others were unfurled, people read aloud, the crowd swelled.

The lanky pharmacist had the *Strassberger Neue Zeitung*; he read: "Shreds." People cried: "Louder." Then so many crowded around that he asked the druggist to take the medicine bag, they're squashing it. He paused while someone brought a stool from the shop and thrust it at him. He stared bewildered at the man who'd brought the stool, but he had to climb onto it. He read about "Wilhelm the Second" who had threatened to "tear the Alsatian constitution to shreds." But now, clinging so ignobly to the throne, he had brought matters to a head: "The entire German constitution lies in shreds."

The pharmacist turned about up on the stool, looked for the druggist. "Please bring me my coat, and the cap." The wind was gusting, the newspaper flapped against his chest. When someone called: "Read more," he shouted back, "My hands are numb." They had to be patient until in front of the whole world he had struggled into his coat, set the cap on his head and pulled on his gloves. As he did so he held the newspaper clamped between his knees, and glared savagely at the man who tried to pull it free. The narrow street was filled to its whole width with people, and more were streaming in from side lanes. Several leaned out of windows, ran downstairs.

As he stood overlooking the crowd, the pharmacist grew into his role. "It is from this standpoint," he read louder and with more gusto, "that all so-called solutions to the question of Alsace and Lorraine must be considered, from an autonomous federal state, to neutrality, to a plebiscite; and as democrats we do not shy from declaring that today we reject any plebiscite, whose only purpose would be to hoodwink France: a purpose which, moreover, as we firmly believe, could be carried out only with the most powerful methods of suppression."

The crowd below was breathless with excitement. Their pupils had widened. That this could be said out loud, that the air could convey it, that it could echo from their ancient silent house walls. And reservists there in their field-grey uniforms, nodding along! The pharmacist saw how people stood open-mouthed, turned to neighbours with a grin, he himself fell into a formal, heightened declamatory style that had lain dormant since schooldays:

"We know what we want! Our fathers protested not

only in Bordeaux but also in the elections of 1873 and in Berlin, and so it is false to claim that the population of Alsace and Lorraine has never been asked for its views on annexation. This is clear and unambiguous, and known to the whole world for half a century."

Scattered applause, hisses: "Read on". The pharmacist waved the paper: "And so if we are to speak of a popular vote, it can only be in the sense of the French asking us if we wish to remain with them. We burn to answer this question from the French."

The pharmacist lowered the paper and turned his face, blue with cold, from side to side. They cried "Bravo", he was flattered, attributed it to his heroic style, his mother had often said when he gave readings at school that one day he would become a member of parliament. Making little bows he clambered down from the stool, the podium of his triumph. People shouted over one another. He was exhilarated to see how he had aroused them. Even the two reservists with pipes in their mouths were clapping. Some shouted: "Swabians out!" He carried the stool a couple of steps, then a woman respectfully took it from him, he followed with pounding heart, thanked her. After a few minutes' consideration he telephoned upstairs to tell his wife how he had spoken. She'd been asleep still. What is it? – I read from the newspaper. – What, you? – Yes, outside the shop. – I'll be down in a moment.

*

Meanwhile the druggist came from the shed in the yard where he had parked the buggy, through the back door into the shop. He closed the front door, which the owner had left open, and changed his shoes behind the counter. As he hung up his sheepskin coat he stood lost in thought.

The officer silent beside him on the buggy had spent the night upstairs in the bed of an assistant off sick. Hanna will arrive soon and explain. And he was seized with a desire to dash up the spiral stairs to the room the officer had left. A small room, cosily furnished, the bedside stand shoved untidily aside, bed unmade. The little druggist entered in felt slippers, closed the door, sniffed the room. He sat on the bed. From downstairs he could hear the pharmacist's voice: "Clear and unambiguous, and known to the whole world for half a century."

His hand slid under the blanket. The bed was warm. Hanna's beloved. It was both of them. His hands absorbed the warmth. He slipped furtively out with his prize.

Hanna, proud, slim, entered the shop once the crowd dispersed. She hurried across to the druggist, who was by the till making entries in the big ledger. He flushed deep red when he saw her. She whispered: "What did he tell you?"

"We didn't talk."

"No? The whole journey? He was, how was he then?"

"I don't know the gentleman."

She frowned. "That ... that's all you can tell me?"

"He got down in Broglie Square."

She stood silent, the counter between them (warm bed upstairs). "I already knew that." She leaned over the counter, breathed at him: "You'd never forgive yourself for being even a little bit friendly to him!" And off she went, slim and upright with her black feather boa.

He stayed a while longer at the counter, looking after the vanished figure, until a young woman stormed in, just like Hanna, needed a worming powder for her child. And right behind her an ordinary looking man in civvies, blinking shyly, wearing tall leather army spats that looked brand new. He offered the druggist half a dozen new hernia trusses wrapped in newspaper, three Mark each for an instant deal. The lanky pharmacist came over at once and negotiated quietly with him at the window. He called to the druggist: "Jakob, please, the digitalis decoction at eleven, it's simmering now." The druggist hurried to the laboratory.

★

On Parade Square outside the hotel only a few people were standing about. Music had started up. At once, as if at a signal, windows opened, people in hats and overcoats leaned out, they filled the balconies next to the hotel and the café to the left, and at the printing house that produced the *General-Anzeiger*. Drumbeats and a bugle, then loud blaring and drumming from a narrow street accompanied by a howling seething mob, and then from a side street the first boys and exhilarated youths with children's flags. The square soon overflowed with people, they came from other streets as well, and now the music, out from the narrow ravine, blared and boomed down the long funnel of Parade Square, greeted by clapping. Handkerchiefs waving from windows, people flourishing hats and caps. The square was not suited to musical performances, there were echoes and re-echoes, each drumbeat sounded three times, like a canon the music was repeated twice and pursued, it enhanced the tumult and was amusing.

Amid the booms and counter-booms hordes of soldiers pour onto the sunny square. There are little single-storey buildings and taller ones with shingle roofs, the hotel and the printing house have broad frontages, they are four storeys high, grey and flat-roofed. On both roofs men move about waving red flags. Four lie on their stomachs on the printing house, try to lower a huge banner down the front of the building and nail it across the top. But as two of them hammer away, a window opens on the fourth floor behind the banner. You see how the window pushes the banner out, an arm shoves it aside, you see an outraged old man (it's his arm) glare upwards with an angry shout. The man lives here, it's his private apartment, they're blocking his view, the men on the roof bellow back, the man yanks the cloth to one side, it hangs by just one corner, there's discussion up there, in the end they nail it firmly to the side.

The café has been completely taken over by high society: they occupy the first floor saloon which is usually closed in the mornings, as well as the regular café below. Even in this cold weather, tables and chairs have been set up outside, two rows, all occupied. That morning the landlord had wrestled with his conscience: should he open up or not? He'd gone very early to the infantry barracks to see what was happening, then the old Procurator had come over and told him that the newly-formed local committee would hire the café for the morning, upper and lower floors, the bill for all consumption through the morning to be presented to him. So, despite the anxiety, his resistance crumbled. A loud jolly crowd now filled the premises, the best families of the town, it's the new committee. Asked brusquely by the Procurator, as he poured him a grog, whether he wouldn't join the committee, there were urgent and important tasks to be done, serious matters from which no responsible man should shy, he'd raised both arms and replied in a mock-injured tone: "But of course I will!"

A jumble of voices below. People are freezing, shouting. Soldiers with a red cockade in the cap take over the middle of the square. Two trestles have been carried from the printing house and piled one atop the other, that'll be the speaker's podium.

The tall pharmacist wanders excitedly among the upstairs tables, now and then squeezes a hand. Here comes his young wife, tall as he but slimmer and more graceful, she's wearing a lorgnette, he got to know her in the east, where she was a nursing assistant and he the pharmacist. She gives him her hand. "Where are you sitting?" When he's sat her down she turns to him: "And you? Will you make another speech?" He smiles uncertainly, looks to see if others heard, at once she's telling the ladies on either side her news, he lets go of her chair, listens eagerly to what she says and how the others react, and maybe he will have a chance to speak. He cleared his throat. But where should he speak. They've all read the papers, of course. Still, he really wants to speak. But to his dismay he sees the ladies tuck into their cakes, and his legend fades. Someone's making a speech out there, you can't hear much, the windows are closed now against the cold. If you want to hear you have to go downstairs, where the doors and windows are kept open because of the guests seated outside in the street. Drinks and cakes are passed to them through the windows.

The old Procurator has been seated, as he wished, by the tiled stove upstairs. His son went missing in the first weeks of the war, no suspicion is ever voiced that he went over to the enemy, but the mother and then the father cling to this hope that dare not be spoken, the mother is dying of grief, the Procurator holds fast to the belief that he's still alive the nearer the war comes to ending and the Allies are victorious, everyone in town supports his conviction. And now his hour is here. Many come to shake his hand. Soon, when his fellow lawyer the mayor, formerly state tax assessor, has taken a seat nearby, he'll throw up the question of the measures taken yesterday.

Some gentlemen are brought up from below, Hanna's father and the pharmacist put in an appearance, ladies make room, form a rectangle of tables around the stove and the old Procurator.

The Procurator, a humane, clean-shaven gentleman with a fringe of white hair on his skull, was tall and thin as the hop-poles that grew in the fields outside the town. He scratched at a corner of his mouth, and mischievously proposed to the assembly that the door to downstairs be closed for half an hour. And the grey cavalier gave a slight bow to the next table; how charming if one or other of the young ladies were to place herself near the door like an angel in paradise with the flaming sword. This led to a gallant argument between two of the ladies and a gentleman who put himself forward too; it was agreed they should take turns, the Procurator proposed that at the end of the meeting each of the ladies be presented with a box of chocolates in gratitude; the ladies protested.

In this excited atmosphere, the portly bureaucrat beside the Procurator, mayor up until this moment, an elderly grinning baldhead housed in loose-fitting clothes, began to make little remarks across the table and then turn back complacently to his grog, to prepare himself for the coming announcements. He mumbled: "We're on our own, the lines are down, nothing but silence from Strassburg, Berlin. Paris not yet here. We're in a primordial state." They all smiled sweetly at him. "A primordial state can be lovely, it can be Paradise, but can also …"

"Surely you don't allude to original sin, your worship?" This from a Catholic priest, sitting here in civvies. The bureaucrat raised his hands: "Careful, no stepping outside one's competence! I meant disorder." And he mentioned a little of what had been happening at the airfield, in the military warehouses et cetera. His final words were delivered in a whisper.

The pharmacist would have loved to speak. He kept a close eye out for a gap in the conversation, and exchanged glances with his wife, who was likewise alert. From outside came a mighty storm of applause, music blared and boomed again, a speech had ended. Upstairs they spoke even more softly, conspiratorially. The Procurator had replaced his horn-rimmed glasses and together with the priest scrutinised a sheet of paper, now and then glancing at the audience; the priest took the paper around the room, it was the attendance list, he inscribed a cross against each name. The discussion continued. They declared themselves the provisional Town Committee, confidence was expressed in the mayor. The Procurator said: "That is the real reason for our assembly." The whispering bureaucrat: "Many thanks. I always like to have a committee over me." Five men were swiftly appointed as a Town Board, the Procurator clarified to both sides and across the rectangle of tables: It's all provisional of course, could all be over by morning, news is all snarled up.

This was the pharmacist's moment: the news. He stood, lied instanter, every inch of him, that he'd been in Strassburg that morning to fetch serum for some urgent cases (the pathetic tone did not yet want to take over). In the city of Strassburg there was great unrest (shreds) and enthusiasm, everyone awaited the day of occupation. (It flowed better now.) The Procurator stretched a long friendly arm out to him: "But please, sit down!" He sat down in confusion, silent for a moment, he couldn't declaim whilst seated, and especially not with the emporium manager at his side. Then the priest asked from across the table: "Is it true that the mutineers in Strassburg are sacking and burning churches?"

General consternation. The pharmacist stammered: "I

... know nothing of that."

At once the priest expressed outrage at such events, everyone shared his sentiment. The pharmacist was forgotten. As they discussed forming a self-defence force, a citizen's militia (there are churches here too), he dared not even look at his wife.

★

On the square, among recruits and reservists, are officers without epaulettes. Now and then recruits and civilians come past to check if they're wearing a red cockade. There's empty space around them, they don't speak, they're pale, puff nervously on cigarettes.

More music. A pack of infantry comes marching in. Cheers ripple across the square. A red flag dances in the hand of the merry childlike recruit at the front. Everyone can see he's looking forward to home. Behind him they march arm in arm, civilians move out of the way, they push through to the artillery and infect them with their high spirits. For whole minutes there's nothing but cheering. The upstairs windows of the café have been opened, the mayor shows his face, two soldiers standing on the speaker's tables give him a military salute, and he inclines his head.

The soldiers have just declared that they've thrown off the Hohenzollern yoke, they want peace, peace for everyone, and bring to the people of Alsace freedom and fraternity. Ladies and girls upstairs in the café shriek and laugh in excitement. They hug one another: "It's so wonderful." Some hurry over to the Procurator, still claiming his cosy place by the stove, and kiss him. Three or four kiss him, one after the other. They hug other men too, it's like carnival. The pharmacist's wife on a sudden whim runs at her husband, the ice is broken, and hugs him,

Citizens and Soldiers

embraces him, and then everyone hugs everyone else and shakes hands. Hanna fends off the hugs, runs to her father, who has stood up like the rest, flings her arms around his neck and sobs. He wonders why she's trembling, tries to see her face but she runs downstairs. Other women too are weeping.

But the pharmacist has caught the bug. His wife's hug excited him, he needs action, has to show her. He dashes onto the square, pushes through the civilians, signals to the man up there beside the speaker, the speaker's glad to stop, they've run out of speakers, they need civilians. Now the tall pharmacist is up there: "People of Alsace, the hour has struck, shreds, we greet you, as democrats we speak it out loud and promise formally before all the world, and peace shall reign, peace!" Loud cheers. "Let no one tangle with us! The people of Alsace need freedom like everyone else. We extend to you a fraternal hand." It was magnificent. He had to shake dozens of fraternal hands. Upstairs they were done with the kissing and now thronged at the windows to hear him. When he came back in there was a storm of applause, his wife flew to him, embraced him proudly. Among others the inclination to bestow hugs and kisses had abated. The Procurator blurted from the stove: "You're one in a thousand!" He gave a proud modest bow and pulled on his coat, he had them bring him a glass of hot grog, and then for the rest of the day was senseless and incapable of work. He wanted to go to the barracks and give a speech there. The work of the shop rested entirely on the druggist's shoulders.

For a full half-hour during the spectacle, the senior garrison officer had paced stiff-kneed in his gaudy general's uniform back and forth behind the crowd, along the pavement to the police station. The crowd made way for him. He had a monocle in his right eye. No one greeted

MONDAY, 11TH NOVEMBER

him. There was whispering behind his back. He no longer spread fear. And he slipped unnoticed down a side lane into the Hotel Europe.

The music trailed off. The square emptied to singing and halloos. Outside the printing house a tight group of very young people at the back of the crowd came to a halt. The middle of the square had hardly become free when they took a running jump at the vacated trestles. One trumpeted through his hands: "Esteemed ladies and gents! Because it's so lovely, we sing once more our rendition of 'Deutschland, Deutschland über alles'!" Peals of laughter from the windows, on the square. They growled out the words.

A few reservists from the rearguard were stunned enough to remove the obligatory pipe from their mouths and run at the lads, but these had younger legs and hightailed it towards Town Hall Square.

★

The Palace of Justice in Strassburg that same morning had become a veritable military citadel. In the big ominous Assizes court the enlarged Soldiers' Council had established its base, one hundred and twenty delegates from thirty formations. Clouds of smoke from pipes, cigars, cigarettes, filled the room, the walls were bare, the heavy cast iron busts of the Kaiser and all the pictures had been pulled down to lie in a heap by the judge's bench like a pile of slaughtered sheep. But happy noisy field-greys sat and clambered over the jury bench and public seats. Sergeant Rebholz rang his bell and shouted down from the judge's bench.

The first information to emerge was that commissions had been set up, Transport in Brandgasse, Finance in the district court, Demobilisation in the Bank of Mulhäusen, commissions for Security, Passes, Pay and Provisioning. In the next few days individuals would be demobilised, then whole units would be disbanded. A representative of the garrison doctor stood to request that the release of medical personnel be delayed.

Icy silence at the news that the Cologne Workers' and Soldiers' Council had been invited by Hindenburg to Supreme Headquarters, comrades Sollmann, Schulte and Fuchsius had also made the trip and reported that Hindenburg had placed himself and the army of the new government at their disposal in order to avert chaos. "Well now," Rebholz observed drily, knowing he had to express the opinion of the assembly, "such reports already sound comical. As you can see, the heads of the old powers-that-be haven't yet blown clear of fog. (Calls of "Cold rub-down!") Meanwhile there's a telegram from the current government in Berlin to us, yes indeed, to the Workers' and Soldiers' Council of Strassburg, that the imminent military occupation of Alsace by the Entente, the French, cannot prejudice the eventual fate of Alsace and Lorraine, which means: when the occupation comes, it's a long way from saying whether Alsace will become French, or neutral, or stay German."

Silence. Rebholz' eyes strained into the big space, the wall behind him had an eerie look, a rectangular picture, the Kaiser of course, had hung there, now the wall seemed paler, and the dark patch made a hole in it. Two men sat on each side of Rebholz at the bench; soldiers occupied the jury benches. It was the deepest moment of silence the room had known since the two sentries burst open the doors with their guns. A voice from the hall, clearly Alsatian, not very loud, suggested: "Proceed with the agenda." Rebholz remained remarkably frozen: "That won't do. We won't get out of it that way. Everyone must have a say, one way or another." But the dumb silence would not be broken. The room was not just struck dumb and uncertain, but dangerously tense. Here were contradictions, and Rebholz' face showed that he knew the contradictions, and would state his own view with vigour.

Until a bearded man stood up under the window of the jury bench, assumed a military posture and called out in deep strong voice: "Alsace is German, and shall remain German." Whereupon, as if ignited by a spark, a voice below called: "Long live the world revolution!"

And already, sung quietly by two, three men, the Internationale. The song seized hold of the jury bench, climbed down into the room, engulfed it within a few moments, roared. And from dark ancient walls that had never heard anything but accusations, probing questions, lies and confessions, and within which, up till now, only black-robed judges, jurymen, criminals, human beings broken and to be broken had eyed one another in the presence of curious onlookers, the song echoed and re-echoed. The mere fact of singing in this place was unprecedented. And the Internationale! Many of the soldiers hardly knew either words or tune. But as the song roared around them, they had a desire to sing along and felt: no school song, but the war's end, peace, freedom for mankind. "Arise, ye wretched of the earth!"

At the second verse someone stepped up from behind to Rebholz, who kept singing as he turned his head. They whispered together. The messenger handed him a note. Seemingly unconcerned, the chairman sang to the end, and then, as they all sat noisily down, made an official announcement that there would be a short break while the committee prepared the next agenda items. His face did not reveal to the other four who followed him into the judge's chamber the fury he felt at the news that the Berlin government had expressly invited the Army High Command to retain control, and that officers were to be allowed to retain sword and epaulettes. As he closed the door behind the others, his face twisted, he screwed up his nose, grabbed the nearest chair and banged it hard on the floor; angry words formed:

"So it's all to stay the same. Everything's to stay the same."

Fifteen minutes later the chairman appeared back in the courtroom. Rebholz, tight-lipped, cleared his throat, rang the bell, and spoke in a penetrating voice: he must make known the contents of a telegraphed instruction from the government in Berlin. According to which those gentlemen, the officers, are to retain sword and epaulettes pending demobilisation.

Wild uproar, scornful laughter! The sergeant waited for it to die down. He remained expressionless.

A laughter-choir set up on the jury benches. Someone directed the infectious attacks of laughter. "That's enough," roared the chairman finally. Calm returned. He put down the paper, asked: "Have we taken note?" A hearty "Yes". Then a clear voice, someone pushed forward: "Give me that bumph." The sergeant waved him away.

Debate continued. How should symbols be treated, many are running around with the tricolour. Someone rose to speak: "The tricolour no less than the black-white-red is a false symbol of liberty, equality and fraternity." A shout: "Let everyone find bliss his own way."

"Quite right," decided the chairman, and proceeded to the next item.

Now a reservist stood up from the throng, bushy head low between the shoulders, hot bearded face. When he turned to those who were still laughing, they fell silent. In a Baden accent he uttered a single sentence: "All punishment lists must be destroyed." And sat down.

★

As the crowd surged forward during the singing, Heiberg managed to elude Bottrowski. The door was wide open, there was singing in the corridors as well. Heiberg slipped unnoticed from the courtroom, the building. He hurried over a bridge.

He heaved a sigh of relief, forced himself, teeth clenched, to regain control. At any moment someone may recognise me, call my name. How can I get home, how can I cross the Rhine to Kehl. Oh how they dog me, it's revolution, it's the end. Cheering troops rampaging outside German businesses pull him along. How to escape this hell? At the Casino on Theatre Place he bumps gloomily into a friend, adjutant to the chief of staff, who doesn't know him at first, then sees what a state he's in, takes him to his lodging behind Broglie Square. Heiberg: "If only I'd known you live here. A pharmacist brought me here a few hours ago from my garrison." And talks and talks, the adjutant listens fascinated, hugs him. "They've already reported your case, I didn't match the name to you." Heiberg should stay quietly here till morning. Maybe the wind would change. "Be proud of what you've done, it'll all be worth it. The Reds want to negotiate with us, our leaders are invited to secret talks this evening."

Heiberg exhausted on the sofa, a blanket over him, murmurs half asleep: "Alsace is German and shall remain German." A memory from the courtroom. When Meissner asked what he'd said, he gave details of the meeting. The little adjutant rubbed his hands and made ready to go out. "Heiberg, the wind will change."

Citizens and Soldiers

★

Back in the little town, when the procession of demonstrators hived off a detachment at the infantry barracks – recruits turning aside into the school, the rest led by drums and trumpets past the water-tower to enter Barracks Road – the Pastor opened his window. Marching music, and Hello, lovely weather. But he closed the window.

He paced up and down in his cosy study. Two walls were lined floor to ceiling with bookcases, books lay on the desk and the chaise longue, in his disquiet he had picked them out, leafed briefly through them, put them down any old where. On the wall over the chaise longue was the Kaiser's portrait. He had been pacing up and down in the study since early morning. All morning the town had been heaving, this dear old town where he'd spent a good fifteen years preaching, baptising, marrying, blessing. His wife was in Stuttgart, his son in the east, and what must it be like in the east, the Bolsheviks will advance and overwhelm the Fatherland. Oh my poor Germany.

And now there was another blast from outside as a procession drew near, mounted this time, a small orderly procession, so there still are such things, they were playing "O Germany high in honour". He sank onto the divan beside his books and listened to the familiar tune, and when it came to the words "Stand fast, stand fast in the raging storm" he lost control and buried his face in his hands. Oh God, oh God, what do you intend for us, what are you doing to our Germany, "thou ancient stalwart land".

I shall pray, he told himself; let his arms fall and stared into space. Surely I should pray. And he plodded as if to a chore over to his desk where he took up the silver crucifix and placed it at the edge. He had to sink to his knees, the blaring receded: "O Germany high in honour, stand fast in the raging storm". He whispered on his knees by the desk, grasped the crucifix in both hands, head pressed to the wood:

"Almighty God, I have much to ask of you. I am an old man. I need your infinite forgiveness. And if I did not know who you are, if I conceived of you only in the way of humans, I would not dare turn now to you. But your goodness is immeasurable, your mercy without end, without end. You are the all-merciful in Heaven, who created us and whose name is daily on my lips and of whom I now know nothing, nothing of his existence, of his power, and of his love. You must attend to me less than to the hundred of my flock, for they are small and ignorant while I know you and yet am now losing you. Oh, now I am defeated, Lord. Now I come to you crawling on my knees. With your son whose image I hold in my hands, I implore you, great almighty judge, save us! Do not let us perish! Save our Germany! Give me a sign so I know that the impossible, the unthinkable cannot happen. The Kaiser has fled, the Reich is crumbling. Great God in Heaven, number every least one of my sins, my derelictions as they deserve, demand of me everything. I have been, despite everything, your servant, an ungrateful dilatory one; comforts and habitude have corrupted me. Oh my Saviour, dearest Lord Jesus, you who know the ways of men because you were made flesh, help me to attain forgiveness, I am already a stubborn old man, restore hope to me in my last days. Do not destroy us, Lord! Do not destroy us."

And he squeezed the crucifix and ground his teeth. He stood, replaced the crucifix on its little marble stand, sank painfully into his desk chair. He felt: it's hopeless, I can't pray.

Citizens and Soldiers

Bitter tears slowly blinded his eyes and trickled into his mouth; he pulled out his handkerchief: better if they had chased us all into a heap and shot us, one and all.

He blew his nose, stared at the metal image of Christ. Incredible. I can't reach him. All my life I've managed to bring others to him. But not me. And suddenly he went whimpering through the study, he was forced to his feet, what is it, what is it? He bit his finger, his wrist. Why can't I reach him, why can't I find my Saviour? He pushed books off the chaise longue and lay stretched out on his back. He lay stiff as a corpse. Then he turned on his side. After a while he crept about the room, put books back on shelves. He touched and stroked the crucifix as he passed, but it felt icy.

He went into the corridor, pulled on his padded jacket, glanced at the clock on the desk: half past ten. He already thought he'd heard tapping, now came a loud knock. He called: "One moment," opened a small cupboard next to the desk where manuscripts, bottles and glasses were kept, poured himself a cognac, then another. Must keep my nerve. He wiped his mouth.

It was Fräulein Köpp the milliner, a hardworking rather poor girl, with a baby on the way. Why must she come just now, I've nothing to say to her. She sat, he made a place for himself on the chaise longue, lit a cigarette (if you don't mind, dear girl). She was tight-faced, stared into her lap, yes, you are sinful and bad like me, God cannot help us, I cannot help you, whyever do you come to me.

"And what's the situation today, my little Köpp?"

"Now he's gone off." (Music. They'll be parading all day.) "He's not at the barracks, no one knows where he is."

"Oh, he'll be back, my girl." She meant the father of her child, we've all lost our Fatherland, help, where can we find help, my child.

"My mum sent me down to look for him first thing this morning, because they're making revolution. Yesterday we had so many orders for officers' wives, we never heard anything in our workshop about revolution. He's not at the barracks."

"Well, well," the Pastor puffed away and said no more. I must take pity on myself so that even I may be pitied. The girl, the hard worker, sat with an accusing look. He pulled himself together, said: "Now, I shall write to the regiment, I know the colonel." She didn't react. He added, gently, much more gently than before: "But we must find a father for the child."

I shan't last here until it's born, I shall have to pass her on to my successor, who'd have thought such a thing possible.

"He's from Bavaria, he'll have gone back there. I can do without him for a father. My mum says so too."

The Pastor mumbled, hadn't really been listening. "Well, well." Then, just to say something, he changed the subject to one that always came in handy when he had no idea what to say, it mostly produced a magical effect: "How's the money situation?" She turned to him, cheeks flushed, nodded vigorously: "We have work just now, reverend, the officers' ladies are going away. But once they're gone we'll be in difficulties."

"I'm sorry to hear it. Others are coming."

"Who, the French? They won't come to us. We had a good clientele. We don't work for peasants."

The Pastor made soothing noises; he hadn't expected this. He thought: there's no way I can drum up customers, where shall I be a week from now, his eye wandered to the silver Christ, to the books, the many books, the removal, dear Lord, the removal.

"And it was the son of Director Koch."

He pricked up his ears. What was she saying. "What was?"

"When he was on leave." What? I don't understand. What was he?

"Here."

"Good, dear girl, good. I understand. And what then?"

"So he comes to us one Sunday, at the shop, I was finishing off the director's wife's hat. He'd come to pick it up. I wasn't properly dressed yet, and he threw himself on me, poor girl." And she blubbed as if on a bell pull, when she saw the Pastor's eyes grow big and round.

The Pastor sat there, suddenly no longer thinking of victory and defeat. He was alert. Priestly wrath swept through him. He puffed on his cigar, I've come this far, I'll roll in like thunder. "What happened there?"

She blubbed: "When he was on leave. Next day, when the director's missus came to pay, he'd already gone."

"The son of Director Koch, the first lieutenant?" The Pastor ogled the pitiful girl as if he meant to gobble her up. "When do you say this happened?"

"We'll have to look it up in our delivery ledger. When we made the last autumn hat for the director's missus. Because she ordered her winter hat from Strassburg."

"My dear girl, I have to know. Was it the same time as … the other? You must know."

"Yes it was."

"What was?"

"That."

"You had two at the same time?"

"Not the same time." She bleated: "He threw himself on me." She feared the Pastor.

He marched snorting up and down the room into which she had brought such depravity. He planted himself before her: "And what am I supposed to do, my fine young

MONDAY, 11TH NOVEMBER

lady? With this horrid mess? And you feel no shame telling me this? This, a scandal, a scandal is what it is!"

Defeat, revolution, Germany in the abyss, I plant myself before it, I will not tolerate it, cast down all criminals. He wheezed: "How dare you bring this to me, hey?"

"Because the Bavarian's gone. One of them must pay, reverend." Aha, his query about money was bringing results. He roared in angry despair: "For sure. One of them must." And one of them would. And he marched up and down the room. Arise, my Germany, shield your houses, set up your watchposts. She: "Else I'll file a complaint." The Pastor wrung his hands, she kept stubbornly mum.

He soon sent the girl away, had a cognac to wash down the mess, opened the door to a cabinet maker reporting the birth of a son, who seemed less than overjoyed when the Pastor congratulated him: "Kids is one thing we're not short of."

Then he felt impelled to go down to old Hegen in the porter's lodge. Could they keep an eye on his house, perhaps take care of the removal if it wouldn't overtax them. And then to the military hospital. To the final victims of this wicked war.

Another burial.

*

Out of the wide barred gate to the left of the main entrance, four men came from the cadaver store through the trees carrying the coffin with young Richard in his status of soldier, lieutenant, airman. The only officers behind the Pastor were the tall Chief Medical Officer, the doctors of the Internal and Surgical Stations, the oculist, unrecognisable without sword and cap. No music. They went rapidly up the frozen road, as instructed by the senior garrison officer so as not to arouse attention.

Behind the coffin marched, or rather ran, two privates with red cockades, they were from the main ward next to Richard's private room, and had now and then provided him some service. A paramedic pushed thickly swaddled First Lieutenant Becker at a trot in a wheelchair. At Becker's side, likewise swaddled, Lieutenant Maus. Flowers in her arms, the staff nurse of the Station, and tall Nurse Hilde in a long blue overcoat.

By the wall a hole had been opened in the earth for Richard, who had flitted in the air like a dragonfly, and fallen. The coffin had to be manoeuvred around two fresh piles of earth from the graves dug for the two soldiers shot by Heiberg at the barracks. The Pastor unbuttoned his coat, heads were uncovered, he drew a little book from his pocket and read. He blessed the one he referred to as the Sleeping. But he was doing more than sleep.

The first clods clattered onto the coffin.

Hilde bit her lip, they're in such a hurry, they threw him in the grave like a dog. On the way back Maus tried to get close, she stuck to the staff nurse. Chief and Pastor simultaneously made as if to go home, men were already assembling, they'd left the barracks. The oculist growled: "One company, two machine guns, and the whole monkey business would be over in no time." The tall Chief, angry, pulled up his collar: "No speeches, colleague, you'll catch cold. Tell me, why did you become an oculist."

★

All the men were summoned to the big training ground of the artillery barracks for an early afternoon meeting. From a first-floor window soldiers shouted, a little red flag waved beside them. This was the Soldiers' Council.

"There's looting. Patrols will be issued with live ammo. There'll be checks going out and coming in." Absolute silence. A roar from above: "Anyone caught will be put on trial." A few voices below: "And who's the judge?"

"Comrades, order must be maintained. Any who don't know yet what revolution is and they compromise it will be taught a lesson. There are traitors among us. There are enemies of the revolution among us. Anyone who steals is an enemy of the revolution. The Alsatians will attack us."

"We have weapons."

"So do they. Rifles and machine guns have gone from the airfield. Where are they?"

Indignation below. Someone cried: "Pull out!" Men upstairs: "Easy to say. We're waiting for transport."

"You'll have a long wait. We want to leave."

The message was spread that at five o'clock, before rations were distributed, there would be another assembly, following a session of the Soldiers' Council.

*

In the echoing corridor on the first floor of the barracks, the major-general who was senior garrison officer met up with the major of the Dragoons regiment. Both wore field-grey greatcoats to conceal their epaulettes, their caps had no cockade. The Major opened the door for the General to the junior officers' mess, a plain long room, its centre occupied by a table with chairs along both sides. The room was filled with the gloom of a winter afternoon. Cold air, food smells. On the dirty linen tablecloth beer bottles stood or lay, empty and half-empty beer and wine glasses, fragments of bread. At the head, marked by a wicker chair, was a dinner half eaten, meat and veg on three plates, crumpled napkins at the side, a fork on the floor.

"Please open the window, Major," the General requested. The window overlooked the barracks yard, the Major pushed it up, whispered: "Keep to the side, General, they're looking up." The General sank into the wicker chair. "See how they guzzle. Do you think I've taken a single bite today? It sticks in the throat."

"They're swine. They never learned any better."

The General pushed the plates aside with a forearm, placed his cap on the table: "Here you see what calls itself a ruling class. This is how they begin." The Major closed one eye, bent down to the General: "I think we should leave them to it." The General fixed his monocle, looked up: "What?" and held a hand to his ear. The Major, of a shorter build, grey-brown moustache, hair the same colour upstanding on a narrow skull, very pale grave face with a funnel-shaped blood-red scar below the left cheek, sat down beside him. "They're making a good start." The General: "You call this good? They're ruining everything." The Major shrugged, twiddled his moustache.

The General: "The widow has reclaimed our colonel, she was with me, she looked ... frightful, vengeance in female form, refused to have him buried here among murderers and bandits, he'll be well away already."

"Bravo."

"Where's the adjutant, Lieutenant von Heiberg?"

"Over the hills and far away."

"If you see him, convey my thanks, thank all the officers. You can be open about it."

"I'll take care, General."

The General turned to the wall. "Switch on the light." The switch was to the right, between the sideboard and a cupboard. When two bulbs came aglow on the ceiling, the General could see what he was looking for. "Off, please." On the rear wall the Kaiser's portrait was completely ruined, it hung loose and askew, just scraps along the frame, at the top you could make out the bright head with the gleaming helmet and one shoulder, it was a picture of him mounted. "Take the whole thing down," hissed the General, slamming both arms on the table. "Can you manage it?"

"Right away." The Major climbed from his chair, laid the frame against the wall, looked at the clock set into the wall above.

"It's ... oh, the clock's stopped." He glanced at his wrist. "It's ten past. Our gentlemen aren't here yet."

"So we wait."

As they made themselves comfortable in the small side room on the sofa next to the piano – dirty coffee cups and cigarette stubs on the table – the dining room grew noisy, lights came on, voices, someone pulled open the door to the little room: "Ah." The officers stood. People were standing around the table, one roared: "Clear it up." It was swiftly cleared. There were ten soldier-councillors, one glared across at the officers until they sat. Among the councillors were one officer representative and two NCOs. The wicker chair at the head was taken by a big broad old soldier with bushy eyebrows, long light brown moustache ending in slender points, a very restless man who even sitting was unable to contain himself, he spoke abruptly, began without formalities: "Now then, the pullout." He looked around the table: "Where are the officers sitting?"

""Left, at the end."

"Why only two?"

The Major: "No more were invited."

Men around the table: "They've all run off. We don't need more. Two's enough."

One raised a hand: "Why do you ask, comrade? The soldiers' council are soldiers. We don't need more guests."

The peasant in the head seat stared across at the General and the Major: "Here's general sir and major sir. Where are the staff officers?" No answer. The chairman turned to his neighbour, who had a sheet of paper and was making notes with a pen: "You invited them?"

The other, scribbling: "Staff officers? Couldn't find any." Laughter. They all stared at the officers. The Major: "Perhaps I can be of use." The chairman: "If it comes to that. Thanks." The General whispered: "This is torture." There was a pause. The chairman kept staring at the officers: "Have the two gentlemen meanwhile discovered anything of Lieutenant von Heiberg's whereabouts?" The Major shook his head. The chairman: "Where's he gone to? He's a Berliner." The caustic scribe: "The murderer's a fugitive. We know his address. The funerals of the two victims will take place tomorrow, garrison cemetery, starting from the barracks."

Pause. The chairman, still glaring at the two guests: "All officers of the garrison will attend." The two officers kept quite still.

Then came discussion of the pullout. It would have to head across the Rhine and into Baden territory. First, when should it happen? It emerged little by little that they would have to enquire at General Headquarters to find where they stand in the queue; the troops here can do nothing on their own, they're to march out in formation. The chairman's neighbour made notes, said: "I'll do the telephoning." The officers whispered. The chairman: "Do the gentlemen have something to say." The General: "It is possible that indignities will be inflicted on troops by the population. There may be shooting. I recommend keeping to the main roads for safety."

Two reservists sitting opposite, jackets unbuttoned, challenged the officers with a mocking look. The younger said: "Alsace is not a war zone. And anyway I object to the chair, Comrade Henschel, worrying about what these officers think."

"You can have your say."

"As I see it, this is no zone of unrest, no war zone. Because there's no war. The officers have lost the war, and now it's over."

"Bravo."

"You finished?"

"Yes. But if anyone starts asking the officers again how it should be done …"

"We can ask their opinion."

"Then that will be a mistake. For then the war will be continuing."

The chairman banged a teaspoon on the table. "The regiments will pull out, you've had your say and the officers too. So we'll send a patrol to Strassburg to ascertain the security situation along the main roads."

The young reservist who had just spoken interrupted angrily: "By thunder, why shouldn't the roads be secure? I was there yesterday. We are not at war."

The chairman in a singsong: "And suppose other regiments are on the march at the same time, artillery maybe, we'll never get through."

"So we wait half an hour. We'll come to an understanding with the comrades."

"So you don't want us to send a patrol to Strassburg."

"We shall not allow them to play war with us any longer. A patrol is superfluous. Always the same old way. Always do what the brass says. So we haven't actually made a revolution! You just need to ask general sir to issue more orders."

"The general's merely senior man of the garrison. There's no longer a colonel, as you know. So we vote whether to send a patrol to Strassburg or not. Two against, eight for."

The young reservist, hands in pockets, legs stretched: "Just keep on like that."

The chairman to his neighbour: "You made a note." Sotto voce: "What are you scribbling away at all the time?"

"It's private, for a letter."

The chairman stared in confusion, he keeps scribbling away, what's he up to?

They discussed stores. The clothing and equipment storerooms on the second floor were packed to the roof with uniforms, greatcoats, munitions, boots, spats, underwear, supplies for several thousand men. The General whispered to the Major: "Say nothing." Major: "Still, I'm curious." Agreement was soon reached that it would be impossible to cart the stores away. So every soldier was to acquire new clothing and carry off any item he lacked. The rest would stay put. They sat pondering this solution. The chairman swore: "The brass leave us to deal with all this clobber, a scandal, they should be strung up."

"Are they the only ones," the reservist piped up again. "That lot ran off in their thousands, like their Supreme War Commander." The scribe at the chairman's side clapped hands in delight. Now the reservist pulled himself up from his slouch: "If you'll allow me, comrade, and if that matter is now settled, I'd like to say something. Why did comrade Georg, our chairman, invite us here? To talk about pulling out, and transport? Good. Have we no other concerns? Us soldiers? Our homes are waiting for us. When we're back they'll ask us what's to happen after four years of mass murder. How we're to settle accounts. This trivial transport matter didn't need all of us to meet together. Comrade Georg could have dealt with it with just one of us. How will the regiments take the revolution forward? What sort of task will they assign themselves?"

MONDAY, 11TH NOVEMBER

The NCO: "You're going too far, comrade. We all want to go home. One's from this place, another from that. Everyone will do his duty."

The scribe threw down his pen. "Disgraceful. And calls itself a Soldiers' Council."

Tumult. Everyone stood. The General and the Major approached the chairman, who was coming towards them. In the corridor the old officer leaned against the wall: "Give me your arm, Major." They went slowly down the stairs. The Major: "They have strong people. The Reich will have a hard time with them."

"I shall stay until the regiments have pulled out. Once the last company has gone I shall take off my tunic and … I cannot bear it."

Curfew in the little town had been set for eight o'clock, but people thronged the streets and dark lanes until late. They came streaming from side streets onto the wide square outside the post office opposite the theatre, not currently performing. Normally they would climb the last two steps to the post office where a little box hung, lit by a gloomy gas flame. In the box, behind a wire screen, the final daily bulletin from the Supreme Army Command dated 8th November was still posted. It read:

> The French, who NE of Oudenarde had taken up
> new positions on the E bank of the Scheldt, were
> forced back across the river by our counter-attack.
> Between Scheldt and Maas we undertook night
> movements according to plan. Rearguard actions
> developed in front of our new lines, which S of
> the Valenciennes-Mons road on the Sambre N of
> Avesnes and on the Maas heights SW of Sedan took
> on considerable scope. These ended everywhere
> with the enemy in retreat.

Tonight they did not climb the steps, or even look up. Some led horses, little clusters of powerful beasts had been brought through the town since afternoon, they came from the Dragoons barracks, from the training ground, soldiers were selling them.

★

Jund the tinsmith stepped from his single-storey cottage into the darkness of the empty street, pulled up his coat collar. Across the way a light was burning in the cake shop beside the little stationers'. The light came through the curtain of a living room, the shop itself was dark, closed. Jund knocked on the lit window, the curtain was drawn back, a nose pressed against the glass. Jund showed his face in the lamplight, the curtain fell back, the house door creaked. He went in. The woman gestured to keep quiet. In the living room a child was asleep in a brass bed, the lamp was shaded by newspaper. Jund took off his coat while the woman stood arms crossed by the bed, regarded him silently. "I can only stay half an hour," he said. Her nostrils flared, she pressed her lips together, made no reply. She was much younger than he, late twenties, small, plump, he was in his forties, had dark hair cut short, deepset eyes, a small dark moustache, his movements slow. "You're talkative tonight," he said and sat down. She whispered: "The child's not asleep yet. And you shouldn't be here." He passed a hand over his face: "I know. But he's not around."

"What if he comes."

"But he won't be here just yet. There's no way they'll be here before the fifteenth."

"How do you know?"

"You can count it on your fingers. Apart from which …"

She stopped him with a vigorous hand gesture and shook her head. She crossed her arms again. Silence.

The man started up again: "How much ready money have you got? At home, or in the savings bank? Because you should be buying."

"Buying what?"

"It's all going for a song. Depends what you want and how much you're willing to pay. The Swabians are leaving everything behind. The barracks is pulling out tomorrow, the officials can't stay once they're gone. You can take whatever you want."

She leaned against the table, attentive. "You off buying, Hermann? Is that why you can only stay half an hour?"

"Lots are leaving all their stuff behind, others are going with debts unpaid. Have all of yours paid up?"

"I only sell for cash. Well, well, they're all going." Her mouth stayed open, she heaved slow breaths. "It'll be hard for me."

"And I won't be here, Walli."

She, after a pause: "What are you going to buy?"

"I thought you could buy that little café of Knapp's in Weissenburg Strasse, the man's already approached me." Excitement flamed in her. He smiled: "Should I? The man must have his money tomorrow."

"I don't have that much, Hermann."

"I'll put it up, Walli."

They stared at one another. He reached for his coat. At the living room door the buxom little woman came up to him, pressed hands to his chest: "But Hermann, when he does come back. Believe me, he will come."

"And what will you do then?"

"And you?"

He smiled at her.

TUESDAY THE 12TH

The Major is up ready, very early. Together with the General he is quartered in a villa abandoned by its owner. Envoys from the Soldiers' Council came early with an order specifying place and time of the funeral for the two murdered soldiers. As garrison senior officer the General has to sign the order. He gouges his name into the paper.

That's why it's a scrawl. In the early hours he was woken by shooting nearby, rang for his orderly, the lout never appeared. Now the lad's helping the old man dress, the old man's berating him, he wants to know what was going on in the night time. The lad said it was Bavarians – what kind of Bavarians – at the station, they were moving through, didn't want to go on, they unhitched the carriages, and then they shot at the signals. "Swine," the General growls. And then it was a motor, continues the lad, who wants to brighten the General's day, it was coming from Strassburg and wouldn't stop. The patrols in town shot at it, but it got away – what kind of motor – the lad helps him on with the jacket, grins behind his back – they said it was Alsatians, they'd stolen an army car, they were heading for Oberhoffen. "Swine." The old man leaves his coffee untouched. Then he listens for the Major's footsteps. He waits a long time. He grows impatient. He summons the lad, asks if the order went up to the Major as well. He says yes. Now the General picks up his cap and climbs the little stairs. But when he has the first flight behind him he hears laughter above. Someone's snorting with laughter, stops, bursts out again. Can it be from the Major's room. The General keeps climbing, tentative, what's the Major up to. He turns his head, sees the lad looking up at him. He beckons to him. "Who's with the Major?"

"No one, General sir."

"No one, wretch, of course there's someone."

"No, General sir." The young chubby-cheeked lad smoothed his tunic, his grin shameless. The General felt for his monocle, he's left it downstairs, ask him to fetch it? No, must look in at once. In the upstairs corridor the Major's lad was sweeping the carpet, stood straight when the General appeared. In the room a salvo of laughter was in progress. Then a smacking sound, another. The General knew which door was the Major's, he stood paralysed until the attack within was over, then he stumbled towards the lad with the broom. "Who is with the Major?"

"No one, General sir."

"The Major is alone?"

"Aye aye, sir." This lad had better control of his face than the one below.

Now the old man knocked on the door. From inside came more smacking noises. And then a shout: "Enter." When the General failed to react to this impertinence, again the shout: "Enter, damn it!" The Major, without a doubt. The lad with the broom was standing behind his back stiff as a post, the General glared at him, I'll wager my lad's lurking on the stairs, but he pressed the handle, stepped quickly in and closed the door behind him.

The Major was sitting in shirt and trousers, barefoot, on a red armchair by the window, back to the door. Braces hung over each arm of the chair. His head was fiery red. He turned in irritation to the door, mouth ready for a damn. His right hand wielded a thin cane with a short piece of rag at the end, a kind of fly-swat. As the General stepped in he leapt to his feet, the stick fell to the floor, he clutched at his trousers, pulled the braces up over his shoulders: "Beg pardon, General." A newspaper on the chair arm slithered to the carpet. The General at the door bowed stiffly: "Please don't let me inconvenience you," and stared at the Major. He glanced around the room.

Citizens and Soldiers

Coffee things on the table, ink pot and pen beside them, so he did sign as well, otherwise there's no one here, the Major really is on his own. "I permitted myself to knock, Major, thought you had company."

The Major: "One minute. Won't you take a seat, General." And vanished into the next room. He soon came back out in housecoat and boots, sat in the armchair next to the old man, who was gripping the cap on his knees, and who at once began:

"It's about the so-called funeral ceremony for those two fellows." He looked keenly at the Major, maybe he's gone mad: "Like to know how you intend to comport yourself there."

The Major, who had not yet combed his hair, pushed grey strands back from his temples with both hands:

"Yes, exactly what I've been thinking. The men sent me an order, I signed it, it's for ten o' clock, you signed it too, General."

"Signed, yes."

"Have to attend, General."

The pale nostrils constricted: "For those murderers? Not I." The Major's face became noticeably pale and pinched, his normal expression returned, his eyes glinted, his look was cold: "I would recommend attendance."

"They want to humble us, can't you see."

"Of course. Nothing we can do. They'll bump us all off eventually."

"One can evade them. Before they come, one can …"

"Of course. Naturally. But that's beside the point."

"So what is the point? You seem in especially high spirits today, Major."

It was an accusation. The Major bent to gather the newspaper, glanced at the fly-spattered wall, whispered: "Lots of insects here, General. I've been hunting them."

His look was sly: "There they are, squashed."

"Who?"

"Young flies, and …" the Major held a hand to his lips, leaned close to the old man: "others."

So he is mad.

"With your permission, General, I shall read some items from the newspaper. They brought it up along with the order." The old man shrugged. The Major, undeterred, began: "First, some items that come as no surprise. Our troops are now east of the Maas, fighting splendidly. Are you acquainted with First Lieutenant Hennings of the 207th Brandenburg Reserve Infantry Regiment? I know his father. The boy was mentioned in despatches, along with a Saxon first lieutenant."

The old man, grim-faced: "Know neither of 'em." The Major, soothing: "They're resisting. Then a government appeal to the Home Army."

"Who signed that bit of bumph?"

"Three people. The socialist Ebert's playing at Reich Chancellor, one's called Göhre, member of the Reichstag, War Minister Schëuch."

"Wouldn't like to be in his shoes."

"His Majesty is in Holland. The Dutch government has decided to intern him."

The old man held hands over his ears: "Stop."

"Now to the point. If you'll forgive me." And as the old man flicked the cap impatiently back and forth across his knees, the Major sucked in his cheeks, pursed his lips and perused the newspaper. There were twitches about the eyes and the corners of his mouth. In a low controlled voice he read out: "The new government had taken over the conduct of business in order to protect the German people from civil war and starvation, and to implement justified demands for self-determination."

He fell silent, eyes on the paper. The old man's cap flicked back and forth: "Continue." The Major's nostrils flared, his face began to redden again: "Nice, what, General: protect the German people from civil war and starvation."

"Absurd," the General crowed, "who is causing civil war and starvation. They are!"

"No, not them exactly." He lifted the paper in the manner one picks up a puppy by the neck: "They're not the cause. Listen, General." And he lowered the paper, laid it over his knees and leapt at his prey: "We were at 'justified demands for self-determination'. Self-determination is all the rage, Wilson included it in his Fourteen Points, in our country the workers, the socialists, the little man, want their voices heard for once. 'This task for the new government can be accomplished only if all institutions and officials in town and country extend a helping hand.'"

"Absurd. They'll be waiting a long time."

The Major, paper in hand, strode across the room, around the table: "Don't say that, General. The helping hand will be extended by us to the new government. But our helping hand shan't lift them out of their little jam too hastily."

And here again the same laughter: "I know, he writes, the new Reich Chancellor, that many will find it difficult to work with the new men who have undertaken to steer the Reich. He knows well how to read our thoughts, he can sense something, he's afraid, but he's canvassing, he's not giving up. He says: I appeal to your love for our nation." The Major stood, leaned with his hand on the table, and tittered contentedly to himself, waving the paper: "Yes, that's how it is. It will sometimes be difficult. But he appeals to our love for the nation. It's like a death in the family, you forgive all the aggravations, don't you, he's taken over the government, it's no joke, no joke for

Comrade Ebert."

The General smacked his thigh with an open palm and cried: "These fellows have no shame, they should be seen off with a horsewhip."

"He's inviting us. He's in the seat of power, otherwise, General, you and I would not be sitting here and would not have been forced to sign that bit of bumph. He's in the seat of power, and invites us ..."

"And what do you think of it?"

"That he's an enormous donkey, such a donkey as you could never imagine. He's a yellow chicken. He's an utterly common jackass. He'd be ten times happier to have this whole ruling business behind him."

"Then he should leave us be, and stop maltreating us."

It was as if the Major had waited only for a spark to send him marching around the table. This was the march step the General heard stomping every morning over this head: "Maltreat! Us!" He laughed, jeered: "That pack, maltreat us! That jackass! Who'd like to maltreat me! Ripping off my epaulettes ..."

He dashed to the door, called the lads: "Both lads to the garden, this minute! Dig!" He positioned himself by the window, and when he saw them pushed it open, called: "To the fence!" He closed the window: "They're taken care of. Please excuse me."

"Ripping off epaulettes," the General repeated from his chair; waited. The Major stood in front of him, brought his blood-red head so low that the General recoiled, the Major blew into his ear: "And so we shall rip off their heads." The General, shocked, reached out an arm: "In God's good hands."

Slowly, lips twitching, the Major moved back to the table. The paper lay there, his face paled, he picked it up: "So, this bit of nonsense from the new government, to tackle the situation with gloves and wooden pegs: 'I appeal to your love of the nation.' Further on: 'A refusal by any organisation at this grave hour would deliver Germany up to disorder and the gravest distress. Therefore support the Fatherland with fearless and undaunted cooperation, everyone at his post, until the hour of the new dispensation has arrived. Berlin, 9th November.'"

The Major stood with both hands pressing on the table, the paper crumpled under his left hand: "He'd better brace himself. The hour of the new dispensation is coming." He banged his fist on the table: "And that's who the Kaiser fled from."

The General: "He was advised to do so."

"Shouldn't have done it. All words on the matter are superfluous … What do you have in mind, General?"

"About what?"

"You came to take me off to the funeral of those two scoundrels."

"You're going?"

"Naturally."

The General climbed wearily to his feet. "I thank you most sincerely for this tactic."

"I hope you'll come along. You will not abandon your post."

"I am fully occupied here with the withdrawal, I am unavailable for other matters."

"They'll drag you out of the house."

"I think, Major, that you will follow me in this."

"My thanks."

"What?"

"Thank you."

"Since I am your superior officer, and order you to accompany me to the barracks on official business."

The Major stood at the table, head down in

contemplation. "With the utmost respect, I request a statement from the General of what he hopes to accomplish at the barracks, since in accordance with his signature he is required to attend the funeral."

"So I'm too busy. Cannot permit myself, neither can you, to take part in this performance."

A pause. The Major looks directly at the General, the old man stands stiffly erect. The Major bowed slightly, a smile opened his lips: "Beg permission to shake the General's hand. Would only remark that I have made my opinion known."

The old man waved him away. The Major stared in puzzlement.

As they went down the stairs the General said: "Don't forget to call the lads back in from the garden, or they'll be fooling about all morning."

No one at the barracks paid them any attention. But after the two officers had walked the lower corridors, they encountered two men carrying an enormous wreath with red ribbons, who continued on without a greeting and then came to a stop behind them. One walked back to the officers, looked them sideways in the face, pulled out a watch: "It's half past eight, funeral's at nine." The officers walked on, the man whistled for others. Two Soldiers' Council men with black crepe on their arms were coming downstairs. The man hurried to meet them, said something, the pair – Chairman Henschel and his secretary – stood where they were until the officers came level with them. Henschel brandished a watch: "Half past eight, gentlemen."

The officers greeted him, nodded, went on up without a word. The soldiers followed them, the men with the wreath came along, others arrived, they were in the first floor corridor. After a brief conversation with his companions, Henschel overtook the officers, blocked the way, at once they were surrounded by a cluster of men. Henschel: "Gentlemen, nine o' clock." The General, curt: "The garrison will pull out tomorrow or the next day. When will you make preparations." At once the Major jumped in: "Beg to suggest that this discussion take place in a closed room." Before the councillors could formulate a reply he pulled open the nearest door, it was an empty dormitory, three-tier bunks, window wide open, the General followed on the Major's heels, the two councillors followed hesitantly; before the next man could enter the Major shut the door in his face: "One moment please."

The discussion was brief. The General declared himself unable to reconcile with his sense of duty occupying with ceremonies the short time before the withdrawal; if he were to die at this moment, they could throw him into the grave without formality.

The Major, seeing the danger, leaped in heedless of what it might cost. He adopted a rather harsh tone. They would withdraw into the Fatherland like a band of robbers. Henschel, annoyed and uncertain, said there was no need to remind them of their duty, but whispered to the secretary, who made furious grimaces and strode to the door, but the Major had placed himself in front of it. Then the chairman asked what the officers thought should happen now. And when the old man, who would not be deterred, declared obstinately that organisation was the thing, not celebrations, the secretary hissed: "Who's celebrating?" Henschel grunted: "Are we celebrating? The funeral will take place anyway as announced, nine o' clock. Of course we don't all need to head off there. All it needs is for the Soldiers' Council and the officer corps, such as there is, to be represented. So you gentlemen need to decide which one of you will go."

The General: "You have heard my opinion." The chairman turned to the Major: "Then it'll have to be you, Major." General and Major exchanged glances, the General understood the little twitch in the Major's face. The Major: "Then I shall represent the officer corps, but on the understanding that everything will be conducted in an orderly fashion." Henschel was about to speak, but the secretary had pulled open the door, the corridor was crowded with men. The officers and councillors pushed their way through, Henschel vented his fury in curses: "Look sharp now, to the yard, fall in."

The Major and the General marched downstairs, unhurried, the Major gripped the old man's arm, whispered: "Stick close to me in the yard."

The men were lining up, the officers walked unhindered all across the yard to the gate. The General took his leave, the Major returned to the yard to stand alongside the Soldiers' Council. A dirge began to play. Two coffins were carried from the central doorway. Drumroll.

A slow march down Barracks Road to the nearby graveyard. The soldiers marched in loose formation, four abreast. The road was lined with civilians and military. The menacing procession with the coffins pressed on. The Major, in a rank with three councillors, stared rigidly ahead at the two hearse wagons. As they grouped themselves around the graves that lay ready to receive the coffins, the atmosphere grew sinister. After prayers by a Catholic priest, a soldier spoke. The murderer was cursed, the thricefold "struck down" ended in a menacing cry. When the Major had thrown the customary three handfuls of sand from the shovel into the grave, a civilian, apparently trying to reach the grave, whispered from behind: "Be sure to get away, Major, they're plotting something." He had already noticed. But how to get away from a thousand men in broad daylight.

"You promised I'd be safe," he said to Henschel, as they moved back from the grave. Henschel angrily pulled the secretary closer: "The band must play. A few sure men to me." And as "I had a comrade dear" rose from the crowd's throats over the graveyard, the Major was able to make his escape behind a group of soldiers, first to the sexton's house, then homeward in the sexton's cape and peaked cap.

Edgy and grim, he changed into civvies upstairs, went down to the General, who extended a hand with a big smile. The Major quickly filled him in, his voice shaking. "Are you afraid?" the old man asked. The Major rasped: "Pointless letting ourselves be killed like rats, they'll be outside the house in half an hour."

Ten minutes later they were riding in a small forage cart driven by the two loyal lads. The cart bounced about horribly, they sat stiffly facing each other under the canvas awning, the lads drove as if possessed. Now and then someone shouted at them from the street, now and then a shot rang out. Once the General turned his small narrow old man's face towards the Major with the green felt cap, the round hard eyes blazed: "Do you feel no shame, Major?"

The Major had been grinding his teeth all the while, squeezing the cap on his knees. He answered, not looking up from his feet: "Amputation without anaesthetic. Better to be clubbed to death." They bounced up and down in the cart.

*

Around this time Lieutenant von Heiberg, the hunted man, was at long last leaving Strassburg. The wind had not changed, as his friend the adjutant had hoped. General von Lossberg, commanding general from the Prince

Albrecht Army, and Lieutenant Colonel von Holleben had spoken bravely and cleverly before the Soldiers' Council, had offered resistance, had said No – and then from the Supreme Command came the order: Give way! From the Supreme Command itself! The little adjutant, shocked, took his leave of Heiberg: "Be proud, my boy, that you fired a shot before they forbade it! I've rustled up a ticket to Berlin for you, from Kehl, using a random name, here's the paybook. They'll bring you a soldier's greatcoat and cap."

"Leaving right away?"

"Yes, across the bridge with all the others. Farewell, Heiberg! See you in Berlin!"

Moving east along the railway track, he was drawn on by a veritable river of humanity. Soldiers and civilians weighed down with baggage, heading out of the city towards the Rhine. In the east of the city gangs of ruffians came running, jeering, howling, waving tricolours, vanished as rapidly as they appeared. A few times shots came from side streets. The crowd pushed silently on.

It was half past eleven before they neared the bridge, and then had to wait. For people were coming in the other direction too, from Kehl, many, many. They were welcomed by uniformed nurses and elegant ladies. Trucks, ambulances, steaming soup cauldrons stood waiting. Among them were soldiers wearing the same uniform as those leaving the city. These were Alsatians in military service, civilians, freed prisoners, they too were weighed down with baggage. The weak, the old, the sick.

Before Heiberg had a chance to commit a blunder, he was pushed forward, trudged amidst the crowd of men, women, children, over the bridge. The good old Rhine swirled by below. A barrage of catcalls pursued them from the Strassburg end. Then they were across, on German soil.

used to making his views known in public, or even in a moderately large gathering, he normally dealt one on one. But his soul burned with news he had read with his own eyes this very morning, touching on the same matter reported to the local Soldiers' Council by this Herr Hintze from the unknown HQ. It informed the manager that the Entente would not conclude peace with a Bolshevik Germany, because in an entity of that kind no durable and authoritative governmental power could be found, and so the Entente would have no alternative but to march into Germany and restore order. It was hard to know this and be unable to speak it out, but Anton Ringermüller managed with the help of his innate shyness. Only when he extricated himself from the throng and came face to face with someone he knew, the tinsmith Jund out on a buying spree, did he dare to reveal his knowledge. Jund reacted with equanimity, remarking: "The French will be here after the fifteenth, the date's not certain, and then we'll see."

At which Ringermüller too calmed down, and his thoughts slid at once to the problem his boss had set him this morning: to acquire red and blue canvas for flags and bunting. There was enough red available from German flaggery, and white from bedsheets – but blue? Blue? He confessed this problem to Jund as well. Jund was expansive: there's lots of possibilities. He put a jovial arm over Ringermüller's shoulders, pulled him to a seat, and started giving him advice.

*

Around two in the afternoon, the deserter and malingerer Walter Ziweck from Kaiserslautern slipped out of the military hospital, where they were about to put him back in the cell on account of his erratic behaviour. He'd caught wind of it, and had also reconnoitred the location of the two rifles the hospital sentries kept tucked away in the building. When Ziweck appeared on the stairs in hospital gown, over it a soldier's greatcoat, cap and rifle, the porter, still ensconced in his room by the entrance because it was his post and he was paid to be there, was unwilling to open the door. Ziweck took underarm aim at him, and the porter cringed. He let Ziweck out, you never know who it is confronting you. The deserter ran, gripping the rifle butt-first, down the road to the town. It was noon, people ahead screamed, moved out of his way, no one stopped him. There were soldiers along the way, they signalled grinning to the shouters to keep calm, he's just letting himself go, people have to let it out after holding themselves in for so long.

Ziweck knew the town, he had been house servant, delivery man and carter for an ironmonger's, the owner had sacked him. That's where he was headed, he meant to settle accounts. He found the place easily, didn't enter the shop but at once climbed the stairs inside the building and rang the bell. The owner was in the shop, the woman and her daughter were in town, the housemaid opened up, he shoved her aside, she squealed, fell dumb with terror when he raised the rifle butt, she didn't know him. She had to tell him where the master and mistress were, he searched all the rooms with her in tow to assure himself they weren't there. Then he declared that he was seizing the apartment and its contents, the master and mistress no longer had any claim on it. He locked and bolted the door, barricaded the kitchen exit with chairs. The rifle stayed with him all the while. In the kitchen she had to finish what she was cooking, with him beside her. He calmed her as she did so, handed her flour and salt, took a taste.

Within half an hour, Ziweck and the girl – he said he can see she's a sensible person – were engaged in friendly chat. She felt a certain attraction to him. He explained among other things that they'd locked him up and wouldn't let him out even with the revolution going on, the authorities still like to act large. He told her of his service at the front, of torments and malingerers, and now he and the girl had the same opinion of the boss class. It seemed only right that she'd once put one over madam and daughter during a big cleanup, they tyrannised and maltreated the staff; but Ziweck kept saying: "That's over and done with now."

After a while they sat down amicably in the dining room at the table they'd both helped lay. He invited her to sit, there's nothing to worry about. She laughed shyly, she'd no idea the revolution included domestics as well, and was so nice for the common people. "How's that," he said, stuffing bread into his mouth, "you think the oppressors will stay on top in the revolution? The military police are on the case."

Encouraged, she fetched the best wine from the larder, cognac, she knew where the mistress hid the good coffee and tinned milk. In this way the meal stretched over one and a half hours, then he lit the master's cigars, she smoked cigarettes. And then he wound up the gramophone and played popular tunes. They danced a bit, had a little kiss. They drifted to the master bedroom, she carefully drew back the bedding, he stood the rifle against the mirrored wardrobe and declared: "I'll shave after, then we'll go down to the shop and have it out with the boss." The housemaid felt happy as she undressed, the revolution was just like a birthday: "What would madam say if she found us in her bed?" Ziweck, holding her in a wild embrace and groaning with excitement – how long since he'd felt a woman against his skin: "They'd all just better notice that there's revolution."

TUESDAY THE 12TH

It was almost five when she woke him. He didn't want to wake up. The doorbell had rung. She crept in a shirt to the door and peeped through the spyhole, it was the postman, he rang again, then went slowly back downstairs. In the bedroom she found Ziweck silently pulling on socks and trousers, yawning and grumpy. When he had the heavy army boots on and was buttoning the braces, he stood up, and she looked at him. She had lain down again, wanted to go back to sleep, she was a silly happy creature from the countryside, thought what had happened here was the revolution, soldiers in the street had already told her so many wonderful things about it, and now it had come to her. But she was frightened by his silent demeanour and the innocuous facial tic that now reappeared; his mouth formed a pout, there was a snort, then the mouth went back to normal. She dressed uneasily, and suddenly had a dreadful fear. She said nothing, he said nothing. She said: "I'll be right back," and disappeared into the corridor. But he heard her working at the lock and asked: "What are you doing?" She whimpered: "I thought ... I thought, because the doorbell rang."

"Come back," he ordered, quite composed, "we shan't be frightened of anyone." Then she flung her arms about his neck and gave him a big kiss, no, it's revolution. Then the bell really did ring. He said, "Come into the living room." And when she didn't move, he pulled her in.

The owner was standing outside. There now developed the scene that by evening became the talk of the town. The ironmonger banged on the door, Ziweck wouldn't stand for noise and warned he'd shoot through the door, there was nothing here for the owner. So the ironmonger withdrew and went to the police. The two policemen who were sent along negotiated with Ziweck through the door, he was rude to them, they'll be put up against a wall by his comrades if they don't skedaddle. They weren't sure what to do, it's a military matter, we'd rather not be involved. The ironmonger's shouting attracted a small crowd in the street, which didn't take his side. A window opened, Ziweck yelled down threats, suddenly a shot rang out, at once the street cleared, no one was hit. Ten minutes later a truck pulled up with ten armed men. One, wearing a Soldiers' Council armband, called boldly from behind the truck: "Comrade!" Again, "Comrade!" Ziweck showed himself, rifle aimed: "What d'you want?"

"We're from the Soldiers' Council. Nothing will happen to you. Come down."

A curse was the answer. The man below tried again to negotiate, he thought Ziweck was drunk like everyone else. "Comrade, this won't do, come down now, what will the good citizens here think." Another curse. Now the man below roared a warning. Ziweck spat down at him, and tapped his brow: "You're just horned cattle. Call yourselves revolutionaries? Rabble." And fired. It hit the truck, they flung themselves behind it for cover, and directed a regular fusillade at the building. Windowpanes shattered, women screamed from neighbouring houses.

The man upstairs gave no more thought to the girl. And gradually through the fear it dawned on her that he was no longer watching her. All he did was hurl insults. They had already brought him to a reprise of his cell situation, barricaded behind the bed. Bullets whizzed merrily through the gaping windows, into masonry. But Ziweck was back at the table, drinking master's cognac. Barbara from Ensisheim was for sure a blend of goose and calf, as the ironmonger's wife told herself daily. But beneath her peasant ineptness lay hidden instincts and knowledge, and just now she was governed by the well-known blend of curiosity, libidinousness and respect for a man that in so many females counts as attraction and gives them second sight. This was Barbara's first amorous adventure, at least since she'd left the village, she'd never come close to any man in town. Now, even though she was frightened of Ziweck, who'd descended to her so suddenly from Heaven, still she liked him very much and didn't want to lose him at any price. She was obstinate, especially in matters of love. They'd made him ill in the war, now he was out of hospital and she had to stand by him. And she left him at it because he was the man after all, but for her part did what she thought would help.

First she sat on his knee at the table, a habit from her village days. Then, to the astonishment of the men below, she closed the green shutters, they stopped firing as she did so and for quite a while afterwards, believing the girl he was holding hostage to be their confederate who would deliver the man up to them. She left one shutter open for observation, and considered what to do. She'd love to know from him why these other soldiers were bothering them, him being a soldier too, and making revolution. "That's what I'd like to know," Ziweck replied in between threats, and he wanted to stand at the window and hurl curses. But bullets ploughed into the ceiling, stucco fell, she pushed the armchair in which he was now fixed, and the table together with the bottle, up against the door. He tried to stand, eyes on the damaged ceiling. Swore some more, eyes bulging, damned traitors to the people, but he overdid the next swig. Barbara knew how men drank, she knew too it was dangerous to interfere. She stood there perplexed, determined to help but with no idea how.

Then it dawned on her: all I need do is tell the soldiers we're in the revolution too. Suddenly she was disgusted by the soldiers still firing away. They were screwy. Ziweck tried to stand, but as he swayed she pushed him gently

Citizens and Soldiers

back into the chair. Eyes flashing, he offered her a little glass of cognac, she took a sip, but had to empty the glass. And now, as he continued to pay close attention to the tracks of bullets in the ceiling, such a remarkable play of nature, she slipped away to the front door.

The assault squad beside and behind the truck saw her at the street door, two men ran across. So Barbara the presumed hostage had escaped. The man must be dead. That's what they thought. Instead the girl went for them, screamed and clawed like a maenad. Blonde hair hung loose over her shoulder, she wore no blouse, only a green dressing gown, shirt and socks just as she'd climbed out of bed. She went for the men spitting and shrieking: "What are you doing, what's all this shooting, he's a soldier like you, he's ill, he's come from the hospital, and you're shooting. But it's revolution."

They crept perplexed and embarrassed out from behind the truck, one by one each with his rifle. What had they landed themselves in. The girl screamed: "Why" and again "Why". They really didn't know why. One said: "The police raised the alarm, it's not his apartment." But it caused consternation that the girl had suddenly taken his side, and they listened to her. Actually she was quite right. What are the police to us? To crown it all, the ironmonger now pushed forward to hear what was going on. But words stuck in his throat when he saw Barbara in his wife's green dressing gown, holding it closed in front of all these men. The soldiers angrily shoved the ironmonger back, they really shouldn't have got themselves stirred up for the likes of him. They said: "Now, gorgeous, what state is he in?"

"What are you going to do with him?"

"Is he wounded?"

"He's asleep. Why don't you leave." Now the men laughed at her, two grabbed her and held her tight, others stormed into the building and up the stairs, she screamed "Ziweck, they're coming, Ziweck, Ziweck!" But he didn't hear.

When the first man entered, rifle at the ready – the girl had left all the doors open, and they could see the man from the doorway – there was Ziweck in the armchair with its little wheels, struggling with what consciousness remained to steer the chair out of the living room into the corridor, no doubt intending to prolong the conflict. And he did strike out at them as they entered and leapt on him, he yelled in fury. But he soon slid helpless to the floor.

They dragged him out, legs flailing, they hauled him down the stairs, into the truck. Barbara tussled with the men. They didn't do anything to him, they recognised a hospital patient from the gown, off they drove. They made slow progress, Barracks Road was thronged with a dangerous crowd.

But Barbara was taken to the police. She was wearing the ironmonger's wife's dressing gown, and was complicit in Ziweck's spree.

*

At the same time a festive atmosphere was building in the town. People had various reasons to rejoice, some because the French would be here by morning, and there'd be an end to the rationing of bread, butter, meat and coal; others reckoned on the fifteenth at the earliest, but were just as happy as the others; the soldiers were happy because they were in marching mood, we're going home, home, back home. Meanwhile others were nervous for various reasons, in part the same reasons that caused others to rejoice.

Everyone sensed that a lot would happen today. What

would it be: rioting, shooting, or what? And to take part in it, from midday on everything with legs was out in the streets. Shopkeepers were at their wits' end, should they close or stay open, people were spending but on the other hand there might be looting, and they were reluctant to let anyone in.

Wandering through the crowds were many who were seldom or never seen here, certainly never in such numbers! Hordes of peasant men and women, honest to goodness Alsatians in short jackets, shiny buttons, flat hats and, following behind, their female adjuncts in wide swaying skirts from which short sturdy legs in bright coloured stockings came into view. On the heads huge white bonnets like big airy birds that had settled on them out in the forests, they wouldn't be parted from them and so brought them along into town as their insignia. Like their husbands and brothers they were a strapping red-cheeked race. They didn't stroll like townsfolk one by one along pavements and into shops, but had equipped themselves with horse carts, oxcarts, horse-drawn wagons, some pushed wheelbarrows, and the barrows were empty, the owners left them standing in alleys as they made themselves comfortable in taverns. It wasn't clear what they wanted here in such numbers and with such modes of transport – they who so seldom showed up in town because townies (greedy, cajoling) collected what they produced from the source. But now these lords and ladies loitered here. News of the revolution had penetrated to every nearby village, meaning: it's all topsy-turvy in town, there's no authority any more, you take what you can, haul away whatever you find. This is why they had turned up, many from early morning. But since nothing was happening, they passed the time drinking.

There were men, too, of quite another sort, for whom

people stepped aside. These wandered in twos, threes, fours and fives along the road, poor tattered men, mostly of a big powerful build with wild brown or blond beards. They wore high black army boots, some had only slippers or ruined shoes. Military tunics hung on the bodies, long black greatcoats, some showed evidence of what had once been a fur. Most were pale and hollow-eyed. They were half-starved Russians from the prison camp, relics of the glorious Battle of the Masurian Lakes. For a day or two after the guards ran away they kept outside the town, then they had to disperse, do what they could to save themselves, for who was going to feed them. The bundles in their hands contained eating utensils, little wooden playthings in the shape of mobile lizards, snakes, carved with care and artistry and crudely painted. These they offered in return for a hunk of bread. There were whole squads in possession of little barrows in which they transported their sick and their bedding. Some came along dragging mattress-sacks from the camp. These processions became dammed up in the marketplace. The town's society ladies had set up a kind of rest stop for them outside the café. In nurses' uniforms and civvies they distributed bread and milky coffee, a few pressed coins into the poor men's hands.

Soldiers' Council patrols moving armed through the streets were uneasy in the crowds. They felt a lack of respect, indeed it seemed some of the youngsters loitering about so cheekily paid them no attention at all. Some patrols decided to withdraw to barracks, and declared that unless reinforced they couldn't bring undisciplined troops to heel. Then representatives of the Council who happened to be around started to debate whether or not they should send out reinforcements, it might provoke trouble, better cooperate with the good old police who are still at their posts.

But already the first wounded soldiers were being led to the barracks, to be taken straight to the military hospital. They were only slightly hurt, the men were obviously using trivial wounds as an excuse to be released from their unwelcome task. Fights had broken out in very dispiriting circumstances, namely in debates with the so-called Citizens' Defence, of which the soldiers raised bitter complaints. These were young civilians, locals of course, with red and white armbands bearing a stamp, some had rifles, they violated decrees and used their fists. They said they'd been entrusted by the mayor to keep order in the streets.

As if a command had been given, around three in the afternoon the turmoil withdrew from the town centre to the periphery. Every lane and alleyway was jammed full of people and carts, all heading to where the landscape was barest and most haunted, to the barracks district, long wide Barracks Road. Why? Did unarmed citizens mean to storm the barracks and take troops prisoner?

Even in the barracks, no one at first realised quite what was happening. They weren't frightened, because they were keyed up and there were plenty of weapons. The people outside, townsmen and women, peasant men and women with barrows and oxcarts certainly didn't look ready to storm the Bastille. They'd been drawn here by a rumour that the barracks were about to be ransacked. The promised looting that had drawn them all to town – everyone had known this with certainty for the past hour – was to take place right now.

Lines of removal vans crowded the north end of Barracks Road. Some were stationed outside villas, where furniture was being carried into the road. Civil officials moving out watched appalled as a pillage-hungry mob shoved its way through and surrounded the vans. There were shouts and threats. But nothing more serious, people still respected private property. In every group were a few calm men and women holding back the hotheads. "Let the Swabs leave in peace! Else they'll go on calling us a pack of thieves." And so the removal men saw that, though the vans were besieged by a noisy crowd, not a single item was taken.

But outside the barracks, that huge long structure with firmly closed gates, was a seething mass of townsmen and women and those in flat hats and short black waistcoats, peasant lasses with bulging calves and healthy faces, wrinkled matrons.

And towards three o' clock a window on the second floor halfway along the block was opened as far as it would go, soldiers, bareheaded, stood there laughing and calling down, and like a swarm of bees drawn by the scent of blossom, the mob flooded across the roadway. The soldiers vanished, but reappeared to hurl armfuls of stuff out of the window. First came boots, hobnails landed on the pavement with just a patter, then the rustle and clatter of leather goods, field dressings, belts, slings, cartridge pouches, paramedic packs.

From other windows masses of objects were ejected that bounced about, utensils of all kinds, a rain of trousers, jackets, braces, gaiter fastenings, leather gaiters. Other windows extruded woollen underwear, socks. From another came the crash of shovels and iron cooking pots. Surging smashing drumming without pause. And howling human voices too. Now and then a consignment was preceded by a warning whistle.

How eagerly the soldiers up there grubbed and shovelled at the stores of clothing and kit. With what sense of release did they scatter the stuff down onto the road. For they knew the meaning of the underwear, the shovels, boots: materiel for a new winter campaign. There they go, shovels for trenches and our own graves. Those greatcoats were meant to clothe new regiments who would be shot to pieces wearing them. Death, blood, cannon's roar from every piece. They dragged them as far as they could, hurled them out of the window, down to the voracious civilians. They'll be in good hands there. From there it can never come again.

They did what they could to put an end to this war. And so they disobeyed the Council's order to protect the stores of clothing and equipment. That's why there were arguments in the barracks all morning. A majority of the Council wanted only to provide the soldiers with fresh clothing, everything else that couldn't be carried off was to be left where it was. No one was to "encroach on State property". And what if the huge inventory should fall into French hands, that would still be in order, and no one had any further rights over the goods. But a majority of the rank and file were unconvinced. Finally the sentries posted by the Council itself outside the storerooms were taken by surprise, and the word went out: all stores are property of the soldiers. And they honoured this motto and acted accordingly, hour after hour.

Soldiers young and old walk unchallenged in and out of the gates. They wear new clothes, carry stuff out. Peasants and townsfolk on the other side of the long road stand in clumps waiting for them. There's buying and selling. Sacks are stuffed full, peasant carts load up.

Citizens uninvolved up till now are drawn by the noise and bustle. Lurking among them are army officers and government officials, still in town to ensure their belongings get away safely. In civilian dress they push through the throngs of peasants and townsfolk and gaze at the outrageous spectacle. Some are squashed for a while against the iron railings of the house where the blind captain used to live; the shutters are closed. They brave the dreadful devastating scene for a long while, it's as mesmerising as a volcanic eruption. For they too know: what is being thrown from the windows is the last chance of a final resistance. It would still have been possible to salvage some honour. In anger and disgust they watch as the toil of thousands, day and night, incessant wartime activity in factories to protect the front and the homeland, is simply thrown away. What is being despoiled here and snapped up by these beasts of peasants and townsfolk is the German Fatherland, the Reich, the officer corps, the entire state. They try to endure the sight. Bartering on every side. They push on. How the soldiers laugh and wave from every window in the barracks, how they howl. Calamity.

After five o' clock soldiers exit the main gate, armed. Others sweep the corridors and prevent the final emptying of the storerooms. Word is: there are still many comrades to be considered. With that the upstairs windows are closed at last. Barracks Road slowly empties.

Darkness. A few lanterns.

Again the rattle of moving vans. They go creaking along the streets. They make haste towards the main roads, and away.

★

The peasants are back in their villages with their loot. Many are drunk. Fellow villagers, the old, children, gather round and listen to their stories. It's a joy.

In the town, on dark Theatre Place near the Hotel Europe formerly frequented by officers, the army bulletin of 8th November is still on display in its frame behind the wire screen. Rain has loosened the top half. Anyone climbing the steps can still take note of the fighting south of the Valenciennes-Mons road, that ended with the enemy in retreat. Only a few days have passed, but Time marches on with enormous vigour.

Strong patrols criss-cross the town until midnight, the barracks gates are barred shut, barbed wire barriers have been set up inside. Order has been re-imposed by an outburst of rage from Henschel, chairman of the Soldiers' Council. He had noticed already that morning at the graveyard that the reins were slipping from his hands, and behind his back soldiers were being incited to violence. The town lies in total silence under endless rain, cocooned by night. The Tuesday that has floated by has brought a great deal into the world.

No longer here are the General (the senior officer) and the Major. They have fled to Strassburg. No longer here are many families of army officers and government officials, who until today were in hiding.

Stretched in their graves beneath fresh mounds of earth covered in big wreaths with red ribbons, drenched in cold rain, the two soldiers who were shot by the adjutant during the brush with the colonel. One a farm labourer from Donaueschingen, an illegitimate child, the other a cabinetmaker's apprentice, elder of two brothers, both strong young men, their strength now no more, extinguished, in this condition differing not at all from an eighty year old man who enjoyed a long life and died of old age, no different from the hundreds around them in the graveyard from more civil times.

Barbara from Ensisheim, silly truculent maidservant, young revolutionary, is snoring in a cell at the police station. Instead of her mistress's lovely green dressing gown she is again wearing the threadbare little costume she had left lying in the bedroom. The policeman on watch is snoring on a chaise longue in the office.

The life of Barbara's lover Ziweck hasn't changed. He's sleeping as usual in his bare cell. Whatever the days bring, whether the revolution makes great strides, whether it's victorious or defeated, Ziweck always lands back in the cell. He's an unruly spirit, a vigorous man who ponders action and undertakes much. The cell is the calm centre of his life.

The Chief Medical Officer had to return to the hospital to visit Ziweck. His medical orderly advised him to have the corn on his left foot removed. It was done. This was a fateful decision. The Chief and his chubby wife are now also asleep.

The Tuesday that has drifted by is an insignificant data point in the Spanish Flu's ongoing rampage of Dark private houses, barracks are wide open to it. People lie asleep and feel nothing of its activity within them. Invisible demons sink into the throat, descend to the lungs. The body will soon be in a state of alarm. The person with all his knowledge is still asleep, in the morning he'll be listless and not understand and be reluctant to rise, he'll touch his forehead and feel hot. In the meantime his flesh, his doughty body, has recognised the opponent and taken up arms against the demons.

They're awake in the homes of the Procurator, of the mayor, of the ladies of the Patriotic Women's League. Dozens of seamstresses bend over their machines, paid assistants, even the ladies join in, they're rushing full speed ahead to sew flags big and small in blue-white-red. For after Tuesday comes Wednesday, after Wednesday come Thursday and Friday, and by Saturday the French may already be here. The work is distributed among all the rooms. They cut up bales of proud black white and red cloth supplied dirt cheap by fabric dealers. The black is flung aside in a heap, red and white go to the cutters and seamstresses, they still need blue, but a solution has been found: they're dying white cloth. Everywhere there's whispering, the ladies look after their guests, keep them awake with strong tea, they may be paying, but don't want it thought the work is done only for money.

Mamselle Köpp, the milliner with the two-fathered unborn baby, is there at her whirring treadle. She doesn't sing, like Faust's Gretchen: "My peace is gone, my heart is sore". She's happy, for she has an item in her pocket that means promotion. She went this morning to the wife of the factory director, mother of the first lieutenant her ravager, to lay out her tragic salvation. The house was magnificent, overwhelming, more opulent even than a film. The lady was distraught, and after questioning her on this and that gave her the husband's visiting card, and she's to look him up in his office in the morning.

*

Someone is running in the dark, blithe as a butterfly across fields.

It's the Jewish hop dealer Julius Bernt, resident of the town.

He took part in the Romanian campaign and was sent back months ago with chronic dysentery. He got over it, but remained weak and had to battle to stay at home, had to drag himself to one assessment after another. And now it's all over. Ever since the first revolutionary troops appeared in the streets, he's sat quietly up till now in his tiny dark ground floor flat on Station Square. No more requirement to report to barracks, attend at the military hospital, no one to fetch him, no one's bothered about him, he's free! He lay two days in bed. His wife was worried, he said so little.

TUESDAY THE 12TH

Today he got up and at midday strolled about the excited town, but in the afternoon, when everyone was heading to the barracks district where looting was in progress, he walked arm in arm with his wife to Parade Square, where they sat down at the café among the happy people and drank coffee and allowed themselves cake. In the evening, despite the garrison decree, he couldn't bear to stay home. He wanted open fields, had to run till he'd had enough.

Wind whistled, rain fell in gouts, the man knew all the paths big and small that led across hop fields he hadn't visited since his return from Romania. And now here he was wandering the zigzag paths, bubbling out words and gesticulating.

He cursed the NCOs, corporals who maltreated him, whose palms he had to grease, he'd had to crawl before them. He cursed the staff doctor at the police station: "What? Still have pains, weak? It's nice at home, no? FAS." Fit for Active Service: the little man whispered to all four wind directions: "FAS, FAS, FAS, the little Jew's a shirker, Jew-pigs are all shirkers, only Jews are shirkers, everyone else runs off eager to the front! And they should shirk, the Jews, they should – should, I say. What for, why should they sit in a trench when all they are is Jew-pigs? Ah, you're not even human to them if you're a Jew. You're not human if you're a soldier. Are you a human to those corporals, those officer swells? Now you've had it! You swellheads!"

He strained his voicebox. He bleated and screamed meaningless words into the wind, crowed. Then he stuffed his hands into the greatcoat pockets and plodded on, calm and refreshed. He looked at the ground and the stalks, tried to orient himself, which fields are these. He thought of Nuremberg, of business, what's the market price for hops now, Württemberger, local varieties. I shall set to work. Deflated now, a harmless merchant, he went on his meditative way.

★

The hops that grew here were a tall vine. The ground was tilled and manured for them. Frames eleven meters high were planted in the soil, fastened with strong cables from which slender wires hung down to meet the climbing plants that twined about them. In rows two meters apart the plants climbed on tall grey stems from which floppy leaves hung. These were creatures that favoured a temperate climate, damp and mist caused them to shrivel, their roots needed deep soil containing humus, chalk and potassium. When they bloomed in summer they were a total gynocracy: only female plants were allowed to grow tall, because they bore little fruit-spigots that formed yellow glands with a bitter substance that gave to the beer humans liked so much such a pleasant taste.

In summer the plants needed lots of water, in May, June, July they formed umbels and were ripe for picking. One hectare of land could produce ten hundredweight of umbels, but the yield varied, and on average in any decade there were two good years, three average and five with a poor yield.

Now it's winter and everything has been harvested, dried and stored in big cool cellars behind Station Square, sulphurated in metal boxes. The time for manuring and cutting the stalks was not yet. On some days men came to hoe weeds.

The plants bided their time quietly in the soil. Day followed day, it was as if they were filled with explosives, one detonation and a wildfire would rage.

Red and yellow spider mites waited near the plants.

They sat in linden trees, on the underside of leaves, covered them in fine threads. Tiny as they were, these mites were armed with a sucking proboscis and puncturing bristles. They'll use these to tap into the young plants. They'll turn the leaves brown and withered. The farmer will complain of "copper blight".

When it's about to come into flower and the people are preparing for the harvest, aphids come across from sloe bushes. They're green. Wherever they settle, leaves curl up and die, and shoots wither from the top.

And sooty mould, a fungal blight, lurks in last season's hop stalks. It waits for the hour to come, at the moment it's all in gestation. There's a black powder on the old stalks. When summer comes with its warmth, the spores will bestir themselves and drill long thin wells into the young plants and suck them dry.

WEDNESDAY THE 13TH

During the night the long-awaited alert reached the barracks. No blare of trumpet, no beating drum. As if in a besieged fortress from which you slip away along furtive paths, around one o' clock they gathered with dimmed lanterns in the huge yard, towards two they began moving out, men and wagons, riders and conveyances. A few Alsatians remained behind as watchmen.

Hooves clattered, dragoons rode out, artillery rattled, trundling cannon, munition wagons of wood and wrought iron, infantry with rifles and knapsacks, steel helmet at the side, they trampled the ground, marched, youngsters, old 'uns, war's lost, the night's icy, we must go home, *must leave the little town, the little town behind, and you, my love, stay here.* Can't see a hand before your face, only those at the front have lanterns and pocket torches, and can see the road.

Forest girdled the town, they plodded and plodded and for them it was enough. Many of the infantry closed their eyes, let themselves be pushed along, held to others' arms half asleep, must keep walking, Mariental, Bischweiler, Weyersheim and Vendenheim and Lampertheim, long way still to our own sweet heim.

Artillery rattled, wagons squeaked, first we head for Strassburg and then it's the road home. We shan't sit in the muck, not till we're bruised and smashed and torn to shreds. Vendenheim and Lampertheim and Schiltigheim, we'll make it heim one day.

O Strassburg, O Strassburg, town so wondrous fair, wish I'd never seen you my whole life long. This campaign is no express train. *So many a soldier lad lies buried there.*

★

Hooves clattered, dragoons headed out, artillery rattled, cannon, munition wagons, infantry, youngsters, old folk.

The Pastor heard the clip-clop, the rattling and rolling, he emerged from sleep, got dressed. In a fur coat, felt slippers, hat on his head he stood a quarter of an hour or more at the open window gazing onto the dark road. He stood erect as a soldier. He kept his hands deep in the pockets, his face immobile. Thus did he greet the soldiers, the German army withdrawing. Gravely, ceremoniously he closed the window behind the last forage wagon. *Holy flame, glow and glow, ne'er forsake the Fatherland.*

He sat in an armchair without removing his hat, kept hands in his pockets, as if he was still at the window and troops were marching by. The phrase "historical moment" occurred to him. He was almost asleep again when he began to feel cold, rose from the armchair and undressed. Sitting in his underwear on the edge of the bed, barefoot, he reproached himself: I am not up to the situation. I am a bad selfish person.

But this was merely prologue to other thoughts, of his wife who was far away, gone ahead of him, and his hopeless worries about the furniture. Now with the regiments gone he was quite alone, no one would stand by him, he would have to flee.

And he lay down.

Hooves clattered, artillery, infantry. *Holy flame, glow and glow, ne'er forsake the Fatherland.* So much loyalty. So many tears.

★

On this same dark night the old woman got up without needing to be wakened. She would use the day that had not yet broken to finish what was left undone yesterday, with that looting.

The noise of ransacking had washed from the barracks over the female complement at the military hospital, the opportunity was there, the first attempt made. A blend of camaraderie and rivalry grew among nurses, kitchen staff and auxiliaries. It involved an onslaught on linen stores, and minds turned to big porcelain bowls, cups and plates. Others dreamed of conserves.

The old woman woke her husband: Drink your coffee. He didn't understand: why so early. He climbed obediently out of bed, she said nothing of her plan. Now he sat before a lit paraffin lamp in his usual place, half asleep, little cap on the bald head, he held the big hot cup in both hands and warmed himself. She handed him his glasses and the newspaper, mumbled a farewell, clattered off.

He began to slurp the coffee, lay back in the chair, his hands dropped to his thighs, he slept, head on chest.

It was daylight when he awoke. There was hammering in the yard, the Major on the second floor was moving out. He noticed with a start that the lamp was still burning, and blew it out. Then he hobbled with the crutch to the bed, and when he'd washed and was back in his chair with the pipe, he began his day, said aloud: "So. It's the 13th of November." He took a big pull on the pipe, and put on his glasses.

Today the old man did not reach for the newspaper. He poked at his toolbox with one of the crutches and hooked it closer. He bent down and rummaged among the tools. He pulled out a crumpled blue envelope. He smoothed the envelope, it was open, pulled from it a folded paper, an official communication concerning the confiscation, surrender and sequestration of items in accordance with Decree M325/7.15 KRA and/or M325e/7.15 KRA of 10 November 1915. The old man kept it hidden in the box under the table, and now and then took a furtive look in order to give himself a treat.

After glancing around to convince himself all was quiet, he puffed away and read out in a low voice: "The following decree is hereby made public on instructions from His Majesty's Minister of War with notice that any contravention ..." With his index finger he carefully followed the text and turned the paper over: on what date did His Majesty's Minister of War instruct that any contravention ...

"Here it is, 3 December 1915. Governor Vietinghoff-Scheel p.p. Why p.p.? Why not the actual governor, since the War Minister addressed it to him?" The old man stumbled every time on this point. The governor was away on a trip, but then they could telephone, maybe the governor's position was a bit wobbly, or the War Minister

WEDNESDAY THE 13TH

and he had some conflicts, the governor refused to accept this War Minister's decrees, had his deputy sign. Good Lord, he said with a big outtake of breath, having let all these thoughts pass by, the things these high-ups get up to, especially in the military.

He turned the paper back over and took a puff.

A lot goes on in the world, much of it was no longer valid, including the business with Vietinghoff-Scheel, the deputy, maybe even the War Minister; what's happened to him? He weighed the document doubtfully in his hand. Outside there was hammering. He squinted towards the noise, shook his head, turned back to his document.

And as his eyes read slowly syllable by syllable, the man with the hammer came in and they had a chat about glue, because a pretty Chinese smoking set had got broken in the packing. Bet the Chinese have the best glue! The old man had no idea, they carefully inspected the broken lid of the black lacquer box and felt over the break without result, until the man left.

> Items affected by the decree, Class A, objects of copper and brass:
> 1. Vessels and trade equipment of all kinds for cooking and baking, for example pots for cooking and pickling, jam kettles and ice cream tubs, saucepans and fruit boilers, pans, baking moulds, casseroles, dishes, mortars.

The old man read each word out in a low voice, and there before his eyes were the objects and the uses to which they were put: jam kettles, ice cream tubs, the fruit that goes into them after you've picked or bought it, add lots of sugar, boil a long time. He recalled his mother in nearby Drusenheim, how she made preserves, he was just a boy, she poured it into metal tubs and it went down to the cellar, and now and then a procession went down, every child held a bowl for the ration doled out by Mother.

After "mortars" there was a little cross, which pointed to an annex with an alphabetical list of copper and brass moulds used in cooking and trade, and for the old man this was a delight. There the wonderful things appeared one after the other, it was for them he kept this document. For although he'd been only a cobbler and the wife had been able to find only cleaning jobs and they'd had to be modest in their eating and drinking, still he had secretly remained a gourmet. All the while he was working he never had the chance, he sat behind his cobbler's globe smelling old leather and hammering and stitching. But after his stroke he took himself in hand, he became a doorman and was able to take better care of himself. Then he noticed what a taste he still had for good things, his wife and the Pastor's wife brought him cigars, cakes, pastries, and then he discovered for himself this bit of reading matter. Which he read with relish: stirring pot, aspic mould, aspic ruffs, pudding moulds, baking tins, baking moulds of every kind, mixing spoons (here he sighed with deep emotion, sweet white cake dough dripped from the spoon, as children they'd been allowed to lick the spoon), oven spatulas, biscuit moulds, egg boilers, egg poaching pans. For a quarter of an hour he was silently transported in his clouds of smoke.

Now he'd had enough, he smoothed the document and placed it gently back in the envelope as a well known clipclop of clogs sounded in the yard. Right, it's the wife, the envelope slid quickly into the box, the wife clipclopped past the front door, didn't come in. And since she didn't come in – she had disappeared towards the vegetable plot at the back – he stood up and made his way on crutches into the corridor. Just then she came up behind him pushing an old pram. "Back in the room," she cried; he hobbled obediently back, she followed, closed the door, and as she searched around on her bed, he still standing on his crutches by the table, she said: "I need a blanket." She rummaged silently in the cupboard. "Here it is." It was an ancient counterpane, she folded it: "I have to go back to the hospital. We're fetching stuff away."

"What stuff?"

She was outside, jolting her little wagon across the yard.

The man sat down shocked. They're stealing. The Pastor said something about it. The woman's mad, she'll be shot. What should I do? The hospital, that's too far for me.

An anxious hour later she was back. She pushed the pram into the room, closed the door behind her. Kitchen cloths, hand towels, whole packages emerged to be stacked on the bed. He loomed over her on his crutches. "Woman, they'll shoot you."

She held a hand to his mouth, tapped him on the forehead. "I'll be off again. Crockery."

He watched as she spread the loot out on the bed, smoothed it with her hands, bedding, hand towels, serviettes. What does she need all this for. How she strokes it. Now she turns around, opens the cupboard, puts the stuff away. The wrinkles in her cheeks fade, the crow's feet at the eyes blur. When she picks up a bundle of linens she does it like lifting a baby. Like there's a light gleaming from the bundle. The old man's rheumatism twinges; that's how she was when the boy was alive.

She gathered up the counterpane again, clipclopped with the pram down the corridor, past men hammering at crates.

Involuntarily, after a while his foot felt under the table

for the box with the emergency decree, but he didn't take it out again.

★

The garrison had withdrawn.

There they stood, familiar yellow walls of the barracks from which largesse had rained down yesterday, menacing walls with arrow-slit windows like a fortress, heaving with dangerous men. But they had marched furtively away, it was incredible, it left behind a monstrous vacancy. Citizens stood about and chatted and marvelled.

It was peace, true and unimaginable, peace! How lovely! No more would alarm sirens, bells, moonlit nights, planes bother them. They had skated onto firm ground.

Gradually in streets, houses and shops people became visible, like a log that floats all day on water and at night waves drag it under and then up it comes again.

Every day left these humans with a slight sense of desolation. In homes, on the street piles of refuse accumulated, dirt, all kinds of rubbish. Spoons, doorknobs, jugs lost their shine. And people themselves sank day by day, skin flaking, waste matter collecting inside them, the skin smelled and made clothing rotten. When night fell they had to lie down and give up living. But where yesterday ended, today it all began again.

So when the nurses and ladies of the Prisoners' Committee remembered that poor Russians from the camp were sleeping in the school, they got out of bed, and were at once portioning out coffee and bread, at every sink on the steps bare male chests were washed, scrubbed, bristly heads sputtered under streams of water. Food was handed out in haste, they were glad to be rid of these men; that very morning, stomachs filled, they packed their little bundles. They wanted to go home, to Russia, home. They had no money, no train would take them, they would march, hunger was not the worst, they'd already survived that, the thousands who hadn't survived lay long buried in the earth. But they weren't all of one mind: some wanted to march through Germany with red flags, as combat troops, others wanted to slip quietly back to Russia.

But first of all they wanted to be gone from Alsace. For now the French were coming to gobble them up. They no longer saw any soldier as their friend.

And as they formed up in front of the school and rain mixed with hail fell on them, the town that no longer housed any regiment began to take on a new colour. The poor Pastor was not spared the sight of his little town's new "whoredom".

Red flags had vanished along with the regiments. This Wednesday saw blue-white-red blaze forth in their stead. Flag cloth swept out of sewing rooms, flew into general stores, soap shops, department stores.

For weeks already, in parallel with the daily bulletins, statuettes, pictures and picture-postcards of German princes and generals had disappeared from displays, patriotic sentiment had fallen to a furtive zero point, and now brushes, combs, braces and corkscrews showed themselves in all their naked objectivity. It seemed that shopkeepers meant to revert to their primal realm: trade.

Today it became clear that the zero point was merely a pivot. A previously unknown series of princes and generals suddenly popped up among the corkscrews and braces, taking over the spots freed by the German generals (who now lay stashed away behind the counter, or as statuettes straw-wrapped like fallen soldiers in boxes in the passage). The Wilsons, Kings of England, Presidents of France, Allied marshals and admirals pulled in and installed themselves among the combs, soaps and writing materials. People rejoicing at the withdrawal of the regiments and sheltering under umbrellas were invited, when shopping optimistically for butter, for meat, to content themselves for the time being with the purchase of a Lloyd George, a Wilson, a Poincaré in plaster, oil or wax. Sales were meagre among ordinary citizens, but a few nervous officials stepped up.

The Pastor visited a First Lieutenant's Widow; her husband had been in the garrison here and was killed in the second month of the war. He found her. She was pleased to tell him that the van with her furniture had finally left. He understood. In the kitchen a rickety chair had been left behind, she wanted to sit the Pastor on it, he politely offered it to her and stood there gravely, stiff hat in his hands, in the obligatory grave Pastor stance. She reached for his hand: "I thank you once again for all the kindness you've shown to me in these difficult times." And the Pastor was puzzled to see that in recalling the past and the difficult present she shed no tears, but heaved a deep sigh of relief: "And I'm so glad the things have gone and I'm free to go. I've been sitting in our little place like a watchdog. I'm sure you agree, reverend, that it won't be so bad?"

He answered in confusion: "No, dear lady, for sure it won't."

"That's what I say. I used to think: if they remove our Kaiser, I'd rather not go on living. And our Crown Prince, such a dashing fellow. It's dreadful. But in the end they won't tear everything down. For example, my brother is a District Administrator, he lives like a king in his district."

He nodded, and as he seemed troubled she asked about his own furniture, she expressed her disgust when he reported his quarrel with the landlord, offered to go herself to the landlord and have a robust conversation. "Look here, reverend, I'll take this off your shoulders, and early tomorrow you shall travel with me."

The Pastor thanked her: "But no, I still have time till this afternoon." But she wouldn't let it go, and he had to acquiesce as she dogged his footsteps and held a pointless conversation with the landlord, but in a brisk tone that he found refreshing – so that he allowed his arm to be twisted to (as he put it) march away from the front together with her because as a single lady she requires male protection (and he the opportunity to make use of her furniture van).

The final visitors to his house he fobbed off with no regrets. He had thought he would fling his arms in grief around everyone from whom he must part, such a parting, under these conditions. But he felt only annoyance and distaste that they would be staying and were no longer loyal. Not one of the Evangelical Maidens' Union showed her face, such enormous ingratitude.

★

One who did show up and horribly disturb his final half hour was the servant girl Barbara, who wanted to free her dear friend of yesterday afternoon, the deserter and malingerer Ziweck. She'd sent someone to ask this morning. For the ironmonger himself had turned up very early all meek at the police station and made a statement that for such and such a reason he preferred not to press charges; the circumstances being such he wouldn't feel comfortable doing so, there might be repercussions. So Barbara silently packed her bundle before sir and madam; madam found it necessary to say: "I await your apology, Barbara." Barbara made no apology. She spat on the corridor floor, banged the door shut. Sir had to restrain his wife.

The Pastor was elated when they came to him with this business. Really, this woman made it easier for him to quit Alsace. He'd had more than enough to do with stupid people of both sexes, knew that the church had a particular duty to accept the simpleminded. But Barbara was a special case. She was aggressive, espoused the rights of the "revolution" – to him! Here's the Köpp girl, insisting he go along with lies and extortion; and here's this one, demanding that he spend his final solemn hours in this lost region with all its historical baggage, attempting to free a madman. As if Germany (*O Germany high in honour*) were not tottering in the greatest peril! And this Barbara was a Catholic! Perhaps the hospital people were playing games with her, sending her to the Protestant Pastor. The Pastor was outraged: "You say he's from Kaiserslautern? Then he's a Reich German, and he'll be coming with us!"

She screamed: "No, no!"

In a fury now he phoned the Catholic priest. Who invited him in icy tones to send the girl over. With smarmy courtesy he ushered Barbara, there with her umbrella and handbag, out of the door, my Catholic colleague will eat her for lunch, it's revenge for the lost half hour (Holy God, if I'm wicked then I'm wicked, this is already a washup, and anyway all of us in our poor great Germany are atoning; the punishment's really too severe, it's over-compensation).

He forgot these blasphemous thoughts as he bumped along at the side of the First Lieutenant's Widow on the way to Strassburg. He was in an improbably good and happy mood – even the weather had turned fine and dry.

★

WEDNESDAY THE 13TH

The flu pandemic raged through the town. Ambulances of the municipal public health department rushed back and forth between town and military hospital, which was in the midst of evacuation; its days were numbered. The seriously ill were transferred to the municipal hospital. They would soon be prisoners of the French; but only a few thought of this, most never mentioned it even once, they viewed the transfer as one of many, were glad the journey wasn't longer, and lay in other beds in older wards, civilian doctors walked about, even some of the nurses had stayed.

But many of the sick were dethroned. There was the pale lanky young man just to the left in the main ward of the Internal Station who lay under a wildly fluctuating temperature chart. He'd been lying there for months. He was a demonstration case, distinguished by a complex heart defect following severe general rheumatism of the joints that exercised all its malice on him. The effusion that formed in one lung had been punctured a few times. But when that improved and the heart could more clearly be heard and seen in X-rays, inflammation of the pericardial sac became evident, and for sure the valves were abnormal. So no big visit came unaccompanied by a little council gathered about his bed. Doctors young and old, permanent and just passing through, tapped and auscultated the heart, it scraped, it rasped, hard to tell whether from the heart or the pleura, or if it was possible to distinguish what came from the valves and what from the pericardial derma. When the clever brown-bearded "consultant" appeared, the professor, he for sure had young Johannes in mind. The meter-long chart was at once unfurled across the bed, the patient saw what had been going on with him, they discussed him as if he was a house with pipes and conduits still not working as they should. Time and again his thin arms were pierced so that the veins would yield up the bacteria they sought. The blood was dripped onto dishes and little tubes of broth, and then put away in incubators. From there, from the laboratories, the dishes and tubes were brought back to the military hospital and inspected at the bedside through magnifying glasses. They went back and forth between bed and window, and lengthy discussions ensued as to whether these were actually cocci, and not simply contaminants. Johannes learned Bacteriology. If something proliferated quickly and coloured the dish yellow and filled it entirely, or the clear broth became cloudy and clumped, then it was contaminants, and they were annoyed and sometimes blamed the patient, he must have twitched as they took the blood, which he always denied. More interesting were the delicate discolorations of the nutritive medium that were eventually discovered, but even here there were arguments, for hardly had these been spotted when some asserted that, at this stage of the disease, bacteria were no longer circulating in the blood, they had localised in the heart, the pleura. Johannes noticed how hard Medicine was, and discussed his case with nurses and auxiliary doctors. Gradually all concerned contented themselves at visits with letting him explain how it had all come about. He could explicate his own charts, some thought him a medical student. Then the visitors leapt on him with their hearing-trumpets and stethoscopes to listen to the heart as long as they liked. Johannes studied the doctors' faces when they stood straight again, he found their ignorance amusing.

Johannes had lain like this in the main ward of the Internal Station for months now; he was an orphan from Würzburg; every two weeks a letter or a picture postcard came from an aunt, he had been an energetic, somewhat rough lad, who responded well to subtle handling and opportunities to learn.

Now suddenly here he lay in the big smoky hospital ward in a row with twelve other beds along the wall. He counted: I'm sixth from the door, and on that side there's another six. He was annoyed: what's wrong with them, those malingerers. And already a long-forgotten beast awoke within him, strong and savage and able to bite. In one little hour he … recovered. For the first time in months he sat up by himself, and ate without assistance.

*

Just after noon, the young woman can no longer contain her unease when Jund fails to appear. She scribbles a note, asks what happened to the business he told her about; her customers have been eager to take black market stuff off her hands as usual, sugar, two hens, some bacon, and she's handed them over but at such bad prices. Quite shakily she writes: what's to happen, there's nothing doing with stationery. Herr Jund shows up, looks quickly over her note, jumps close, only has two words: all done, the café bought already, is she still in, he can always sell it on to someone else, she's ecstatic, of course she's in, where is it, he's far too busy to talk, gives her the address, I'll settle the contract with the procurator this evening, so make up your mind, but of course I will, she flings her arms around him, his mind is elsewhere, another matter is preying on him, but he might be biting off more than he can chew, a printing shop, half given away, only a few thousand Mark, he steams off, no time today for love.

*

After dinner old people appear on the street, of a kind not seen for a long time. Two grey men make a leisurely approach, sticks tapping, they shuffle along stiff and bent, in their younger days they had seen Frenchmen in the town, now they smile and mumble, their shoes are falling apart, crumpled trousers given out by the old folk's home, two little brown dachshunds trot behind. And the stroll proceeds very slowly, heads and hands nod and shake, long stops in front of shop windows, eyes astonished at the blue-white-red ribbons that call up memories of the time before 1870, and the ancient nags set themselves again in motion, their smiles are sly and mischievous, the laugh-muscles are the only things that follow. They're like a rusty harp blown on by the breeze, dully twanging.

How funny, the lanky young dog behind the two dachshunds being walked by the broad-shouldered man in a brown leather jacket. The creature has shot up tall, longlegged and clumsy. When a dachshund turns round, the dog flinches back. It hasn't even learned the technique of sniffing yet. It hasn't yet grown into its young limbs. But that's a general rule: the command of one's organs is attained only slowly, even then is incomplete. How much of our great capacious body actually belongs to us. Our spoon merely skims the surface of the soup.

A narrow-faced woman is pushed in a wheelchair. The peaceful world comes into view. The woman is pale and sallow, for a whole year she's had no outing for fear of aeroplanes, now her husband has encouraged her. The housemaid is pushing. The husband, big, strong, dressed in black, is employed in the tax office, he strokes the thick moustache, walks behind the other two. He's supervising the transport.

★

From four in the afternoon to the stoke of seven, three whole hours, Fräulein Köpp reads newspapers in the poorly lit back room of her milliner's shop, but nothing about politics. A German lady she visited to collect payment left her a big pile of papers, she'd been collecting them in hopes of victory, as mementos, now there's no victory, only the papers. Fräulein Köpp devours them, she sits at the long narrow work bench, sits elbows splayed over the outspread sheets, and knows nothing of the world.

> *Strassberger Latest News*, Sunday Edition,
> 13th October 1918.
> 'German Oath 1813', by Friedrich Rückert:
>
>> *Into a knot our hands we braid,*
>> *Lift our eyes to heaven and this we swear:*
>> *All ye living shall our oath hear,*
>> *So too, if you wish, ye who are dead.*

She lingers at the righthand corner, the "visiting card puzzle", Erich Tubannak, Senneheim, the name on the card conceals the profession, with *a* some pick up the thread, with *n* all wear it on the head. As a milliner, she found it deeply intriguing, what did everyone, male and female, wear on the head with an *n*, or was it a *u*, hat, cap, bonnet, what else do people wear on the head, in annoyance she skimmed over to health care, had another look, maybe it was an *e*. Worst toothache, remedy for every kind of eczema, in case of nasal catarrh, what's this, nasal bath three or four times with water at 8 degrees, where did the worst case of dividing a fruit occur, in William Tell, only one apple on the head, she knew nothing of William Tell, worst toothache. The novel on the previous page: "She lowered her eyes and played with her muff. He could not see the expression on her face. Had he perhaps said too much after all, and fatally insulted her good intentions. He bent down to her, to read her face: 'Are you cross with me, Miss Viviana?' he gently asked. Her mouth twitched in vexed defiance."

The shop door tinkled, she jumped up, a neighbour's child asking if her mother was here, no, again she laid her arms on the bench.

"Imperial Chancellor Prince Max of Baden, Vice-chancellor von Payer. In accordance with the Imperial decree of 30th September, the political leadership of the German Reich has undergone a fundamental change. As successor to the Graf von Hertling, who provided the highest services to the Fatherland, I – in the conviction that I have behind me the will of the majority of the nation –."

"You are such a child, Miss Viviana! It was not intended that way at all! I shall for sure never forget your friendship." She lifted her tear-streaked visage up to him: "Do you regret not having understood me?"

Little Köpp puffed her cheeks and blew air, men are always so mean, she's right, just leave him cold.

Another page. A glance at the top, where men went about their business, such comical names, Tewfik Pasha, a Turk, in Russia they're called Bolsheviks, Wilson's response is a charter, which for all its brevity is clearly the outcome of careful deliberation. The Entente armies have liberated and conquered the towns of St Quentin etc., destroying them in the process. "For weeks the town of Cambrai suffered daily air raids by Entente squadrons, dropping their bombs so that house after house, street after street was turned to rubble, the inhabitants no longer dared to leave their cellars. As the Entente armies approached, heavy calibre grenades followed the aerial bombs, the civilian population had to be brought to safety, the front approached ever closer to the town (but this is horrible!), after the grenades came trench mortars, the outlying areas were turned to rubble, and devastation spread ever wider. The ancient buildings on the marketplace, which during the tank battle of the previous year (what's this now) first came into contact with English grenades, received extensive damage. During the night of 8th October, when the last German rearguard, having put up such a valorous defence along the canal on the eastern edge of the town, withdrew through the abandoned devastated streets, they had to stumble across the chasms of destroyed houses. Streets barricaded by rubble, horse carcases along the roadside, the sky red with flames soaring from houses hit by English incendiary grenades."

The English, aren't they the thing. Breathless, she placed a hand over her breast, read some of it again, the front approached ever closer to the town, heavy grenades followed by mortars, but it wasn't as much fun the second time.

Draught ox, sweet as a lamb, good puller, must be passed on. Fritz Grab, corset clinic. At the bottom of the page she landed up in Fr. Lehne's *The Three Pretty Bernhausens.* "Thora's tender neck bent low, as if weighed down by the expensive string of big pearls that her betrothed had just placed about her neck as a wedding gift. But with an almost wild motion she straightened up as she felt his lips at her throat, so that the Commercial Counsellor drew back almost in shock. Her eyes flamed angrily at him. Had he forgotten the condition she imposed at the time of their betrothal? He understood, with an almost sheepish smile he passed a handkerchief across his blushing face and drew her hand respectfully to his lips. 'My dear Thora, it is still five days away.' 'Yes, five more days,' she whispered, her lips pale. The Commercial Counsellor had ordered coffee, whipped cream, and various cakes."

There are nice gentlemen, maybe the first lieutenant will marry me, officers have their code of honour, she looked through the Letters to the Editor in case there was something about the code of honour when a girl's in the family way. Apply to the Red Cross Prisoner Care Centre, Maria Magdalena. From 1st October you have the right to demand higher rent. Chicory root must first be washed thoroughly.

She sat, her bottom far back on the chair, chest aslant the work bench, ears flushed bright red. The room was overheated, utterly silent. She easily felt sick, the baby, her property. In future she would take things easy.

In the toilet she vomited proudly, bent over the pan, said: Cheers.

★

First Lieutenant Becker and Lieutenant Maus spent the day quietly in their room. Becker had spent a year already in the little town, in bed. He should have been transferred long ago to the military hospital in Berlin, his home town, but he had requested to remain outside, "outside", here at least. He had been hit by grenade shrapnel on the Somme. Lamed, he was carried to the rear. The metal tore a huge hole in the sacrum, disturbed the spinal marrow. At first he could do nothing with his entire lower body. It was a dead thing, an appendage. Becker, high school teacher by profession, classicist, told the specialists and everyone who came to visit him in the hospital: I'm an antique centaur, the horse under me has been shot, but his human body is seated firmly on top. For a while it was the custom for visitors to ask Becker: "How's the horse doing?" But more often it was the patient who interrogated doctors and nurses. Gradually he became a focus of attention in the Surgical Station. They had to perform plastic surgery on the sacrum, there was a crater-like depression, and a fistula that gave him no peace.

Afternoon.

Young rosy-cheeked Lieutenant Maus with the big dressing on his shoulders tried his best to cross his arms and maintain a posture of grim determination. But with the left arm bandaged, all the right arm could do was fold itself nicely around it, and the impression given was more of pain than strength of character. Becker, in the lounger by the window of the twin-bedded room observed him with friendly interest, tender and gently mocking. Finally Maus growled: "Dog's breakfast. No checkup, no corporal. It's two o' clock, we're supposed to fetch our own lunch. We'd have had no breakfast if I hadn't raised hell."

Becker, calmly: "Revolutions alter the divisions of time. The French Revolution, for example, brought in a new calendar. Maybe breakfast would have arrived this evening, in accordance with the new timings. And anyway, we're now on French soil."

Maus paid no attention, he gazed out tragically from sombre eyes. Becker came benignly to his aid: "Nurse Hilde still not found?"

"I came across her in the kitchen."

"Voilà. The kitchen, Aphrodite's favourite hangout."

The younger man sat down reflectively and laid the splinted arm on his knee. "I don't understand her. I thought it must be about Richard, the chap who died Sunday."

"Why not. Wouldn't you, if you were lying in hospital and there was no one else, at least want to be mourned by her?"

"It's connected with the trip she took last week. I asked her why she won't talk, says nothing of what it's like over there. She waved me away and told me not to ask, it was bad, horrible. Anyway she's an Alsatian, her father's with the Strassburg Cathedral architect's office, but she'd rather go across into Germany, they have relatives in Württemberg. I thought it might have been about me, a little. A self-inflicted wound, it seems. It must truly be dreadful there. What's become of our great prosperous Germany, Becker! She told me: no housing, or only at horrendous prices, spivs everywhere, cheating, racketeering."

"Interesting," Becker remarked when he paused, "and that's where we're heading."

"And the railway carriages. Seats ripped apart, no curtains, they even steal the string nets from the luggage racks. No heating in the carriages, the engines can hardly pull, no coal, mechanical defects."

"And the town?"

"People begging for bread in the street."

The first lieutenant with the long tired face nodded from his lounge: "That's defeat. That's how it looked with the Russians."

The window was wide open. In the garden someone was practising the trumpet.

A junior ambulance officer came to Becker and Maus and informed them that the hospital, such as it was, would head out from the station by the airfield, tomorrow Thursday, towards evening. They can if they wish be transferred today to Strassburg by express transport, but they're free to join the general transport. When Maus looked enquiringly to his older friend, his mouth was already open to say: We'll take the general transport. This greatly relieved the junior officer; he confided: a few officers on board will hopefully keep troublemakers in check.

Becker shrugged, and when the officer had closed the door behind him said: "These fine fellows don't seem to have much confidence in their revolution." He turned his head to the window: "Novelties. Earlier, in peacetime, you sat in your study, prepared next day's lessons, waited for the post, for something or other, it was eerily quiet. Now novelties pour down on our heads. And what else did Nurse Hilde say? Will she no longer grace our corridor?"

"She has her little ways."

"As do we all."

"Because of Richard. And now, yes, because of Germany. All for nothing. All gone. He's dead, I have my shoulder, you your back, and everything that creeps and crawls around here."

"Or lies in the earth."

"Yes, Becker, all for nothing. It's true. Is it thinkable?"

A change had come over Becker. He sat up straighter. Without moving his head he directed his gaze at the ceiling, his jaw muscles twitched: No. Truly, it's unthinkable. Completely unthinkable. I refuse to think it. That it all is. It simply is.

The younger rosy-cheeked man complained to the room like a beaten recalcitrant child: "And then ..." he pulled a folded sheet of newspaper from his jacket pocket: "then they demand from us five thousand cannon, two thousand aeroplanes, three hundred thousand machine guns, evacuation of Alsace-Lorraine within fourteen days, evacuation from the left bank of the Rhine, occupation of Cologne, Koblenz, Mainz. Becker, it's intolerable, no one could bear it, better to be beaten to death with cudgels."

"They've already signed. You're already enjoying the Armistice."

"And the colonies, and Posen, and parts of Schleswig-Holstein, and the Kaiser. Yesterday in the English House of Commons they said the Kaiser, the Crown Prince, generals would be put on a list of war criminals to be handed over.

An indescribable insult. We're besmirched from head to toe. And this on top of it. Revolution. I'd rather not live. I'd rather take a knife and run amok." Maus covered his ears: "I wish that fellow would stop his blaring."

"He's practising, he won't be interrupted. Playing the trumpet's the only thing he'll bring home from the war."

"Just stop," growled the other. Becker: "The man's given me pleasure ever since I arrived. Earlier, when they changed my dressings, I thought the world was ending, I wouldn't make it out of the procedure alive, another splinter of bone, yet another splinter of bone. But then he'd blare away, he's been blaring away the whole time, and earlier. I knew he'd go on blaring, and that brought me across the abyss."

Maus sighed: "You should see what's going on in the hospital, Becker. They're carrying it away, bit by bit."

"Who are?"

"Ravens, thieves, our German compatriots, men and women, all stealing. No one stops them. Hilde says she'll be gone in an hour, doesn't want to fall under suspicion."

The man in the garden was practising *What do the trumpets say*.

Becker shook his head: "I'll not acknowledge it. I shall never acknowledge it. It is not true." His hand stroked the air, as if giving an order or wiping something away. "They can describe it or print is as they like. It *is* not. It *is* not."

Maus stepped closer, he was puzzled to see Becker so quiet: "Are you in pain?"

Becker breathed: "Not too bad."

"My God, Becker, what's the matter? I've over-excited you."

Becker's teeth were chattering, he made a weary gesture: "We're cripples. They can do what they want with us."

Maus stroked his arm: "Becker, I'll find a bottle of wine, we'll drink to withdrawal." But a minute later, while he was still away from the room, Nurse Hilde appeared and found Becker on his own. He lay there, his face empty: "Lieutenant Maus has gone out for a moment."

"Good morning, first lieutenant. I'll close the window. You seem to be freezing."

He pulled himself together: "Tell me something, Nurse Hilde."

"What?"

"Will you be leaving too? Is the hospital falling apart?"

She hung her head. Her face was closed, she said: "I'm going to my father, in Strassburg. He's nearly seventy."

"So you have a home here. You've been across to Germany, Maus tells me."

There were tears in her eyes; she looked away: "For the last fortnight I've been behaving like the stupidest kitchen maid. I understand nothing, all I can do is weep. I'm sorry. I wish you all the best, lieutenant."

He held her hand: "Why the hurry? The old man in Strassburg spent the whole long war without you, another half hour won't hurt. Maus is finding wine for a farewell party."

"Let go. I'm not on the mood."

"There's no reason here to weep and drown in tears. There'll be no calamity. They're redrawing the frontier, and we'll keep our heads down until it's all settled."

"All right for you to joke."

"Well, if the prophet won't go to the mountain, the mountain must come to the prophet. Every week you've picked bone fragments from my back, that's why I try to make you feel better. Look at Maus: he collects newspapers, every day he shoves them down my throat. I'm supposed to learn the numbers of submarines, cannon and machine guns off by heart. I can't."

"What do you mean, lieutenant?"

"I mean that to all these facts, from wherever they come, I set up a categorical denial. I reject them." She regarded him attentively. "Look at my chart, Nurse Hilde. 36.8, it's nothing. I apply the law that Schiller expressed:

> *No, there's a limit to a despot's power.*
> *When the oppressed for justice looks in vain,*
> *when his sore burden may no more be borne,*
> *with fearless heart he makes appeal to Heaven,*
> *and thence brings down his everlasting rights,*
> *which there abide, inalienably his,*
> *and indestructible as are the stars.*
> *Nature's primeval state returns again."*

Maus came in, the knuckles of the left hand held a string from which two unmatched bottles dangled like bell clappers. She stepped over to him: "I came to say goodbye."

"She's staying, Maus."

"Of course," Maus said, placing the bottles on the floor and taking her by the arm.

She: "What are you doing?" Maus pressed her onto the chair, she sat, spread her arms across the table, laid her head on them. They heard weeping. When she sat up and apologised, she accepted a glass of wine from Maus.

They stayed together for half an hour. At Becker's request, the sentimental trumpet player joined them, but didn't drink, said he had five bottles in his possession and drank only in the afternoons. And anyway, preparations for the departure of the hospital train included just as much wine as food, so he wanted to spend at least one more day sober. There was little conversation. Becker drank more than the other two. He was unusually excited. He exclaimed from his chair: "So glum! So glum! You're letting yourselves be fooled. You're staring facts in the face. I see a time coming when people do nothing but stare so-called facts in the face and know nothing else. Even lovers will extol their realism. A fine world! I swear on the rainbow! What *is* today, tomorrow is *nothing*, hocus pocus, fidibus."

He was in truth a little tipsy: "I'm building my strength for the trip through Germany. You should not embark on it without precautions. My inner eye has lit up, so that I can guard myself against facts. I shall thrust them back into their inherent nullity, the defective locomotives, the lack of coal, the ripped up seats."

And he demanded something that infuriated Maus – but he would not be deflected: Maus must go down to the garden below his window and make an auto da fé of the newspapers lying there on the table. That's not on, Maus demurred, you can't light fires here, the revolution's not that far gone. Becker insisted, and Hilde, suddenly changed, agreed with him and with a wild expression and not a word spoken she flung the papers out of the window. The fire must be lit below Becker's window. To orderlies and patients who came to watch, Maus explained in embarrassment that it was correspondence that mustn't fall into enemy hands.

Stern, fists clenched, Becker watched smoke drift up past the window.

Left arm raised, seemingly free of pain, he preached to the window: "In old books we find accounts of a war fought many years ago on the soil of this region of Europe; it lasted several years, some say four. In this war, it is said, certain nations were defeated, their wealth taken, their lands, their honour insulted. It took a long time before these reports with their momentous impact were seen to be legends, based on nothing more than commonplace twists of fate. Appearance was defeated. Truth triumphed. It was a test. People passed it."

At last Hilde ran back into the building – Maus down below furtively rescuing a few papers – and could not help but mark her departure by embracing the victor with all her heart and soul, at length, passionately, and thinking of the whole war.

*

Late that afternoon, in the gathering dusk, Nurse Hilde slipped along the corridor through the general confusion once more to Becker. She hugged him, kissed him again and again, wouldn't let go, he whimpered: "Why can I no longer be with you, I can't stand up, I'm a nothing." He sobbed in her face. He begged: "Do stay."

She opened her blouse and pressed her breasts to his face. He buried himself in them. The final kisses.

*

An hour later Maus pursued her through the melee in the corridor as she was about to leave the hospital, coat over her arm. He pulled her into the empty private room where Richard, the airman, had died on Sunday. She tried to leave, whispered: "It's Richard's room, open the door."

"You loved him."

She: "None of your business. Yes."

"Tell me the truth before we part, because I love you."

"What do you all want from me. It is the truth."

"And you're abandoning me, just like that."

She made no answer. He struggled with her. He pushed her to the iron bedstead. She resisted, pushed back and hissed: "What are you up to!" They tumbled onto the bedsprings. She twisted and turned, clawed at his head, his throat, his ears, pulled his hair and tried to wiggle free. He fought back with his right arm, and his heavy flexible body. Suddenly she gave in and became slack. His face on hers, he felt tears coursing down her hot cheeks. She stretched out and wept, uttered not a sound. He kissed her passionately, breathed words of endearment. She made no reply and let him have his way. Her convulsive shudders ceased as she lay in his embrace and a dreadful bliss took away consciousness.

When she departed from the hospital that evening in her dark raincoat amid all the comings and goings of people carrying away whatever they could, and crossed diagonally over the main road into the little wood, she sat down on the first fallen trunk, in the dark. She was just close enough to the road to orient herself by a street lamp.

She sat and sat. Now this as well. This as well. A trembling in the limbs. Until the cold forced her to her feet.

In the road, before the bend, she turned around to the bright-lit hospital complex. Life returned to her. She stood tall, cheerful.

And that's how she went on into town, strong and proud.

*

In one of the houses across the fields that she strode past so proudly, her gaze directed at the lights of the little town, there lived another woman who had been torn from her lover. In this state of hope and dread, of waiting and yearning, Hanna was some days ahead of young Nurse Hilde. How often does she pore over the map of Germany and trace the route his train must be taking, how often does her gaze rest hypnotised on the black railway hub Berlin. Lines embed themselves there from all directions, but the gaze fixates as it seeks to isolate just this one dark point and draw it closer to her. How often in the afternoons, when her parents are out to another meeting of the Welcoming Committee, does she climb to the maid's room and sit on a stool and wait and feel communion with the absent man. But no emotion can grip and hold him in reality. And so she lived with her arms and legs, her head and body, in the little town that the absent man had trod – but she wasn't really there, she'd been banished beyond it, every thought wafted her away from the town, and only gravity, the weight of her limbs, held her back.

How to go to him?

"My darling, my whole life. Perhaps this letter will reach you. Perhaps it will not, like all the others you surely would have answered if you had received them. I begin every letter with My darling, my whole life, and that tells you I have none, that I await a letter from you, must wait, because I would like to come to myself. Darling, I cannot hold out any longer. Darling, I am tearing myself to pieces. If I don't hear from you soon, if I am not filled soon by a word from you, I shall break down. Only a few days have passed since you were here with me together in this room, I look at the calendar, it was November 10th, last Sunday, not even one more Sunday has come by since then. But I experienced again something in common with you when they bore the coffins of those two, you know who I mean, past the house. I watched them come down our street, and the many, many following behind, and was unable to look away. I should have felt like an accomplice, a guilty person, for you of course are me, my life, but all I did was resent them, because they took you away from me. All I could feel, God forgive me, was hatred and resentment.

"I write, and write. I think, and think. I look about me. I wait for someone or other to offer advice. Early this morning I was at the pharmacy, with the druggist who drove you to Strassburg. I had him speak of you. He told me what he knew. It was nothing.

"Darling, my whole life, it cannot go on like this. You will receive other letters from me, tomorrow, next day, maybe in two or three days. But the days are so full of torment, I cannot bear them! What else will happen I do not know. Write to me, Hans, write to me, write, come to me, be here, do not abandon me.

"My God, Hans, my wrist watch is lying here by my side, I took it off because I don't want to look at it. It's six in the evening, my God, I have to wait for half past six, seven, half past seven, eight, half past eight, I cannot, it's an impossible task for me, a sentence of hard labour, it's too much for me, I cannot …"

Now she stopped writing. In utter despair, beside herself, she pushed the letter to one side, laid her head on the table, and wept.

Why so fretful, dear child? Why make your life so hard. You have too much imagination. On the other hand you have too little imagination, or else you'd know this, for example: soon you'll stand up, look despairing around the room in case there's someone there to help, to talk to, in whose presence you can shed a few tears. You know your mother has long steered well clear of you. You'll sit back down and chew your fingers and curse your parents for leaving you like this, busying themselves with this stupid committee stuff while you're nearly dying.

And now a jealous outraged creature will emerge, and you'll be impelled and urgently advised to put on your best coat, look out nice overshoes, powder yourself, apply lipstick, hat on, and away into town. There you'll drink chocolate, not look at the clock, and before you know it you've calmed down, grown quite calm, not just from the chocolate – the café owner gives of his best, because he knows the French will be here soon and shortages will be a thing of the past – but also because two ladies you know are sitting next to him enthusing about Nancy and Paris, speaking French, and you join in. You recall how Paris was once your dream.

Oh how good it is to sit quietly in this café on the red plush bench by the wall, with others, looking out on Parade Square, almost opposite the police station, a pharmacy, so much to see, and you're already almost a long way from yourself. All this is known to the writer. For him it is no novelty, he almost always goes about so quietly, and figures take shape within him, as yet vague, they move in him as in a pleasant damp garden, a greenhouse, but after a while he opens the door – he must, to make room for new figures – and out they go, he follows them, his loving gaze takes them all in for one last time, and they vanish.

I foresee, and I look at my watch, and exactly to the second I can say when in your torment and confusion you will stand up and when you will go to the wardrobe, open it, which coat you will choose. And I confess to you, Fräulein Hanna, that even though I've taken part in your conversations and encounters with the most decent reticence proper to a narrator, still I rejoice to see you stand up, and while admiring your so tender yet robust body I can help to clothe it – for I help you into your fur boots, I straighten your hat before the mirror, I gaze with you into the mirror and dab powder on your saucy little nose and accompany you down the street in order to help you emerge from your grief.

But you – we make a big detour across the desolate space by the water tower, past the evacuated school, here's the pretentious museum building, there's the church, the main road bends here, on the other side is the barred gate of the Hop Market – you can speak for yourself how this walk that has brought you out of the overheated room allows you to become clearer, let us say calmer, more sensible. Yesterday you were at the post office and you know: rail links to the outside are unreliable, you write via Switzerland, how long will it take for a letter to reach there, and Germany's in the grip of revolution. You know the mail is uncertain, and how could a reply come today or tomorrow, today, only the Wednesday after that dreadful Sunday.

But there's one other matter you daren't touch on. Shall I reveal it? In that last letter you left lying on the table you alluded to it, but were not explicit. The two coffins with the shot soldiers passed by your house! Who shot them, who was the murderer? "Murderer": let us say it out loud. For a while you pretended it had nothing to do with you, then it seized hold of you. You don't know why and what it is. Two men murdered by him, by Hans, you can't keep it away from your image of him, as you watch it draw near to that image like smoke that will soon become fire. You already feel the fire within you. When he was with you in the maid's room and told you about it, it touched only your ears. He stood shivering, dirty, hungry, hunted, and the the long-feared pain of parting. It couldn't penetrate to you, now it penetrates, crashes into the railway station concourse of your heart and you twist and turn and want to block it and sweep it from you. I don't know if he knows about the Furies, but you sense something of it, maybe for him, you cling to him, love him, but the horror grows. And you labour day and night, in vain, to keep it far from him.

Operating Theatre Nurse Hilde – you don't know her,

she's been brought into contact with you only through my breath – depressed and newly awakened, who now heads twenty, thirty paces behind you down Long Road, the main road into the little town, does not engage in so much interior monologue. This is because she is simpler, calmer and more secure. She bears within her the legacy of her father, a patient artist and artisan. Such a nature goes calmly about its business, has no fear of that business because it senses an intimate bond with her.

What would you say if you knew that proud Hilde, this Brunhilde – you encounter her in Parade Square, by the café entrance, she wanders across into the Municipal Hospital and you think as she crosses the marketplace how good she has it, going so peacefully about her work – that this Hilde will soon leave the little town to set for herself a murky and difficult task?

She will travel this Wednesday evening to Strassburg. She has already made the trip to Württemberg. She came back in shock. The distress at everything she saw, and then the tumult, the dissolution of the military hospital, the complete upheaval finally overwhelmed her. Then came those hours with Maus and Becker. Now, in Strassburg, she is awaited by her father's assistant, who is a barbarian, a tiger. A young architect, a demonic fellow before whom she is powerless. Ever since she met him, the doors to her own being, to her nature, have been closed. Before he came along she was human. She spent the war a long way from him. She knows he was wounded at the start of the war, and returned to Strassburg. They have never written, never sent each other a greeting.

She means to pass this test.

STRASSBURG

Strassburg, as always, was beautiful and charming.

It lay gently in the embrace of broad green ramparts, relics of earlier wars. A little river trickled beneath its bridges past lawns and leafy trees, washerwomen knelt with tucked-up skirts and beat their linen in the greygreen stream, conversations floated on the air, white soapy foam came adrift from their toil in clumps and balls borne by the kindly current. Old-fashioned low half-timbered houses reflected in the water found themselves just as comely as two centuries ago. "Not a day older," they told themselves each morning as day broke. Men in peaked caps lounged at bridge railings lost in thought, stared drowsily down. Others of their kind sat in gloomy taverns at bare wooden tables behind a glass, and smoked. Later they'll climb into a boat and fetch vegetables and occasionally reflect on prices but mostly think of nothing at all and merely steer the boat, blow the nose now and then, set the cap straight, and know that this is the Thomas Quay and they're standing on their own two legs.

On this Wednesday, the day when the regiments withdrew before dawn from the little town, and the seriously ill were transported from the military hospital, and the last occupants of the hospital made ready to leave next day, on this 13th November the Strassburg newspapers announced the formation of a National Assembly for Alsace-Lorraine. The Second Chamber of the former Regional Council took the business of government in hand, but not too formally, everyone knows this government won't last long, for next Monday at noon the French will come marching in through White Tower Gate and at an opportune moment snuff out the infant National Assembly's candle.

On this same day the People's Delegate in Berlin,

Citizens and Soldiers

Ebert, a fine stocky fellow from Social Democracy, received a representative of the Dutch press who loomed two heads taller and was dressed very elegantly; the shorter of the two revealed to the taller that the cause of freedom in Germany had achieved its day of victory. The German people were victorious and the firmly anchored dominion of the Zollerns, Wittelsbachs and so on had collapsed. With that, Germany had completed its revolution. Such were the authentic reports reaching the People's Delegate, some by word of mouth, i.e. directly, some by telephone. With a veritable sigh of relief Herr Ebert, forename Friedrich, added: "Our victory has been almost bloodless, I must say, achieved easily and completely. That the old power could still mount a challenge seems out of the question." The Dutch representative got to his feet, they stood facing one another on the thick carpet. The Dutchman dared to have doubts: "It's almost too good to be true. We have a proverb, Chancellor, it goes: there'll be the Devil to pay."

"We have the same proverb," the other man responded, "but stay a while in the city and tell us what you see, and whether our victory is not complete."

"Gladly," said the gentleman of the press, and sent off his telegram of the day's interview.

In the course of the morning two ordinary men in Strassburg, a registry clerk and his office assistant, put into action a scheme they had carefully matured together. The clerk was attached to a commissary, he and his assistant belonged to the same convalescent company of the 3rd Reserve Battalion of an infantry regiment. They were stolid locals who worked in the same military office. Their work had languished ever since Sunday, when in line with the general example they simply stayed at home. Now they went one step farther. The clerk and his crony fetched a little handcart from a log and coal cellar and pulled it along busy Meisengasse. They stopped in a side street. Then they climbed the stairs they had climbed hundreds of times these past years, always one in official uniform and the other in common squaddie's garb, up to their office. But today they were in civvies, their thoughts blithesome of all the time that had passed and the tricks and intrigues they had employed to survive the times and be able to climb up and down these stairs. How much money, anxiety, humiliation had it cost them not to be redeployed. Now they hung up their jackets in the chilly lobby and set about the business in shirtsleeves. Piece by piece they carried down the steps a big desk, a chair, and a huge metal cabinet. These three objects were claimed by the clerk. He needed them at home, to keep his papers. The metal cabinet: because he was a nervous legally-minded man concerned above all to be in possession of total legitimacy and an absolutely uninterrupted existence. He had undertaken genealogical researches and possessed attested excerpts from church registers, mayoral offices, proving that his family had emigrated here three hundred years before from Switzerland. Up till now he had no confidence that these papers would withstand a fire. His wife thought his researches frivolous, and kept moving items from place to place in the house. Now he would install himself securely with the papers and this big metal cabinet in their shared domicile, and his opinions would gain an unarguable status. Desk and chair served the same purpose.

As they loaded up, companies of German troops passed by in the narrow street at slow march; they were heading across town to evacuate the left bank of the Rhine, and spared not a glance for the clerk and his helper. Who made a second trip, to fetch the small iron stove that stood in the lobby. It took them a good hour to dismantle the flue that reached up to the ceiling without damaging it, the assistant had brought tools along. They also carried down the coal scuttle and shovel. These were for the assistant, who for years had suffered from a malfunctioning stove.

★

The ancient porter at the little hotel near the cathedral grinned silently through the gap in the door into the room where his boss Anton Erbe sat on the high office stool at his desk over an opened ledger, pen behind his ear, doing nothing. Herr Erbe was so idle, or so deep in thought, that he didn't even turn his head to the door to hear more clearly what it was the man had been mumbling for a good while now. Herr Erbe had acquired the habit of contemplative sitting and doing nothing while in the prison from which he had made his exit only this past Saturday. At last Herr Erbe, a mild-looking man with glasses, did turn his head because of the draught, and he saw old man Hubert grinning through the door and moving his lips. Herr Erbe thought: either I'm deaf or he's mad, because I can't make a word out. But this failed to exercise him, he being so phlegmatic. He just kept looking at Hubert. Who now nodded vigorously several times and rasped that his voice was gone because he'd swallowed food the wrong way. Now he croaked: "Here's another one." He'd already said this, albeit not audibly, some fifteen times, but he too was a patient fellow, who had outlasted the tempestuous Herr Erbe the elder, founder of the little hotel, late father of Herr Anton on the high stool.

"Another what?" Instead of answering, Hubert pointed his right thumb back over his shoulder. He was pushed aside, and a tall elderly gentleman came into view. This gentleman, who had a small suitcase in his left hand and a knobbly walking stick in the right and in consequence did not remove his hat, was – our Major.

"You are the owner of this hotel? I would like a room."

Herr Erbe asked with a meaning look: "To whom do I owe the pleasure?" Whereat the Major fixed him with a glare of command and asked pointedly: "Is this place a hotel?" The hotelier nodded. "Then I would like a room."

"I only ask because it seems you're acquainted with Hubert. And you've stayed here before."

"Who is Hubert?"

Herr Erbe removed his glasses and pointed to the doorway. The Major put down his little case, and stepped up to the desk: "Now I really would beg of you, my dear sir, I need a room."

"Just because you're acquainted with Hubert, there's really no need to shove past him like that. The man's been in service at our hotel a good thirty years."

At which the Major picked his case up again, then thought of the hard night he had behind him, and pulled himself together. "Well, do you have a room?"

"But of course. We can always find one, why not. Certainly the only question is, two nights or three?" And without waiting for the Major's response – he really wanted to respond to this civilian familiarity with an about-face – Herr Erbe came out from behind his barrier, pulled a little wicker chair forward from the wall, into which the Major, despite everything, slowly deposited himself, and then talked calmly down at him from his lazy office chair: "You see, here's Hubert, he's not all…; he'll take your suitcase up right away, second floor, Hubert, the twin-bedded room, it became vacant just yesterday, a couple from Vendenheim spent their honeymoon there, happy young things, ah, if only we were still so young. You must know Vendenheim? Beautiful country, Alsace. I had to leave for a while, a year sister that anyone can read. I tell her: Girl, it's not on, it arouses suspicion. She says: I feel a quarrel coming on. I give in, and why should I break with our relations."

"Was your good lady detained as well?"

Mild Herr Erbe laughed on his high office stool:

"No. My wife acted very sensibly. After they'd snooped around a couple of times, the police, she packed her little bundle and said: Anton, I won't stay here, they mean us no good and I mean them no good, but they're stronger, come with me! And I, stupid idiot, out of sheer obstinacy, said no, and so off she goes to her sister via Switzerland. And when the first letters from her arrived I was well and truly suspicious, openly collaborating with foreign powers."

The Major cast a quick sharp glance: "In your place I'd have taken to my heels as well." Herr Erbe spread his arms: "Why? Why, Major? Run from whom? This is my hotel. Business was booming. I'd done nothing to anyone. But they hauled me in as anti-German, a traitor, and so I had to sit there from spring of 1917, a year and a half, Major. They found nothing to charge me with."

"Errors were made," the Major muttered, yielding to fate. The mild hotelier raised his head:

"My wife is still over there, she'll not come back until the French are here. Not a minute sooner. I use the time to feed myself up, otherwise she'll have too big a shock when she sees her old man. Today's Wednesday, on Saturday they fetched me out of Fadengasse, feels like a whole month already. I wept, Major, when they unlocked the cell and said we can go, we can leave, go wherever we like, and they're all standing there, crowds, Alsatians, they all felt as we did, and they cried and hugged us, strangers, but everyone friends, and they led me back to the hotel in triumph with music and song, back here where my good old father used to live. Now, Major, why do I tell you this? Because you must take this with you back home, back to Germany, so they know it too. I'm easy-going and good-natured, my wife thinks I'm too much so, but that's another story. Here I never gave cause for suspicion, I was no friend of Germany but also no enemy, and certainly no traitor. And when I emerged from the holding pen in Fadengasse and there were dozens of others like me, and I stood in the street, here outside my hotel ... well, damnation." Herr Erbe gritted his teeth and stared before him, brow furrowed, he spoke softly. "At that moment no Prussian had better let me lay hands on him, but there were none to see, suddenly they were all gone from the street, and then I realised they were right to call me anti-German. I was now. And still am ... But I've nothing against soldiers."

The Major kept quite still. Herr Erbe cleaned his glasses, replaced them carefully on his nose, settled the earpieces one by one, wiped his forehead. The Major waited a while longer. Since Herr Erbe did nothing but stare into space, the Major stood up. Erbe said: "The room is at your disposal." The Major, his throat tight, said: "I am most grateful," and let Hubert lead the way. On the stairs he gave the porter money for newspapers, any will do, local or foreign.

*

At two in the afternoon the General, pale, came to the big room. "What, two beds?"

"For ... wedding trips, General, honeymooners, a chicken coop."

"Did you scour the whole town – permit me to take

this chair. So you couldn't stand the noise."

"Shameless mob, these Alsatians, night-long drunken sprees right above other people's heads. Intentionally, of course. I went up, told them to stop, complained to the night porter. Nothing to be done, one as brazen as the next."

"We're surrounded by enemies. The hatred, the hatred, they literally trumpet it, out in the open now. Devil take the hindmost. They should have gone about the evacuation in quite another way. Is something the matter, Major?"

He sat there in his greatcoat, collar turned up, hands buried in his pockets, and now he spat into his handkerchief. The floor around him was buried in newspapers. "I couldn't care less about these people. I must respectfully report that just before you arrived, I threw up."

"No, the flu?"

"Stomach upset. Bile." He kicked at the pile of papers.

The General: "Don't keep reading that rubbish. Ten paces distance."

"I can't bear it, General. They used to print our army communiqués, now the enemy is speaking. Have to know what he intends. I am and remain Prussian, by profession."

"Yes, and?"

"In Berlin they've established a new ministry, for Prussia, there's a Comrade Hirsch, forename Paul, a certain Braun, Ernst, and Adolf Hoffmann. Do you know who Hoffmann is?"

"I have a tailor of that name. Why do you make a note of it?"

"Because I'll be binning the papers. He's called 'Ten Commandments' Hoffmann. Illiterate. Prussian Minister of Culture. Where's old Fritz with his walking stick?"

"I wouldn't throw up just for that."

A knock at the door. They exchanged glances, the

Major turned his head, shouted "Enter." A youngish bearded man in a raincoat, holding a small dripping huntsman's hat, stood in the doorway. The General on his feet, arms lifted in surprise: "Heinz."

"Uncle, sorry, I didn't recognise you in civvies."

"Shut the door, my lad. Well."

He introduced the others. "My nephew's a forester hereabouts. And what are you doing in Strassburg, with wife and child?"

He carefully hung up his wet things and moved the clothes hanger off the carpet. The General laughed: "There you see a married man. Why bother about a carpet belonging to those people?"

The Forester slumped in his chair: "Major, please forgive me seeking out my uncle here. I thought if I don't catch him in time, maybe he'll be gone by tomorrow."

"Makes sense, my lad. I won't stay here a day longer."

A long pause. The General: "And where is the family?"

"Over there already. Ludwigshafen, weeks ago. There was no way to hang on in our little village, once the front was no longer advancing. Lousy scoundrels. Everything undermined."

"Did the manager downstairs try to engage you in conversation?"

"That sort won't try it on, I had my hunting dagger with me, and my dog whip." He drew from one of his high boots a short leather whip. "But the way it is now, I could never have believed it possible after all the long years I've spent here, fifteen years. Either these people are hypocrites who run with whoever's winning, or they're perjurers, liars and traitors."

"No, well," the Major responded, "what's so strange about that. Anyway, what can a civilian do except comply."

"In peacetime, Major!"

"What about peacetime?"

"Before, they could speak their minds, you could have a good discussion with them. Whenever I received an army communiqué over the phone, I took it into the village and read it out that evening, and we all shared the same opinion."

The Major: "So it seemed to you."

"We sat long into the night, drank, argued, and there were some, they brought up prickly terms like annexation and so on. One of them, I tell you, a young peasant ..."

The Major: "Why wasn't he with the troops?"

"Fell sick, apparently, came back. That's peasants for you, they have their sides of bacon and ham, he managed to stay where he was."

The Major: "Don't we know it. Many of you lot profited from it, as well."

"But the fellow opened his big mouth and he wanted for Germany everything the geography books said, and all the others were staunchly with him apart from a couple who held their tongues and I thought them suspicious. Eventually ... there wasn't one in the whole village and the surroundings who stood by me. My wife and kids came running, they were frightened, I had to send them away. And now I've had to leave, they shot at me one night in the forest lodge. I know the fellow that did it." He wiped his eyes. "I would never have believed it. Not a hand lifted in support."

"Dear God, what on earth are you doing gadding about here still?"

"A chap has to know if it's really like that, because I cannot believe it. This was my home. The kids were born in my forest lodge, now they're away, supposedly never to return. My wife writes: Don't leave Alsace too soon, or you'll never get back in, the people are fickle, it'll all come right again. She's as much attached to the country as I am. And so I sit around and wait."

He wept silently behind his handkerchief as the two officers looked on.

The Major: "How old are you?"

The General stroked his moustache uneasily, and waved the Major off: "Leave him be. You're a bachelor, Major, know nothing of families."

"Thank God."

The Major made no objection when uncle and nephew, who sat for a while sombre and maudlin, took their leave. He promised to visit them later that evening.

★

Left alone he stretched his legs, covered his ears when the cathedral bells launched their massive pealing, his face showed torment. When the bells kept ringing he banged open the window and looked down onto the narrow street where people were calmly strolling. Then he trampled across the mound of newspapers, pushed past the honeymoon bed, and rang for hot chocolate. He swore out loud.

As he sipped, trembling and angry, two drips landed on the brown tabletop.

Unnoticed at first; only when he pushed the crockery aside did his glance fall on the two drips of chocolate. He regarded them without interest, set down the cup and saucer. Then he drank a second cup, and felt better. He cursed this place, this country. He accidentally nudged the saucer. Two brown blobs, one now somewhat smeared. Annoyed, he covered them again with the saucer, sat by the window in the chair beside the newspaper mountain. Now he sat quite still. Suddenly he felt impelled to stop reading, push past the obnoxious hotelier's honeymoon bed, and like a dog lured on by a hunk of sausage head for the table, the crockery. He had to lift the saucer. Two damnable round blobs, still there. He ground his teeth, banged his fist on the table so that the crockery rattled, glared venomously at the blobs, fists clenched, but dared not touch them. He stomped over to the clothes stand, on with the coat, the soft hat, and down the stairs. In the street he expelled a deep breath, forgot all about it.

When he returned late in the evening from the Officers' Casino, where he'd bumped into several acquaintances, and clicked on the light, he remembered the two drips. He was seized with anxiety. The table was cleared, clean! He passed his palm across the surface. Still, he washed his hands with extra care before going to bed, before climbing into the ridiculous honeymoon bed installed by the Alsatian downstairs, the stupid hotelier. The whole pack should have been dealt with by other means.

★

She strolled through the delightful city of Strassburg.

She had spent her first night back in her home town. Good and deep, wonderfully deep her sleep had been. She hadn't been home, her mouth was still closed. As she moved through the streets she still tasted of night. Not for ever so long, not since she was a little girl had she felt so in possession of her limbs, such reconciliation between body and feeling. She sauntered deep in thought along the bank of the little grey-green river. And as she strolled and her limbs moved she was the betrothed of the slow opaque stream, and ancient St Nikolai Church. At Kaufhausgasse she turned towards the city centre and was drawn down Küfergasse.

A silvery mist lay over far-off buildings and houses, embedding roofs and distant spires in a glassy haze. Here was Gutenberg Square. She wasn't surprised to see flower-stalls and everything as it used to be, long-ago in peacetime. Women had always stood here, always their baskets and stalls with bright flowers piled in front. For this was Gutenberg Square.

Meanwhile she had seen battlefield and frontline medical stations, and the military hospital, endless soldiers, fit, marching, convalescing, sick, wounded, dying. Four years gone by, on the margins of death. Now the old life came rushing, and with an obscure sense of wellbeing she surged to meet it. In the street were greetings, movements this way and that. No way to exchange a word with anyone, since yesterday speech had been knocked from her.

Up there is old Gutenberg, black, black all over, the black of printer's ink as is only fitting. At school Fräulein Mohr had explained the reliefs.

She stared at the reliefs, found a bit of life in them, took them in and augmented herself.

She wanted to go on like this. But she sensed her mother taking the little girl to school, a serious silent expedition … Hilde screwed her eyes up remembering – no talking, the child must learn to keep silent, at home Father wants peace and quiet. Mother was long dead, she had spoiled Father, and so he fell to pieces when she died. Bernhard appeared in the house. Father wouldn't have gone on living if Bernhard hadn't come along to be his assistant. Father disliked him, couldn't stand anyone independent around him, so why keep him on? And Hilde was astonished, her eyes resting once more on the reliefs, when the thought came that Father had kept Bernhard by his side precisely to quarrel with him, having now nothing to love.

Her eyes glanced to the side.

Flowers, pigeons, and the big arcades over there, lovely dark walkways. Nice when it rains. They still sell photos and picture postcards to visitors, souvenirs, pokerwork. Slovenly solitary soldiers passed by, hands in coat pockets. A loving thought took aim at someone far away, in a lounger. Her hand lifted, felt for buttons, the coat was fastened over her breast.

She followed a meandering course down streets growing busier. She had her long dark coat on, and the dark nurse's cap. And when she came past the theatre and over the bridge to Kaiser Square – always soldiers, columns rumbling – she dropped down onto a bench, affected suddenly by the sight of an empty plinth: it was the Kaiser Monument. The war was over, the whole long difficult war, four years, and she was home again. And she was rocked for an immeasurably brief moment by the war, Bernhard, flight, freedom, dying, defeat, looting, chaos at the hospital. When she breathed out (for there had been only a single pause in her breathing) she felt chilled as if her clothes had been ripped off. She shivered, her gaze fixed unconsciously on the tips of her shoes, she knew what they were, wiggled her foot and found her way back to her limbs, her clothes. She stood, she must move, vigorously. And her feet moved, pursued a scent somewhere or other, back over the bridge, up Hohenlohe Strasse, her old route to school, to the Higher Girls' School.

And there before her stood a sturdy old woman in a little poke bonnet, a woman with a robust back and posterior. Hilde tried to go past, but the woman held her firmly by the hand, smiled. It was Mother's sister, Aunt Eckhard, they kissed in the street, I'm on my way, I'm just now going to see Father ... Hilde, of course you'll come to me this afternoon, with Father, for coffee, yes, we have coffee, where from I won't tell you, only there's no milk.

The sun is shining to the left behind the cathedral. Hilde approached along the side of the cathedral down Bruderhofgasse, saw a little door, then ahead over there the tall mass of the tower. She stopped by the ancient Kammerzell House. Sunlight flooded the almost empty square. Silver-grey mist swirled up past the tower. It thickened as it rose, whiter, a glaze that carried light higher. What did she feel as the freed herself from the Kammerzell House and dared to step into the square, the huge structure looming over her, beside her? She was in the vicinity of a giant protective overshadowing being. Nothing in her but gratitude, joy and delight. Oh, she knew she would soon step into a darkly shimmering gigantic space, and go down on her knees beside a pillar, before a statue of the Virgin Mary.

There on the square, little human, young woman, a nurse, she gazed up to the heights. The confusion of spires and points and pillars acquired light. Many lines drew the eye upward, but lower down were three rounded portals, and over the middle portal a huge rose window revolved, it dampened the running and shooting of spires and points and lines, but only for a while, to right and left the lines shot high again. Each window was surmounted by pointed tracery. The spire to the left was no longer visible in the misty haze. It was like looking up at a giant's legs and having to stop at the stomach.

The bell struck two notes. That was the call. She stepped into the church, the cathedral accepted her, the vast gloomy space took hold and closed her in. When she found herself again among the arches and pillars and at the distant altar, she had a wish: to pour out and yield up from her overflowing heart the profusion of strength and joy that she felt.

suffer being jostled, ignored, no salutes, what a dreadful way to leave. It's a scandal, Hilde."

"They say the French will be here soon."

He drummed his fingers on the table. "That's when it will really start for us. They'll be giving the orders. Our new masters. We're to learn new ways. Learn new ways, you know?"

(Father dear, how long do you still have to live?)

"You can speak French, Father."

"Speak yes. But think, no. And I have no reason to think in French. What I think and have thought, is good." He said this adamantly, as if to an invisible opponent, his bald head drooped, the skull's incredibly strong. "And I have no wish to, whatever my age. I will not betray my life. I have no reason to." He regarded her from beneath knitted brows, ah, such strength from Father, ah, how good to have him sit here in the parlour, it's my parlour too. And she was able to respond, tense and expectant: "You're right, Father."

★

Outside the Palace of Justice on Finkmatt Quay the Pastor was wandering up and down amid crowds of people, scruffy soldiers, rowdies, the curious. He really wanted to enter the building, read the riot act to those inside. But security was tight. The First Lieutenant's Widow was still sticking to him. She peered around eagerly from under her coquettish widow's veil, it was all so heavenly in the city, she was glad they wouldn't allow her Pastor into the building, she needed a companion. His heart wasn't in it, she'd long realised how reluctant he was. If only she'd found someone else in time.

STRASSBURG

★

All this and more could not sketch even an outline of the lovely old city. Although newspapers brought wild reports, and although journalists, shirtsleeves rolled up, exercised their mighty profession of hot-air blowing, the good city was concerned first and foremost with ... being there, accepting in resolute calm the place that Fate had decreed for her on the Earth, letting the little River Ill flow through, straddling the water with bridges, calmly laying out her little lanes, streets and squares so that people could live. For a long time the commonality had not exactly had enough to eat in the city. So they were deluged with garish food-ration cards, ration stamps for fruit and vegetables that were to be kept safe because they would remain valid until further notice, but the stamps, as stated by the words printed on them, were intended only to regulate trade and conferred no claim to any foodstuff. A gaudy green the Fruit Card of the City of Strassburg, the Fats Card a ruddy hue, each stamp valid for 62.5 grams of edible fat or 1/10 litre of edible oil, valid also in Schiltigheim, Bischheim or Hönheim. For bread there was the violet Bread Card, each stamp valid for 50 grams of bread or 33 grams of flour and three stamps were valid for 100 grams of flour, all this simply to regulate trade.

Unable to console the body, the idea was hit upon to gratify the soul. And so people found on their Bread Cards pictures of the lovely River Ill with its bridges, and they could stare at the vapid Virgin at the South Transept.

Since noon a red flag had flown from the cathedral spire, the organ inside played no better for it, hardly anyone looked up. Farther away, Mr Lloyd George in London had made a speech, Emperor Karl was no longer in Vienna but on the run, arousing, apparently, mighty jubilation among sundry nationalities. The truth of this was a matter on which opinions were divided. The eye alighted on other news: that a joiner in Knoblauch Lane was now exclusively occupied with making flagpoles. In the small ads section, an elderly lady had placed a large notice for the public sale of ultra-modern hats of hair-felt and satin, priced between 15 and 30 Mark. She hoped to clear old stock rapidly. Sweetened Alsatian white wines 1918 were brought in on carts and offered at 240 Mark per hectolitre, these could expect rapid clearance. It's almost superfluous to note that prams and pushchairs were on sale cheap at various locations, that modern bedrooms, oak-panelled dining rooms and washing facilities continued uninterrupted their eternal march towards newly-wedded couples. As surely as the famous Moon continued to follow its course around the Earth, so surely did new or hardly-worn fur coats now importune new wearers with the capacity to pay. Flower shops sought well-presented girls to make deliveries. A plumber paid a visit with his little cart to a gentleman who summoned him. A teacher of Hungarian had sought long and fruitlessly in Hohenlohe Strasse for the house of the lady who had hired him for lessons, the number was not clearly written. Farmer Ruhe, visiting his meadow near Schiltigheim one afternoon and finding a cherry tree cut down, just like that, by a ruthless hand, felt afterwards the world had come to a stop. But this was already the second such incident in a year. A harmless little three year old girl, to whom no one could maliciously ascribe a link to any belligerent power (her own father, coffin-maker in Strassburg, had even declared himself neutral) – on Wednesday evening this little girl was hit by a military motorcycle and dragged along for several yards. But she suffered only slight abrasions.

None of it revealed anything of the old city, as it

quivered gently in the tumult.

And none of it revealed the yearning of lovers searching for the beloved that streamed in from afar and licked at the city like a pale flame from a distant blaze. Many such flames burned in the city itself.

★

And a very long way off, on this same evening in Breilly near Amiens, a young French soldier emerged crouching from the cellar of a peasant's cottage and climbed cautiously up the dark steps. He had heard a little knock at the cellar door, a signal. It was Clementine, a peasant woman, wife of a fallen friend, summoning him to supper. The signal meant the coast is clear, it's dark, door's locked.

By 14th September 1914, when the Battle of the Marne had just ended, Denis had already had enough of fighting. When his best friend fell at his side he felt he'd already done his bit for the war. He dared not go to his parents in the nearby village. Clementine, who had lost her husband, seemed a safer bet. Which proved true. They lived peacefully in friendship and love unnoticed on the isolated farm near Amiens all through the long war. He hid, she protected him. He was idle, she fed him up. But now as the war ended the silly fellow wanted out one way or another, and that would mean running headfirst into death and she would lose him. And so she coddled him and worked on him three times a day.

In the end Clementine and fear of the law prevailed. They eat in the kitchen, and drink.

At their feet is a wide box for the dogs, the bitch whelped yesterday, brought eight little yowling beings into the world.

"What about malaria, or Volhynian fever?"

They both smiled. The senior doctor shrugged: "Best just to wait, take quinine by mouth. Your good lady wife will keep an eye on your digestion. You yourself, Chief, always insist that fever must be diverted to the bowels, my opinion too."

He took his leave. "I shall call round again this evening, with your permission?"

Antonia pursued him down the hall, steered him into the living room; she looked worried. The senior doctor, cap in hand: "There's no cause for concern, dear lady. A certain contamination has occurred, but we can localise it."

"The redness?"

"Inflammation."

"And the fever? I'm so worried. He's already had so much trouble with his corns."

The doctor shook her hand, saying nothing, urging confidence.

"But, but …"

He left. She dared not return at once to the bedroom. Then she slapped on some untroubled good cheer, hummed as she went down the hall to let him know she was coming. In the room she leaned against the bed and smiled at her old man: "Well now! So we're to fall into the hands of the French, at the very end!" This was an opening for him to contradict her.

He laughed: "We'll be taking some bedbound cases along. I'll be comfortable enough," and he grew enthusiastic: "I'll be able to lie down all day!"

"Lazybones!"

"Now I know why people like to lie in bed so much: you truly get a good rest. I'm glad of it, really, Antonia, it's all coming together: war's over, I'm closing down the whole tedious doctor business, and I'll ease into retirement travelling in comfort, as a patient." He slurped coffee, pushed the cup away, said: "One minute." She left him on his own. No lad in the kitchen, no help, the dishes. Oh this revolution. And now the corn.

The window should be closed, he thought after he had lain by himself long enough, and he gave it a hard stare: it seems to be shut, but there's a draught, I'm freezing. How funny, I'm freezing. When the shivering stopped he realised: it's the chills, I'm anxious, I'll keep a good grip on myself so Antonia won't notice. – Pooh, how it puts one out, crazy. His teeth chattered. Am I a fearful old fusspot, they always told me I was, but I never believed them. But I'd better call for Antonia. He shouted. No answer came. She'll be upstairs packing. I must find another blanket. He would make his way to the bell-pull by the door. He climbed out of bed in his nightshirt, couldn't stand, the dressing on his left leg hindered him. He crept on all fours like a dog towards the door, rang. He listened for her approach, and tried to return to the bed when he heard her. But she was already there, frightened to death to see him kneeling at the bedside unable to climb up.

"Sorry, Antonia, I needed a warm blanket." He shivered horribly, and gave a crooked smile.

*

"You're alive this same day, this hour, this minute, I have no news of you, you've abandoned me. I begin in the grey of dawn to reach for paper to write to you, you'd never believe what I have to see and hear and live with here. If anyone knew what you once were to me, and are, they'd beat me to death. And they are spiteful and everyone holds some grudge against others. In the little town you know so well, repugnant and horrible things are about to happen, they'll put their little hatreds into action. No Germans to be seen now. What you're doing now, how you're managing, whether you're safe, the newspapers are full of such dreadful news from over there. I curse those who have brought defeat on the Germans, on you and me."

Then she crumpled the letter, threw it in the wastepaper basket, and later she picked it out and smoothed it and laid it aside.

★

Closedown of the military hospital. The final hours. No trumpeter practising in the garden, he's stowed the trumpet in his luggage along with a pair of newly-nailed army boots, not to mention bed linen for his wife.

Bed linen is what the nurses and all else in the hospital that was female have helped themselves to since yesterday evening. They were generous enough to bring in women from outside, and looted on such a scale that by midday it was "sold out".

Our taciturn old girl, the Pastor's doorkeeper: where do we find her? She who for a decade guided the blind captain so punctually and collected horse-dung so diligently from the street, sensitive to any disturbance to her routine - what has happened to her! What a change at such a great age, a revolution in miniature. She joined in the dance at the hospital to the very end. For the first time nurses and patients saw the old woman chatting and tittering. She singlehandedly freed an orderly from the claws of another who was trying to prevent the marble nameplate of the Surgical Station being loaded onto a pram and taken away. The old woman battered him with such violence they had to hold her back.

And will peace prevail with her husband, who is rectitude itself and suffers from a mania for order? You should see the angel of rectitude this Thursday morning, standing outside the house door opposite the water-tower, a crutch under each armpit. He chats with passers-by and everyone coming out and in, and announces: "Now at last a man can let his heart breathe. Prussians, those oppressors!" So said the former NCO, who still kept the wonderful decree about the confiscation of baking tins and cake-lids in a box under his table. He stood in the doorway like a war victim. It wouldn't take much for him to seize the very last crate being nailed up in the yard.

He even became assertive towards his wife. His suddenly awakened rapaciousness borne on a new patriotism made him savage. He drove the wife, who'd already brought back enough stuff, to return to the hospital. He enquired in the street what was happening at the barracks, the Officers' Casino, and when he heard that local patrols were all over the place, he swore. What sort of patrols? They're armed, it's the civil defence, they've occupied the town to keep order, prevent any unpleasantness with the French. He tried to incite acquaintances to stab or disarm the patrols, but encountered no corresponding sentiment. He chewed over this news of a civil defence, and that afternoon hobbled about the town for the first time in years, to find out what this civil defence was up to, and took a good look at those people, none of whom he knew. He was convinced they were simply guarding what was left of the property of the rich, and looting it themselves. And found agreement among little people of his acquaintance, Alsatians infected with the revolutionary bug. They came together: "Who gave them the right? Should we let them go on like this? They'd better not think they'll get away with it when the French come." But all it was, was bluster.

★

The few dozen patients laid out side by side in the Internal Station building were having a holiday. Together with the orderlies they formed a closed group, keeping under their wing everything needed for a long journey across Germany. Word was they'd be en route a good ten days.

The war was over. The heavens were not exactly full of violins, but they were to some extent rocket-bright. An Alsatian farmer, once a patient at the hospital, donated a live pig. Everyone came running to see it, and inspect the huge stock of provisions, enough for a polar expedition. The hospital's food stores had been protected against the onslaught of women – who were diverted to the bedding and crockery stores.

At noon they ate and drank, and there was extra beer. The jollity rose rapidly. Strangely the same song kept ringing out through the building – the *Wacht am Rhein*: "The cry resounds like thunder's peal." If you want to know why, here's the explanation: firstly, they wanted their song to ring out so that people in the road outside would shake their heads; and secondly their journey would be taking them "to the Rhine, the Rhine, the German Rhine".

Towards three it began to grow dark. Around five o' clock Becker woke his friend, who was lying in bed, by trailing a wet hankie over his face and whispering in his ear: "It's raining." Maus slept on a little while, then opened his eyes without waking up. Becker patiently trailed the hankie back and forth until Maus grabbed at it. Maus looked at the window: "Weather's bad." Becker smiled:

DEPARTURE

"Up now. We must change. You looked so happy just now."

"She came to visit me again, in my dreams. Can't believe how soppy I am about her." And as he sat on the edge of the bed he let his youthful blooming head slump to his chest. He jumped up: "So, we must change for our big journey into the unknown. No sentimentality."

The act of standing caused Becker considerable pain, he forced himself, Maus was amazed at his progress. At six, pitch dark outside, they sat fully dressed, greatcoat over the shoulders, in their little room, caps on the bed.

At one point there were shouts in the corridor, it seemed the last few minutes were being devoted to looting, the din was very loud, a few people ran past their door, then came swearing and laughter. They listened glowering, Becker groaned: "Holy God" and clenched his fist. Maus: "Don't lose your nerve, we still need it."

But what was happening outside was not, as they thought, a chase after thieves, but the freeing of the mentally disturbed malingerer, deserter actually, Ziweck; they wanted to take him along, being a Bavarian. But he fled, and was brought back forcibly by two men in army uniform who'd been alerted by the rebellious Barbara, two men from her home village.

★

By eight everything was assembled at the railway station next to the airfield, lit by magnesium flares. Flu victims were carried on stretchers. Tall and slow, wrapped in a thick greatcoat, cane in the right hand and another in the left, First Lieutenant Becker made his way, the fleshless face in the pitiless glare that knew only black and white was like a death mask. On either side, for support and protection, Lieutenant Maus and an orderly. Finally a stretcher brought the seriously ill Chief Medical Officer to a special compartment, where his wife too took a seat. It all proceeded in a serious businesslike manner.

The hospital on the big road lay empty, except for the corpse-washer asleep in the little dormitory.

During the night Ziweck climbed onto the roof and hoisted the red flag.

On the Train

And now the train headed out.

The locomotive was ancient, on her last legs; she did what she could, she had a ridiculously tall smokestack, she'd slept a long while in sheds, and her dream was for her last days to fade gently away in a museum somewhere. It was not to be, she was called up like the last man. Behind her came the familiar goods cars for men and horses, three cars. These had crossed every frontier during the war, scattering men and steeds all across the world, at the war's outbreak they were hung with garlands, the doors stood open and young freshly kitted soldiers gazed out as if from a hay-strewn barn and waved at the towns. Merrily they had plastered the sides and doors with chalk slogans, we're off to war, into a new life. Now the last of the goods wagons bore a faded inscription on one of the sliding doors, scrawled by an unskilled hand.

The three cars served with good civic modesty as kitchen, food store and stall. For this is where they kept the living pig, and an offering to the expiring god of war in the form of a few cheerily cackling hens from two women whose husbands had been restored to them. In the ancient wooden public car with benches people lay stacked, on benches, between benches; and in the aisles between benches they had managed to spread bedding.

On the Train

Those who were still sick arranged their beds for the long haul; more cars with compartments were hooked on to accommodate the seriously ill, the last few flu cases, and families. The few remaining officers understood that this was where they should take cover.

Wheezing, the little granny of an ancient locomotive with her dry throat set about her work, cautiously hauling her little children along. The wagons began to move, from every window people gazed back at the last of the flares. Into darkness the little granny hauled the cars, the lights behind disappeared, and they slipped into a silent dark forest. A solitary bass voice sang in one of the leading cars: *Ah how could it be, that I could ever leave you. I love you with all my heart, please believe me.*

★

Lights in the cars went out. Outside the moon shone, heads lifted from benches and peeped out. Cold rushed in, they snuggled under blankets.

In their private compartment, Becker lay on the bench opposite Maus.

"You awake, Maus?"

"Yes."

"Stay alert, Maus, the war will soon be over."

"The war's already over."

"Another half hour, just half an hour, don't fall asleep, then you'll see, then you'll see, the war is over. Stay awake, Maus. So we can savour the moment when this war is at an end. You don't see it yet, Maus. Don't think of your shoulder. I'm not thinking of my spine. Don't look back. Lift your head. If you can, lie on your stomach. You'll see more clearly."

Maus lay on his side. He lifted his head. They were

passing through a forest. The little granny hauling. Sometimes the forest opened up, they saw moonlight flooding into deep bays. Now and then sparks flew past. The cars trundled and trundled.

Nothing more of the little town.

The cars trundled.

"We've been going a long time," Maus whispered. A new landscape was spreading out, a rise and fall of ground, hills, valleys.

"Don't worry, Maus, we'll be going like this a lot longer. A lot longer. Oh to think we're alive to see it. That it's coming once again to meet us. Now it's all over, now, now even that's fading." He was stuttering, Maus couldn't follow him. Puzzled, he said: "The things you say, Becker."

Becker lay with his head against the windowpane, his face tense. He whispered: "It's peace. Life. Life. I greet you, dearest Peace. Here you are. Stay here. Stay for ever. Never abandon me again, dearest Peace. We're returning from the war – the long, cruel, hard war. We did what we could. We went into it as youngsters. Now we return, lamed, mutilated. And thirsting, hungering for you, feverish. War was the alarm clock, it rang just beside us, we kept thinking yes we're here, stop ringing, it never stopped, but now it's silent. We're on our way, we're coming, Peace, here we are. Ah to see you once more, to try everything once more. We had lost all hope of being granted this."

Becker lay on his stomach, he lifted his head higher against the window. "We lost hundreds of thousands, dear ones, good ones, young ones. They lie out there in the mud, gunfire in their ears still. Dearest Peace, be merciful with us who are returning."

Maus listened in astonishment: "What are you saying, Becker?"

The cars trundled, trundled. On through white

moonlight and deep shadow the train glided.

"We must have committed egregious sins for this to have happened to us, for us to be returning like this, defeated." He stretched out on the bench, pulled the blanket over him, he didn't stop. Oh Peace, Life, you are still our face. Our face, oh our face.

Reveal yourself to us. Reveal us. Here we are, we're coming. Deal mercifully with us.

They lay, one on his stomach, the other on his side, and dreamed. The carriage's rocking matched the mood. Unresisting they took it in.

★

Becker slept.

From an expanse of meadow, or was it a water-mirror, a figure emerged and spoke to him: "You're going away."

"We're going home."

"Why are you going home? Day after day your trains grind along."

"We've been defeated. We must evacuate from this country. Come closer, I can't hear you properly."

"Stay! Stay! Why would you leave?"

"With reluctance I leave this land where I lay for so long."

"Oh, stay here, do. I have no business with warriors. We are peaceable. Look around you."

"I saw."

"Look harder. You are devout and good. Stay."

"Who are you? Who's speaking to me?"

"You can see me."

"Your name."

"I am an old man, a blessing to his country. I am called Johannes Tauler."

"Johannes Tauler! You!"

"I once lived here. In times gone by. Oh you dear Christian, listen to me."

"I'm but a poor Christian."

"You *are* one. To the extent that you can lead people to God's truth. You can turn to the miraculous workings of God and reflect on the inexpressible gifts he has revealed to us, that flow out from him."

"You think so ...?"

"Yes, good man. Why do I pursue you out of the darkness, like a mother who hears her child call? You have rejoiced and expressed delight at Peace, the sweet face of Peace, which is one of the countless blessings revealed to us, and to all creatures."

Becker murmured in his sleep: "How can I stay."

"Stay, so that you can know more. God stirs you and draws you to him. He wishes to sink his love into you."

"Come closer. Be clearer."

"Lift yourself to me so I can see into your eyes. Ah, such a sad look."

"I've been ill a long while."

"So speak new words to your sickness. Say: God greets you, oh you most bitter of bitternesses, you shall be my dear sister, you are full of grace."

"I shall."

"You have not done so yet. You are hard and proud, a great soul, a high mountain. Do not shut your eyes, my child. You must pray for patience and a merciful outcome. The Lord comes with a silent gentle rustling."

The carriages trundled. Becker lay there.

"You persist in your own comfort zone, my child. That will be no way out. You must turn. Repeat after me: Oh most bitter of bitternesses, you shall be my dear sister."

He murmured, murmured it again. He heard the voice: "Oh you good Christian. Your wretched forsaken soul, in

On the Train

what distress is it caught up. It cannot even lament properly. Come. Do not forsake me. Do not forget my country. One day I shall send you a sign, a helpful sign."

Becker's lips parted, he raised himself, questioning.

But he found nothing, and went back to sleep.

★

The train travelled in a wide northerly arc towards Germany. The vast retreating army had taken over all the lines. When day dawned, they had just trundled wordlessly past the ancient peaceful town of Weissenburg. None saw the grey monument erected beside the railway to commemorate the German victory here of fifty years before. The monument stood there grey, the victors, now the defeated, left it standing, it receded into the dawn gloom. They crossed the Lauter; as they slept amid the rattling trundling they quit sweet Alsace, now it's the Pfalz, they're trundling on through Landau and beyond. To the left, the hills of the Hardt. They have not yet crossed the Rhine.

In the big communal car they sleep on benches and on the floor of the aisles. They've travelled this way and that, from east to west and west to east, they've fallen ill, recovered, now they lie here being conveyed back home. As the wind in spring blows so much fine gossamer of blossoms across fields and along streets, onto soil fertile and stony, so have they been scattered here and there, and where they land, there they settle.

In the kitchen car a few men wake up early, one thinks: "This is no longer Alsace, what it is I don't know, and couldn't care less."

They're competent lads, one or other of them has laid by a quantity of stuff in the provisions car, well packed and bundled, a week ago none of it was theirs; if anyone asks where they got it from, they claim it's from the former military hospital by the airfield, from the regiment's clothing stores, they have propeller wood, greatcoats, boots, fabrics – but why do we speak of these, clothing stores, regiments, airfield, they're up early in the Lord's good morning, they've brewed a fabulous jug of coffee from which they pour a few hot mugfuls, bread and jam to go with it. They smack lips, slurp and laugh into the misty countryside. Soon they'll make their way to the others.

The Chief Medical Officer's wife, thick dressing gown over her shoulders, in blue slippers, no stockings, pushes the curtain aside. "You've had such a good sleep, Otto." She's happy, he's happy. There's still hot coffee in the Thermos, he gulps it down, lies back in bliss. "It's wonderful, quite wonderful." Both are in a remarkably good mood, what's the cause of their joy, it's over, the war, every dream will be fulfilled, she puts her arms around his neck, the situation is so enticing, arousing, they're on the move, being looked after, they're like young newlyweds. They shake their heads and laugh at the red flags that hang here and there from buildings, but whole villages are adorned as well in the Reich colours, with flags and flowers, from some late report of victory or already as a welcome to the retreating troops.

THE PASTOR AND THE WIDOW

The First Lieutenant's Widow strolled at the side of her Pastor through delightful Strassburg and couldn't stop the giggling that grated so on the Pastor's nerves. It was the afternoon of the military hospital evacuation. What a hussy, he thought; how could the late lieutenant who lay now on the Marne have been devoted to such a thing. But it did not escape him that in Strassburg one was surrounded by many such hussies.

The Pastor and the Widow

In Gutenberg Square, at the Widow's side, he gazed gloomily on the same flower women who brought such joy to our Nurse Hilde, and pigeons were flying and pecking between the cobbles, rather hungry pigeons, they don't even have Bread Cards, for heaven's sake feed them.

"Madam ..." ("But don't keep calling me that, what will people think of us here on our travels. You're ... I know, my uncle. I'm Frau Gusta, or simply Gusta, incognito, Pastor, we're in a war zone.") "Well then, dear lady (O God), may I offer you flowers?"

She was delighted, brandished the little bunch and pointed at the "old'un" up there.

"It's Gutenberg, they named the square after him."

"I prefer you, dear uncle. I hope you're happier strolling with me rather than standing up there in the cold, with the pigeons ..." She tittered. He walked at her side, grave, telling himself: enough is not yet enough. But he was immensely curious, for what he saw in her company he would never have seen on his own.

Behold the officers, behaving as if we're not in the midst of a world-historical catastrophe! But perhaps they just want to drink themselves into a last taste of happiness, into numbness.

What's this? He pulled her to a stop by an advertising pillar:

Proclamation to Comrades of Army Detachment A

> The conditions of the Armistice Agreement require the transfer of the whole of Alsace-Lorraine to the forces of the Entente. With a heavy heart ... But, Comrades, it behooves us with dignity ... Wherever the population of Alsace confronts us with violence, corresponding counter-measures will at once be put

in place by your leaders.
Army High Command, Chief of the General Staff
**Central Workers' and Soldiers' Council of Strassburg,
To the People**:
Stay calm! The German soldier is not your enemy. The German people and German soldiers have delivered the final blow to the much-hated system.

The Pastor stood there speechless. He glanced right, left, people walking by, soldiers, officers, all going along with it! For the first time Frau Gusta felt his arm slide under hers; so the old bear's waking up, but he'll creep back into his stuffy old den soon enough; contentedly she squeezed his arm, her cavalier at last, but he was simply knocked back by it all, and looking for support. But his arm would not be released so quickly. Oh, this jolly old Strassburg! Rat and mouse killer, Millimors is cheap and easy to use, goose liver pâté, modern villas for sale in sought-after location, Christmas, cigars for Christmas, whatever will this Christmas be like, this dear festival of Christ, grand hare dinners at the Stadt Thann.

A squad of troops in Meisengasse is singing a German song, it's sad and moving: *Forlorn, forlorn am I*, but no, they're laughing, making merry: *Demobbed, demobbed, demobbed am I! Done with all the hating, how glad am I!*

"Allo, Djong old plum, come on, gi'ssa kiss!" The men stand outside a private house, fists raised, what are they shouting? *Haw haw haw, Robespierre's at yer door.* They shout this a dozen times, move on. Gusta, nervous: "What are they up to?"

"Shush," he whispered down to her. "They're provoking Reich Germans."

"But why?"

The Pastor and the Widow

All the distraught Pastor could say was: "They're Alsatians."

She pulled him on to Kleber Place. Sun, sun, sun. Field-grey officers still cross Kleber Place, soon the French will be here, no less tense, with intelligent sharp faces, and they'll greet old Kleber on his high four-cornered pedestal as one of their own. Behind Kleber there's a modern hotel, the Red House, but why's it called red, shops, galleries, restaurants. To the right the cathedral spire towers over the buildings, the many little chimneys on the red roofs send it their smoke. Cars and trucks are parked on the wide expanse. Madam First Lieutenant wants to sit in the Café Aubette. The Pastor trails along in her wake.

The place is full, she wants to sit right in the hubbub, among all the laughing, drinking, cake-eating, the clatter of plates. But he spots a table at the window, and they set themselves down.

Sunshine on the square. Fat men in civvies go past. An elderly man with a white moustache is carrying a big parcel, he's coatless and wears high bucket-top boots like a cavalryman. A chap pulling a little dog on a leash. A motorcyclist rattles onto the square, stops, climbs off. Ah you lovely square, I can already see alien regiments riding across you, officers with kepis and gold ribbons, with narrow trousers and in the hand a short cane.

Merry Widow Gusta throws back her veil to reveal her little red snub nose, she's enjoying herself tremendously, imagines herself a provincial goose come to the big city. A tall maitre d' snakes his way through the room and bows at every table. She's interested in the ladies. Such elegance, how straight they sit, short skirts, really short, how they show off their legs, lovely stockings. Such taste, Parisians, I'll buy myself stockings like that, but are my calves too big.

An elegant lady in a sleek black dress, black fur stole over her shoulders, looks around in the entrance, she's pretty, carefully made up, so well groomed, she rustles beaming past Gusta, who feels very small. She's located two ladies adjacent to Gusta's table, one pale with outrageously blonde hair falling in curls to her neck, hovering over it is a black and white felt hat with a boldly upturned brim. Gusta is delighted to identify points of similarity with this lady, she's plump too, no longer young, looks nice, she'll bring pleasure to lots more yet. See how the eyes that gaze out so benignly are set deep in the sockets, she must have been ill. The woman beside her has a red felt hat, not my taste, she doesn't look around much. See all these men sitting here. A lot must be officers, getting away from it all for once, like me. And there are fat elderly men too, why do they rest their heavy fleshy hands on the table, just so everyone can see their rings, probably. Bet they've tucked the wedding ring in the waistcoat pocket. But the girls aren't biting.

Ah, a young man from the next table has got up and is standing over the two ladies. They squeeze his hand, they know him. At once they put their heads together. The young elegant man, officer for sure, turns his cropped head and points to a table where other young gentlemen sit silently smoking cigarettes. It's all so interesting! So nice to be part of it. What a life that is. The three of them chat away quite easily, why don't they invite the young man to sit, people in the aisle can't push by.

The ladies stand up, seems someone's coming. Ah, the new woman. Wonderful. I could fall in love with her. But she's not young. She's like the pale woman with the sickly eyes. Under her arm she has a little monkey-terrier, they all fuss over it. How reserved she is as she speaks to the man, her face is small, such delicate features. Now she

The Pastor and the Widow

listens to the other two, they're trying to persuade her or the dog, her little face is inscrutable as an aristocrat's.

They sat nearly an hour in the Café Aubette, then it was time to go. The Pastor rose wearily from his seat, what a boring fellow, like all the men from our garrison, and I've spent four whole years with that sort, you become a complete bumpkin.

But the First Lieutenant's Widow was destined to encounter much more enjoyable experiences than she expected at the time of their withdrawal from the Aubette. For with her little red nose, now covered again by the widow's veil, she resembled a dog that sniffs the wind and detects thunder and will not be diverted.

Outside she looked left and right, it was still damp and chilly, still Thursday the 14th, Kleber still up there on his monument, the sun had disappeared, darkness was falling. There they were, drifting towards the newspaper kiosk. In the street to the right people, men and women, were vanishing into an abyss, what was it, oh yes, toilets. Facing them, however, across the street flooded with people and vehicles where the first lights were being lit, the harshest glare streamed from shops and cafés dansants. The Pastor seemed to have no interest in them, he walked along head down, hands deep in his coat pockets, saying not a word. But Gusta's agile eye had spotted a winking café signboard advertising in large letters: concert, dancing. And dance, dance, it was a magic spell that took root in her. For almost a decade she'd never been dancing, her husband had liked sports, but didn't dance. Shouldn't we go dancing? She walked slowly, the Pastor strode on a minute more at his long pace, but now he fell into line, said: "Sorry," aroused from his dream. (He must be thinking of his burrow in Westphalia or Pomerania, or of that old war like all the other men; they're not the slightest bit concerned about what will become of us.)

She made tiny little tripping steps and wouldn't move from the dazzling sign, it's on the first floor for sure, if I only knew when. And as she was still considering how best to whisper it to the Pastor, he himself suggested: "You want to cross the street? Let's go back a little way." And he led her right up to the glaring sign so she was able to stand amazed looking at it and as he waited patient and unsuspecting said "Ah," and studied the poster: "Dancing from 4.30 to 11." She tapped him cheekily on the shoulder (see how fast it happens: faster than when you think about it) and pointed to the poster. His eyes, which for so long had run over nothing but proclamations and war bulletins, perceived with indifference the phrase "Dancing from half past four to eleven", the letters left no trace in his brain. They had as little import for him as for an ant that has found a little scrap of cheese at the edge of a village, and as it drags it back to the nest a peasant procession comes along singing, so little importance did the singing have for the ant as it dragged the scrap along, totally absorbed in studying fissures in the terrain.

But snuffling Gusta was not so easily diverted from her thunderstorm. "Uncle dear, do come along, I'd like so much to see how they dance."

Now he was shocked, and consciousness returned. She had dropped her formal tone with him. He furrowed his brow and looked sternly at her, had every intention of opening his mouth, and from his mouth there should slip unambiguous well-prepared words of protest and earnest admonition. But now (he had no idea why, she had only made a rash move, but a clever one) she had thrown back her veil to show him such a childlike and imploring face and with it such an appealing roguish smile that he was thrown into a difficult struggle. But no such

The Pastor and the Widow

difficult struggle can be waged silently to the bitter end on the streets of Strassburg next to such a poster and a lady, contrary to what literature and the Temptation of Saint Anthony would have you believe. Rather, you must respond right away. And the response comes sooner than you yourself would expect, and while you're still debating fearfully with yourself she has already formed on her lips, her very own lips, the words that will change the whole situation.

"I really don't know, dear lady," the Pastor had replied, already with such hesitation, confusion, conceding, protesting, but already pleading. She sensed he was reluctant but couldn't deny her. She dared once more her "dear little uncle", he was furious, saw himself already half lost against this barrage. She said with a pout: "We'll just go in, look around for fifteen minutes. Just a wittle quarter of an hour, please oh please, uncle dear."

Oh the minx. Oh Eve, must the Fall be ever repeated, the Adam in us knows everything, they told him everything, presented all the consequences, and (oh how true the Bible is) it's happening, just like then.

And with a heavy sense of being a new Adam, the words of the Bible weighing on him, he accompanies skipping Gusta up the stairs to the first floor, from where music wafts. Here's the cloakroom, he puts his stiff felt hat down, won't the gentleman wish to leave his overcoat as well, it's very warm inside. – Well, if it must be. Now what's the First Lieutenant's Widow up to, they're hanging her dark coat up with a smile, and the hat and the veil, where's she gone; the gentleman is looking for the lady? She'll be in the washroom; so we'll wait, how strange that I'm here, dear God, the defeat, our retreat, oh Strassburg, oh Strassburg, thou wonderful town. There ... is that her tripping towards me? Nice plump little lady in a smart blue dress, she has a rose in her hand, shall I pin it on, or what would you like, uncle dear, always this uncle dear, and I'm really not that old.

They sit at a little marble table, now she'd like a port, he has one too, it's a spacious room, lots of customers, the band is four musicians, chatting and smoking at the moment, the Pastor's completely deflated. Gusta beams, pats his hand encouragingly: "I'm so grateful to you, Pastor." One of the musicians starts to sing, it's the pianist. A few couples step onto the dance floor. What is this dance, is it a tango, Gusta whispers in excitement: "They're singing in English, come, Pastor, yes, just once, just this once."

"Please, I beg you."

"Once, just this once."

"But I really cannot, look at how they're dancing, no, I don't want to."

"Just once, what harm can a little dance do?"

So he gets to his feet in God's name and twirls with her in a kind of polka, but it doesn't work, he's embarrassed, at last she gives up, they sit down, she sulks, he keeps quiet and sips from his glass. Then it starts up again, and as she's still staring moodily at her rose someone whispers behind her, she turns round, a man bows to the Pastor, to her: "With your permission, sir, gracious lady." He doesn't understand, she doesn't understand, oh yes she does, she blushes, smiles at the Pastor, eyes opened wide in delight, and she's already on her feet, on the dance floor, in his arms.

For this man is, as she recognised at once, the same exact man from the Aubette, and he tells her straight away that he's already seen her in the Aubette with her good husband, and she remembers him and the lady with the dog, there she is, oh yes, all three of them are sitting there, but you should be dancing with your lovely wife, sometimes one likes a change when a young woman has a husband she loves and who loves her, I don't understand these modern steps, they're easy for a lady to learn, and so it turns out, and she's in another world, and afterwards he takes her gravely back to her table where the Pastor is still gazing into his glass, but he tugs suspiciously at his black bow tie and finally, without looking at her, clears his throat and says: "We can leave now." She wheedles and edges closer to him, the next dance has begun, it's a tango, and as she turns her head in expectation the serious young man is already there bowing, she stands up with a flourish, beaming, and now the tango. She already knows the man, she knows his arms, his chest and his bow tie, he's a wonderful dancer, she sees that the others dance the same steps, but he makes it so formal and serious and elegant, and when he whispers, his face betraying not the slightest flicker, God you're so beautiful, the world is untethered, I don't know him, and he doesn't know me. How one moves this way and that, stopping and turning, some of the steps are really rather risqué, but everyone's doing it, these are the new dances. When the swaying and turning and stepping and stopping are over and he takes her hand to lead her back to her table, she has a sense of having experienced something tremendous, and he leads her to the table and there's no one there, the man bows.

Where is the Pastor? The waiter approaches as she's peering around: "The gentleman is waiting for madam in the cloakroom." Once there she pulls him aside, he is adamant: "I never promised you more than this." What had happened to make him so formal all of a sudden? As he watched her dancing, a memory had come to him of Fräulein Köpp the milliner with the dubious baby, and of several similar cases, and the memory had spoiled the occasion for him, and he no longer wanted to see this First Lieutenant's Widow. He had already put on his coat and was holding his hat, she couldn't call him "uncle dear", she thought "spoilsport, pah", gave him her hand, "well then, byebye until dinner," and back into the salon, angry. And then two more dances and a date for tomorrow with the man and back to the hotel, where she bumped into the Pastor in the lobby and said a cool farewell when he declared he had to leave that very evening. She thought: shall I make another move on him? ... but she saw that the man was wounded in his pride.

When finally they came to shake hands in the dining room, he dared to suggest that she might travel with him. "I believe, dear lady, that neither you nor I understand enough of the customs of a city such as this." She thanked him with jutted chin for the advice, and span a yarn about a captain's lady who lived here, and of course she absolutely must pay her a visit. He was glad to see that she had returned to normal life, and left. As far as he was concerned, old Adam had been decisively defeated, his biblical duty fulfilled.

But the Widow lingered another quarter of an hour in the dining room among the dirty plates, and mulled revenge as she cracked bonbons.

THE WILHELMSHAVEN SAILORS

Smokestack flaring, wheels rattling, never once stopping, a special train came on its way from Wilhelmshaven via Osnabrück, Münster, Düsseldorf, Cologne. On board were two hundred and twenty sailors of the High Seas Fleet belonging to the revolution's avant garde, Alsatians, now all asleep on benches, in the aisles. They meant to save Alsace from the French.

They were some of the twenty thousand or so naval conscripts from Alsace and Lorraine in Kiel and

Wilhelmshaven. Why so many? Every year a representative in the Alsace Territorial Assembly asked this question. From the government desk he received the curiously mocking reply: They withstand the tropical climate so well, so very well. Being now in the navy at Kiel, they had joined the revolt of the 1st and 3rd squadrons of Admiral von Hippe, and were present when the red flag was hoisted on the battleships *König, Kronprinz Wilhelm, Kurfürst, Thüringen, Helgoland, Markgraf.*

How it came over the sailors at the beginning of November is easily explained. All through the war they had languished in their home base. And they would have held out comfortably enough for the last one or two weeks of the war. But then their officers brewed up a scheme not to their liking. They were supposed, all eighty thousand men, to leave harbour and head into certain death, which they, like every human being, abhorred. The officers had not intended to betray the plan, rather, sailors intercepted farewell letters from officers to their loved ones in which they could read between the lines. The naval officers meant to engage the English, lurking outside in much greater strength than they. For now that it was at last certain in these November days that victory was impossible by land or sea, they wanted at least to go down with flying colours. Who did? The officers. But the sailors took the view that there were two parties here. For the vessels in which the officers proposed to die also contained them, the sailors. And they were not available for any such scheme.

And so as the hour of the mandated sailing approached, no fires burned in boiler rooms. Not even the stokers wanted to die. Frederick the Great once had to deal, at the battle of Kunersdorf, with the curious reluctance of people, soldiers even, to head into clearly signposted death. He had roared: "Do you mean to live forever?" But even

Citizens and Soldiers

that animated only a few. Field commanders often notice: people are reluctant to die when it's as plain as the nose on their face. Of course, once they're over the tricky matter of dying they lie quite calm, but are no longer much use to the field commander.

In Kiel, the officers screaming at the sailors and agitators received the blunt response: "We won't obey. You've lost the war. It wasn't our war." This response was sealed with blood on both sides, and confirmed as final.

The events at Kiel were repeated at Wilhelmshaven, Altona, Bremen. These were the most appalling, final, absolutely final days for the German army, when the US General Pershing broke through in the Argonne and pushed on towards Metz.

When the Alsatian sailors read in the newspapers over the next few days what kind of armistice conditions were being imposed, and that Alsace-Lorraine, their own land, was mentioned, they pricked up their ears. Oho, we might have a little something to say about that. So swiftly had these bawled-out underlings turned into free, even proud people, who would not have their rights taken from them.

Seaman Thomas, from Weissenburg, was a temperate man who'd served eighteen years in the imperial fleet. People listened when he spoke. Sailors quizzed him. They swore: "The Entente's plotting a mean trick on our Alsace, they're going to swallow it up." They cursed the deceitful imperialism of Mr Wilson from America. Where was this right of self-determination he so loved to peddle? Mischievous Reich Germans wormed their way in, stoked up steam behind them even though they had other goals in mind. But the sailors swore an oath: "We demand our Alsace. We shall never let anyone take our Alsace." They felt the power of the revolution in their bones. "We shall bring the revolution to Alsace. Kleber was *our* general."

A special train was put together for them at Wilhelmshaven. The fires from the North Sea coast raging across the whole of Germany would now be hurled at Alsace.

Through the night the train sped, smokestack flaring, never stopping, past Osnabrück, Münster, Düsseldorf, Cologne. It was Wednesday the 13th. Now they had arrived in Strassburg, on Thursday, a hundred and eighty men. For forty of them had been given over to Metz and Saarbrücken. All hundred and eighty assembled in Strassburg on wide Station Square, slung the rifle on the back and set off, red flag to the fore, in close formation, not losing a minute, down narrow Küssstrasse, left onto St John's Quay, then along Kleber Quay, and there already is the Palace of Justice. They were in a great hurry, for they had already worked out that in war and revolution it all depends on speed. If you're not quick the other will be quick, and if you're quicker than the other then you're already halfway to winning the encounter.

The Regional Court building stood on Finkmatt Quay. Excited people followed them from the station. A big crowd had already gathered outside the Palace of Justice opposite. But you mustn't think that all those who, ever since the revolution, had gathered day in day out before the Palace of Justice or come thronging in little columns, were impassioned politicians. Among the many remarkable changes wrought on the sinister court building during those days was its conversion to a feeding station. For soldiers passing through or searching, demobbed men wandering about with no roof over their heads, naturally turned first to their Soldiers' Council. And the councillors, well aware of what was most important in the life of a human being, simply had several field kitchens brought into the ground floor of the Regional Court building, and there people ate, warmed themselves no questions asked, and various questions were thereby in many cases rendered moot. They made a din, sang, and now and then, from the upper corridor where the governing was going on, thunder rumbled down – but it was milder than many a judge's pronouncement. For the people making a din up there in the courtroom, Room 45, were the same kind of people as the ones downstairs eating and warming themselves.

It is almost noon, and Staff Sergeant Hueber is presiding. They've debated and thundered about yesterday's looting, the security patrols had tried to hold people back, they'd threatened, in the end they'd been forced to fire, some had been wounded, some scoundrels even set fires among the provisions to facilitate looting – and now a tremendous roar rises up from below, not the ordinary din silenced by thunder from above – cheers, shouts of joy, boots marching up the stairs, the doors to the courtroom burst open, and preceded by a red flag, tree-tall Thomas at the head, sailors come marching in! The courtroom erupts.

When the general jubilation subsides and the bluejackets have distributed themselves around the courtroom to find a seat and greet acquaintances, Thomas the giant steps solemnly onto the podium and from there declares to those below how happy they all are to be back in dear old Strassburg. They've come from Wilhelmshaven in the name of sixteen thousand Alsatian sailors at the naval base to convey cordial greetings to their homeland! And now they're here and wish to act in the spirit of the Internationale to help their compatriots too to share in this new age of golden freedom and reconciliation among nations. Endless applause, handshakes, clapping of shoulders, fraternal embraces.

That was Thursday morning.

THE WILHELMSHAVEN SAILORS

While the Pastor was sitting with his Widow in the Aubette looking on at all the cheerful happenings at neighbouring tables, running battles were already taking place in the Regional Court building among the "Inner Council", and yes, sailors and soldiers and the new mayor of Strassburg, Herr Peirotes, were also present.

The sailors declared without preamble that it was their intention immediately to declare the Republic of Alsace-Lorraine. It proved very difficult to talk them out of it.

Peirotes was a clever man, Jacques Laurent his forenames, he was born in Strassburg. As typesetter and journeyman he had travelled all through Central Europe, had even visited the distant Balkans. But then he grew mindful of the pleasures of his homeland, and from a typesetter, Strassburg made of him a writer, and a member of the Second Chamber. The much-travelled man was short and stocky, almost fifty years old now, with a grave honest face, high forehead, thick moustache. He spoke in a firm rasping voice. He took the sailors on.

Peirotes said: "There's nothing to prevent you going to Kleber Place, which you know well, and having one of you, say Comrade Thomas himself, declare the new republic. But what will it achieve? Recently so much has been happening in Kleber Place, people have almost grown used to such goings on. In the evenings youths come running and make a spectacle, they set off firecrackers to make people think there's shooting, and yesterday some of them stuck a cigarette in Kleber's mouth up there on his plinth, and placed a garish cap on his head. Then they sang songs to provoke the people. Who would go along with that sort of thing. If someone wants to declare a republic, there must also be some who are receptive to the idea."

"It is necessary," Thomas declared calmly; "we will not hand our Alsace over to French capitalism. What we

Citizens and Soldiers

achieved in Kiel and Wilhelmshaven we'll achieve here for the long term."

Peirotes was amazed: "Think about it, Comrade Thomas! Why? In Kiel and Wilhelmshaven you chased away admirals and naval officers. Here we have no admirals on our little River Ill, we have no ship's captains. There are Prussians. But they're withdrawing all by themselves. On the twenty-first, at noon on the dot, the last of them will march across Kehl Bridge. The French have achieved this. And so we have no need to make revolution."

"So. What will we have then? The French."

Honest Peirotes gazed frankly at the wild Goliath in the sailor's blouse. He thought: what mighty arms and hairy hands you have, you with your thirty-five years clambering like a monkey up masts, my hair's already falling out. But what must first be ascertained is, which of us two can do more here. Peirotes said to Thomas: "Indeed, the French. The people of Alsace have nothing against the French. After all, once upon a time we were French here. As you must know. In 1870 the Prussian boot heel came and stomped on our parents. You are Alsatian, you'll have heard about it at home. We never stopped protesting about it. And then, afterwards – let the townsfolk tell you what they've endured during this war. Yes, frankly and honestly, the whole world here is glad the French are coming."

Thomas thrust his hands into his pockets, straightened himself in his seat, laughed out loud and looked around to his friend Eisenring: "What do you say to that? They want their French. So we can just steam back to where we came from."

Peirotes: "The people want them. And we comrades from Strassburg and all of Alsace, we want them too. Yes, glare at me. We're all of one mind. And if you should perhaps head off to Kleber Place, friend Thomas, and there declare

THE WILHELMSHAVEN SAILORS

the Republic of Alsace-Lorraine, let me make a prediction."

"I'm all ears."

"When you're on the square, there will be not a single socialist, not a single Alsatian! Not one single soul! The only ones there will be ... Old Germans. Old Germans, patriots of the Kaiser. And the Alsatians will say out loud what they're already muttering: you lot are delegates from Germany, you were sent here with German money, from Berlin, to place us once again under the whip."

Thomas crossed his arms. "Listen to this fellow. Just listen to him. To think that of us. To say that to our faces."

Peirotes: "Convince the people, Comrade Thomas. Go there. Have some fun, take the test in Kleber Place."

Thomas, coarse and loud: "I've nothing to do with Wilhelm and the Prussians. I've proved that. I'm just as good an Alsatian as you. I'm a socialist as well. And you're a Frenchy stooge."

Peirotes was unfazed: "I'm a socialist. I've been in the party all my life. You mustn't think that because you come from Wilhelmshaven you know more than I do of socialism. Socialism requires preparation. Here there is nothing to be done. Not now. Socialism comes not from you or from me, but from the masses. Show me the masses."

"Then we must enlighten them, lead them, the situation is not so bad, now the war's over. Everyone knows what capitalism and imperialism are up to."

Peirotes shrugged: "So give it a try. You are new people. You have revolutionary experience. Tell the people what you know. If you wish (it's not us who should have the say) we can call assemblies. Today is Thursday. When will you speak?"

Thomas glanced at his young friend Eisenring, he was a good-humoured fellow but smouldered now with ardent fury: "So that's how it is. You come from a country where the revolution is victorious and knock on your neighbour's door where the same thing's happening, and say to him: open your window, neighbour, take a look, see what's going on in the world. And he babbles: I've got a headache, my back hurts, I can't today, maybe tomorrow. The French are coming! As if the French can be against socialism and revolution. French soldiers, Peirotes, are our comrades, workers, peasants, little people who've had enough. They'll fall into our hands like the 17th German Reserve Division tomorrow, when it marches through here with its officers. What do you say, Eisenring, shall we try it?"

Peirotes, uneasy: "What?"

"What do you say, Eisenring? This lot have bungled it all. As you can see. Here they're all fired up with chauvinism. We came just in time. Fine socialists! A dozy lot, devil take you! We shall assemble revolutionary soldiers, arouse the population."

Peirotes was silent at first, then nodded: "Yes, you do that. You still have a good week, until the twenty-first, at twelve noon."

Thomas leaned back and stared at Peirotes, his face hard: "This is what an Alsatian socialist look like. Take a good look, Eisenring. He's thinking of French generals. He's longing for them, he's waiting for the same generals who suppressed the Commune so brutally. He'll crawl before them, like the social democrats did in Germany. He'll knock us flat. And if it comes to it he'll have us shot, just like Köbis and Reichpietsch last month."

Peirotes, quite calm: "I won't stand in your way. You have the power. I spoke only as a native Alsatian who knows the situation."

Thomas sat glowering, and smoked his pipe. When Peirotes asked what he intended, he roared, banging his fist on the table: "Call themselves socialists! Revolutionaries! If only we could sweep you all away."

Eisenring begged him to calm down. Peirotes stroked his moustache, stood up, knocked back his chair. He is a man too. Off he went.

But only a few paces. He was also the mayor.

OF DEATH AND LOVE

When it was evening once more in the train (Friday evening now) and an orderly came clambering along the corridor and asked those in the compartment if they'd like anything, Maus let down the window and said: "How nice that you've come. If you could rustle up a hot toddy, lots of sugar, a bit of lemon as well, we'd be very happy."

"I don't want to sleep so early tonight," he told Becker, buried in his corner under cushions and blankets. "It's hard to dream in a train. And you have thoughts that never reach the end."

The orderly did indeed manage the perilous trek all the way down the train with a little basket; he handed them arrack, sugar, lemon, glasses and spoons. Glasses and spoons were superfluous, they already had some. And for the first time Maus set on the bench the spirit stove that was part of his field equipment, sent to him by his mother for the winter. He was amazed to find that it worked. They drank the hot brew.

The train trundled, trundled. Darkness laid itself upon the earth. Where was sky, where the ground? The light in their car flickered glumly. Maus said: "Now we're two monks alone in a cell. Tell me about yourself, Becker." Becker from behind, half sitting under his blankets: "What would you like to hear?"

"Up to you."

"I'll tell you about my second birth ... Until the war came, things went pretty well with me. Then I was with the regiment in the east for a few months, and then we sat in the west. I had an easy life, if you must know, Maus, ever since school, ever since I can remember. Whenever I think about it, good memories, friendships that remain with me, loves that ended without pain. I often noticed how young people reacted bitterly to some experience or other. I never had such experiences. I became a teacher, and my boys were fond of me. In my teaching, in the old classics and wherever I could I impressed on them how sublime the human being is. You know the chorus from *Antigone*:

> 'Wonders are many, yet of all things Man is most wonderful, the power that crosses the white sea, driven by the stormy south-wind, making a path under surges that threaten to engulf him;
> – And the light-hearted race of birds, and the tribes of savage beasts and the sea-brood of the deep he snares in the meshes of his woven toils, he leads captive, man excellent in wit.
> – And speech, and wind-swift thought hath he taught himself.'

Of this, Maus, I was assured; happy in my inheritance, a child of good fortune, people said it of me, I was born on a Sunday."

"It's your character. You said as much in the hospital."

"My father was of no great account, a customs inspector. I hardly remember him, he died early, he took my mother from around here, the Rhineland. Then she had me all to herself and let me do what I wanted, Mother is still alive. You'll meet her."

"Is she – like you?"

"Ten times better. Ten times more. But I can't explain to you how. You'll notice when you see her. Then you'll understand how I could be happy and carefree, who I got it from. That's how I know what kind of reception she'll give me when I'm home."

"Did she never visit you?"

"I begged her not to. She didn't write for a long time after that."

"I don't understand."

"Not until Tuesday, last Tuesday, I received a letter from her: 'Now you'll no doubt be glad to return home.' But I was going to tell you about myself."

And then he was silent and gazed at the half-lit bulb.

"Come on, Becker, please."

He had to pause, then gave himself a shake.

"Maus, it really is something remarkable I've often observed, and now confirm. So, you're travelling with me in this carriage, I lie here, lie ... do you really believe I'm thinking about something? I don't think at all. Now and then something might bounce around in my head, but mostly not even that. You know I lay there in the hospital for more than a year, and there they were and people came to me and sometimes I seemed even to myself to be an oracle that people consult. But I hardly ever thought, all I did was speak. You're puzzled. You believe ... when someone says something and it's halfway sensible, then he must have thought about it. That's really what astonishes me, as well. I lie there like a cow, ruminating, chewing the cud, I look around, I can hear, I can feel, I can do all that, but I cannot think. I've experienced the same thing wonderfully again, here now on our travels. Unless I deliberately decide to reflect on something – and that almost never happens – I do not think. But when I open my mouth, I know all sorts of things. And so I conclude:

thinking and knowing are like eating and drinking. You stuff something into yourself, and that's it. But it nourishes you, no need to worry about it. And so I lay there like a log of wood for months, and now I'm lying here, my head's empty or confused, and only when I open my mouth do I occasionally make sense. You have to speak to know what you are."

"I really can't follow much of what you're saying. I'm sorry, Becker."

"Including my medical condition. I'm lying with my company in a trench. When it's time and we leap up and start running, after just ten meters I hear a shell burst nearby, then it's all over. That too is a remarkable leap from Being into Nothingness, or into something else. I have no memory of a transition. Suddenly and simply I was not there. Maybe I've forgotten the impact that sent me across that boundary. Anyway, all of a sudden I'm in a ghastly room, old, low, dirty windows, lying on a bed. At that moment, Maus, I was a totally unconscious lump of meat, my name wasn't Becker, I wasn't in a war, all I was was pain. Was it pain? I don't even know if it was pain, whether I took it for pain. A horrible sinister presence. I imagine myself a jellyfish, the kind that little boys spear on a stick at the seaside. It still has its tentacles, its feelers, mouth and guts, but its entire presence is pain. Where my ego had gone I have no idea. I couldn't even tell what was arms, head, legs. All sorts of things moved about around me, I never asked questions, I had nothing to ask, there was nothing to ask about, for everything simply was, it was, and I myself was a nagging pain. This, as I later heard, was the third day after I was wounded.

"Then I became aware of other transitions, shadings, cross-hatchings, until I came to a different region. I saw apparitions approach my bed, some dark, some light. They moved lips, I heard something, but didn't understand. My face must have looked stupid. They said: not himself yet. Then one evening a great big world jolted over me. If I have to describe it: all at once I flowed together and congealed. I understood what the nurse was saying to the patient in the next bed, and his reply. I saw the blanket, the room, and knew I was lying in a bed like his, and I'm ill, I wondered what sort of illness it might be. Measles, but where's Mother, or have I had an accident, which hospital did they bring me to, then I see the bread tin and the name board hanging at the end of my neighbour's bed, and now an orderly comes along with a basin. The next thing is: war, attack, First Lieutenant Becker, and a villainous pain in my back. All this while the nurse at the next bed kept looking across at me, she saw my face, and there she is, she takes my hand and starts talking, I can understand her, I am again First Lieutenant Becker. Reporting back from a trip. Next day they all smiled at me as if I was a little child just woken up. But then, Maus," he raised his left index finger, "only at that point was I dead. Only then did it descend into death."

Maus poured another glass of toddy, and shook himself: "You're horrible today. You shouldn't talk about that old stuff."

"Better stuff to come, Maus. Pour one for me, one gulp before the descent into the underworld. Do you know Wagner's *Tristan and Isolde*? A wonderful opera, it's been my delight for years."

They listened to the squeaking shuddering train, rail joints announced themselves with little jolts, the glass in the window frames chinked, a long long steady roar set in, deafening, it enveloped them completely, they were going through a tunnel.

When it grew quieter and the wheels resumed their

old song, Becker's voice could again be heard: "In Wagner's *Tristan* there's lots of talk of a magic potion. Angry that Tristan has demeaned her by taking her to old King Mark as a prisoner of war, Isolde wants to die together with him. He accepts the goblet as a propitiatory drink. But it's a love potion. Isolde's mother had given her a little apothecary's kit for her journey to foreign parts. It had balms for woe and wounds, antidotes to poisons; for deepest grief and highest joy it had the death-potion. Isolde's maid mixed the propitiatory drink using the love-potion. It took Tristan and Isolde from their normal waking state into a strangely altered one, between being and not-being, in which they always desire total not-being. For normal days keep them constantly apart. And so they come to yearn for a love-death. Love-death, it sounds so crazy. When you hear the music you believe it. It has that sound."

And Becker sang the love-death motif:

> "'Thus might we die, that together, ever one, without end, never waking, never fearing, namelessly enveloped in love, given up to each other, to live only for love!

And such a love-death really does occur in this magical opera, the ending's famous, Isolde sings over Tristan's corpse the same love-death motif, but now it rises to a tempestuous volume, yearning, desire, craving, love itself." From his corner Becker now partly spoke, partly hummed Isolde's concluding aria, suggesting the melody:

> "How softly and gently he smiles, how sweetly his eyes open – can you see, my friends, do you not see it? How he glows ever brighter, raising himself high amidst the stars? Do you not see it? How his heart swells with courage, gushing full and majestic in his

breast? How in tender bliss sweet breath wafts gently from his lips – Friends! Look! Do you not feel and see it? Do I alone hear this melody so wondrously and gently sounding from within him, in bliss lamenting, all-expressing, gently reconciling, piercing me, soaring aloft, its sweet echoes resounding about me? Are they gentle aerial waves ringing out clearly, surging around me? Are they billows of blissful fragrance? As they seethe and roar about me, shall I breathe, shall I give ear? Shall I drink of them, plunge beneath them? Breathe my life away in sweet scents? In the heaving swell, in the resounding echoes, in the universal stream of the world-breath – to drown, to founder – unconscious – utmost rapture!"

Maus had slid up very close on the opposite bench, after gently placing the spirit stove on the floor beside the bottle and his glass. He listened attentive as a schoolboy. By the end he had closed his eyes, and he nodded to Becker: "Marvellous!"

Becker ended with a brisk hand gesture: "Lovely. Unforgettable. You should get to know it, not in the theatre, I'll show you on the piano. – It's different in real life. Nobody in our world switches a death-potion. And so life is not yet as elevated as a dream. For example, I wasn't quite dead as I lay in the hospital. But lying there for three, four months, actually I was. I won't tell you, Maus, how it progressed, how I gradually gave up wanting to live, and actually was no longer alive. They could sedate me, leave me unsedated, take me on a stretcher cart to the X-ray room, to the operating theatre for an exploration, or to a spinal tap, clear up cutaneous gangrene. I was tainted by the cold hunk attached to me, my legs, my body, and no longer had any part in it. It was all too much for me, too much! But enough of that ... So in the end it was a matter of staying alive. And then ... I could no longer do so. You never realised, Maus, you were ill too, but you recovered quickly, I remember it well. In my case it was as if Fate meant to wreak vengeance on me for all the good times I'd had before. It did a thorough job. When my legs regained feeling, something I'd awaited eagerly in the first months, it failed to reach all the way to me. I'd forgotten everything, laughing, crying, joy, anger. Can you imagine? It's not the same as Isolde's love-death. *In the heaving swell, in the resounding echoes, in the universal stream of the world-breath - to drown, to founder - unconscious - utmost rapture!* No highest rapture, no heaving swell, a monotonous grey flat plain without end, an inert moon crater now sunlit, now in shadow. In those days they used to stand around my bed and make me wiggle my toes. And when I could, they erupted in delight, the nurses' faces glowed, everyone around me was delighted. And to be polite I said yes, so as not to upset them, and understood none of it. What was it to me if my toes wiggled. Doctors came by in the mornings and were already girded up to relish me; they had pins tucked into the flap of their white gown that they stuck in my skin, and if I said Ow, they beamed. 'It's coming on,' they said. That was the slogan: 'It's coming on.' And now they set to work on me, and I can't tell you, Maus, what it was they did. But if I'm alive in the future, and now, they are to blame. My mother's been replaced. The part for which I have to thank my parents has died away. They brought me to my second birth. That's the man you see and hear. They lifted me and gave me electric shocks, they massaged and stretched my limbs. They wouldn't give up. Now and then you read about a mining disaster, a calamitous storm, and so and so many are trapped, buried alive, and must be rescued, and people toil day after day to uncover what they can, until they reach the shaft. Sometimes they down tools, time has gone by, they can calculate, every effort's hopeless now. The team that rescued me, their names be praised, didn't give up. It was one great imploring chorus that gathered about my bed and forced me up out of my grave. I couldn't tell you which of them did more to summon me, cajole me, I sing the song of praises to all those who helped. That's why I did not leave them to go to another hospital – and that's why I didn't want my mother to intervene. It would have been a shock to me, in the weeks when these others brought me into the world."

Becker paused. Maus cautiously lit the stove on the floor. When they had warm glasses in their hands, Maus asked: "Will you tell the ending today?"

Becker: "The ending, Maus, you'll see and hear for yourself every day that we're together: peace, sweet peace! I'm waiting. I want to be in Berlin ... How did I come back up, how did I find the world again? I haven't the foggiest memory. A work of discovery awaits, very slow, bit by bit. You begin to see light, recognise objects, people, trees. You think I should have seen and noticed everything already, since I wasn't unconscious. Correct: seen and not seen. For a long time something was missing – myself. One day my self suddenly popped up, when it noticed sunlight streaming into the room. I saw: it's light. I knew light. I comprehended light. Because I had become blind and deaf. Without feeling, like my legs. For me there was no light or sound. That day I lay troubled until evening. They noticed something was up. There was to be a change of dressings, they thought I was scared, pushing them away. But it wasn't that. I was bewildered. I had no idea what might come next. I sensed something.

"And yes, now there came blow after blow. The biggest was ... our trumpeter in the garden. I'll have fond memories of him as long as I live. When I heard a sound again for the first time, understood a tone, tumbled into a tone ... you'll be amazed: I was so bewildered I slept exhausted for hours after. The nurses all looked serious, the doctor sat at my bedside and tapped my neck and head; he had some particular concern. For the whole of the next week I had to pull myself dreadfully together in order to bear it. You know, Maus, I still didn't want to. I felt a distinct repugnance when a whole song, some gramophone music, came to me. A bitter feeling: there are still such things, and I must go to them again. Dreadfully hard to overcome the repugnance. Anyway, it happened. After a week or two there was still a bit of fear ... and fearful shocks later on, when the old grey feeling returned. Birth pangs. And now ... we're heading home, Maus.

"And now I'm back again. And I want to be back, ten times more than before, when I went to war and leapt up from the trench and the shrapnel hit me. Now, I demand something. Peace. Sweet heavenly peace. We are here. It has our face. I cling to it with claws of iron, Maus, I shan't let it take me, not take me once again, this thing that has my face. See the moon above the clouds, see the white drifting clouds, hear the rattle of the wheels, look at us here, Maus, you and me! Escaped from death. It's life, peace. We'll never let it be stolen away, by anyone."

"I'm a reluctant passenger, Becker," Maus said, elbows on knees, head in his hands.

Becker: "I'd noticed."

*

"No news of you. They are all gone now, those who reminded me of you. I'm worried about you. I write every day to the address in Switzerland that you gave me. You don't reply. People say the postal service isn't working, the retreat has jammed everything up. I wonder if I should come looking for you, the trains are all packed. But surely I will, one day. I should feel ashamed to write to you like this."

★

Officers came together in droves at the Officers' Casino in Strassburg. One left another his address, the war had brought them together, it was a slice of life; everyone wanted to know from someone else what was going to happen. The staircases in the Casino building on Theatre Place were covered in notices, final War Loan, appeal by the Army High Command to adapt with dignity to the inevitable, advice about bread rations for the journey. Someone had amused himself by stapling to the door of a big busy dining hall a long thin strip of paper. Visitors crowded around and read in wonderment a typewritten text:

Horoscope for the Astronomical Year 1914 by Madame Thèbes

The world remains in the ambit of Mars, but in a constellation with Saturn and not with the Moon, so that difficult bloody times are coming which will heap fame and victories on France despite all the blood and all the tears. 1914 will be famous among all famous years, it will be a year of unrest, and then of peace, a year of hatred and then a year of those who love, a year of unrest among the peoples of Europe that ends as a year of rapprochement, which signifies the collapse of Germany. Even Italy, which has made itself unloved, will be chastened; for Austria-Hungary it will go even worse. – In Germany there are upheavals and sensational abscondings, just as in

> Austria-Hungary. – Belgium has already survived
> longer than it will yet survive. Only Spain and King
> Alfonso have nothing to fear. – The Balkan wars
> continue. – The spring in 1914 is lovely.

The sheet was ripped down; within half an hour another copy was pinned in the same spot.

The daily newspapers that lay about by the dozen were excitable: "What does the red flag on the cathedral signify? (They read with furrowed brows, had to read, these are the new overlords.) It is the external sign of international Socialism ... reconciliation of peoples ... The red flag on the cathedral is proof that this theory has won. Reaction and capitalism are defeated. Who would not rejoice?" (They read without comprehending a word, angry that it had to be read.)

"Profiteering has not yet lost all its adherents. There are still those who try to build their fortune on the poverty of others. But their power is broken. May it remain broken, to the benefit of mankind. In the red flag, after long and brutish travails (These fellows are stark staring mad) a solution on the side of humanity has made its reappearance. Why should it not find resonance in the soldiers of France? Prussian militarism has been buried! The German nation has emerged from its chrysalis, it is the same fully-fledged Butterfly of Freedom as the French nation. In Socialism there lies the spring of eternal youth. A new age has dawned."

This was attributed to Gaffer Tailor and Glovemaker. But anyone who picked up the paper could not put it down without a sense of shock.

It was Friday morning, 15th November. The Pastor paced up and down the corridors with the Major, both in civvies. Once they'd ingested enough poison from the day's news, they kept an eye out for acquaintances. The Pastor kept up a repetitive tedious wailing about the general collapse, lack of discipline in the army out there, it went in one of the Major's ears and out the other. He drew the Pastor's attention to the item about the red flag on the cathedral and said acidly: "Prussian militarism is buried, the German nation has emerged from its chrysalis. What d'you say to that? In Socialism lies the spring of eternal youth. That's their trade now. What d'you say to that?"

The Pastor wrung his hands: "Slogans."

"Effective."

"Who can say."

"There's the rub. You church fellows should have thrown the people a few crumbs. Maybe it'll happen yet. What? Always look for connections. Don't let the reins slip from your hands."

The Pastor looked doubtful: "You think, Major, that we've somehow been remiss?"

"It all became too much for us. Seems to me you'll have to buck your ideas up soon enough with these slogans. Spring of eternal youth. Isn't that something. Don't you think?"

"Of course."

"Soup, cooking, loyalty to the Fatherland are well enough. But they won't do on their own."

At this point other transients drifting like them through the corridors greeted each other and exchanged views. There was no sloganising, each eyed the others with mistrust. When the Major bumped into the Pastor again he cursed: "It's disgusting. Surrounded by lily-livered cowards. Can't believe they were comrades once, daren't open their mouths in front of anyone. If they're that cowardly they deserve their fate."

Citizens and Soldiers

He fumed, strode along, the Pastor had to hurry to keep up.

The Major came to a stop in a corner by a coatstand: "How long will you stay in Strassburg? I've had enough. The French won't be here before the twentieth. The staff are useless, they had it too easy. I'll wait back inside, I'm thinking Berlin, wait for comrades from the front." He laid a hand on the Pastor's shoulder, whispered in his ear: "Yorck! Convention of Tauroggen!"

The Pastor stared at him, he understood at once: "You don't mean another revolt?"

"I didn't say that. That's a long way off. No idea if you or I will ever see it. The enemy ... is inside the country! Red flag on the cathedral. If I had my hands on some artillery, I'd fetch it down today with cannon. I'm thinking of armed civilians, a kind of reserve militia, setting up a new kind of Landsturm."

"Homeland protection."

"You have to join in, Pastor. It's all about slogans. We'll do it differently than under Napoleon. But we must make a start before the army disbands. The Reds will do their utmost to disband the army as quickly as possible. It must stay together as long as possible." The Pastor squeezed his hand. The Major: "I'm glad. I'll head to Berlin, to my detachment. I have your address, and you have mine."

"I'll have a lot of spare time in the next few months, Major. I shall look you up."

"Bravo. Can you stay here a few more days, to spread the word here and there? You know lots of people, Westphalian detachments, in an emergency you could be across the Rhine in half an hour, in Kehl."

"Many heartfelt thanks, Major. Already my heart beats more calmly."

"Forget about your heart, Pastor. Take care that no

one does the dirty on you. The Reds have some sharp fellows among them, who'll give you short shrift. You saw how they grabbed hold of us for the funeral of those two mutineers."

Now the Major very hastily took his leave, as the distraught Forester, the General's relative, hove into view. Let the Pastor deal with him. So the pair slouched for hours through the streets, along the quays, over bridges. Neither Pastor nor Forester could bear to part from this land. They carried their woes through the dear old city of Strassburg, and the city relished their ever-recycled maudlin blather.

★

The lovely old city had to put up with much else besides. A young woman, a servant girl, grumbled away her sentence quietly in the women's prison, the revolution hadn't lifted it from her. She'd been employed in a munitions plant and had come to know an engineer; she'd do anything not to lose him. First she lied that she was expecting his child – he remained cool; then she cut the skin over the pulse in her wrists, which made him no more tender; finally she borrowed an infant and showed it him as his. Now his patience was at an end. The public prosecutor stuck her in jail for a year, for this was worse than love, it was false testimony.

And for a young married couple named Hass, who worked in the suburb of Schiltigheim, the good old city prepared a particularly mischievous surprise. In the morning before setting off they carefully closed the shutters of their ground floor apartment. In the evening when they came back from Schiltigheim, the shutters were open, the living room was a complete mess, and they

Citizens and Soldiers

were missing a bunch of money, a new cap, a new pair of men's shoes, as well as a number of valuable leather belts and boots that just last Tuesday they'd hauled with a great deal of trouble from a clothing depot, and regarded as a stable asset for the impending change of currency.

That the city showed no harshness towards individual women goes without saying. On this Friday afternoon the chubby Widow, the Pastor's companion, found what she'd been looking for. Everything's slipping the reins, why shouldn't she? Afternoon with the elegant man from the dance floor stretched into evening. And early on Saturday in her hotel room she wondered if the new day shouldn't lead her back to where she'd left him yesterday, and after a lengthy internal struggle she paid the cavalier one more farewell visit, and her morning stretched out ... She thought: it's war, it's revolution, when shall we have war and revolution again.

But in the afternoon she was seized with fear that the French might be coming. And so she planted herself in a train, after a passionate parting from her now-sworn friend (so she had after all found at least one friend in her life), and blissful and satisfied, black widow's veil over her face again so as not to betray too much of her joy, armed with high spirits and gratitude, she headed across the Rhine.

★

To the north, the hospital train trundled slowly through the countryside.

At every station the locomotive found herself the butt of ridicule. She wasn't bothered, the whole country was in the grip of an emergency. When they reached the Ludwigshafen area they managed to cross the venerable stately waters of the Rhine, and then, fulfilled and calmed by the sight, chugged peacefully on through a landscape wonderfully reminiscent of Alsace, every village a "heim", and in one of these "homesteads" where they had to spend the night, partly to let the locomotive recuperate and partly because the route ahead was congested, the pig they'd brought along was slaughtered with the help of the local butcher. Then the train set itself again in motion, and a blessed feast spread joy over all the travellers.

As they slurped their soup, smacked their lips and chewed, they looked out of the windows, admired the pretty region, and were glad that dear piggy would be with them for one more evening and tomorrow's lunch. Beer had been donated at the last stop.

At that last "heim", while the slaughter was in progress, Becker set off down the train on his two canes. He, a tall man, went bent and very slow. Like a blind man he placed each foot very carefully on the floor in front of him, and when the leg stood on it he swung himself forward as if on a bar and pressed down on the other foot. Every muscle and muscle group had to be summoned up separately, he couldn't be distracted while this was going on, the work required close concentration. Afterwards he sat back exhausted and silent in the compartment, and chain-smoked cigarettes.

Before coffee, Maus, who still couldn't give up his newspaper habit, threw the sheets out of the window in accord with their silent agreement. After coffee (the crockery remained on the floor, not cleared away until evening) Maus studied Becker's face, it seemed benign. He gathered his courage: "Did it take a lot out of you?"

Becker nodded: "Deciphering a corrupt text would be easier. Did you want something?" They sat facing one another in the window corner. Maus couldn't find the right words to begin. He smiled tentatively: "A small question. But I haven't the faintest idea if you'll engage with it."

"Courage, Maus. Is it about women?"

Maus, relieved: "Yes." But said nothing more. Becker chuckled, took a deep breath, waited.

Maus: "I'm embarrassed to ask. It's ... no fun for me. The whole thing's a torment."

"And that's why you haven't been able to sleep since we set off. Yearning for Hilde, or someone else?"

"Yearning of course, naturally. But the lack of clarity, the anguish."

"Now now, Maus."

"I'm embarrassed."

"In front of me, Maus?"

"No, no. Or rather, that too. But with myself. It torments me so. There seems to be something ... not quite right with me."

"Now you really pique my curiosity, lad. Fire away. You're an awful sight, moping like this. You're really not the poor sinner, and me the beadle with the whip."

"I've been doing my own whipping, Becker, ever since we set off. Oh, if only you could provide me with a good solution. You know, about Hilde."

"Yes."

"She said goodbye to us two days ago, on Wednesday. You remember. I ... wasn't satisfied just with a goodbye, it was too formal. I saw her again."

"When?"

"That afternoon, on Wednesday, Becker. She was hanging around in the main ward and with the patients, I kept an eye out for her, I had to see her just one last time and speak to her. There was a lot at stake for me."

Becker: "So it's that serious! I had no idea."

Maus sat up straight: "You had no idea? You thought it

was just flirting, a passing hospital romance?"

"Of course. If it was anything more than that you kept it well hidden. So ... it was more than that."

Maus considered: "You're right, during those last days."

Becker as always was propped up on many cushions, because of his wounds. He adjusted them under him, then crossed his arms over his chest, and sat there.

Maus was at last in full flow: "What you should say to me now, what you need to clarify for me, is a very delicate matter. I submit it to you in deepest confidence. I trust you, Becker. I won't demand, on your word of honour, that you keep it to yourself ... If a woman gives herself to a man, is she then really his? Is that what she has in mind?"

Becker turned his face to the wall. After a while he said: "Wait a minute. I have to consider." He fussed with his pillows. Maus helped, he lay flat. "That's better." He said in his calm voice, his gaze directed at Maus: "In principle, I think – sure. She considers him hers. Why do you doubt it?"

"Because of the circumstances."

Maus groaned and raked his hair, and in misery implored Becker: "Help me, Becker, please. I've been wrestling and wrestling with it. I've been accusing myself of all sorts of things. Maybe I insulted her, abused her, worse than that. Maybe it's all over now between her and me. She didn't want to. It was that evening with all the uproar, everyone stealing. At last I tracked her down in our corridor. And I wanted to – had to – talk with her. I was so agitated, so inexpressibly agitated, it was the last time I'd see her, when would I ever see her again, like this, and so close and all alone. And she wanted to leave. And there we were outside Richard's room, you know, the one where he used to lie, and we went in, I closed the door."

"And?" Becker asked.

Citizens and Soldiers

"I was jealous of Richard, even though he's dead. Oh god, I don't know what I'm telling you. She resisted, I was so agitated, I could feel her against me, I wanted to have her, I had to have her, I believe, Becker, I was prepared at that moment to murder anyone who tried to take her from me. She didn't want to. I asked her: Is it because of Richard? Did you love Richard? And she said yes, but she only did it to vex me, I know that, and it made me even more agitated. I could not, could not bear rejection."

Becker stared at the ceiling: "So in fact, you raped her."

"That's what I accuse myself of, Becker, and that's why I'm suffering so horribly. Because I love her! I've loved her since the first time I saw her. And I'd like to wash it all away. But Becker, I've heard so often, and I believe: it's impossible to rape a woman if she really doesn't want it. In the end she has to want it. Unless she's actually unconscious. And she wasn't."

"How do you know?"

"She could talk. She had her arms around me."

"Around you?"

"At the end, anyway. What she said I have no idea. And that's my hope: at the end, at least, she wasn't angry. I couldn't make out her face in the corridor. – Oh Becker, how ashamed I was afterwards. And still am. I could tear myself to pieces."

"It seems that in the end she forgave you."

Maus, relieved, grabbed Becker's left hand that was dangling slack: "Yes, tell me that. She's forgiven me, she doesn't despise me. I didn't violate her, I would never have forgiven myself."

"You regret it so much, Maus?"

"Dreadfully, terribly. When I recall it I suffer the torments of hell. I beg you, Becker, help me. Ever since it happened I'm no longer a human being."

Becker slowly turned his head towards Maus, and observed him as he sat collapsed, face buried in his hands. Now Maus lifted his face: "So what do you say, Becker?"

"That you've been severely punished. That you punish yourself too much. – Tell me again: she had her arms around you? And how did you part afterwards, the final, final goodbye?"

"She was silent, embarrassed. Just stood there."

Becker looked again at the ceiling. "I don't think there's any grievance, Maus. Women ... like to be taken by surprise. She has fond thoughts of you now."

Maud flung himself on his knees and pressed Becker's arm to his breast: "Becker, is it true? Tell me, is it true?" Suddenly Maus was sobbing into Becker's arm. Becker spoke down to him from the bench: "My young friend, you're ill."

Maus, stammering: "It's so despicable what I got myself into there, and really I didn't want to. What sort of caddish behaviour, to have to do what I really don't want to do. I hate myself. I spit on myself. I don't understand."

"One doesn't have to understand everything, my young friend. Don't make yourself mad. What a tender conscience you do have."

"I never did before, Becker. Only in this instance. I love her so very much and would so like to hold on to her."

"You will."

Maus rose to his feet and settled back onto the bench. "Oh I'm so happy. I've been freed. Now she's there again. Now I'm back to myself. Thanks be to God."

★

That night it seemed to Becker in his dreams that a voice sounded within him, a deep male voice, and a pale fatherly figure stood in the corridor of the train and bent down to him.

In joy and sweetness his insides melted.

"You poor abandoned soul, lost in such distress. You cannot even sigh or moan."

"Don't leave so soon, today."

"A long story you told, as you lay dead in your body and returned to life. And did you return to life?"

"Don't leave so soon."

"The abominable foe is always on the lookout. Wherever a breach opens, there he is. Do not permit it. Any plant not planted by the Heavenly Father shall be uprooted."

"Help me."

"Forget me not, poor abandoned soul. Think on the words of the two people who entered the temple to pray, one a Pharisee, the other a tax collector. The Pharisee stood and thanked God that he was not like other people, like robbers, adulterers, or this tax collector. The tax collector dared not raise his eyes to God, beat his breast and said: God have mercy on my soul. He returned home vindicated. For sinners, the suffering, the poor shall have their share of mercy, and be blessed."

"And ..." Becker wanted to say something. Then his own groans awoke him. The car was dark, Maus fast asleep. Becker tidied his bedding. Sleepy and without thoughts he laid his head back down.

The train trundled on.

THE CHIEF MEDICAL OFFICER

The Chief Medical Officer's condition pursued its course. The red flush in the left leg had spread above the knee, poultices were applied every day, salves were tried one day but they couldn't identify the right one. They painted iodine along the edges and placed a thin adhesive bandage over it, this was meant to hold back the redness, it seemed to work, but suddenly it sent feelers out under the dressing, and advanced. "We'll soon be on top of it," the doctor in charge said soothingly, "we'll isolate the breakaways," and again he set to with his magical iodine painting and with the help of the Chief's wife wound a pink adhesive bandage around the whole thing. His temperature went up and down. When it went up they said scientifically: "Just as we expected;" when it went down they were pleased: "You see?" And the good Chief, whose body was now so much under their administration, beamed contentedly from on high at both the ups and the downs.

He was always in good spirits. He said that his heart had never at any time been so robust. He enjoyed lying down, having a thorough rest, you can only do that when you're ill. In the afternoons (but he never mentioned this) the dreams were wonderful; he soon realised they were linked to the fever. He strongly resisted attempts by the doctor in charge to give him an antipyretic: "It weakens the body, it weakens one's resistance," he declared; "I want to know my body. You surgeons don't pay attention to that. Keep your poisons away from me." They were able to reach agreement on one point raised by the patient: "The antipyretic messes up the chart." That made sense to the doctor, and the Chief was able to resume his rest and his extraordinary dreams.

On Sunday a wonderful blood sausage made an appearance in the train, the kitchen delivered its best efforts, and the firkin of wine that had been donated to them back in the little town was also opened on this Sunday. It was 17th November.

Citizens and Soldiers

And already more than eight days had passed since the revolution broke out. On the very same day something disquieting happened in the Chief's compartment. As lunch things were being collected at a little station where once again they had come to a stop, and everything that could walk was promenading alongside the train, asking for news, besieging the station master to know how they would be proceeding, how long it would still last. At this stop even the Chief's wife had left the compartment and was chatting farther back with Lieutenant Maus, who had stuck his head out of the window. As she stood there several people came running, calling for her. She ran back in shock, Maus too climbed down. Up ahead a little disturbance had developed. The sick Chief was trying to descend the steps from his compartment in his nightshirt, people had noticed him at once, he chatted with the soldiers amiably but incoherently, they took hold of him and manoeuvred him back with little difficulty. He was already smiling again at his wife from his bed; his bandages lay on the floor. The doctor in charge soon came along. The patient was cold, shivering. Towards evening his face was grey-white, there was an obvious change, the eyes looked out as calm as ever, but they were sunken, the skin around them yellow.

The Chief lay now in the corridor car, where special cases were being looked after. The doctor in charge drew the Chief's wife into the corridor.

They looked at one another under the light bulb, the doctor rubbed the leather lining of his cap: "We shall be in Würzburg in an hour. I can no longer take responsibility. There must be blood tests, doses of serum, we have nothing here."

"You want to unload him in Würzburg," she said, her eyes indignant. "I don't know a single soul there."

THE CHIEF MEDICAL OFFICER

"It's Germany, dear lady. The doctors are the same, Würzburg is a big city."

She was almost in a rage. "Why didn't you bring any serum along. You told us you had everything you needed."

He calmly placed the cap back on his head, his hand on the door handle. "I don't know what kind of serum, it can only be ascertained after a blood test."

She at his side, anxious, imploring: "So ... it's blood poisoning?"

He, shrugging: "That cannot be excluded."

"From corns, from a corn?" She pouted, wept bitterly protesting like a child, both hands clung to the window frame; the train was travelling unusually fast, and swaying.

In Würzburg at the goods yard there was enormous activity. Already on the way in they could see red flags in the city. All the doors of the train opened, it was late afternoon, the conductor announced that they would be here for the night and maybe tomorrow morning too; in fifteen minutes they'd be shunted to another track, so no one should leave the train. They peered out of the windows. Ambulance men with a stretcher went along the train, looking for something. Jeers from some windows: "Not us, we're off to see mummy!" But towards the rear they saw the men stop, another one's croaked, they jumped down to see who it was. A lady alighted, it was the Chief Medical Officer's wife, yes, the old man, he must live in the area, then the ambulance men carefully lifted the stretcher off the train, they've covered his face, he's dead already, the doctor in charge followed slowly behind the stretcher as it was carried all the way down the platform and across the tracks. The old Chief! He lives here, no, they say he was poorly, his heart. They all felt sorry for him, then the shunting took all their attention, and they made ready as far as they could to march into town, and adorned themselves with red armbands.

At the hospital they kept the wife waiting outside for two hours. When she went in – he had a bare private room, a single electric bulb glowing – he at once stretched out his hand towards her in his old loving way, he rubbed her cold hands between his and thanked her for overcoming her objections and bringing him off the train to lie here. "I sometimes thought of it, Antonia, the train rattled so, but I didn't want to suggest it." He was visibly improved, but he soon grew quieter, graver and curiously mysterious in his tall nest of cushions.

"Do you want anything, Otto?"

"No."

"Did you nod off?"

"What? I … was just thinking about the eastern front. Their journey is much longer than ours. Hm." He'd had a blood sample and a serum injection, he said.

"Thank God, that's why I had to take you off, the doctor couldn't do it on the train."

"No, we had no supplies of serum."

Strange, he never asked why he needed serum, was just glad to have it. "Tomorrow you can bring me the plant catalogue from my briefcase," he said, half asleep.

Early next morning around six o'clock, when she turned up at the hospital all smiles – she was happy, for the first time in days she'd had a good night's sleep in a hotel – the night nurse was just coming out of his room holding a bottle of champagne and a bottle of cognac.

"How is he, nurse?"

The nurse didn't immediately recognise her. "The night was all right at first. Then the fever rose, I gave him champagne, the pulse was irregular."

The wife wanted to go in. The nurse blocked the doorway. "We must wait for the doctor, I've sent to wake him up." They stood mutely outside the door, the nurse with her hands full. The wife begged: "But let me see him, won't you." She could hear a curious sound from the room, regular, and became agitated. "He's asleep. I suppose? But I can just sit with him."

Now along came the doctor, unkempt, collarless, in a white medical gown, a pale long-legged fellow with a cold face, without greeting her he opened the door, the nurse followed. They closed the door behind them. After several long minutes they came out, the doctor peered down at her, tugged at the narrow collar of his gown, and cleared his throat: "You wish to visit the Chief Medical Officer?"

At her frightened stare he asked hesitantly: "Did the nurse not put you in the picture? So. Yes. It's not going well. We gave him another injection. How did it all begin? How many days now?"

"Since Tuesday, doctor."

"Not so long then. Yes. So. The heart." He gazed at her a while, clearly without seeing her, seemed very sleepy, gave a nod, went off.

In the room she at once took everything in. It stank of alcohol and camphor. The sister was cleaning needles in bowls at the little white table. He lay with his upper body raised, arms on top of the blankets. He was snoring noisily. His eyes were closed. His red sunken face twitched and flamed without pause. Chills ran down her spine as she cautiously touched his hand. He didn't react.

He was enormously hard at work, clearly. He snored lustily, like a saw, dreadfully deep and loud, regular, as if at an important task. Often he puffed out his cheeks, and the breath escaped through his mouth, pushing the lips out and forming bubbles of spittle that dribbled down the white stubble on his chin.

She saw this, observed with emotions she did not

trust herself to acknowledge in front of the nurse: anguish, fear, embarrassment. This regular snoring and sawing and inflated cheeks. She turned to the nurse, who was wiping a long syringe with her back turned, asked: "Has he ... been like this for long?"

"Oh. He grew restless after four. Then it all kicked off. I've just given him caffeine."

The wife stood there uncertain, look back and forth between the nurse and the bed: "Why ... is he doing this? Is it the lungs? Can't he get enough air?"

The nurse looked at her in surprise: "Aren't you a doctor's wife? Haven't you seen sick people?"

"My husband's a medical officer in the service."

"Ah. The snoring always happens. They do it when ... well, you can see."

The wife took a chair and sat for an hour, two hours at the bedside. The sick man continued to labour. "You can see": clearly she meant when someone's dying. She wiped his sweat with a handkerchief, then a face cloth. As she wiped, the expression death-sweat came to her, and she paused paralysed with horror and dropped the cloth. It was terrifying. She opened the door, and was glad when the day nurse came in; she'd been in discussion with the staff nurse just outside, which ended with the day nurse praising the staff nurse's acumen, for if the Chief Medical Officer had been transferred to the two-bed ward with the cardiac colonel there'd have been trouble, and they'd have had to bring the new patient back to the private room now anyway. The day nurse, a strapping elderly person with metal-rimmed glasses, studied the patient carefully. The wife held her hands to her eyes: "How long will it last, nurse?"

"A few hours, maybe the whole day, we've had some who lasted two days like this."

THE CHIEF MEDICAL OFFICER

"Is he in much pain?"

"He? He's not aware of anything."

She bent over him, touched his shoulder, spoke to him: "Chief Medical Officer! Sir! See, he hears nothing." She gave his face a quick wipe, straightened the pillows and his head which had drooped sideways, and said: "So, you just sit there quietly. If anything happens, come out into the corridor."

Frau Antonia obediently sat down, her face to the window. Today's Monday. We set off on Thursday, this is Würzburg, I never imagined I'd come to Würzburg with him. The snoring's horrible, horrible, if only I could block up my ears. Why am I sitting here, actually? The nurse has gone, I have to sit here. That's how they are in a hospital. He would have known that. She watched his face, it was pale with a bluish tinge, little beads of sweat were forming again on his forehead. He's not aware of anything. This is death. Really, he's already gone. I'm a widow. I don't know when the transport train will leave, maybe they'll be at the station till evening, and if it's all over in time I'll be able to go with it, our things will be going straight on to Naumburg. Otherwise I'll have to unload it all, maybe they've already unloaded it without asking me. She gave no thought to the funeral. A restlessness overcame her. They might have simply dumped our things on the platform, no one knows who they belong to, they'll be carried off, stolen, with this revolution. I can't just sit here. She checked her wristwatch. Another half hour, then.

She spent that half hour as if on hot coals, more and more tormented by the snoring, fear too crept in, impatience. There's nothing I can do here. It's up to the nurse. She simply left me here, it's outrageous.

At eight o'clock she shook herself and said softly as she stroked his hand: "Otto, I must see about our things."

(Tears welled in her eyes) "Your crates are there, all your books. If you recover, what will you do without your things, they just left me here."

Outside she wiped her eyes, stood at the door until the nurse appeared, now sobbed out loud: "Nurse, I need air. You have to let me go."

"Yes, off you go, child, off you go. Come back at noon. We're always here. Yes, these are bad times."

As soon as the wife was out of the building she began to run. She ran as if pursued by a nightmare, fearful, distraught, through the horribly complicated hospital gardens. At last she came to the main entrance. At last she was outside and could calm down. And now a cab. I'm going to the station. It was as if she were going to meet her husband. The one back there was not him. And look, there's the train, her train. She walked along it, these are her people, they nod to her, these are the ambulance men, their gurney behind them. No one had yet touched the baggage. Officers stood chatting outside their compartments, smoking. The cook came chasing after her to ask about the Chief, and can he keep something back for them. She climbed into the old untidy compartment, the cook at once brought her coffee and bread, she ate and drank, wiped tears away and then burst into a loud wailing because she was sitting here all alone and Otto was back there and what he was doing didn't bear thinking about. She curled up in fear when she recalled the snores. She'd had him taken to the hospital, and only yesterday, the day before, he'd drunk coffee with her, and his catalogues were scattered around. She couldn't think beyond this. What's to happen if he really does die. It's not a done deal yet, maybe they're wrong, and after all we have our little house, and he has his gardening.

She wept quietly. And when she'd finished the coffee and the bread she hunted around the compartment for his

THE CHIEF MEDICAL OFFICER

briefcase and started to write a letter to her brother, she was now in Würzburg, he's ill, in hospital. And then she felt again so all alone and found it all so incomprehensible that Otto was over there in the hospital, and was said to be dying, really dying, and she was unable to write more.

The kitchen orderly pulled her out of her grieving. He collected the dirty plates, and the fellow, who was quite unknown to her, dared because it was revolution to nod to her and say: "Now now, Mrs Chief, it's all not half so bad. You see how I limp. They took off half my leg, back there with the Russians. But I limp along, and it's still OK."

She looked away, offended. She returned to the hospital, nothing had changed, it was still her husband lying there, but uncertainty had planted itself between them.

The train departed at ten past seven that evening. He survived for one hour past the departure time. She clung to his neck for the final leavetaking, but they pulled her away and tied a napkin under his chin and knotted it over his head, because his lower jaw was hanging slack. The napkin looked horrible and stupid because of the silly knot on top. The nurse said: "It's just for an hour or two, we'll take it off after."

She stood beside the bed, thought of the him, the war, the long years before and how good he was with his idiosyncrasies and how she'd grown used to him. She heard the distant rattle of trains. There goes his hospital train, gliding into the dark without him. It's all finished, the war's over, they've left us here. Wearily she stood up.

Someone asked her something. Funeral, yes, what needs to happen.

For him, as for many others, there was no formal officer's funeral. They had to keep their heads down. His body was left along the way, in a cemetery in Würzburg.

Citizens and Soldiers

They scattered like fallen leaves

The military hospital, having lost its Chief, took but little time to dissolve entirely. They rumbled on out of Bavaria, no longer thinking of the war and the little town in Alsace; Little Granny, the long-necked locomotive, was left behind in Würzburg, A fresh engine was hitched to the front of the cars, to which more were attached. Inside the train thoughts were of home, and they grew quiet and withdrawn. The train roared across Thuringia.

Monday 18th November, the final evening, the final dark rainy night. Dim lights in the compartments. Becker and Maus lay dozing on their benches.

"You asleep, Maus?"

"Trying. But can't."

"Do you recall how we set off? We left the airfield behind, then there was light and dark, it was their famous forest, so in the end I did get to see it, after all. Trees, clearings, it was magical."

"Peace, dearest peace you said. You were actually singing, Becker. I thought you must be dreaming."

"Soon it will all be over, Maus. We'll be demobbed in Naumburg."

"Yes. What will become of us? Surely we'll need further treatment?"

"There are clinics everywhere, hospitals. But for the rest … it's all over."

"And then a new life begins."

"Then it begins."

The car squeaked and shuddered in a steady rhythm, they absorbed the motions, the noises, the shaking they associated still with the military hospital and the war.

Becker: "You remember the trumpeter who practised

in the garden every day?"

"He got off in Hessen."

"Ah. I'd have liked to say farewell to him."

"The men have a lot of worries just now."

"And the old woman who cleaned for us. She became flighty towards the end." Maus gave a honk of laughter: "I saw her, she was nicking stuff like mad, and nattering away!"

"And the blind captain you told me about, who always took solitary walks through the town, counting his paces. And Richard."

"He's in the cemetery on the road to our hospital. I took a look, beside him there's a French airman who crashed in the area."

"Well, well. So they lie there as well. And so everything is packed away and sinks together and becomes the past just like, I don't know, the Seven Years War and the Persian War. I wonder if the dead will ever rise up against the living. But us, Maus, we're shipwrecked sailors on a raft. We're cast up on a beach. Like Odysseus."

"What's going to happen, Becker?"

"No Nausicaa will be there to welcome us and bring us clothes. Pallas Athene breathed courage into Nausicaa's soul and removed fear from her limbs. And she stood waiting for him."

"So where is your peace now, Becker, your dearest peace?"

Becker made no reply. An unsuspected sweetness from somewhere flowed through him. Turn about, say: God greets you, oh you most bitter of bitternesses. You shall be my dear sister. You are full of grace.

Maus: "I'm in low spirits, I can't bear to look out of the window. The country's exhausted, there'll be no more army, my father can't support me on his pension."

Becker was humming, he couldn't identify what it was flitting through him. Again the breath of a word, do not forget my country, one day I shall send you a helpful sign. "And yet, peace. No one in a foxhole, no grenades bursting, something else is coming."

"But what? I don't want to go home."

Becker, who was on his stomach, turned his head to face him. "What do you want? What are you asking for? Look at me, her I lie, with my back, my legs." His face dropped to the pillow. "I shall never again touch a woman."

Maus: "Hush now, many have said the same." Becker covered his eyes, Maus had never heard his friend complain.

"I wish there'd never been a war, and if there were, I wish it had never ended. To awaken me for this."

"I'll stay with you, Becker."

"I tell you, it's a wicked spirit that made this life. I was already dead, it certainly wasn't the 'utmost rapture' of Tristan, but silence and calm, a true and proper condition. Then a wicked spirit roused me, and they call it recovering. And now there's no calm to be found, just hope and wait, desire, and lie there. Because it's wicked, it harries me and allows me no rest. This is what we've been gifted, this is what we're fitted with, with this insanity."

Maus sat silent in the face of this outburst. He didn't understand what Becker was saying, but he could feel the bitter acerbity. He summoned cajolery to help him out: "But it's not at all as you say, it can't be Becker saying such things."

"It is he precisely, this poor so-and-so. I do not permit myself to be deprived of the right of protest. Which I too possess. I shall at least be capable of that, of protesting. Don't make of me some jaunty deity. See my mask fly away."

"Becker, you're letting yourself go."

They scattered like fallen leaves

"And why not. Why them and not me, I shall let myself go, in the end I will and I must let myself go. I protest. I wish I'd remained out there. The ones lying back there are better off than us, they have no need to start all over again, they've already finished the job."

Becker gave a low groan. Maus: "If not even you can manage it, what are we to say."

Becker turned his face to him again, and sought wordlessly for his hand. Maus: "It's OK to be weak now and then, old chap. I really did take you for a kind of god, actually."

★

Early next morning, when they stopped at a little station for a thorough sanitising of men and cars, Becker sat in his corner very pale, withdrawn, cool, but placid. There was already coffee on the bench, Maus brought rolls and spread a clean handkerchief on his side. As he poured coffee he looked back at Becker, who was observing him: "Now, you big picture of suffering, how may I serve you?"

The old mocking smile at Becker's lips: "Stop bothering me, false dog. Open the window."

And when Maus had lowered the window, Becker with a gesture of pathos poured half his coffee cup out of it:

"There! That's for the gods of this land. Saxon soil, I consecrate you with this thin transparent brew."

At this stop they had an opportunity to witness a demonstration preceded by red flags. The little troop seemed to have the intention to approach the train and set up a conversation, but veered away. Maus made sad eyes: "Why don't they come to us? No one should be afraid."

Becker: "Who are they? What are they doing?"

"It's the revolution."

"What! And I was so glad to hear about the revolution. They're off to church, Maus."

"I tell you no. Today's only Tuesday."

They climbed back on the train. Maus packed his friend into the heavy horse blankets that in some mysterious way had strayed to them from the artillery barracks. Becker said carelessly: "Disappointing."

Doors banged. The train proceeded through little Saxon duchies that were no more, they stopped in Saalfeld, Rudolstadt, Weimar, and looked out. Nothing special for them to see.

Naumburg was the final stop.

They had all packed their possessions very carefully, concealing things, because they knew there'd be inspections at the exit. Everything passed without incident, very quickly. There was great upheaval in the station. Before they had a chance to get lost, they found themselves on another platform amid a huge packed mass of soldiers and civilians, all waiting for trains, and all unfamiliar.

They were pushed apart.

In the stationmaster's office and on each platform were uniformed men at little tables, with long lines of people having passes signed and stamped. These were Soldiers' Council men. For those not travelling on at once, hotels and civilian billets were provided. The last flu cases were taken off to hospital.

Like leaves from a withered tree, they fell to earth and were scattered.

Part Two

SHATTERING DEFEAT

Like an unlatched door in a hurricane slamming back and forth until blown off its hinges, just so was the German Army buffeted and battered and unearthed from its tunnels and fortifications.

The German general, Erich Ludendorff, a 53-year-old from the province of Posen, knew that this year was his last chance. In the spring he lunged out with the blow that after forty-four months was to decide the war.

He assembled around him one and a half million men and more than six thousand guns in a tightly defined area of northern France. In close formation, unobserved, fifty divisions marched towards Cambrai and St Quentin. Preparations took three months. At midnight on 20th March, amid gales and rain, he unleashed his armies with the codename *St Michael*. *Mars* was to be the codename for the second push, and the enemy's death blow would be dealt by *St George*. By the end of three days' fighting, the English V. Army of General Gough was almost annihilated, the III. to the north now merely slag. True, the German XVII. Army had been halted near Arras and forced to shelter in a maze of trenches. Near Montdidier a fifteen kilometre gap had opened between English and French forces. In several places fighting took place on open ground. That was on 25th March. On the 26th, Allied reserves began to stream in towards Amiens. On the 27th and 28th, the gap was sealed like a scab on a wound. And on the 29th the enemy front was as firm as ever. The codename *Mars* was never uttered.

The German general knew what was at stake. Shaken already, in May he repeated the attack, and again in July. On 18th July came the first enemy counter-offensive, which brought the German military machine to a standstill.

From 18th July, General Ludendorff's army was

Citizens and Soldiers

subjected to dreadful and deliberate attrition by an enemy whose strength only grew. The blackest day for the general was 8th August, when his II. Army allowed itself to be caught napping near Péronne, east of Amiens. Seven divisions were destroyed, entire sectors handed to enemy tanks without a fight. On 21st March the German still had eighty fresh reserve divisions at his disposal; on 13th August only twenty-five remained behind his front line, many of them already exhausted. He was thrown back over the Aisne and the Somme. Paris, coveted Paris, on which he had hurled shells from his heavy calibre long-distance guns, was no longer his concern. Paris, the flower of the west, was out of danger. Now danger threatened the Germans themselves. For what was being assembled around and in front of the city was steel, fire and an immensely burgeoning Will.

The German general had already abandoned a thousand canon and a million grenades. His front line was overstretched. On 10th September the English thrust the Germans back to the Hindenburg Line. What slaughter now began around Cambrai, Cambrai for the second time in this war the focal point of agonising toil and heroic efforts. It was a small innocuous town on a little river that snaked its way north through rolling countryside into the rushing Scheldt. Here peaceful provincials lived their lives, had their cafés, restaurants, their families, the church, the lace industry was prosperous enough, sugar and beer were produced. Whenever the town's name had come up previously, it was in connection with one of France's finest and most seductive spirits, Fénelon, who centuries before had here his seat and strove as educator, tamer and soother of savages like the young Duc de Bourgogne. "Your victories and conquests, Majesty," he wrote to his king, "no longer give me joy. One is filled with bitterness and grief, tending even to despair. One believes that the suffering of the people is of no concern to you. You place your fame and your sovereignty above all." He left behind some portentous *Dialogues of the Dead*.

The battle raged around his silent seat. For thirty days, for thirty risings and settings of the sun, they murdered and smashed. Tommies attacked to the west of the town. On the 24th and 26th the impregnable fortifications around Selency, north of St Quentin, fell to them. Americans came to their aid, overran lines to north and south of the town. Earth-shaking thunder of big guns, exploding mines, a hail of grenades, days and nights without end. Anneux, the two Sauchys, Beaucamp, the outskirts of Cambrai fell, were in American hands along with three hundred canon. And from the adversary's living wall they extracted twenty-two thousand prisoners.

Meanwhile other American armies were reducing the dreaded St Mihiel salient on the Maas in an uninterrupted forty-eight hour battle. Here the now badly wounded adversary relinquished two hundred canon and twenty thousand prisoners.

The German general did not lose countenance. His icy conclusion: "We made a sortie from a fortress under siege. The sortie failed. The fortress is as strong as ever."

The enemy general was Ferdinand Foch, a god-fearing man from Tarbes in the Pyrenees, not far from miracle-jangling Lourdes. He had distinguished himself in the confusion of the battle of Morhange in the summer of 1914, as part of Castelnau's army he commanded that XX Corps which denied the Kaiser, so certain of victory, entry into the town of Nancy; the parade uniform for the triumphal entry had already been ordered, but Fate corrected human calculation. For the Battle of the Marne Joffre fetched him out of Lorraine at the end of August, soon praises were sung of Maunoury, French and Franchet d'Esperey, who threw back the audacious Kluck, but without Foch their flanking push in the centre of the French lines would never have succeeded. He was almost seventy. He had undergone a painful time of waiting in Versailles as Chief of Staff with no army. Not until 26th March of this year, when Germany's decisive battle seemed to be won, was he summoned to Doullens, where the English General Haig and the Frenchman Pétain were finding it impossible to agree. Supreme command was handed to Foch. The pious Frenchman was not inclined to accept the Prussian's icy words about the fortress strong as ever. He hammered and thrust at the defensive walls thrown up by the invaders of his own land. For these walls were bits of iron and concrete, which can be shattered, but in particular they were men, who can be captured, killed, lamed, and worn out.

Now, with British armies supported by generals Debeney and Humbert, little by little he enticed forty German divisions, including fifteen reserve divisions, to move forward, and with the tenacity of his years subjected them to a merciless process of decimation.

The month elapsed. October could only bring to fruition what September had sown. On 3rd, 4th and 5th October the Allies renewed their attack. Around this time the situation for the German general and his troops was already so far gone that the English General Haig observed Austrian units facing him in the valley of the Somme. Behind his lines the German commander had only forty divisions, of which two-thirds had already been deployed in action. Cambrai was assaulted from north and south. The Hindenburg and Siegfried Lines, which converged at Catelet, were overrun. The Allies advanced from one fortification to the next, every foot of ground, dreadfully secured, was defended with the utmost energy. But the

Germans were not spared a retreat across the Oise.

The war of 1866 lasted two weeks, the war of 1870-71 seven months; this war was now in its fifth year. Again and again some miracle had kept one or other of the adversaries alive, and delayed the weakening of his pulse and the black veil drawn across the brain. But now a sinister gloom betokening the proximity of death spread among the Germans. It was on 29th September that the German general informed his imperial government of the peril. On 2nd October his strength failed him. His nerves gave in. He demanded an armistice, armistice. Not an hour to lose.

But there was the foe, the old pious general from Tarbes. And across the Atlantic Ocean came huge convoys, strongly protected, unmolested by the once-dreaded U-boats, transport vessels from the New World bringing men, strong and dauntless, to the battlefields where, to the astonishment equally of Germans, French and English, they ran in great numbers, heads held high, ahead of their artillery straight into German machine gun fire. Even so, they advanced in such numbers that they eventually overran the enemy positions. Like twittering birds of passage on great migratory wings, like schools of fish at spawning time, nimble little creatures with sparkling scales, all nameless and sent swirling by the boats of fishermen, just so did these men come on, as prophesied by their bard Walt Whitman:

> *Come, I will make the continent indissoluble,*
> *I will make the most splendid race the sun ever shone upon,*
> *I will make divine magnetic lands,*
>   *With the love of comrades,*
>   *With the life-long love of comrades.*
> *I will plant companionship thick as trees along all the rivers of*
> *America, and along the shores of the Great Lakes, and all over*
>   *the prairies,*

Citizens and Soldiers

> *I will make inseparable cities with their arms about each other's necks,*
> *By the love of comrades,*
> *By the manly love of comrades.*
> *For you these from me, O Democracy, to serve you ma femme!*
> *For you, for you I am trilling these songs.*

The German gave way. The Chemin des Dames became free. Now it was mid-October. General Erich Ludendorff had gathered his wits yet again. War is fickle. If you can't fight for a breakthrough, you fight defensively. If you can't fight in France, you fight on the German border, maybe in Germany itself. War is fickle. The fallback line he had prepared along the Serre and the Aisne was blocked to him. He fixed on a line Hirson–Mézières–Metz. The general had so few troops left that he summoned divisions from Upper Alsace and Belgium and threw them at the Argonne, others from Lens to Flanders. He tore a hole in his front here, in order to fill a gap there.

Jubilation in liberated French territory: "Les Boches. Ah, they're fleeing. The hour is approaching for them to atone, and give satisfaction!"

On 16th October the Belgians advanced under their king from Dixmuide towards Ypres. The Belgian North Sea coast came under fire from the guns of the English fleet. The German general is now grown hard again. He still has the vast defence system of Lille, Maubeuge, Sedan, Montmédy, Thionville, Metz. His front is now shorter. War is fickle. His eastern flank between Aisne and Maas holds.

How many canon, how many machine guns have fallen into the hands of the French up to this date, 21st October, since that fateful 17th July? Four thousand five hundred canon, twenty-five thousand machine guns. The English boast of having captured, in August and September alone, one hundred and twenty-three thousand German prisoners, and a prize of fourteen hundred canon.

There is after all no reason to give in, the general thinks, if the Kaiser remains resolute, the army remains resolute, the people remain resolute. But something's going on. He has known it since 8th August. His army is almost dead from exhaustion. The homeland is wavering. The Kaiser is unsettled. A nation consists of people. As long as a hard Will lies over them they bow the head and keep quiet. When they feel pain they grit the teeth. If the Will should slacken they take a deep breath, nudge one another and grumble. The homeland is grumbling. The direction is backwards, ever backwards. New strategic possibilities interest no one, after fifty months of war.

And now, under the unified leadership of Ferdinand Foch, Debeney's army crosses the Oise, Mangin's army forces its way across the Serre, Gouraud marches along the right bank of the Aisne, the English annihilate the foe on the edge of the Mormal Forest. St Gobain, centre of the Siegfried and Hindenburg Lines, is overrun from east and west. It's 26th October.

Now the German general is summoned to his Kaiser at the Bellevue Palace in Berlin. The general knows what this means. But he doesn't know its full extent. A white-haired man of medium build in the uniform of a general stands facing him in the audience chamber, his back to the desk, the well-known face of the Kaiser, an agitated, deeply affected person who only with difficulty restrains himself from letting loose with his full fury, a person whose words conceal hatred and vengeance. The general is dismissed coldly, without thanks.

★

The latter event occurred at the beginning of November. Then the British launched their 1st, 3rd and 4th Armies at the Kaiser's still-persevering troops. Twenty-five German divisions stood facing them between Sambre and Scheldt, cobbled together, exhausted, replenished with units of men too young and too old. The Brits ripped open a thirty mile gap in the enemy line. They advanced in pouring November rain, the Germans had to retreat, abandon whole batteries. The Brits crossed through the Mormal Forest and dug in on a line Barzy–Berlaimont west of Fresnes–Boisin. The front between Bar and the Meuse was overrun at the same time by French and American forces.

FLOORED

Close behind the German front lines lay French and Belgian towns and villages that had lived for years in semi-peace. With the approach of the fiery Allied steamroller, they had enjoyed their peace for long enough. Everywhere orders came from the High Command to evacuate these places. But even when no orders came, the population set itself in motion.

What though could compete for speed with rifle bullets, bomber planes, grenades? How to avoid being caught between the two front lines, and smashed to pieces? The long peace had lulled people into self-deception, the end had to come, now it was here.

Desperate hunt for vehicles. Dutch and Spanish Aid Committees made soothing noises and did what they could, but the people were in a panic as explosions came nearer and German troops came rattling into their towns and villages and dug in among them. People fled and drove away in carts, children in their arms, bedding on the back, and came upon new German lines. They handed over whatever they could for horses and carts. They fled in their thousands from Douai, all at once as canon thundered ever nearer, a thousand French francs for a pram. Peasants loaded up their oxen, cattle and donkeys – horses had been taken long ago; they set wife and children on them, kept going day and night. But there was no fodder for the beasts, they had to be slaughtered at the roadside, refugees came together to cook and eat them beneath canvas awnings in the open air, amid canon fire, bombs exploding, signal flares. Families lay clumped together in heaps, often fear set them moving during the night. Then children lost their parents, and were taken up and led on by other families along the main roads down which an endless stream of refugees came pouring.

The German armies withdrew in good order, they're soldiers, they march under orders, they have wagons and canon. Canon thunder is no novelty to them. They feel no need to scream when aeroplanes appear, they set up camouflage and let their anti-aircraft guns play. In the little places they abandoned, they shot dogs and cats that would otherwise starve. They were besieged by hungry refugees. When they set up their smoking field kitchens, children and women elbowed in among the ranks. You can't make out what these wretched frost-bitten groups are saying, but any who hold out a mug, a bowl, receive it back, filled. It was no dinner, just what they had. Then quarrels broke out between troops and kitchen orderlies, because they'd not put enough in the cauldrons. The men shared their bread with refugees; they ate, and watched how the children chewed their morsel, it's tough on you kids, what is war, what's it for, we've kids like you back home, maybe the war's coming to us, we've lost the game. The retreat continued. Women and children clung begging to wagons and limbers. Bigger children lying worn out in the road were sat on canon and carried to the next town.

In Liège there had once been a World Exhibition, the empty halls were still there. The stream of refugees that came rolling in was led to these halls under their intact roofs. Parents sat together on straw and wept for their children. During the night, maddened young women screamed, people had to push their way through and take them off to hospital. Many lay completely strengthless, faces immobile, so that soon, into these bright halls that once were filled with happy people, a guest entered, one often encountered on the long highways: Death.

In this town of Liège businesses discovered a special source of pride. In their show windows they exhibited large copper pans that had been held back from the confiscations; the shiny red hollows were filled with pictures of the Belgian royal couple, now returning home.

★

The retreat made haste across lines with heroic names: Siegfried, Hunding, Brunhilde. The beaten army fought forlornly on the Hermann Line, defended itself in Champagne, on the Maas. Rearguard actions took place outside Antwerp. The I., III., and V. Armies took up a defensive stance in Champagne and on the Maas until 11th November; the II., XVII., and XVIII. Armies fought on the Hermann Line until it collapsed. During the retreat from the Maas positions, almost every Army, remnant, detritus of an army took part: the I., II., III., IV., VII., XVII., XVIII. Entire battalions and companies were wiped out. The Allies assailed them with an inexhaustible deluge of fresh troops, immeasurable wealth of canon, tanks, aeroplanes. They were able to deploy abandoned German materiel, directing it at fleeing troops. Germans were poisoned by their own Yellow Cross gases.

Blood flowed, laments of soldiers and civilians filled the November air.

Gripping the tiller with unyielding resolution: Fate.

★

During the night of 7th November, the German Army Command sent a telegram to the commander of the Allied troops seeking an immediate armistice. They received the reply: German plenipotentiaries must present themselves at the French advance posts on the road Chimay-Fourmies-La Capelle-Guise.

At ten that evening they crossed Allied lines near Haudroy, were taken by truck to Soissons, and early Friday morning reached the Forest of Compiègne, headquarters of Marshal Foch. He had them admitted around nine o'clock to his railway carriage. He was flanked by a French general and two admirals, one English and one American. The German spokesman, a civilian, thought it necessary, given the severity of the situation, to broach a few remarks; the Supreme Allied Commander waved him aside with the words: The guns will not fall silent before this treaty is signed. (He himself did not believe it would be accepted.) They were given a seventy-two hour deadline.

At one o'clock a captain with the German delegation was assigned the task of conveying the document with the utmost, *utmost* despatch to the German High Command by car, by plane, by whatever means possible. Every hour meant more deaths. Germans fired wildly when the captain came speeding along in his car, big white flag waving, bugler outside on the footboard sounding a signal, no one could hear it amid all the guns. The delegates wasted five hours casting about this way and that, and then took the desperate decision to break through somewhere even if it cost them their lives. They charged ahead, and had luck.

But they climbed out amazed when they reached the German trenches. What did they find? Nothing but a few machine guns here and there along the parapet, and a tiny handful of troops firing like men possessed, dead comrades strewn around.

Saturday passed into Sunday at Compiègne, no reply came. French railway workers showed newspapers to the negotiators standing around waiting: headlines finger-thick: the Kaiser has abdicated, the Crown Prince as well. It is now 10th November, tomorrow at 11 o'clock the seventy-two hours will be up.

At eight in the evening a radio telegram reaches Main Headquarters: new conditions are demanded, my God, they've wasted whole days on this, what on Earth will happen. At last the redeeming word: at half past ten a radio message to the Armistice Commission: "The German government accepts the Armistice conditions presented to you on 8th November. Reich Chancellor Ends." The German officers must meet with the French interpreter officer, who asks: Who is this Chancellor Ends? He is known neither here nor in Paris. The head of the German delegation, a stolid man of middle height with straw-blond hair and gold-rimmed pince-nez, the journalist and parliamentarian Erzberger, has to repair the damage and explain: it just means Reich Chancellor. Ends means end, full stop. And, he adds, probably that's what will happen to this chancellor. Which is of no concern to the interpreter.

At five in the morning they signed the treaty.

At this point the Americans have three and a half million men under arms. In the New World a further one point four million, deployment ready, can now be demobilised.

The Battle of Metz was supposed to begin on 13th November. Eight fresh US divisions were standing ready to the north of the fortifications; General Castelnau with three French divisions to the south was to advance on Saarlouis and Saarbrücken, supported by six US divisions.

From the Forest of Compiègne the Allied Supreme Commander was able to inform his generals: "Hostilities along the entire front are to cease at 11 o'clock French time on 11th November. No Allied troops are to cross the lines achieved on this day at this hour without further orders."

*

And when next day the negotiators crossed back over the enemy lines with the signed document, they saw that revolution had arrived, the Kaiser was no more, and in Germany there was no proper government. In those four difficult days the whole world had changed. Even the telegram they had at last received was composed by no government and no Reich Chancellor. In the general confusion it had emanated from the Supreme Army Command.

Because everything was happening so monstrously fast.

*

On the morning of 11th November, the Monday, a solidly built gentleman with white waving hair stepped out of No. 10 Downing Street. On the steps he gestured with both arms and called out in an excited and happy voice to the people gathered in the street and across the road, and to the guardians of the peace. They can't hear what he's saying. The crowd swarmed about him because he gestured so enthusiastically, and clearly wanted to be noticed. Soon the street was packed. The man kept repeating the same news: This morning at eleven o'clock, the war will be over. They surge towards him, shake him by the hand, clap him on the shoulder. He's the Prime Minister, Lloyd George. He had no idea how he made it back inside. Someone must have come to his rescue. Inside he stood between his two secretaries and laughed and laughed.

That afternoon his powerful voice resonated in the House of Commons as he announced the event: "The cruellest and most dreadful war that has ever lacerated mankind ended today. I hope that on this eventful morning the war to end all wars has come to an end *(prolonged, prolonged applause)*. Our hearts are filled with gratitude. I move that this House now adjourn, in order to convey in church our thanks to God for delivering us from great peril."

It was the grey church of Parliament to which they then formally repaired, to the sound of every bell pealing.

The bells had to peal a long time before the black clouds over the ancient church parted to reveal the face of the Eternal, who pushed the clouds aside, gazed down upon the people, and heard what they were saying. He said, and they perceived him as they sang their hymns: "I never showed myself as long as you waged war. I have nothing to do with stubborn, raving lunatics. I have long known how humanity has fallen away from me. I should have created you and then carried you off to the North Pole, to the ice, so you'd be unable to stir. Your cheers and ringing bells make not the slightest impression on me. But because you feel gratitude, I shall listen to you. It makes you feel good. I do not trust you. I do not trust you." Once again he called out: "I do not trust you!"

Thus did the Eternal rage in the black clouds over the church of Parliament. He spoke likewise in Paris, other capitals. People heard Him, and a sombre shudder ran through them.

And so, on that day in London, Paris and other cities, complete strangers hugged in the street, wept, and knew one another as human beings.

But He who had called out from the darkness did not linger over their jubilation, their tears and gratitude. He devoted His attention again to the dreadful activity he had pursued over the last four and a half years: obscurely empathising with the pain, the helplessness, the dumb inward wrath of soldiers, men defenceless in their weaponry; witnessing the general frenzy, striving at least now and then to become their master, but it only showed how badly it had all slipped away from Him.

Like roots of a tree fixed deep and wide in the ground, just so when news of the Armistice came did the German army, shaken and stung, wrench loose its troops from dugouts, trenches and fortifications. They had to make fearful haste.

By 17th November they were to have withdrawn behind the line Antwerp-Dendermonde, and farther south behind Longwy-Briey-Metz-Saverne-Sélestat; in the far south, west of the Rhine, to the Neuf Brisach-Basle road. But they would have no time to rest even then, and regardless of wind and rain, hill or plain, by the 21st they must have marched, fled or ridden as far as Turnhout and the Hasselt Canal, to Diest, to the northern border of Luxemburg. Not one soldier should show his face in Luxemburg or Alsace-Lorraine. By the 27th they should have been chased entirely out of Belgium. Furthermore, by 1st December they must have cleared all regions to the west of Düsseldorf and Neuss, and not be in evidence west

Citizens and Soldiers

of a line running from Düren, Salm, Bernkastel, Rhine to the Swiss frontier. Then, as if this were not enough, they were to remove themselves from the entire Rhineland, and by 9th December vacate the rest of the left bank of the Rhine. The adversary would be at their heels, and pursue them to the east bank of the Rhine, where they would occupy Cologne, Coblenz and Mainz to a depth of thirty kilometres.

Marching, riding, flying: infantry, riflemen, bicycle troops, cavalry, mounted artillery, foot artillery, pioneers and trench mortars, formations of machine gunners and intelligence, airman units, artillery spotters, bomb squadrons, fighter squadrons.

Rain fell. The roads were softened, few locomotives were available. Anything with legs had to march, the highways were chock full of troops, artillery, horses and materiel. Among and alongside them were civilians from villages and towns, with their belongings. Wherever they came, the Field-marshal General's poster had been pasted: "Up until this day we have borne our arms honourably. In loyal submission and fulfilment of its duties the Army has achieved mighty deeds. We depart the field of battle proudly, heads held high."

Their legs, vehicles and aeroplanes were of use now solely for returning home. Their rifles, machine guns and canon seemed not insignificant, for they were marching through enemy territory, and on all sides were people eager to fall on them and exact revenge.

The hospital train from our little town was still on its way, Becker had launched into his paean to sweet peace, the good Chief Medic was still alive in his best of all possible worlds, the donated pig still squealed contentedly in the baggage wagon, for it was being fattened for the coming Sunday. It was now Friday 15th November – and gobbets of the German Army were already crossing the frontier. Five thousand German soldiers forced their way over the Dutch border, because other routes were blocked to them. At their head were ten automobiles carrying officers. Dutch gendarmes and military drivers disarmed them, the officers raised no objection, they handed over what they had. If they needed weapons in future, they'd be given some. Many officers came with no insignia of rank, others still wore theirs. The Dutch had no idea what this meant, the German gentlemen maintained inscrutable faces. The squads arrived in tidy company formations. But once across the Maas bridge they set themselves at ease. A heaving mass of people knew there were pickings to be had. And the soldiers did not disappoint. Without any pangs they said goodbye of steel helmets, gasmasks, just handed them over; they pulled gasmasks with the horrible snout over the heads of toddlers, but many a helmet was sent sailing over the bridge railings with a little farewell benediction. "Customs check!" they cried merrily, "who's got anything to declare." They were allowed across in their hundreds, disarmed, and wandered on their way with a spring in their step. Among them, on bicycles, were figures discreetly dubbed "slime mould" by the officers in their vehicles; these were members of the Soldiers' Council, they had white armbands tagged with mysterious magical letters such as R.R. These councillors received the same treatment as soldiers and officers, and were disarmed. Thus plundered and simplified, everything marched, rode and pedalled across to Germany, escorted by Dutch gendarmes and military vehicles.

On the same Friday, way ahead of them, the first big returning troop transport train passed through Berlin, the confused tumultuous Reich capital (but was it still the Reich capital, capital of what Reich?) – ten corridor cars and several cattle wagons. They proceeded from Charlottenburg to Lichtenberg, at Lichtenberg there were feeding stations on the platform. It was a remarkable sight, this transport, providing a foretaste of what was to come. Soldiers stood on running boards, lay on roofs. The train was hung like a Christmas tree with kitbags, sandbags, boxes. The soldiers sang endlessly their songs of return. Obviously, these were not hymns to the Fatherland.

As they rolled across the flatlands of Mark Brandenburg, along the track telegraph poles stood stiffly to attention, chest out, to set the returnees a good example. Scruffy sparrows perching on the wires announced to the passengers what had just been tapped out about the "Council of Intellectual Workers" in the Reichstag building in Berlin, a poem, a noble poem:

> *Faced with Earth's storm of Freedom*
> *Fall, whoever cannot breathe.*
> *And the rage of Spring: become,*
> *create, what ne'er was dreamed.*

The wires bowed down in pride as this Delphicly obscure pronouncement coursed through them. But the soldiers, totally unimpressed, bombarded the sparrow colonies with apple cores.

HILDE

Hair loosened, face flushed by the hot steam that filled the tiny bathroom, eyes clear and dreamy, Hilde, quite naked, rested her hands on the curved edge of the zinc bathtub, dipped a tentative foot into the very hot water, and slowly lowered it to the bottom of the tub.

She drew up the other leg, and let the foot play over

the water's surface breath. Then she dropped it in. She had both legs in the water, remained standing, it was hot. Heat huffed from below and sniffed at her like a dog, now the tenuous mist curled about her arms, she felt it at her ears, her hair became damp, she tied it behind her neck, and lowered herself into the water. She kept quite still in the water so as not to make the heat worse. She felt her face become fuller, felt she was a little excited. Her breasts were not yet under water, she stretched out, ripples washed tamely against her neck, her throat. Both arms lay slack at her sides.

She stayed in this position. The day was cold, it wasn't raining, so fog from the Rhine had rolled in across the city. It was morning, father had gone out. The bathroom was at the rear of the house, jolts and rumbles from the street, the clop of horses' hooves came through indistinctly; huge disorganised bands of troops were flooding into the city and out again across to Kehl. The evacuation deadline was approaching.

Though she had been back in the city for days, she had not yet seen the one with whom for the whole war she had linked the name of Strassburg. She felt no longing for him, no fear.

Why had she climbed into the bath? Why? Why once again have to lock a door behind her, let steam curl around her. When it spouted scalding from the tap she had greeted it dreamily, put a finger under it. She watched it spread across the tub, and then laid herself down.

Through her head, lying back against the curved rim, scraps of images flowed, distant Russian roads, outside a cottage a pipe-smoking reservist stared after her cart drawn by small sturdy ponies, field mail was distributed, no letter for me, how nice, Bernhard has kept his promise, how unbending he is, he feels so sure of me. If I were at the North Pole sinking beneath ice, he'd remain calm and say: it doesn't matter, you're still mine.

She peered out of narrowed eyeslits. There in the water lay blushing feet and toes, they belonged to her body. How the body stretched itself in the tub, the bulging swell of the legs. In the little hairs on her lower leg, tiny air bubbles lay trapped, like snails, a bright strip on each side, colonies, she smoothed them away, they returned. When she stroked her hand down her body they swirled like champagne bubbles.

She inhaled steam, it carried a slight scent of lavender, her eyes turned aside, she smiled, on the edge of the tub was a sponge, the soap had fallen in the water, she fished it out. She dozed, blood flowed beating through her body, everywhere the same, in her insides, her limbs, through her head, she could feel the heart beat and pulse and never give a moment's peace.

What was melting away from her? Father, mother, here I am, dark in the darkness.

And as she lay quietly in the water – small creature in a zinc bathtub, in a small room in one of those two-storey houses they have in Strassburg – as she dozed and dreamed, she became a battleground for the beating pulsing heart and the rushing torrents of blood. Inside her, intestines moved with sinuous twitchings, little pink villi penetrated the membrane like roots in the liquid flow, and sucked at it.

Neither Hilde, nor from Strassburg was she now, rather a plant, and had nothing to fear, she had only to grow, to bear fruit, and decay. And who had set her this task? It was hers, and she soothed herself with the fact.

Then she remembered her hair. She felt her head: is it wet. Sweat trickled down her cheeks. Slowly she lifted herself, stood and let water drip. Head drooped to breasts.

She thought, as she squinted down at her breasts: here I am, a well-fed cow, and have no idea what I want.

She felt cold, climbed out and sat in a bathrobe, hood over her head, on the stool. "How lovely the world is," her lips said as she opened the robe and again inhaled steamy warmth. Then she shuddered as memories came of the hospital, the cadaver room, pus-soaked bandages. But it passed, she said aloud to herself: "How lovely the world is" and towelled her feet dry. She fished slippers out from under the stool, sat on the sofa in the heated living room.

The rumble of traffic sounded louder here. She was wrapped in a plaid rug, had shoved a sofa cushion behind her head. She was vaguely aware of street sounds, marching boots. The sounds came to her, she kept a little slit of an eye open, tracked the sounds. Ah, I'm such a sinful girl. Heaved a tragic sigh. Wandered across to her little bedroom.

When she was in the street around eleven o'clock, she had on a rough dark green overcoat and a little fur hat. She turned at once into a narrow alley beside the house, to avoid the sight of soldiers. Once again, as on her first day back, she found herself at the rear of the cathedral. People thronged at a side entrance. She strolled across. Someone had tied the hands of a statue and hung a placard on it: *sic transit gloria mundi*. The bound statue had the face of the German Kaiser. Laughing, cursing, handclaps from the crowd. Why am I here? She headed for the other side. The cathedral tower loomed high in the fog, she was on the square, she went in.

Up to the left, the organ with its bright-coloured woodwork, the pipes silver; the grey space shuddered with the force of its sound. The church was quite empty. Stools were stacked untidily around the columns. Something moved in front of the high altar, there were voices. She wandered irresolute through the space. A wedding was taking place in a side chapel. As Hilde approached, the wedding guests were kneeling in two rows. Tall and golden the tabernacle, a double line of candles burning before it. The tiled tabernacle tapered as it rose to a golden spire, and was a model of the cathedral.

Hilde peered through the railing. She could see the bride and groom from behind. The priest wore a white smock with yellow ribbons and scarves. He held a black book in both hands, pale bald head with gold-rimmed glasses, he read aloud, the book close to his nose; at several points he turned to the bridal couple. The table under the tabernacle was covered in white, books and pictures on it. To left and right on the red carpet there were kneeling choirboys, a comforting sight, sometimes they looked around impatiently. But the priest continued reading, about Christian love.

The floor was stone, a chill crept through the space, Hilde couldn't tear herself away from the chapel. She was as one with the bridal couple in glad festive communion. She glanced to the side. The high altar was quite dark, behind it light fell in through a wide window, slowly tall white candles and candelabra emerged, and a red carpet led up some steps. Pillars and columns were all of reddish sandstone. A tall man with a huge staff and yellow scarf was gazing around, she recognised him. Suddenly the organ began to roar. The priest ended his reading and turned from the bridal couple towards the altar. He crossed himself several times, knelt, the organ swelled, the two rows of guests knelt and looked at the golden cross on the priest's back and his pale bald head. Now the priest was searching in a big book, he read and read, silently, for what he was thinking and reading was between himself and the Eternal in whose honour the cathedral had been built. The organ's calmer now, and as it warbles his hands have closed to become paws and he keeps turning to the bridal couple and back again. He spreads his arms wide, and reads from the book, leaning forward as if guarding himself from the flames that pour from the pages. Then he drops his arms, the perilous part is over, again he reads, calm and silent, and sniffles. The organ maunders softly, a little girl in white comes tripping with a little basket between the two rows of guests, they throw coins in. Suddenly a bell, silence, bell.

When Hilde looks up, the enormous space is bright, the high altar is there in its everyday guise with many candelabra, it looks like a workroom for strange tasks. The colourful confusion of glass in the windows. The stone flags on the floor are cold, cold streams in from all sides. And the organ's lamenting imploring is of no use, Hilde rubs her hands, kneels, whispers a prayer at the railing, and leaves.

Grave but happy she strolls towards the exit. She has taken part in a wedding and has shared in the blessing. Calmly she descends the steps into midday brightness, into the town, her lovely old town.

Across by the souvenir shop she can't help laughing. People stand about, reading aloud from the picture postcards stuck to the window from inside. One card, edged in mourning, shows two old boots. The caption beneath read:

General Announcement
With deep grief we announce to all friends and acquaintances that our dearly beloved last pair of leather boots, attended by every means of the repairer's art and embrocated with cow- and axle-grease, at four years of age, so full of hope, has found blessed release from senile frailty and atrophy of the sole. On them stood, on them moved the

Citizens and Soldiers

> entirety of our life. In the mornings when we awoke, there they stood fully dressed at our bedside to bring us their greeting, they sat with us at coffee, they sat with us at mealtimes, they accompanied us to the cinema, the theatre, up into the mountains. With them we enjoyed our sweetest trysts. On our wedding night they stood guard outside the door over our young bliss. Never through all our joys and sorrows did these loyal boots ever abandon us. We shall never lose our memories of them. The funeral will set off from the main gate of the Clothing Office. After the ceremony a ration coupon for a new pair of boots will be raffled. Funeral oration by State Counsellor Doctor Barefoot.

Another card showed a photo of a large loaf of bread: "Final photograph from the life," it said: "This evening at 9 o'clock, in the presence of its family, our good and dearly beloved final loaf of bread, at the age of barely six days, after careful frugality and rationing, was consumed gently and painlessly down to the last crumb. By kind request of the following, please no flowers or visits of condolence: Jeremias Flourgon, the Skinniwisp family, Dorothea Fatless."

Hilde joined in the laughter.

She had a yen to see Bernhard this afternoon: the evil Minotaur in his cave. She wanted to see how he would extend his claws in her direction.

SEAMAN THOMAS

What has become of our sailors who came speeding on Wednesday night asleep on the special train from Wilhelmshaven, thundering past Münster, Osnabrück,

Cologne to show Alsace what a German revolution is? For the Allies were pressing on, Wednesday turned inexorably to Thursday the 14th, and whoever stepped into Thursday's current could be sure that, alive or dead – and he could cling however he liked to Thursday – he would be borne along to Friday the 15th. And now his justified revulsion at Friday and Saturday was no defence.

On the day of the sailors' arrival: jubilation in the Soldiers' Council, spirited speeches, affectionate embraces, but in the afternoon Comrade Peirotes had to say what he had to say. The Allies and the 22nd November cast shadows before them. Now they were no longer so happy. And when Old Germans stepped forward whose bearing was not at all revolutionary, they began to feel quite faint. They came together at the Palace of Justice – what could they do, sulking alone in a corner – and formed the "Marine Council", partly because a soldier's a soldier and a sailor's a sailor, and partly because of their obstinate belief that they had a mandate to fulfil from the sixteen thousand sailors in Wilhelmshaven. But they perceived more and more that they were no longer in the chaos of Wilhelmshaven, but in the dear old Strassburg of their fathers. It wasn't just Peirotes. They swore first sailor-style, then mezzo, then piano, pianissimo.

And this came about because Strassburg not only had its cathedral, and the quiet friendly canals and the River Ill with the washerwomen, and the many brasseries, and wine (so long denied to sailors) was still to be had. They visited acquaintances, relations, where they learned of the pitiless pretentions of Germans during the war, how Alsatians were looked at askance, everyone at risk of being taken for a spy (and who knew better than they, who weren't trusted to join the army but were packed off to ships), and how glad everyone was that the French

Citizens and Soldiers

were coming to liberate them. Ah, it all makes sense! This Alsace, their beloved homeland, proved a hard nut for the revolutionaries. No one wanted their wares. Just one day after their tumultuous arrival, Eisenring, young leader of the sailors, was so brutally challenged that he had to make a strenuous public denial when accused of accepting bribes from Old Germans. "We're Alsatians, committed international socialists." It cannot be concealed that the locals said: "We won't eat that dish, either."

And so they sat and lounged about in the big austere Provincial Court building, patrolled the streets alongside others as a civil defence. Really: the heroes of Wilhelmshaven as a civil defence. And when they arrested someone who had looted too vigorously – maybe more than three pairs of boots, entire bolts of cloth – they confiscated the excess. They paced irresolutely about the Assize Court, during sessions under humourless Sergeant Rebholz, who was an Old German and conducted everything like a club event. And the discussions were a long way from what they wanted. No ocean, no fleet, no revolution, and yet they had put senior officers and cowardly citizens in harness and marched them along with the red flag. And here they were arguing about what to do with five hundred cases of gas masks stored in warehouses, how much had they cost to produce, what should the selling price be set at, maybe they can make a tidy profit. Oh lord, oh lord.

And the debate even stirred up big waves when the question arose: how to hand power over to the French? This caused a lot of teeth-grinding. But 20th November was already an unalterable date. And this Rebholz, the fool, insists that the French will simply occupy Alsace militarily, the civil authorities will remain unchanged. And for the obsequies it was suggested: first, the National Council for Alsace-Lorraine should hand over en bloc, then the mayor should come along with the city of Strassburg, and finally the Central Soldiers' and Workers' Council should present itself, make a bow and say: here's your military power. God have mercy. Alsatians slipped out of the courtroom and whispered in the corridor: did you hear that? Sergeant Rebholz the German means to hand military power to General Gouraud. Better hope he's not picked up by the ears and slung in clink.

Rifles against the wall behind them, cigarette in the mouth, Seaman Jörg and Seaman Baptist, Strassburgers both, newly inducted into the Navy, stood guard outside the little room assigned to the Marine Council. What it was they were guarding they had no idea. The room was empty. But they took notice of what was happening in the corridor, and the bustle outside the big debating chamber. Jörg, the younger, confided to his friend:

"Strassburg people are basically sensible. I was talking with my uncle in Schiltigheim, and a neighbour came by. They take a good look at me, 'cos I'm a sailor, and ask what's all this play-acting about. They scold me, we should be ashamed of ourselves, 'cos why did they stick us in the Navy? It's because we're Alsatians and the Prussians don't trust us. And all the other stuff they did. They said: goodbye and good riddance to the Swabs. The pastor said the same."

"Well then, it'll probably all turn out right."

"We never wanted more than that, that's what that lot all say."

"What do you think?"

"It's not such a dumb idea."

"So you say, Jörg. And how will you deal with the French? We want socialism. Revolution. You saw it in Wilhelmshaven."

Jörg thought for a bit. "We didn't want to sally forth to

engage the British. We managed that. And then we wanted to go home."

"Well now, Jörg, we're at loggerheads. You let your people talk you round. We want revolution, it must all come down. So that we can have some order in the world."

"That's what I told them too, at home. But they were adamant."

"So forget those dumb oxen. As if it's going to affect them, in Schiltigheim. You think my old man says any different? Or my brother? Ha! That's beside the point."

They fell silent. Jörg stood muttering to himself. And after a while he started up again: "I really can't work out what this socialism is about. Whether the French troops want it as well."

"At once. Right away. Let them be here for two weeks and they'll be all fired up, and off it will go across the whole of France."

"Down with officers?"

"Exactly as with us. And if anyone doesn't like it, they can buzz off."

Long pause. Jörg: "Do people work, in socialism?"

"Less than now. Think about it. There's no army or navy, and so there are more people there, and so you get less work. And then there's all the rich."

"They'll have to set to first."

"Of course. They've had it easy long enough. We'll give them a hard time. Bankers and commercial counsellors. Fat bellies. Just imagine."

"Fantastic. And the women."

"That commercial counsellor crowd, all of them, girls too. 'Cos my sister has to work now, and so does your mum."

"Of course."

"Well then."

"And how much will we earn?"

"More than now. It'll all be shared out. We won't let them exploit us any more. Profits go to the state. Which shares them out. You won't have to feed yourself at the field kitchen while Mr Director has five courses in a restaurant, and a young lady beside him. Everything's equal."

"The young lady too?"

"Obviously, Jörg." (They both have broad grins.) "We'll live like commercial counsellors for a good long while." They rocked themselves in pleasant thoughts for a while.

Jörg: "Is Marxism socialism as well?"

"All one and the same. Some say this, others say that. Marxism is all in books. We don't need to know about how they'll do the sharing, what jobs we'll get, and so on."

Jörg was flabbergasted. "Then I don't understand, why doesn't everyone join in."

Baptist gave him a shove: "Now you see it, my lad. Now you get the picture. Now the light's turned on." They lit another cigarette.

Then an alarm sounded, the big courtroom emptied, everyone rushed to the lower floor where machine guns and side-arms were stored. The XVII. Reserve Division had marched in, led by officers with shoulder flashes, cockades and swords, the troops following with strict discipline. The city noticed little of the danger that unfolded.

Noon came, evening. A struggle for the troops began between officers and revolutionaries. By early on Sunday (it's now 17th November) the sailors and soldiers had prevailed. The XVII. Reserve Division disarmed the officers, tore off shoulder flashes and cockades. The revolution showed its power, a victory was won. But what was it put to? O woe! Sailors and soldiers were brought together. Then sailors and units of the mutinous Division with their red and white armbands came together like lambs to man every security post in the city – for the bourgeoisie!

More troops, in loose formation or tight marching order, came flooding through Strassburg and on to the Kehl Bridge. Patrols ensured they would not be provoked by the display of tricolours.

But in Strassburg, after the triumph over the XVII. Reserve Division, it was a gloomy Sunday for the revolution. The Central Council had called for eight big assemblies at noon, under the headings World War, Revolution, Socialism. Soldiers and all citizens of Strassburg and environs were invited. They were meant to shape these assemblies into a powerful statement of the people's good cause. Posters were stuck up on walls and pillars, their red visible from afar: Sunday morning, 11 o'clock. The socialist press talked it up. But even here the stalwart were dismayed to find the proclamation elbowed by all kinds of everyday notices such as one sees in any run-of-the-mill town inhabited by people: New Butcher's Shop Opening in Metzgergiessen; Warm Winter Clothing at the Hoher Steg Emporium; and For Constipation Take Pentapills, at the Iron Man Apothecary.

Powerful statements! The city guarded itself with adamant frostiness against that which it did not want. Seaman Thomas, who could see what was coming, had to be dragged along. He swore: "I'm not going to any courtroom, don't want to, it's all a swindle, even Peirotes is going to speak." He was right, of course. He was forced to expose his impotence to the population. In the Choral Hall and the two theatres, yawning empty spaces, no need to unlock the doors. In the Eden Theatre a mere forty souls, mainly children, sent there to mock him. Totally empty Eldorado and Central Theatre. More attendees at the UT Cinema, where Rebholz was speechifying so as to keep in practice. He started off, the mighty socialist, with none other than Jesus Christ, who had also made world revolution. He concluded by exhorting the honest public to support the efforts of the Soldiers' Council to impede looting.

Tall Leading Seaman Thomas was dragged along to the Aubette. There he was faced with solid smiling citizens and a gaggle of powdered ladies who observed him with interest, some through opera glasses. The good-natured sea-bear stood glowering at the speaker's podium, behind a carafe of water. Since when did they plonk water down when he needed firing up to speak. But his friends encouraged him, it's no tragedy, our time will come, one day. Then he began to relate in general and in detail what it feels like to be a sailor. He gets about, never sticks around in a town or village, voyages over the ocean, and so it's only natural he's international. International, that's the broad view. There, he's stuck it to those bourgeois below the podium. So he let loose on the topic of Wilhelmshaven, and loud applause came when he reported how they were always treated, just because they're Alsatians, and how the fleet was to be deployed on 3rd and 4th November and how they'd given those officer gents one in the eye. To conclude, he turned to the French. Unfortunately they took a different view to him. But he, as a sailor and an international socialist, was under no illusions. Before a year's up, those Strassburgers who love to cry Vive La France will no longer be so full of joy. For Alsace will be a part not of a free German Republic, but of a capitalist and militaristic France. Now, you shouldn't drive a person to happiness with cudgels. Maybe you'd like to think it over. Alsatian is what we should be, and nothing more. That's bomb-proof. But gradually those rusty chains will be shaken off, and the Internationale will be victorious.

So, now he was done, he'd managed it. Because he seemed so pleasant in speech and appearance, the ladies and gentlemen applauded with gusto. Afterwards Thomas stood on Kleber Place and asked his companion, who's our old friend Bottrowski from Neukölln: "Do the kids here still fight with peashooters?"

Bottrowski laughed: "In the evenings."

Thomas: "We fired ours off at midday, at the Aubette."

"But you laid it all out to them so clear like."

Thomas: "Lad, lad. It's very nice in Strassburg. We are and shall remain Alsatians. But you'll see me here for just two more days. I will not stay."

"They'll say you ran off because of the French."

"Let them, they'll also say how we were stabbed in the back by the Swabs and Berlin. No skin off my nose."

They went down several alleys in the direction of Broglie Square, and entered a little shop serving food. A soldier was waiting for them. Thomas asked: "You were at the meeting?"

"No, Thomas, I wasn't." The soldier looked angry. Thomas: "I won't do it again, neither."

Bottrowski's face was back to normal, strong and fresh apart from a yellow bruise under the left eye: "When we got here Thursday, we thought now it'll all break loose in Strassburg."

"Me too."

Bottrowski: "Would have happened if it wasn't for the French. I'd swear an oath on it. But socialism can't compete with them, if you're bourgeois. They like their flags and uniforms and officers and medals. Patriotism. Hail to Thee in Victor's Crown, or the Marseillaise. The capitalists sit on top rubbing their hands."

Thomas: "Maybe I'll go to sea, merchant ship, English

or Dutch. I won't stay here, Bottrowski. When I saw that lot facing me at the Aubette today, I told myself it's no longer an option for Seaman Thomas." He clenched his fists. All three faces looked fierce. Bottrowski picked up his beer mug, they chinked mugs but uttered not a word. Bottrowski, after a pause: "I'll head to Berlin. There's things to attend to there, with Ebert, Scheidemann and Co."

Thomas wasn't yet so far along: "I can swallow the tricolour, but to have these officers traipsing around, and we'd got rid of them, and the moneybags back in charge again."

Bottrowski: "Come to Berlin. I have a particular account to settle with someone, a scoundrel called Heiberg, the lieutenant I took along to the Soldiers' Council, and the villain hoodwinked me and he'd shot two of our people."

"Cut him down. I'm off to Wilhelmshaven." And he looked at the other two soldiers, who said nothing: "Josef, you're Alsatian like me. Tell me, would you have thought it possible? What will they say to us, back in Wilhelmshaven."

STRAYS SWARM LIKE FLIES

The million-strong army tramping its way back was surrounded, as if by a swarm of flies, by a cloud of refugees, deserters, and individuals separated from their units. The huge murderous two-fronted monster had flung itself across a peaceful land. The fertile ground was not greatly put out at being ploughed for a brief while by grenades and bombs. The millions of corpses were a novelty, but the ground had means to manage the business, and took in without distinction men young and old, recruits and reservists, students, peasants. It welcomed them all, astonished that so many should come all at once. But it comforted the new arrivals, and scolded gently: you see what it was like for you up there, so settle in with me down here. And handled them all so kindly they soon forgot the horrors up above.

In settlements big and small, in abandoned and shell-scarred farmyards, in holes in the earth, in dense French forests, bands of stray soldiers and refugees had kept themselves alive. If you were to add them all up there'd be many thousands, and the longer the war went on, the more there'd be. Before the war none of these thousands had heeded calls for a general strike. What no thundering slogan, no political dictat, no pacifist teaching could set in motion was now achieved simply by the confusions of war. French, Russians, Germans, soldiers and civilians squatted side by side and put up a common defence – against war.

How had this urge become possible? Local authorities, military posts at high and low levels on both fronts were in a lather. Strengthening the military police had little effect. If now and then they collared some individual, or even a whole group of vagrants, month by month more came flooding. Every offensive increased their number. This was because in the course of years there was gossip about the war's prospects. Most, willingly or unwillingly, still obeyed the call-up order (how could anyone shirk), but the nearer many came to the front, the stronger the wish grew to be far away from it, and in the course of the fifty long months many found their wish granted. They turned themselves into a species of wild life.

The military police dared not approach those shell-scarred woods and isolated farms. There was a whole gamut of friends of peace, from those who merely hid somewhere in a village, maybe close to their own home, worked, made themselves scarce during inspections, to those who led a notorious bandit existence, seldom solitary, mostly in large bands.

In northern France there were impenetrable forests where outlaw gangs lived for long months of the war, some in groups of two or three, sometimes in bands of up to twenty. They were on good terms with the local civilian population. But some packs practised extortion on civilians, obtained food by begging among them. Then there were other bands who made clever use of circumstances and set up widespread networks that exploited their talents: as middlemen in black market trade. They would shift quarters and create formal organisations, and from their activities even staff officers and the families of troops behind the lines profited.

It was hard to track them down. In the forest some lived underground in well constructed burrows. They had learned to build dugouts, and camouflage them. Though as a rule military police and army patrols never ventured into the thickets, it happened now and then that a simple peasant who had some reason to avoid the open road would suddenly, all alone in the silent forest, feel the ground give way beneath his feet, and he would tumble flailing into a meters-deep abyss. And what kind of abyss? A man trap? No, not at all. He would tumble in among merrily squealing piglets and horribly cackling hens alarmed by the fall. And when the unlucky fellow had tried in vain for a while to clamber back out amid the animal chorus – a hard task, for the walls narrowed like a chimney as they rose, and widened greatly lower down, precisely the opposite of what someone trying to clamber out would wish – after a time, which might be several hours, someone would appear up above, a woman maybe, and then several men shining dark-lanterns down, and after some palaver they would lower a rope ladder and he could climb back into lovely daylight, mucky with soil and the droppings of hens and pigs. The people up there would observe him closely. Any who fell into the pit would likely already know about the outlaws, who would be stern or friendly as the case required. No one would escape without massive threats of penalties. But mostly the mishap would result in new business connections.

Once a butcher from Douai suffered such a calamity. He was an elderly man, with little enough butchering to do. In the interests of his children, every couple of weeks he looked anxi0usly about for livestock that would take pity on hungry humans. Glum and empty-handed, he was making is way one afternoon through the forest, he couldn't bring himself to return home like this, and took the diversion through the trees purely out of chagrin and professional antipathy to the military police, who strove to maintain human beings in a state of hunger. Then he tripped. And something happened he'd never dreamed of: he fell in among pigs. "Can it be possible," the butcher thought, "is this where people hide their goods and chattels? Is this still a human age?" It was pitch dark down there, at least for the moment. He was limited to ears and a sense of touch. There were chickens down there too. But where were the people they belonged to?

Slowly his eyes adjusted, and he gazed with delight on the riches at hand. He didn't mind the dirt and smell, to him they were nourishing aromas. But why did no one show up. The elderly man was reluctant to try climbing as the first option, but it might be half a day at least before the owner showed himself; the fellow would surely come to feed his stock.

Indeed, it had grown dark when finally, as he squatted in a fatherly way among the dear little pigs and good little chickens, he heard voices above, then there was a shout, ah, they'd heard something, then a dark-lantern shone down.

A man's voice said: "Oho, there he is."

"Just the one?"

"Yes. I say, what are you doing down there?" He spoke French.

"I fell in."

"What were you doing in the forest?"

"I'm a butcher from Douai, I lost my way, I was heading home."

"Butcher?" Now there was a burst of laughter up above.

Someone called down: "So you meant to acquire our pigs on the cheap."

"But monsieur."

"You're a burglar. We'll turn you in to the police."

"Let me out, monsieur, I'll explain it all to you once I'm up." The butcher wasn't at all nervous, he could feel the coins in his jacket lining. Someone called down: "Are you hurt?" The question seemed friendly enough, so he replied: "Yes, a little. My knee." A few minutes later, during which the lantern was withdrawn, the question came: "Do you have a gun?"

"No, just money." Now the rope ladder was lowered. He clambered happily up and was greeted by a mighty salvo of laughter, triggered, among other things, by the dreadful state of his clothing. It seemed to him, as he looked around at the circle of ten men (a woman was also present) that he recognised one or other as locals. He apologised if he'd caused any unpleasantness, described the accident, when questioned replied quite openly that he'd been scouting the district for contraband goods, alas without success. He would now like to enter into a business discussion with such good fellows. But now they grew extremely reticent. And to cut a long story short, he was informed, following a confidential discussion out of earshot, that he'd have to stay until tomorrow morning, around midday.

"Here? But where? In the muck?"

"No." There were enquiries about the amount of cash he was carrying on him; he named a considerable sum, somewhat rounded down. And in a satisfied amicable way he was informed they could do nothing more about the present situation without the presence of a certain two persons. They led him for ten minutes or so through the forest, suddenly plunged down some earthen steps, and were under turf in a room with board supports, tolerably warm but alas horribly smoky. Several other rooms adjoined, less warm but even smokier. They told the butcher that this room being a bit higher than the others, smoke was drawn into it. They regretted that they'd have to accommodate him in the last room, which was the highest, where two others were currently asleep. Well, he could console himself with the thought that who comes last eats last. The butcher complained: "A man could suffocate in there." They assured him: "We all have the catarrh, but no one's ever suffocated."

Next morning, lightly smoked but nevertheless well refreshed by his sleep after a solid supper, he crawled together with his two companions in sorrow, the newest recruits to the band, up from his bed of hay into the front room, a kind of communal living room. Wonderful coffee was served in real cups; six of them sat relaxed on benches around the table. The young female, not yet twenty years old, maybe eighteen, maybe even younger, fed the iron stove with damp logs, which were roundly cursed by all as the principal malefactors, i.e. smoke generators, but there's nothing to be done, they're delivered by Nature in that condition. They had red wine and cigarettes, provided on demand; the butcher noticed that the girl wrote everything down, it was run like an actual bar. Apart from an irritating cough, the butcher felt quite at ease.

The sense of ease was accompanied by the thought that his family must be dreadfully worried about him, the accident must have enhanced his value. He himself regarded it not as a deprivation of freedom, but as business pending.

As first the oven alone – then the others – finally he himself began to smoke. He grew curious about how they'd managed so wonderfully to have done with the war, for he found their situation exceptionally pleasant.

When he began asking, they were pleased to introduce him to a certain Scarpini. He wore a flat cap, once white, and played a leading role, not as robber chief, but as cook. He was a young man with a blond moustache in a cheeky face. He apologised to the butcher for the excessively squashed white hat, but showed when he took it off how it had been folded inside. "These rooms are so low," the young man complained, "but it is a proper chef's hat." He was glad to hear the butcher's confirmation.

He explained that for him the war had really been a kind of vacation. In his three years at the front he'd got to know himself really, really well. He'd really got his money's worth. Of all those he'd come to know in his battalion, it was he who took the biscuit. He'd been a machine-gunner. Before, he'd sat around like a stupid monkey with his parents on the farm, it was enough to make you a moron; but he only realised this when he went back on leave. Others in the battalion, his corporal, NCOs, lieutenant, were all amazed, what a remarkably diligent fellow he is, but he'd hardly been aware of it before. And now the ears of the horrified butcher were assailed by depictions of assaults, actions to defend trenches, each more horrible than the last and all delivered in an utterly matter of fact tone. Direct hits and indirect hits mentioned just for the heck of it. Scarpini and four others at their spray-gun, one time they're just standing there, all five of them, crash, they're all down, one's screaming, his legs are gone, the other three are just bloody smithereens that have to be shovelled under, right there and then, one was his best friend, and he himself had a scratch on his arm! "Sometimes it was too much even for me, how we were lodging there so close to the Germans. Finally we had a new lieutenant. Just what I'd been waiting for. He was proud of me. One day he called out Machine-gun Scarpini! and Scarpini was no longer there. The trench angel who'd been despatching the Boche to heaven had done a runner."

"Why?" the puzzled butcher asked. "If everyone scarpers, the Boche will eat us for breakfast." Scarpini happily concurred: "Unfortunately I had no choice. But first thing was, I couldn't stand that lieutenant, him praising me to the skies, it made me nervous, and in the end it seemed so stupid. There you sit in your hole, and you watch a little group approaching, they mean to take us by surprise, but probably they're just lost. So you let them get within fifty metres, if there were more of us we'd take them prisoner, then you bam-bam-bam away with the spray-gun, it only takes a moment and poof, they're gone. It was fun at first, but in the long run …" And the young man in the chef's hat made a courtly exculpatory gesture: "Can't do it. You have to find other things to do. Maybe with the very young."

He puffed away in silence. "Far as we're concerned, they can keep the war going as long as they like. And come to that, do you know why they're at war? Me too neither. But what's certain is there's more and more of us. Take a peek at Hans and Friedrich, my kitchen lads."

The two lads beside him were Germans, very young,

they expressed themselves in a garbled mix of German and French. One, Hans Gruch from Westphalia, honestly confessed he was no hero; he'd become separated from his company during an advance when he fell down a hole; Friedrich was already lying there in a dreadful state, howling and whining and his clothes mucky as always. It was a long story, how they made their way through and reached the forest. Friedrich told the butcher: "They always say Boche and treat us like robbers. How am I a robber? We were called up and sent off right away just behind the lines, we never had any proper training, and then they sent us forward. So why am I a Boche? The whole dirty business was nothing to do with me."

The cook smiled at him: "Friedrich, what does she say now, your mother? What are you now, actually: missing in action, blown up, deserter, in a mass grave, or what?"

"Who knows? Some of them lying there in our position, they'd bought it, and who was supposed to find out who they were."

"And your companions when you advanced."

"They all ran and threw themselves down, you can imagine. And no one was behind me."

Scarpini whistled: "Just think, Friedrich, someone was behind you after all, and saw you and your trousers." Friedrich, the young lad, began to tremble. Tall Hans butted in: "No one saw us. Unless it was a dead 'un. They was lying all around, some a good while already. They wouldn't betray us. And if they did. They'll never catch us. In my company only ten were left ..."

Scarpini helped himself to another glass of red, and sang: "That's how we live, that's how we live, day in day out".

At noon the two ringleaders appeared, everything was tucked out of sight, they studied the butcher and half

Citizens and Soldiers

an hour later came back looking serious. One ringleader was English, the other German. The Englishman dated from the time of the first great battles; the extensive secret organisation that smuggled men across the Dutch frontier had been unable to pass him on; and when Miss Cavell's centre in Brussels was betrayed he abandoned all hope. Because it seemed too risky to give himself up as a prisoner, and he had no stomach for hiding away in some big place with constant German checks, the smart angry man went to others in the forest and armed himself. That way they'd make it through more comfortably. When he had a chance to inflict damage on the Germans he did so, but only at first; concern for the group gradually made him more cautious. And little by little there emerged only one moral imperative: to exercise one's agency.

Meanwhile several groups adapted in very pretty and civil ways. The Englishman knew the butcher, of course, and it turned out they shared reminiscences of the families in Douai who had striven in vain to pass the man (he was from the Royal Engineers) farther up the line. The German ringleader introduced himself, a stout bearded apparition in his forties, he wore new officer's spats and a small worn hunter's cap. A new English macintosh was draped over his shoulders. Such macintoshes popped up in unexpected places, had their origin in a repelled offensive, stripped in the confusion of war from English dead and even from Germans; later the macintoshes turned up in third and fourth hands as contraband through peaceful trade. They served unstintingly to keep off the rain, always the same rain so deprecated in the camps of friend and foe alike.

"Well," said the butcher to Friedrich the kitchen lad as he made ready to leave (for it had all gone very smoothly) and Friedrich set a pair of crispy little sausages before him, "what would your mother say back home if she knew what you're up to here?"

"Why?" Friedrich was stung.

"Well, it's no hero's death."

Little Friedrich fell into a rage, and the Englishmen's brow furrowed in puzzlement to hear him splutter: "What you think of us. As if us Germans ain't human. My mum would rather have me back than not back. So only the French are real people, then."

Scarpini clapped him on the shoulder: "Don't fret, our baby boy. His daddy has a home-leave wound, that's what he told us. That's valid for the whole family."

The butcher had to pay an enormous bill for his stay! But nothing else happened. The adventure was nothing if not encouraging; for example he learned that people seek an exit from endless misery by whatever dubious means. As he strode down the road in the rain, he thought: if I had a son and they wanted to take him away from me or the Germans took him off to dig trenches, I'd rather have him here. That's for sure.

When, in absolute confidence, he told his wife about his adventure, he ended by saying: "Don't look so surprised. You'd talk different if they'd deported us, or I had to go and dig trenches for the Germans."

"But surely a Frenchman should …"

"A Frenchman should and a Frenchman shouldn't. There are brave men at the front. Don't worry about that. But there must be a place in the world for people who aren't brave. For sure everyone has a right not to be brave. The cook, that Scarpini with his little chef's hat, he told awful stories from out there. Shocks and explosions. Could you bear it?"

"But a man!"

"A man. A man is also human. Since when could a man

put up with just anything. I wouldn't put up with the shocks. And hold my bayonet at the ready and stab someone, no. I may be a butcher, but I couldn't do it."

She: "If everyone thought that, Maurice."

Now he was angry: "Enough of your nonsense. People defend themselves. But that doesn't suit everyone. For sure it didn't suit those at the front. So who's really brave, in the end? You women! Only you! You and your big mouths."

This failed to satisfy his wife. He: "You'd rather I was blown to kingdom come? Just say it."

She: "Calm down. You're here, aren't you, and we're content."

"Well then. We make a living, and go about our business." He sat a long while with his furtive red wine and told her of the robber cave, and as he went to bed he crowned his narrative with this declaration: "Of all those I've come across in this war, it's them I like best! And think of me what you will, wife: if I was younger and a war came and I could manage it – for it's not easy to find your way to those people in the forest – I would go to them." He thumped the table. "Yes I would!"

*

The gangs and bands in the forests, to which individuals from the towns still came, did much damage to the retreating armies. All those strays, deserters, were seized with a savage urge to action when the Armistice came. They wanted plunder, many thirsted for revenge. Many tried, and found opportunities at least on the German side, to mingle in among the gaudy hodgepodge of remnant units; and robbers, deserters, strays became quasi-legal once more.

GREETINGS, HOME SWEET HOME!

Towns along the Rhine awaited the returnees, decorated streets, bridges. Fathers, brothers, sons were coming home. They wanted to celebrate all that was still alive, returned from Hell, and celebrate the war's end. All who had dreamt of the glories of war, and now went uneasily about, perked up as their pride and joy (marching regiments, canon, tanks, machine guns, blaring music, flags) again filled the streets. There's still cause to rejoice, not all is lost. Others waited for what would feed the New that must surely come, for there is no state, all is adrift, on some days you seem to have fallen into a veritable bandit existence.

Others waited for what would feed the revolution, total revolution.

In Cologne a hundred schools were made ready to receive returnees, soup kitchens were set up in the streets. The magistracy deployed six hundred reliable men as a civil defence to support the police. The VI. Army came marching from the Belgian frontier.

Ahead of the frontline armies, rearguard support troops flooded south, east, north. What had so meticulously been set up by the General Staff and placed so deliberately in the rear of the frontline forces uprooted itself, rolled back to make way for the slowly retreating armies.

On 18th November the V. Army reached Trier, a hundred thousand soldiers came marching with their General von Marwitz at the head. Enormous jubilation in the town. Tears and joy. So all is not lost, after all. Workers held back. A fierce order was issued by the commanding officer: His soldiers showed brave faces to the enemy, they are entitled to find their route through the homeland unobstructed. He therefore requires unconditional obedience to his orders and decrees. "Good!" said some as they read the poster; others held their tongues, some went hm, hm, and continued on their way.

Mingling with the bivouacking soldiers, in the schools and food stations were people whose intentions were various. Nurses and society ladies offered coffee, beer and little sausages. Around the soldiers' soup kitchens, set up in the open, were throngs of poor women and many children, elderly men, begging for bread and holding out bowls. Those in charge tried to drive beggars away from station forecourts.

Soldiers strolling about town and enjoying the cleanliness and the decorated shop windows encountered comrades who had been back a while already, shell-shocked men with wildly jerking arms and heads, begging. Officers asked indignantly: "Is that old hurdy-gurdy scandal following the 1870 war to begin again?" Police checked papers, and hauled these men off the street; they were told it was undignified to beg, radicals must be stirring them up. There were commotions.

Leaflets were smuggled into the schools with broadcast messages from the Russian Soviet government to the Workers' and Soldiers' Councils: "Don't surrender your weapons! Don't be duped by talk of elections!" Anyone minded to buy a newspaper would find an indignant response from the government in Berlin (which, to the wonder of many, called itself the "Reich Government"): it viewed the radio broadcast as illegitimate interference in German affairs. Another official source augmented this response with a certain scorn, reporting that the Russian Soviet government had offered to send the new German People's Republic some shipments of grain, and had already despatched two trainloads of flour. The Russians, it said, had added that they could provide Germany with an ongoing supply from the rich grain-producing region of the Kuban. Well, this noble offer clearly stems from a benevolent motive (hm, hm), as we are pleased to acknowledge. Nonetheless it is doubtful whether the Russian Soviet government has control over said region. For in precisely the Kuban region, as we have just learned, a new government under Sazonov has been formed. Therefore, in order not to cause the Soviet government any difficulties, we prefer to decline the offer, with our thanks.

★

The first snow fell in Berlin on Monday. It didn't last long. By midday fog filled the streets, so trams had to drive with lights; the snow thawed.

From across the Channel the Northcliffe press shrieked: "Huns whimper for bread, No leniency for Huns, Germany will pay if the Allies keep their nerve." A politician, Arthur Balfour, raged: "Eleven days after their plea for an armistice, they torpedoed the Irish mail packet *RMS Leinster* near Kingstown, four hundred and fifty people lie dead, Germans have always been, and always will be, scoundrels." The voice of balladeer Rudyard Kipling shrilled: "A people with the heart of a savage tiger."

Each side totted up the numbers of dead and wounded and made public what they had kept concealed during the war. Each side acted as if it spoke for the eternally silenced dead. On the English side were 670,986 killed, 1,041,000 wounded, 350,243 missing. But many will die of the wounds which keep them still in hospital, and uncounted are the civilians who succumbed to wartime epidemics and whose lives will be shortened by the miseries and stresses of war.

The Germans revealed the scale of their calamity: 1,580,000 of their men are dead, almost four million wounded, 260,000 are missing. And here too nothing is said of the hundreds of thousands who died at home of wartime diseases, or the many thousands who succumbed to privations caused by the blockade, thousands have yet to die of their wounds, tens of thousands lie crippled or sit blind in institutions.

★

Fog condensed into ever thicker swathes in Berlin. It took on colour from the chimneys and turned yellow, like the air in London.

Lieutenant Maus landed up in this fog when he reached Berlin at midday on Tuesday. In Naumburg, immediately on arriving at the hotel to which they had been directed, he said farewell to his friend Becker. Becker was exhausted by the journey, and would spend a few more days in hospital in Naumburg. But Maus was expecting letters from Strassburg. "Don't stay too long, come back soon to Berlin," he urged Becker.

"Certainly, my son. And don't you betray me to my mother."

And Maus, down the steps like lightning.

Father and mother were both out when he arrived back at Dresdener-strasse. The maid said: Legation Counsellor's at the office, Madame won't be back till evening, she's visiting relatives in Steglitz. Maus rushed to his room: nothing. Desk bare. "Have there been no letters these past few days?"

"Two from Madame Maus to you were returned, Lieutenant. She was surprised not to have any word from you."

Maus sank into a chair. He couldn't believe it. The girl had indeed taken it badly. She hadn't forgiven him. Not one line.

GREETINGS, HOME SWEET HOME!

"Shall I prepare breakfast, Lieutenant?"

"Leave me alone." He threw his cap to the floor. She slipped out. He tore open his coat, shrugged it off, flung it down on the sofa. He paced about, filled with anger. It was too much. The liberties women take. How could Hilde presume? Letting him arrive home without a word.

He pulled open the door and shouted: "Bring breakfast." He sat stiff and livid as the table was laid in front of him. The maid was too scared to open her mouth. The lieutenant, vexed that his mother wasn't home to welcome him, ate and drank absently, his mind elsewhere. Then he went to the wardrobe and changed into civvies. "Law student Johannes Maus, shoulder wound," he said to the mirror. The arm was still useless.

★

But I, thought Becker in Naumburg, alone in his room, a nasty bare blue-papered unheated room – I'd do best to lay myself in a coffin. The war's over. I can't go on living, I can't, cannot.

And overwhelmed by everything he saw, and saw coming, he clenched his fists and ground his teeth. They should see me now, the people from the hospital, their god, their idol. His fists remained clenched, his teeth ground, and now his mood changed. Just let them see me, I will *not* be humiliated, I *shall* endure.

And Maus was hardly fifteen minutes gone from the hotel when the mood changed. At the hospital a surgeon and a neurologist visited him that afternoon, declared the findings at the site of the pelvic wound to be excellent, all treatment should continue as before, electrical stimulation, exercises, generally regain strength. Then he too would be able to live at home. "Much depends on your willpower,

Citizens and Soldiers

your tenacity, First Lieutenant." He wanted to hear nothing more.

One day after Maus (it's now Wednesday 20th November) Becker too was back in Berlin. He had given no prior notice. His mother opened the door.

He stood upright on the arm of the orderly who had been assigned to him at the station to carry his bags and his two crutches. The robust woman, who had a full youthful face, her hair still dark, stared at him from the doorway. Then without a word she pulled him into the hall, and fell to the floor.

"Help me to a chair, Scholtz, then lift my mother up. You can leave the door open."

He sat in the old-fashioned gaslit hallway, his mother, a dark kitchen apron around her waist, lay there on the floor. She was too heavy for the little orderly, he left her lying and went to fetch water.

So, do I want to, do I want to, Becker asked himself. He saw his mother lying there – I can do nothing about it; he felt no emotion – my feelings are gone, I can no longer feel, so I really have died. Then she stirred, the orderly sprinkled water. She sat up surprisingly quickly, unaided, said: "Oh god," and went into the kitchen to dry herself. Becker smiled at the orderly: "You've caused a flood with the jug. You must enjoy drowning your patients."

One arm supported by his mother, the other by the orderly, Becker made, as he put it, his grand entrance to his mother's house. They put pillows under him, sat him on the sofa; mother went off to fetch coffee ("real coffee," she said, eyes blinking sadly). Becker meanwhile chatted with the orderly, who showed himself a sensible man. He'd like to employ him now and then, as a companion, but it probably can't be done. "You're on duty at the station?"

"Only till two in the afternoon, First Lieutenant, and

GREETINGS, HOME SWEET HOME!

that sometimes changes. I'm a paramedic up north. If you like, I can come to the house, but I have no equipment."

This was good news. The man was hired, he was about to leave when mother came back in with the coffee tray. There were three cups; she glanced enquiringly at the orderly. He sat down with a will, and told of his son who was also on his way home. But the mobile troops would probably not be back till early December, after tramping all the way from France and Belgium. The coffee drunk, he took his leave. Mother escorted him to the front door and quietly discussed the timing of further visits.

As they did so, a cloud descended on Becker. His ears were stuffed with cotton wool; his head, close behind his forehead and at the temples, was emptied of all thoughts, and in their place came warm wafting air. His brow felt hot, his hands burned and seemed big and swollen. When his mother came back in she seemed to move through a mist. He knew this feeling: it was the Demon. He had difficulty following what his mother said. Soul and reason had been stolen away. Purely in order to say something and conceal his condition, this condition of utter emptiness, he asked his mother to help him to his study. She gladly took his arm. As they stepped slowly she put her right arm around his waist, her left gripped his left, and she led him safely through the doorway. "How big you are, Friedrich. Or I've shrunk." He gave a vacuous smile, she mustn't know the Demon has me, why has he taken hold of me just at this moment, just as I come back home, it's years since I last encountered him.

He sat on his writing chair, a kind of stool with a big wide backrest. She ran to fetch a thick green sofa cushion. To left and right on the desk were piles of books, on the blotting pad in the middle were letters. But he merely saw them. The Demon had him. He was like a fly sucked dry by a spider, sat there an empty shell. Fleeting thoughts passed through him – this much was he granted – he felt helpless, tried in torment to decipher what his mother was saying; she had taken a seat facing him and held his hands and looked up at him, and it seemed to him that he answered but without her noticing. He managed to ask her to lay him on the sofa for a few minutes, then he'd be all hers.

She gladly led him across, helped him out of his uniform jacket, pulled off the boots. He wanted to lie down, she ran off to bring more pillows from his bed and placed them in the middle of the sofa, she had a clear idea of what he needed. He lay down, she squeezed his hand, he heard her sobbing in the corridor.

It took the Demon a good half hour to be sated and fade away. This time he guzzled so heartily on Becker that Becker had to force himself not to whimper. To be just a shell, unable to compose a thought, to have no sense of who you are, hardly know your own name.

He was profoundly content when a cool weariness drifted across his eyes, over forehead and eyelids, and poured down his arms and legs. He was tired. He wanted to sleep. He slept.

He didn't notice when his mother came in an hour later, saw him lying, watched and watched him. That pale haggard face. What suffering has it endured. But he won't talk, doesn't write, wants no help, wants no one's sympathy, I know him. He almost died, he wouldn't let me come to him. What does it mean that now he's returned home. Maybe he senses that he's very ill and needs help. Friedrich, how he used to laugh, how cheerful he used to be. Everyone liked him. There he is, my one and only.

He slept, a little colour returned to his face. When she came back in he was lying on his stomach, head lifted, he looked at her. He sat up. All things had a voice again, a name. How good that things have a name.

To his mother (she was so happy at his tone, that old confident flirtatiousness, clearly he had slept well) he said: "Mother, I know from the Bible it all began when God created Heaven and Earth from a state of barren and empty uselessness. And then it goes on: He spoke."

Mother: "Right. And there was light."

Friedrich: "He spoke. And then there was light."

Mother: "Well, he is God after all."

Friedrich: "The lord God, the lord God, that's his problem: who can he show himself to, as the lord God? What means can a lord God employ? Would you, Mother, for example, if you found yourself in such a situation, worse than Robinson Crusoe, in a terrible situation, surrounded by nothing but empty wastes, in total darkness (don't stir the Demon, I've escaped him), would you know what to do, how to act? What would you do first, amid all this empty waste? Would it occur to you to ... speak? To say something? Open your mouth, form a word, and expect something to come of it? Voilà: God ... spoke! I'm not too concerned with what he said, only that he lighted on the notion of speaking. A magnificent event."

Mother: "I see that my son Friedrich would have done just the same, as a god."

He gazed at her thoughtfully. Mother, serious: "What is this, about the Creation?"

"How good that we have words to hang onto. You really can cling to words. And then Goethe has Mephistopheles mock: *In sum have words to lean upon, And through that trusty gateway, lexicon, You pass into the shrine of certainty*. As if it were a matter for mockery. There's something tremendous about the Word."

Mother settled into her armchair: "I never thought

we'd have such a good conversation on your first day home."

"You assumed I'd changed? Truly I had. It's just, at the moment I have no idea in what respect. Back there in hospital I knew for sure that I'd changed very greatly. On the journey back I explained it to my friend Maus in terms of Tristan and Isolde."

Mother wiped her eyes: "It makes me so happy to hear you speak like this."

"You've no idea what I'm going to say."

"Who is Maus?"

"Friend from the regiment, we shared a ward in the hospital. He took one in the shoulder, he's almost recovered, I guess it will always be stiff."

"Poor man. Let's be happy that you've both come home."

Now Becker leaned back, his eyes had widened for a moment, he spoke softly: "That's not how it is, Mother, that we're home so everyone can be happy that here we are again. It's good to be back. But what comes next is unclear. Only for those left lying out there is everything clear. But for the rest of us …"

"The war is over, Friedrich."

"Look at me, Mother, and tell me the war is over. It's not my wounds. I'm a hardened sinner, so the wounding had to come, to open my ears. The fact there *was* a war has not ended. Did you not go through it as well, Mother?"

"What are you saying?"

He covered his face with both hands. "The fact that there *was* a war has not ended. It's still going on. It should, it must go on. Mother, I sit here no longer the Friedrich I once was. And it's not just my legs."

"But I know you, Friedrich."

"And you call me by the same name?" She smiled:

"Yes."

So he made an effort to move a little closer. He smiled uncertainly. She wanted to help him; what he wanted was to hold her tight.

★

An hour later she brought tea and rusks, they ate and drank together, he laughed when she fed him rusks, really he'll eat anything, anything good anyway. He looked at her full of gratitude, she whispered: "My dear boy." After she cleared away she found him deep in thought, gazing at the floor. He said: "Here I lie and sit. I think, and I feel. Now I'm here. Here I lived and worked, before the war. Before the war. It's more than the war. Mother, I know that I didn't struggle against death month after month and didn't return home from the war, just to resume my old life. That's not granted me, as you can see. And even if my limbs were stronger, I couldn't allow myself to do it."

A nod: "I see that, Friedrich. None of us will live the same lives as before. But still."

"You're good, I know. I used to live like a butterfly. Touch nothing. Think nothing."

"Whoever did the thinking, if not you?"

"Touched nothing, thought nothing, knew nothing. Mother, we lie in an abyss. How can it all have been swept away, disappear like a puff of dust, everything that sent millions of us into the war and sacrificed and killed young and old, and it vanishes like a ghost at cockcrow, the Reich, the German Reich, the framework of our existence. I haven't read the papers, but I know enough. The Kaiser in Holland, the Crown Prince, all the princes gone, and a pack of people nobody knows sits in their place. And we, how are we to think of this? What an unmasking, mother."

"It's defeat, Friedrich."

"And not even the fact that millions are dead, and millions more maimed, kept them at their post. So shameless, and they were our mainstay, the framework of our existence."

"Friedrich, what were they supposed to do, after the defeat?"

He crossed his arms, and said nothing for a long while. Then he touched mother's hand: "What defeat do you mean?"

"Now. 1918."

"The defeat lies much farther back. I still haven't come upon the roots. One may be defeated, but one does not succumb, and not like that. It's an unmasking. They couldn't die, they feared death as much as any citizen. They didn't have the proper relationship to death and life." And after a while he added: "They were inauthentic."

Mother sat silent as he observed her. She was so happy to see, hear and have him here. She didn't understand him. He was tormented. Ah, he's ill, crippled. It will all slowly come better.

Bitterness, bitterest bitterness, when will you be my dear sister.

FUNERALS FOR THE REVOLUTION'S FALLEN

A fog lies over Berlin. A long street leads from the Linden to the Halle Gate, almost parallel to noisy dubious Friedrich-strasse: it's Wilhelm-strasse. In its northern part are elegant buildings, before it cuts across the crowded shopping street called Leipziger-strasse. Its southern part has come sadly down in the world, and as you approach the Halle Gate, wretched figures of the lower class step from buildings and stand in dark entries. The women and men who pass to and fro in front of the grubby buildings, what do they hold in memory: not Friedrich-strasse, they aren't well-scrubbed enough for that, rather gin shops, black marketeering, types who have reason to hide themselves away.

In one of the low buildings at the far end of Wilhelm-strasse, in a wide low room that looked onto the gloomy courtyard, a light still burned though it was morning. The landlady who sub-let this room and the adjoining living room to Herr Brose-Zenk could see through the frosted glass pane over the door that the light was still on. She thought of fog, the courtyard, but every time just uttered a contemptuous "hm". Either the fat pig's drunk and fell asleep without turning off the light, or there's a woman with him, and he needs illumination.

Herr Brose-Zink was in fact resting. He'd been gambling three nights straight till five in the morning, and luck was with him. Knocked sideways by the excitement he so cherished, knocked wonderfully sideways, he came by night cab from Fasanen-strasse to Wilhelm-strasse. He switched on the light, he'd snoozed in the cab, now he threw off hat and fur coat, boots. And then jacket, trousers, collar tugged open with force, and he hit the sack. In his thoughts he was still dragging on the big cigar that had just fallen from his mouth. He fell asleep.

Is the fellow dead, the landlady wondered in the kitchen. There'd been an incident two years before the war, a respectable gentleman had hanged himself in that room, he'd been with her only a week, some said debts, others some criminal matter. She left her turnips where they were, dried her strong hands, and stepped on determined legs into the corridor. She could handle any Brose-Zenk. If the man had got up to mischief there in her room, hanged himself or there were bloodstains, she'd land him one, alive or dead. She was in her fifties, she'd been attractive once, now she was mainly fat. She applied herself to baths and corsets, struggled to keep her swelling and ever more swelling body under control. She was so slim and elegant once, the darling of ever so many men. Her body was like a field that yielded nothing for ages, and then so much there weren't enough hands to gather in all the corn. She put an ear to his door, the ominous light still shone above. Was the fellow asleep, or dead? Eleven in the morning, we agreed a lump sum for lighting, this is going too far. She didn't listen for long, for a simple reason: all she could hear was her own snuffles, and she couldn't easily bend to the keyhole. She tapped gently, knocked harder, then ... hesitated. She couldn't bear to see a corpse hanging at the window. What to do? Go to the police. She knew a clerk at the Hegemann-strasse office, she sometimes consulted him about dubious tenants who turned up at her place during the war and might be spies, the police always welcomed such information. And ten minutes later she returned with the inspector, and marched on clacking soles along the corridor to her tenant's room. She pointed to the dreadfully mute pane of frosted glass.

The inspector stroked his moustache, cleared his throat, and knocked discreetly. No response. He knocked again, louder. No answer. Frau Kleinbart relished the moment. Now the inspector cleared his throat, shouted: "Herr Brose-Zenk," pushed on the door handle. The door opened all by itself. You could look directly to the bed. An object was lying on it. Must be Brose-Zenk. Not hanging, at least. But not moving either. Suicide or murder. The inspector spurred himself on. Suddenly ... the object shot upright, sat up straight. It looked awful. A man. He rubbed his eyes, his beard was tangled. One foot was booted, the other bare. The starched collar was open, the jacket crumpled. The cheeks showed different colours, the left, which he'd lain on like a block of stone, was striped red as from a lashing, the right had a more natural sallow hue. And then on the right, the legacy of two younger ladies who'd shared his winning streak the night before. So Brose-Zenk sat up straight, wiggled his big toe, and looked at the inspector, who, of course, he recognised at once.

"What d'you want?" he croaked, swung his legs off the bed and hunted for his other boot. The inspector bowed politely, their heads collided, Brose-Zenk's fault, but the officer begged pardon, handed him the boot, and said it was because of the light, people were concerned, especially Frau Kleinbart, and so on.

"That's all?" the mistrustful tenant asked from the bedside. "Absolutely," the inspector spread his arms, "at least, as far as I know. Your papers are in order, I suppose?"

At once, as if at a signal, Herr Brose plunged a hand into his breast pocket and pulled out a pile of crumpled banknotes in which his slim wallet was nested. He stuffed the notes into his trouser pocket. "You like flashing your money around," the officer laughed, and flicked through the pass. The woman stared at her tenant, eyes ablaze, speechless. The officer handed back the pass: "Well, let's be glad it was just a warning shot. And if you don't relish such visits, you'll turn off the gas in good time. Otherwise Frau Kleinbart will be calling the fire brigade."

The two figures stood whispering in the corridor, what sort of a man is he, how did he come by so much money, flashing it around like that.

Herr Brose inside at the bedside judged the whole thing a misfired ambush manoeuvre. Political, of course, everything's political these days. They want to ... steal his correspondence. The landlady's in on it. They're welcome.

His correspondence was in another location, where his name was not Brose-Zenk, but unhyphenated Schröder. He was grateful to the landlady for waking him, today was a big day, funerals for the revolution's Fallen, he wanted to take part as a peaceful onlooker. The fact is, Herr Brose-Zenk is a speculator, he needs to form a picture of what to expect from this revolution.

He had always stuck with the bourgeoisie – of course, where else was the money. The status of true war profiteer had eluded him. He had no access to big industries and the actual war-contractor business. And so petty dealings in foodstuffs, and the gambling to which he was also attracted. But now the dawn air is stirring, his hour has come. The mighty are cast down, the little man's on the rise. There's justice in the world. With such thoughts he dressed, or rather finished undressing. The crumpled suit was unwearable in its present state. He studied the dark suit with white stripes that hung in the wardrobe, it might be repossessed one day, seemed just the thing. As he washed he studied his face, bleary, sure, but with the wet beard it looks benevolent, trustworthy, humorous even, and don't I have imagination? He turned, face still covered in lather, to the table, where an illustrated magazine lay, on the back were medallions showing several members of the government, peoples' representatives and so on. I look just as good as those, he thought; all those councils, workers' councils, soldiers' councils. My mother wanted me to be a commercial counsellor; they don't yet have any commercial councils, I guess they could do with a few.

He changed his clothes, observed himself naked as he did so, admired his masculinity and good health – but without going overboard, for he enjoyed women, just as he ate a lot. His passion, though, remained the gaming table. And he had a friend, not very brisk, lazy even, who was like an offshoot of his, Motz, to whom he granted favours with the ladies who hung around him because of his luck at the table.

Eleven o'clock, my god, they'll already be gathering at Tempelhof Field. He had wagonloads of foodstuffs waiting in Holland and Bavaria, buyers already lined up, but it was all built on sand if there was turmoil here. As he went past, Brose gave a nod to the kitchen where the landlady was cooking, then on to Halle Gate, and Motz.

They took a taxi. Red flags waved from many windows. Belle-Alliance-strasse was black with people, common types, men in shabby army greatcoats. Brose-Zenk, stiff hat fixed firmly on his head, was a short solidly-built man with brown side whiskers trimmed to sharp lines, and thick lips not often visible; he would suck them whenever a memory or the prospect of some pleasure unconsciously popped up; his pale brown eyes radiated unsullied philanthropy.

Motz was a similar size, but beneath his coloured waistcoat was already the bulge of a pot belly. On his large head he balanced a black slouch hat that lent an artistic air. He looked down glumly in the open vehicle at the slush on his wet shoes. It wasn't the dirt that depressed him, but one of his bouts of hypochondria that he cherished and nurtured. He had recently heard of diabetes, and itchy skin was mentioned as one of the symptoms; he'd suffered from it for two weeks now, or more precisely his whole body itched. He sat hunched over himself, diabetes it certainly was, there were few enough cakes, sweet liquor was easier to find, he enjoyed both only with tightly closed eyes and a hasty prayer. All in all Motz, just like Brose-Zenk alias Schröder, appeared very different from what he was. When he removed the hat he revealed a huge bald patch, a forehead that rose like a tower leaning backwards, dropping down to the weakly developed bald occiput. There were bushy fronds of brown hair only over the ears and at the neck. But at the front, a nose like an eagle's beak jutted out of the face. The little dark eyes could radiate spirit and boldness. The face was completed lower down by a pale almost square expanse of cheek from which the chin jutted like a little apple. The opening below the nose and above the chin was a little mouth. And so stocky little Motz without his hat looked like a not quite fully developed Napoleon, or in any case like a man from whom great things might still be expected. He was lucky that way, many thought. For the first few weeks. After that he proved to be a total dead loss who misused his demonic grimaces, and quite clearly Nature had played a blatant deception on him.

The same trick affected his friend Brose. For ever since the war began, Brose entertained big ambitions, but the projects were to be brought to fruition by the coming man, bold swashbuckler Motz, e.g. the project to settle the innumerable war widows in a gated estate where they would provide a model for the whole of Germany, and more of that ilk. For some weeks Motz would have a contemplative air, seemed to be turning over big plans, then he'd come up with a ludicrous proposal: they should produce photos of war dead, reproductions and enlargements in available materials, colourise each photo, print a snappy inscription, and surround it with a green and gold laurel wreath. This would elevate drooping German morale right down to the smallest family, and bring in 50 Mark per photo. As there were two million war dead by now – they could include the badly wounded as well, provide a sort of consolation – even fifty percent coverage would bring in a hundred million Mark, and after deducting twenty percent for costs there'd still be eighty

FUNERALS FOR THE REVOLUTION'S FALLEN

million for themselves. This great work would embrace, in national economy terms, the paper industry, cardboard industry, printing, photography, the chemical industry, and all this, in conjunction with a heightened national morale, would bring a great boost to Germany. This was Napoleon. Still, Brose kept him on. You can always use a fellow with that physiognomy for some as yet unspecified business. Meanwhile, they became friends.

As they bounced along in the cab, Motz fiddled glumly with his hat, wondering how he'd get to the pharmacy this afternoon for another urine analysis.

These all look pretty good, Brose whispered to his friend as they climbed out of the cab at Tempelhof Field. They quickly pushed their way in. A big wooden stage had been erected, the substructure black, on it the coffins of eight victims. Fifteen had fallen in Berlin in the first days, only these eight now resting beneath wreaths were to receive a public burial at state expense. Lying there were a mechanic from Landsberger-strasse, the landlord of a bar, a toolmaker shot in Chaussee-strasse. A saddler and a worker had been felled in an Alexanderplatz firefight. A gas worker and a thirteen year old schoolboy took a bullet on Eichendorff-strasse near Stettiner Station. And finally a young female worker. Someone was already speaking, you couldn't see or hear him, deputations with wreaths were still pushing through the throng. Motz whispered: More than a thousand wreaths, marvellous funeral. A squad from the Marine Air Corps; a few men in civvies bore an enormous wreath donated by the Turkish colony in Berlin, on it you could read "To the Heroes of Freedom". Motz suddenly gave a start: "What are these people actually doing here?"

Brose, surprised: "They're just looking, same as you and me. What's your problem?"

"No, no," the scatterbrained and seriously diabetic Motz pulled himself together, "but the fellow up there ought to speak a bit more clearly."

Brose: "There'll be family members here as well, up front with the government."

Motz slumped back into his introspection.

A new speaker; people whispered: "Haase, the Independent." He shouted: "Never has a political upheaval been accomplished at so little sacrifice. The revolution is not yet completed. It is at its initial stage, and must be safeguarded."

Brose nudged his friend: "Watch out! It's one of them. He means socialism."

Black-draped drays drawn by four horses stood by the podium. Soldiers lifted the eight coffins onto them, laid the wreaths on top, they worked with great care. Music began to play: *Jesus is our Trust*. The crowd parted, and the procession put itself in order. At the head was an honour guard from the Alexander Regiment, then came a delegation of wreath-bearers, then members of the People's Government. Brose-Zenk and Motz had expected the latter, for the names were known not just to them but to workers, they were Molkenbuhr, Müller, Haase. Brose shoved his way roughly to the front to gain a glimpse of the new People's Government; in his agitated thoughts were *freight cars, my freight cars*. He had a better view than Motz, to whom, once the parade had passed, he turned his friendly almost radiant face. Brose stroked his beard: "So that was them. Got it."

At the corner of Belle-Alliance-strasse, outside the department store, Lieutenant Maus had planted himself. He was seething, wanted an end to the aggravations. Why, really, had he come so soon back to Berlin. He was tucked in behind little people, married couples chatting

FUNERALS FOR THE REVOLUTION'S FALLEN

in loud voices about some Max who was with one of the wreath deputations, Gustav's there with his employees, Karl couldn't take the day off today. And as the music drew near and the Alexanders marched past ("Our boys!" some voices crowed), individuals in the procession were pointed out. Maus was startled, and didn't know what came over him when he heard: "The one beside Molkenbuhr, that's Comrade Haase." This was said by a fat woman dressed in black to her husband, who puffed absently on his pipe and nodded complacently. Following behind the government, business enterprises came marching with black-bordered banners. The shields and ribbons proclaimed in huge letters: "Died for the Revolution", "Brothers, we thank you". When the fat woman read these out she sniffled and dabbed her eyes, even the men around her fell silent for a while. A shield was pointed out, borne by a group of young people with educated faces: "The Intellectual Proletariat". Maus was intrigued, his rage evaporated as he gazed on: "Becker should be here to see this. The whole thing's crazy. They look like students."

Maus was bewildered, as if he'd been poleaxed, the procession's so huge, no end in sight, the people seem peaceful enough, but there are so many of them, that's what's so terrifying, that these simple peaceable people, this horde of ordinary people, little men and little women, have come together here in public, on the side of revolutionaries. No dog barks for us, we're dreadfully dead, buried, six feet under. There in uniform are two French prisoners of war, they wave left and right, the crowds applaud, the clapping tracks the two Frenchmen down the street. A pack of Russian prisoners stumbled glumly behind. Even they were carried away by the mood.

The wide procession had been moving past for half an hour – once over the bridge it turned aside onto

Königgrätzer-strasse heading for Brandenburg Gate – and now trumpets and a drum tattoo approached, solemn music, heads along the street were uncovered, the four-horse drays with the coffins were approaching. Three coffins on each of the first two, two on the third. The white coffin was the female worker. Behind the coffins a column of sailors came marching, rifles at the back on leather straps, reversed. Death and the Avengers. This was the climax of the procession. All along the route it cast dread and horror over the people, this is what it looks like, the reason we're here, it's no ordinary parade and us merely gawkers. Watch out, this happens, you too can be struck down. And the menace, the sailors behind the hearses. The spell did not dissolve once the unsettling escort had gone past, it took a while before the deeply affected crowds came to themselves, and conversation started up again. The workers of Berlin came marching, members of electoral alliances, men and women, youth groups, troops from the Berlin garrison (but frontline troops were not yet back).

One marching band faded into the next, always the Internationale, the Marseillaise. Lieutenant Maus had stood empty-headed in the crowd; now he was stuck, unable to work his way out of the throng. Horribly outcast, time has rolled over me before I was even there. How can I come to terms with these little people. I haven't the faintest idea. Always the same lines blaring: *The Internationale unites the human race.* In the school hall we sang *Hail to Thee in Victor's Crown, Deutschland, Deutschland über alles.* Gone, the old times! I ... I'm the old times!

Always more bands marching. People shout, exchange signs of recognition. Then a very old man comes along, alone, white-haired in a grey loden coat, black threadbare slouch hat on his head. The gaunt little man holds a flag on a short pole. Strange colours, black-red-gold, must be the colours of the 1848 March revolution. Here and there people point to the little old man, his parents were proscribed, they took part in that earlier revolution; he marches sadly, slowly; at Brandenburg Gate they'll sit him in an open horse-cab, he's witnessed a triumphant revolution, people call out, wish him well; ah, he no longer has a heart for rejoicing.

★

The two friends Brose and Motz set off in a cab ahead of the procession, in order to arrive in good time for the burials at the little cemetery of the March Fallen in Friedrichshain Park. Motz wondered why Brose kept urging the driver on, he was forced by road closures to take a roundabout route. Motz had no desire to visit the cemetery, he was superstitious: "For God's sake, no one should go to a cemetery of their own free will. It's not healthy."

Brose: "I cannot accept that argument. The Stock Exchange is unhealthy as well. No doubt you have an appointment with someone. Who is it, please?"

"You don't know her."

"Blonde, brunette, black?"

"I don't know."

"What's that supposed to mean?"

"Dyed, titian red, she says."

Brose stared at him in disgust: "You'll take good care, understand? I've warned you often enough about women with dyed hair."

"Brose, I can look after myself."

"Haven't you had enough trouble with dyed women?"

"And with naturals, Brose."

"Dyed women are spies." And he related the events of

Citizens and Soldiers

that very morning. "The police forced their way in. How do I know what lies behind it. Today, you will not see her. Understand? Does she have a telephone?"

"She's waiting for me, we're going to eat together."

Brose, peremptory: "I'll call her." Motz sighed. He was in a dreadful state of dependency.

Brose managed what many would have found impossible: he gained admission to the over-full cemetery thanks to his shameless bearing and the insolent way he flashed a pass. Barth had given a speech by the open graves, Luise Zietz also. Both swore allegiance to the Fallen.

And now several wind instruments began blaring. Their mournful tone suggested they didn't really believe any of it.

Karl Liebknecht, the new People's Tribune, emerged from the forest of red flags.

Motz stood there dopy and irritated, nervous too because it was a cemetery, albeit, as he consoled himself, for people who died a long time ago. Brose-Zenk clutched, nay clawed at his arm when Liebknecht began to speak. From where they stood, separated from the graves by a sea of people, they could look right at the speaker's face. And when this Liebknecht began to speak, it was at once a very different matter from those who'd gone before. Flagbearers hoisted their flags proudly and as one to greet their leader. The rumble from the throng of voices outside subsided, there were cries of "Quiet! Liebknecht!" The cry "quiet" rippled outward; everyone must know all the way to the Schlossplatz that Liebknecht's about to speak. Now, without loudspeakers, across a whole web of streets, half Berlin is to be addressed.

The People's Tribune is a lanky man with a pale restless face, his eyes, bleary, turn from side to side never resting on anything; the dark moustache droops uncombed over

FUNERALS FOR THE REVOLUTION'S FALLEN

his mouth. Now and then the still youthful man grinds his teeth in a kind of perpetual fury and outrage that prevents his thoughts from cohering. He seems to be the only one at the cemetery who does not realise how the throng hangs on his every word. He speaks loudly, with vigour, in irregular bursts, and at the same time croaks and often stumbles.

Shrill as a song of vengeance and victory was his opening:

"The Hohenzollerns hoped to parade victorious at the war's end through Brandenburg Gate. But instead the proletariat intervened. The Hohenzollerns ran away, every throne in Germany was overturned. These lordly beings and their cowardly hangers-on are now nowhere to be seen, they have slunk into their mouseholes. They dare not, these generals, these cabbage Junkers, dare not stand before us and account for themselves, with good reason, the exploiters, the bloodsuckers, parasites on the poor toiling workers from whose sweat they have lived and who have now shaken them off and squashed them underfoot. The time of mass murder is past, the game is over at last for the criminals on the throne; covered in contumely and shame, cursed and hated by the whole world, they have fled away condemned, pathetic, along with their blue eyeglasses, those incorrigible bloodsuckers. Even into foreign parts shall the hatred and curses of the starved, murdered, bludgeoned people pursue them."

The People's Tribune wore a black frock-coat that hung on him loose and wrinkled. His nervous head, the hair on it drifting over forehead and ears, turned with these last phrases up to the grey sky; it was to this that he screamed his rage. Now the man ground his teeth and surrendered to his spleen. A curious unrestrained hatred had ignited, a mere dram of this hatred. Why did they listen

Citizens and Soldiers

to him with such enormous excitement? Because he was no orator, because as he spoke he was not addressing them, because he was only giving expression in their presence to his grief, but it was genuine emotion, a torrent of grief, and as the torrent swept downhill it carried them along, and who after such a war did not bear within themselves bitterness, anger, hatred. Ah, those times of impotence are gone. We shall be raised once more to the heights of humanity.

Now Liebknecht crossed his arms and gazed into the open grave at his feet.

Dark holes. Now it was not about princes and mass murderers. Now it was the turn of the dead, the Fallen. He would sing a hymn to their courage. But he tendered them only a few words, his voice low, as if embarrassed to address close relatives in front of so many people. "There you lie, you've shown what you are. The blood that flowed from you is our blood. They shot you, they shot us. Everyone should know it, and know that we feel the agony of these wounds. Accept our thanks, friends."

Already his eyes had lifted from the dark embrace of the graves, his eyes bored into the red of a flag in front of him, his arms travelled through the air:

"Their agony shall not be forgotten. We know what the target was of the bullets that hit them. The awakened proletariat was the target. The murderers had not yet had enough. They flailed away on every front, they threw the people's property out of every window, squandered the people's energies, exploited everything to the hilt in order to triumph, in order to force upon the world their insolent wicked yoke. The whole world rose against them. In the end, when all was lost, they murdered you to save themselves. And even now they do not stand idle. They have accomplices and supporters in places where none would have expected."

Now he yelled, lifted his shoulders, cried out with arms stretched high; it seemed he was trying to lift himself off the ground: "Conspiracies are in train to disrupt the dictatorship of the proletariat, place it once again at their mercy. After such defeats, after such crimes the murderers and assassins still have the gall to forge new schemes, and find accomplices. Their conscience has not awoken, and they know how to befog the conscience of others who are in league with them. We shall block their path! Be on your guard! Comrades, colleagues, friends! Using every means, even by putting our own lives on the line, we must fight for the revolution."

The coffins were lowered, sailors with rifles lined the graveside, a triple salute rang out.

It was dark, the cemetery began emptying as wreath deputations were still arriving. The huge procession that had surged up from Tempelhof Field pushed on to Brandenburg Gate, where it dispersed. For hours the Internationale resounded across Königstor Plaza.

BLUEBOTTLES AND CORPSE-ROBBERS

Not a cab could be found until Brose and Motz reached the exit to Landsbergerstrasse, level with the Georgenkirche. Alexanderplatz was jammed with a flood of people. The cabman, attempting to head west, turned round to them in despair: "There's nothing doing here, gents, and Münzstrasse's no better."

"Alexanderstrasse."

"Can't get past police HQ, they say it's barricaded."

"Go where you like," Brose cried, and banged the little window shut. Motz, glad to have the cemetery and

Citizens and Soldiers

the speeches behind him, said: "What's the point. I'd like to know where we'll find a hot dinner today, between four and five in the afternoon."

"We can find a hot meal anywhere! Don't turn your hair grey worrying."

Brose whistled angrily, fists at his beard as if he meant to tear it out. With great difficulty the cab made a U-turn, they diverted into a side street, found themselves on Schilling-strasse, Blumen-strasse, turned off towards Jannowitz Bridge. Down there flowed the gloomy Spree, a grey-black narrow channel between grubby buildings, past tall unsmoking chimneys: dumb, broken Berlin.

Brose-Zenk unleashed his vexation onto harmless Motz. "Ha! What d' you say now about this business? Will they set Berlin ablaze tomorrow, or are they just pretending?"

"They won't set Berlin ablaze just yet," Motz trilled; he tried to light a cigarette but Brose prevented him: "Don't light up now, our entire existence is at stake. Answer me."

"I've heard Liebknecht lots of times. He always talks like that. That's all I know."

"And?"

"What?"

"If he actually does it, if he sets the place on fire? What then? Did you see the rage in the man! And they were marching for hours! And listening to him, that arsonist, that Nero. And we're supposed to keep calm."

Motz seemed not to care. Brose nudged him: "Who do you bet on? Liebknecht, or who?"

"Who do I bet on? I don't know. Liebknecht could be a good bet. Why d'you like gambling so much?"

"Let me worry about that."

"Liebknecht might well be a good bet."

"That he'll set Berlin ablaze?"

"No, that he'll do nothing. He'll do nothing, Brose, trust me. He won't set anything ablaze. He won't cause any damage."

"But he can talk."

"That's true, he can talk. And how. The others too. Don't let it bug you. They're happy enough to wave their flags and have their marching bands and be able to print what they like. And why shouldn't they be allowed to, after the long war? They're not getting any more to eat, but at least they can let off steam."

Brose was fascinated: "So that's what you think?"

"Flags and marching bands, yes indeed. For the rest" (He whispered, they were riding on asphalt, the cabby might hear) "if their lovely Kaiser had won the war they'd have been ecstatic, and instead of the Internationale all you'd hear in Berlin all day long would be 'Hail to thee in victor's wreath, with your horrid herring breath' and the same Tom Dick and Harry would be out in the streets with their flags and drums, marching along. It's just that a different lot would be giving speeches."

"More pleasant speeches, I think."

"I wouldn't have paid them any more attention. Brose, why do you let these people get to you? If their Wilhelm had won, you'd be bragging along with them. Now they relish his downfall, and blame him for the mess, and curse because they can't get their hands on him. How on earth will it affect anything? Nobody has a clue. So off they go marching and think: now the world will see, we'll give it a piece of our mind. And when it's all gone up in smoke they march and Barth and Molkenbuhr and that Liebknecht have to make their speeches."

Brose eyed his friend thoughtfully: "Go on."

"It'll all calm down again."

"You're an optimist."

"On the contrary, I'm a pessimist," said Motz, sticking a cigarette between his lips regardless. "Sorry, but after two o'clock my stomach can't hold out any longer. A pessimist, because what will come of all the marching and speechifying in the end? Today's Wednesday the twentieth. They started their revolution on the ninth, and you and I are running around as free as we were on first November or first October. That doesn't fit the notion of revolution. If I was a revolutionary, people like you and me would be the first behind bars."

Brose, outraged: "Why me?"

Motz responded in falsetto: "Why me? Why you? Why? – Me, because all through this war I've been a layabout, a parasite, and because I felt no compunction to make any effort at the sight of the dreadful misery around me every day. I steered well clear of it. Because I respond with fatalism to the collapse of the Reich. Brose, you know I'm telling the truth. It's how I am. Here we are in a cab. Later we'll have a meal together. I was just as content yesterday, happy by the hour. It won't do. They would have to arrest me for being a parasite. And you …"

"Now, why me? Anyway, when these workers stroll around all day, going on strike or attending a funeral, doesn't that also count as doing nothing?"

Motz: "I'd certainly count them in. But they do work, though, now and then. Still, you'd be on the arrest list, first because you let me go on being a parasite, that's a crime against me, you should be educating me to become a conscious member of human society. And secondly –" he waved his outspread hand slowly back and forth, his expression ambiguous, "because" (He whispered in Brose's ear) "you're a black-marketeer."

Brose chuckled: "It's in God's hands." Motz: "Amen."

While the bluebottles buzzed away in their cab, the

sombre procession was still rolling along Berlin tarmac. Countless throngs jammed the pavements and crowded at windows. The black solemn menacing procession came past like a giant stock-pot whose aromas they inhaled. For this was a mighty city, stretching many kilometres to all four points of the compass, with long lines of streets rich and poor, full of buildings decrepit and new, innumerable grey rental barracks and their associated dark courtyards with side-wings and secondary structures. Factories and workshops, shops, department stores, slaughterhouses, dairies had grown up here. Gas mains, lighting cables had been laid across the city, water mains and sewers linked the buildings. Underground trains, trams, motor buses sped ceaselessly in all directions, telephone lines connected people of distant neighbourhoods, they could hold conversations without leaving home. Gradually they had brought forth what it means to be a big city, through heavy toil, tenacious striving; their restless industry created it under their hands. For they toiled, toiled beyond measure, knew only toil, wanted only work, thirsted and hungered only for work. When natural hunger and thirst intruded it seemed like an interruption, they dealt with it and went again about their work. When no work was to be found they loitered disconsolate. They dreamed of earning money. Many yearned for honours, for luxury, and this was the primum mobile for work. To whip themselves on and because they had no idea what their problems were, they rooted around in the clamour of newspapers that brought them irritations, hatreds, grudges, now and then fun, malicious glee. They went to the cinema and allowed themselves to imagine love, beauty, adventures. In the street they came face to face with prostitution. They sat in a circus where boxers knocked each other down.

In their thousands now they formed an honour

guard along pavements and watched saucer-eyed. The majestic giant beast that was the public, the wide-mawed lindworm crawled past them, led on by music. They had experienced the howling flag-waving giant called War; this new monster they regarded dubiously – a revolution that looked so much like war.

★

Strays, deserters, conscientious objectors gazed upon these events. They dared emerge once more into light.

Hans Bruch, a Westphalian in a greenish worn-out soldier's uniform, stood at Halle Gate not far from despairing Lieutenant Maus. Hans had been knocking around with two others, first in Liege, then in Krefeld, where they came across some men they knew. Then, when revolution broke out, they fluttered like moths to the light. On to Berlin. In those first weeks they had their work cut out to find food and drink. Big posters urged everyone with no business in Berlin to leave the city, go into the countryside, the city cannot feed you, in the countryside you can find jobs and wages. The three of them knew all about those jobs and wages and had no appetite for them, the last thing they were looking for was a life of carting dung for some common peasant, and digging potatoes. The revolution appealed to them, several times already they had hurried to a barracks to hear Liebknecht – maybe he'll make sense of it. But soon, please! You can't go on waiting too long, else you'll croak on the bloody Berlin paving, or bash someone to death. Which was the most probable outcome.

This was Hans Bruch's opinion too, after he'd stood freezing for an hour with the other two at Halle Gate: "No point standing around here. They'll be marching another five hours yet. What are they thinking of." The second man, fiercely: "No good will come of it."

Bruch: "I must make an announcement on behalf of my legs. We must find something hot for our stomachs. But no begging."

"So I don't know how, then," the second man said. "Nor me," said the third, "I'd rather stay here, maybe something'll turn up."

Hans: "Nothing will turn up, unless you stick your hand in the wrong pocket – but you won't come into a fortune on these streets."

So our pilgrims wended their way through the city to Weber-strasse, where they knew of a little bar. In a back room a handful of Spartacus people were holding a meeting, most wore army greatcoats, sat at beer tables and harangued each other with contrary views. Two intellectuals were there as well, they urged caution, whispered among themselves, one was Russian, he was their great white hope, for only from Russia could salvation come, with Russia it can be done, without Russia we're doomed. And they whispered about news, promises, about intercepted letters from the Reich government, about a threatened putsch by the right. The second man muttered to Hans Bruch: "Why've you brought us here? We'll starve before they make it that far." The third man was of the same mind. Hans asked: "You have a better idea?" The two younger men dragged him out, and as they passed the church on Weberstrasse they let loose with a broadside on the bletherskites back in the bar. Hans observed: "Out in the trenches, if we'd spent as long as those fellows expecting an attack and given away all our plans, they'd have finished us off in a month, and you'd not hear another peep from any of us."

"And they run around," raged the second man, "with those donkeys, those spectacled eggheads." The third man:

"Eggheads are always the dumbest. How anyone can take them seriously I've never in my life understood."

Hans impatient by the church: "So what's to happen?" The second man whispered in his ear a word he'd heard in the bar: "expropriate".

Hans, annoyed: "Don't be stupid. Where do you want to eat? You want to line up again at the soup kitchen and play pat-a-cake?"

But the second man knew what he was saying. In the bar he had made contact with two other men, West Prussians whose home towns back east had been destroyed; now they were looking to make good in Berlin. These men of "direct action" had formed brand new "expropriation groups", with headquarters in changeable locations around Silesian Station. They promised themselves nothing less than the immediate destruction of society, or some such. A few sailors had gravitated to them.

That evening, while the huge procession of mourners had still not come to an end and meetings to stoke up the fires were being held all over the city, Hans Bruch, his two friends and five other men drove in three cars, rifles on their backs, first to a jeweller's in Spandau-strasse and then to a wholesale butcher's. Both businesses being closed for Sunday, they at once went to the owner's apartment and put into effect a well-laid plan. They wore black masks and thick leather gloves. Once the door opened to their polite knocks and rings, they identified themselves as the "Henschel Revolutionary Committee", showed a piece of bumph one of them pulled officiously from his belt. Then they cut the telephone wires, and forced the jeweller to hand over a massive pile of watches, rings, bracelets, for which they provided a one-line receipt with an illegible signature in the name of the Committee. The butcher had to go down to his cellar and haul up meat, bacon, ham and sausages. He too was provided with a piece of paper in the aforesaid manner. Family members were meanwhile kept closeted in a back room. They were warned severely against opening a window, they'd be shot at once. So they understood what revolution meant. Quick as a flash the intruders were gone. The few people in the street who saw the cars and the armed men shrank timorously back.

★

The cab bearing Brose and Motz jolted along dark streets that kept a dumb diabolical silence. Hardly any street lamps. Brose was feeling more and more relaxed about the afternoon. He settled back and embarked on the solemn intricate procedure of lighting a cigar. "Pah. They come up with all kinds of slogans because there's nothing else they can do. Vultures, corpse-robbers and what have you. They should turn their minds a bit more to surfacing the streets. Capitalism is rotten, on its last legs, they say. So we're in good company, Motz. Criticising is so very easy in these stormy times. But where can you find enterprising natures, actual entrepreneurs who can take the necessary steps so that we can make progress? They have to stir up the right forces. The way ahead is clear. If nothing's done, we'll have chaos."

Motz proffered a light. "Havana? Way beyond my means."

Brose: "Not everyone can have everything, and it's not every day I have one. A complete conceptual muddle has taken root."

Motz: "The masses. The masses are wading in."

"Nail on the head. Once they'd have called someone like me a condottiere. Now they say black-marketeer. You supply food, coal, foreign currency, and that's all the thanks you get."

Citizens and Soldiers

"Sadly, you only supply the well to do, Brose."

"Pah," Brose exclaimed, "quite right. Am I supposed to give money to the poor so they can buy the food I bring in with so much trouble from Holland, from Denmark? I'm not a famine relief agency. They should turn to the state. *I* can't make anyone well to do. Unfortunately."

"It seems they want to become well to do through violence. I freely admit, if that was my purpose I wouldn't be going to church."

They laughed complacently. Brose: "There you have the mass mentality, life size! An individual like me – like you – takes another path. The good thing is, as I saw today," (He whispered in Motz's ear, the cab was rattling) "they always rely on somebody else. On their songs, and their flags." He chuckled: "Just think if I had to rely on you in my dealings, and you on me. Anyway, I worked in the Commissariat, army administration. And if this wretched humpus-rumpus hadn't come along, I'd have a Service Cross or similar in my buttonhole. Some there are who even flaunt an Iron Cross."

Motz: "If I was a revolutionary, I'd string you up for the very same reason."

After endless snaking through dark streets they arrived in Prinz Albert Strasse behind the House of Representatives. Now the cabbie swore. He whipped up the nag, there were loud voices, a stone rattled against a window. A shout: "Out! If we walk, so must you." The two men inside cowered together, the cabbie roared, they were dragged out. Brose and Motz stood in dim light amid a small crowd of men with a big red flag, clearly an offshoot of the march.

"Smash the swells!" "Exploiters!"

Motz laughed in the faces of the men shaking their fists at him: "I'd like to see the man I've exploited. You must all be mad. Let us go on our way. How's the cabbie to earn a living."

"Smash him on the snout, make it a real humdinger."

Motz already felt a shove at his back. "So you pay the cabbie now, and then quick march, shitbag." Brose, all of a dither, paid, he had to cover the cracked window as well. Then they were free to go on. When they looked back from the corner of Königgrätzer-strasse the cab was still surrounded by the crowd, the outraged cabbie was trapped in endless debate, he swore at them, they tried to lecture him.

And so the two men trudged across Potsdamer Platz and took the tram to Bülow-strasse. There Brose lived in a not very lordly building under the name "Schröder, Financing". An ancient maidservant opened for him. Behind the office was a kitchen with small side rooms. Brose wanted to eat, they sat in the living area under a gas flame side by side on a wide sofa that clearly did duty as a bed. They said nothing until Brose suddenly declared angrily that the procession had brought him no farther forward. The broad masses of the people look good and instil confidence, but that Liebknecht. Motz said as he ate: "You shouldn't stake it all on one class. We of course belong to the better classes on whose behalf you are active, and they pay you. Me too, indirectly, through you. Otherwise I'm an impoverished petty bourgeois, ruined by the war. And finally I've recently rented a plot in the garden colony, we've formed an association of small peasants and agricultural workers, and if needs must I shall let myself be elected as peasant representative."

"Not bad," said Brose, astonished. "But me? My freight cars?"

"I shall obtain passes for you from the revolutionaries." Brose: "Really?"

"True as I'm sitting here eating tender roast lamb, alas

without sauce."

Brose shouted: "Augusta, bring some sauce, but hot."

Motz, chewing: "The maid's a good cook."

Motz even had to accompany the restless Brose-Zenk to the gambling club in Fasanen-strasse, for no other purpose than to listen to Brose and add his two pfennigs worth. It was in an elegant private apartment. They were greeted by a middle-aged lady with a martial aspect and a raffish moustache, and presented to the gentlemen already standing around reading or chatting. Brose knew them all. Motz thought at first it was a brothel. But Brose, as he confided to Motz, was tonight after an important personality who sometimes came here to gamble, a newspaper man who had contact with another who for his part stood in an excellent relationship to the present government. And that man must surely know where matters are heading. "Why should he?" Motz whispered. "Maybe not even Ebert knows."

Brose shook him by the arm: "Your confounded scepticism. Don't let it spoil you. Our very existence is at stake, I tell you! Either Ebert or the Kaiser or" (a groan) "Liebknecht. Nothing is certain. How can we find our way out of this. I'll be ruined overnight if they seize my freight cars at the Dutch border."

"You said yourself, money's losing its value. Meanwhile you're still earning."

Brose blocked his ears: "You say earnings, and I see it all melt away. Where on earth has Schneider got to?"

"Who's Schneider?"

"That's the editor's name."

And here he comes, waddling along, looks pale, faded, old, small, like a sleepy infant with his bald pate, you really feel like putting him to bed. Brose made haste to greet him. The gaming must have started, for no one was there apart from two gentlemen reading and the lady with the raffish moustache. Brose introduced Motz to the editor: "My friend Motz, chief steward on a Brandenburg manor, farmers' representative."

The editor made a gesture of respect: "Ah, you're here for the Farmers' Congress. You must let me know what happens, the peasant question could be decisive."

Motz at once began: "We complain particularly about feedstuffs, fodder material."

The editor was in a hurry, but Brose held him tight by the shoulder: "Esteemed colleague, were you at the funeral?"

"So who's died now?"

"At the March Fallen."

The weary man wailed: "What do you think. I've been on my feet all day just for that. Spare me the evening, my dear sir. But what do you think of Liebknecht?"

"Yes, what do you think," Brose whispered in great excitement, "is it true, is he like Lenin?"

Weary editor: "We need a strong hand. Maybe he's the one. Letting such a man out of jail. He's an entire enemy army." (He whispered, looking at the floor.) "'Beat to death!' He's crazy. A fire-raiser, belongs in a loony bin."

Brose, enthused: "You think so? And what about events abroad?"

"The people want peace." The weary man's every pocket was stuffed full of newspapers. He fumbled and wriggled and pulled out a great big paper, foreign format. He glanced around, the room was empty, even the lady had disappeared, he led Brose to a tall bright standing lamp in the smoking corner. "Listen to this," he wailed, and put on a pair of horn-rimmed glasses, "he has foreign support."

"Russia, Moscow."

"No, the Entente! Last week Ebert did something

Citizens and Soldiers

really clever. In the name of the government he asked the USA for aid, food shipments. Here's the text, it's so clever, it's in French, *Le Temps*, I shall translate: 'The German Government requests the government of the United States to inform the German Reich Chancellor by wireless whether he can count on the readiness of the United States to despatch foodstuffs to Germany, on condition that order is maintained in Germany and a fair distribution of the foodstuffs is guaranteed.'"

Brose: "That's right, that's right, he's thinking of the poor."

"Of course. And now listen to the Entente's version. *Le Temps*: 'The formula was suggested to Wilson via the Reich Chancellor. When Herr Ebert offered to present the conditions to his fellow citizens, he was not only thinking of caring for his country, but was also seeking to secure the position of his government. He intended to say to his colleagues from the minority fraction: we shall receive food aid if you allow me to maintain order. With the greatest firmness, President Wilson (who was in principle willing to accede) – President Wilson had no intention of delivering either to Herr Ebert (well well!) or to Herr Solf or to Herr Erzberger such a dreadful means of coercion. But it will be astonishing if the Majority Socialists and the former servants of Wilhelm II do not make haste, with their accustomed lack of honour, to exploit the response given them so frankly by President Wilson.'"

Brose: "In that case probably Liebknecht should do the distribution. And of course there's the fact that they're capitalists themselves, the French."

Schneider removed his glasses, and flourished the newspaper in despair: "The people over there have no idea. They don't know Ebert. Of course he held his nerve through the war and didn't betray Germany to the Entente, but he hates revolution just as much as the Entente do! Everyone who knows him knows that."

"You know him?" Brose asked, awestruck.

"Known him for a long time. You can depend on him." (He whispered in Brose's ear.) "Even the Kaiser said, when things were getting dicey: I am prepared to work with Herr Ebert."

Brose: "Just imagine. Wonderful."

"So there's your proof. And now they slander him." He stuffed the paper back in his jacket pocket. Brose wanted to ask if Ebert was strong enough, if he had enough troops, but the editor would be detained no longer, he'd just wanted to speak from the heart. He hurried to the gaming room. They rushed after him like bulls released to the arena.

Motz settles by the wall. He watches Brose at the long table in full gambling frenzy. He pulls out his watch and thinks of his new girlfriend. He slips away. His hour, too, has come.

★

The building where they were gambling was of some interest.

Reigning over the porter's lodge was a person not exactly young but also not exactly old, who was invested in this position two years ago when the previous long-serving porter showed too great an interest in the visitors and wasn't clever enough in dealings with the criminal police. So the lady of martial aspect, to whom the building belonged, replaced him with Frau or Fräulein Julie, who sewed for her. Julie was discreet, but the promotion wasn't yet adequate to her ambitions. She took in an interesting guest, one who didn't entirely please the landlady, though she didn't openly object: a man blinded in the war. The unmarried war-blinded were gladly handed over by medical authorities and care facilities to reliable women, the war-blinded were favoured by many women over other kinds of severely wounded and those incapable of a full day's work, because they received a full pension; this could be cashed in for a lump sum under certain circumstances – though the authorities proceeded very cautiously – and the invalid could buy a little property, or open a shop. As a rule it started off with marriage. But Schurz, Frau Julie's war-blinded man, hadn't yet gone that far, and Frau Julie was doing her utmost to achieve this end. She tackled the pensioner with all her loving ways. But he was obstinate and mistrustful and wanted to go on receiving his monthly pension. This caused her endless irritation, but she forced herself to hold it in, for the claims he made on her were horrendous, entirely those of a married man.

The woman naively thought she could clean the blind man out, but instead he cleaned her out. He hatched an ignoble plan. He thought: if she has me in her pocket and takes on my name, I'll be nothing and the pension office will no longer protect me. Then it will just be a marriage. On the other hand, if I push it too far the other way, the woman will finish with me, and the office will dump me in a home for the blind. And so his plan was to keep her as long as possible in a state of suspense, to temporise and not listen to anything. "We can't go on forever being engaged," Julie the concierge implored. "My relatives are already asking what fault you find in me."

He spoke rudely of her family, and promised to give their first and best a crack on the noggin with a stool if he ever came near enough. He acted out attacks of rage, trench madness, his sly way of cutting short arguments and driving her to despair. That's where matters stood in the porter's lodge. But the obstinate blind man was already a kind of support to Frau Julie; being blind, he could sleep any time, day or night. And so she set him to sleeping by day and keeping watch for her at night, to open and shut the front door for the procession of visitors that made the building so lively from eleven p.m. until four in the morning. Now and then he would hold brief conversations through his little window, and tuck away little tips that he kept concealed from Frau Julie; during the day she sought to pilfer these back while he slept, which led to further underground warfare.

By contrast, the elegant first floor (this is an old building, with no lift) is leased by a gloomy troubled family left behind by a colonel. The husband fell early in the war, the only son disappeared during the retreat from the Marne. Now the big rooms accommodate the mother and her daughters, two of them still at school, the eldest has just obtained her schoolmistress certificate. This respectable family's main source of income was the wife's Baltic estates, but since the start of the war, and now with the Bolshevik revolution, all that has gone. The brave widow has some support. She's confined the family to three rooms, and sublets the four best; she and the daughters help with the housekeeping. Her apartment receives just as many visitors as the apartment opposite, but only in the afternoon hours. They're stiff upright men, young and old, clearly of the military class. These persons never tip the concierge, and so Frau Julie on the day shift comes off less well than her blind man. Which however does not deter the blind man, a former soldier, from taking a lively interest in these visitors, the kind who were once his superior officers, and he tells the woman cock and bull stories about them. The landlady is not unaware of the curious comings and goings at the respectable family's apartment. She tolerates it gladly. They're gentlemen (she's gleaned a few names from the daughters) with the best connections, even men from ministries.

We shall not be surprised (for we know how small the world is) when this Wednesday, the day of the funerals of the revolutionary victims, we see a figure climbing with heavy tread up to the first floor, someone, it seems, we know. The robust elderly man wears a black leather overcoat, on his head a greenish hunter's cap, the face is pale, gloomy, grave. A narrow gray brush moustache sits over his upper lip. A girl opens the door, she hesitates, a door inside opens, a man looks out, hurries up, stares at the other. He states his name. "Ah!" It's our Major, whom we last saw in Strassburg. He's invited in with a little bow, and looks around astonished at the elegance of the room, a blend of salon and office. No fewer than three young ladies are typing away by the window. Maps hang on the walls, charts, newspaper cuttings.

The Major's eyes are wide: "What an operation. A little ahead of the times." Disingenuous smiles in response: "What do you mean? We're an advice service for decommissioned officers. Has the Major come from the funeral ceremonies?"

"Hah, not at all. Don't need to freeze my feet."

"The Major must have heard Liebknecht."

"Thank you for asking. All Berlin's a riddle to me. There's a lot going on that might well have been swiftly ended."

At the very top of the building, the third floor has stood empty since early in the war. For the past year masses of eager prospective tenants have come forward, but the landlady's reluctant to take in just anyone, she herself plans to use the space, but doesn't yet know how. She has a justified sense that one or other of the activities already in the building might flourish, and require more room.

MAURICE BARRÈS

The American army moved past Longwy towards Luxemburg. It entered a hilly mist-wreathed landscape. On the hills were autumnal black tree-skeletons, beneath the trees dead leaves lay thickly compacted by rain, decomposing to soil. Houses stood on many of the heights, labourers' cottages, uniformly small. Greenish-grey brooks and water-courses on all sides. On some heights, amid sad grey stumps, huge fir trees soared, proud dark-green beings that gazed motionless down upon the troops. Here and there grey-green meadows opened up, the grass frozen, or drowned. No creature running, no bird flying. But the columns marched with their canon and machine guns and cheerful singing. They saw trees tinged poisonous green, some swaddled foot to crown in leafy vines. In clearings trees had shed whole clouds of reddish foliage, it lay there blazing.

Huge chimneys came into view, this was a zone of blast-furnaces. Near St Martin giant retorts rose into the air, tall as a house, grey and rusted, alongside were rail tracks, halls and barracks. Nearby railway trains afflicted the ears with their whistles. And yet more grey-green levels, and on the horizon smoke from chimneys.

On the 21st the Americans reached the city of Luxemburg. The Germans were gone. On Station Square were the burnt-out remains of a big warehouse where bread had been stored. It went up in flames before they marched off.

Americans!

The Germans had scoffed: it's Barnum's Circus entering the war.

In the spring of 1917, was there not dreadful gossip among the French, who had already lost so much blood: the Americans will come, they'll supply locomotives and vehicles, steel and copper for our munitions, material for aeroplanes, they'll manage their own transport, provisioning, hospitals – but our soldiers will remain in the frontline of terrible battles, and when the call comes for blood to be spilled, who's going to step forth and say: here I am?

On ships across the ocean came representatives of every race and shade of skin colour, lumberjacks, earthmovers, track-layers, radio installers. So much Red Cross, so much spiritual support for the troops. There came men who at Verdun would race, standing tall, ahead of their artillery fire straight into enemy machine-gun fire, fall in their thousands – but the positions would be taken. Who in forty-eight hours of incessant fighting would squash the Saint-Mihiel salient and extract twenty thousand prisoners and two hundred canon from the German bastion. From their mouths came blunt words: "For a long time we considered the mosquito a harmless little creature. Then we discovered the dangers in letting them proliferate. It is now proven that the Germans are a focus of discord in the world. They forced this war on us. We shall take the opportunity to destroy as many as possible."

Luxemburg was such a pleasant little city. The people were joyful, had hung out flags. The Americans piped and drummed and went into their barracks and private quarters. And when they felt like going sightseeing, they were led along the main street to a mighty bridge with big pylons for tramway cables. They gazed into an abyss. In the background a misty height rose, pale green meadows climbed the slope. There were broad paths, and even a flowing stream. They asked if it was all natural. Proud Luxemburgers answered: yes. Only the bridge was not natural, they'd built it. When the Americans looked down on the other side, the stream flowed there too, with actual rapids. There was also a low fortress-like wall with many black windows. And a little bridge crossed the stream. All of it so endlessly cute for men from Mississippi and Missouri, from the Great Lakes and Niagara Falls.

When they returned to Station Square, a colossally steaming locomotive aroused curiosity and amazement. Hauling squeaky-clean carriages, four in number, white above and green below, it came trundling onto Station Square with truly enormous wheezes. When it stopped, the locomotive made an elegant diversion around the four carriages, which meanwhile stood still and filled with people, and now the whole thing pulled out again, carriages and people, man and mouse, away from Luxemburg city.

The Americans brought into Luxemburg their little leather pouches with yellow tobacco, also chewing gum, which thereafter never left the city. And when they came to their quarters, wherever there was a bigger boy or girl, the first thing they did was hand out boxing gloves and at once indulge with the children in their national sport.

Following behind came the French CIX. Line Regiment. More jubilation. They were welcomed by Herr Paul Stümper, assisted by the mayor of Hollerich and Luxemburg: "You held out against the first blow. Your blood flowed in rivers. We are proud to welcome the CIX. Line Regiment with the Military Medal in its colours, and four times mentioned in despatches."

Later on, at dinners and receptions, whispers started about the five hundred French prisoners of war who had arrived in the city eight days earlier from Germany, starving, exhausted, clothes in tatters. And then the Germans (people now spoke boldly in the street of "Prussian swine"), they're gone at last. But during the long occupation they'd carried out arrest after arrest, jail for being a French sympathiser, at least five hundred cases.

And then, very quietly: "As for Grand Duchess Adelaide, the Kaiser dined with her, and she raised a toast to the glorious German army, oho, the Grand Duchess Adelaide."

★

Maurice Barrès – deputy in the French parliament, member of the Académie, a man from Charmes on the Moselle who as a child witnessed the entry of the Prussians in 1870 and never forgot it – was invited to participate in the return of French troops to the regained areas. He was now fifty-six years old, famous beyond the nation's borders as a writer, and during the war had shown himself a passionate friend of the army and a tireless drummer. In parliament he formed his own party, which he called the Nationalists. He left Nancy (where he had spent unhappy years of schooling) together with French troops crossing the former enemy lines with heavy sombre steps. They came to a wilderness zone, ruined villages, torn-up ground. The troops at first advanced in field grey, no singing. Over them hung a pale snow-heavy sky. Then the car carrying Barrès and some officers turned aside, they sped on, he wanted to greet an old friend, a man who had stepped out in August 1914, bright and confident like many others, and that same August had fallen, along with others, at the nearby hill of Delme. Up till now the dead man had been separated from family and friends by enemy lines, no flowers had been laid on his grave, was there in fact a grave? Barrès' car roared through villages that lay totally deserted, the surroundings silent, silent; they were the first to penetrate this region.

They stopped in Fonteny. A window opened, a head popped out, a voice cried: "The French! The French!" The spell was broken, children came running. And then the mayor, holding both hands out to them, tears ran down his cheeks, he stammered: "We've waited for you – forty-seven years!" There were hugs.

And as people began to set out flags, Barrès enquired about the dead man, Guy de Cassagnac. The mayor led him to a nearby farmyard, a tall young woman came up and began to relate what happened on 20th August 1914, after the battle. How a young dying man, a French officer, was wheeled in a barrow, he was smiling, and already so weak he couldn't be carried into the house. He had to be lifted down to a bed laid on the grass. There, his head held by the young woman, the young soldier died. And as the young woman reached the end of her report her lips began to quiver, her face became flushed, she lifted her hands and wept. A peasant stepped to her side and continued the tale: "We wanted to bury the officer under this here tree, but it was forbidden. German soldiers came, stripped the body, took away medals. So the dead man was placed with all the rest in a mass grave."

– *"The room was brighter than today, you sat by the window, slightly hunched, a book on your knees that you had taken from my library, the illustrated Venice volume. You leafed through it, immersed yourself in some of the pictures. Your expression was one of joyful musing, enraptured even, intoxicated. I sat in my armchair and watched you. The whole room, thanks to you, became a picture."*

Children from the farm led the visitors to a nearby quarry where the fallen were buried. Flowers on the ground, on the broad grave mound. There the young officer lay, as he had wished in his last letter: "If I die, they must bury me alongside my men."

Barrès and the officers returned to their car and drove on towards Metz. In Metz the ancient town bell, the Mutte, was pealing. It kept on and on pealing. Cast on it were the words: "I ring out justice."

It was yesterday that General Mangin said to Barrès, and repeated it today to Marshal Pétain: "Now we may lay down our lives. We have done our duty, our days are fulfilled."

They came to Metz, Barrès and the officers with him, just in time to see the last German troops move out under a leaden sky, flanked by huge still crowds. Nothing to be heard apart from the soldiers' heavy marching tread, the rumble, squeak and rattle of wagons, clip-clop of hooves. Officers and men stared straight ahead. Not a sound from the crowd. Here and there a whisper.

The voice of Barrès the Hellenist, friend of Venice, the overpowering voice of one who never gave rest to his revulsion and hatred: "I was in Gerbéviller, I launched a thorough enquiry, like others in Nomény and Louvain, in the whole of Belgium. Should we allow them to depart unpunished, General Claus and his soldiers who beat, stole, hanged, shot, including women, children and old men from Lorraine, should they be left to lose themselves among the hordes of the defeated? What we want is to liberate Germany from its Bocherie. We want to annihilate that which just now was all set to bring about the destruction of the whole world. We want to separate decent Germans from the despicable Boche.

"M. Louis Renault has rightly said: anyone who contravenes the Convention of the Court of Judgement in The Hague is a common criminal and must be brought before the courts of the country in which he committed his crime. The guilty must be located and detained. I'm told a German officer forced civilians to walk ahead of his troops. Let him be found.

"If one wants the Germans to cease being half-human, and slaves capable of committing the most execrable crimes under the most irone discipline, then a hand that is stronger than the ringleaders must seize these ringleaders and bring them to justice, so that there, in the full glare of publicity, under the necessary guarantees of a fair trial, they can be sentenced and condemned in the eyes of the whole world.

"Germans! See the Germans of 1914-18. They are in retreat. They were trained to goose-step, and believed themselves strong as iron. They shouted: Might makes Right. Their intoxication by the doctrines of Bernhardi will evaporate in the hour of atonement now approaching, when the scourge of justice shall lash the guilty."

THE LAST GERMAN DAYS OF STRASSBURG

From what infernal abyss must it have emerged, the black smoky cloud pulsing with the glare of fires and composed of hate, calamity, pain, vengeance, that lay over Europe during those years, and would not dissipate.

From what invisible roots did that noxious thorny weed shoot high and spread across the whole world, to tear the flesh of any who tried to come close to others, who therefore had to remain spellbound helplessly in place.

For almost fifty years the Germans, conquerors of 1870, had remained in Alsace. Now their hour had struck. Divorce was inevitable. Regiments and civil offices began to move out of the former Reich Territory. Left behind their buildings, memorials to old victories, monuments to the German Kaiser, and several tens of thousands of Old German citizens.

★

The Reich Territory of Alsace and Lorraine, the object of so much pondering and debate and expense of energy by so many, had collapsed. No longer valid was the Law of the Constitution of Alsace-Lorraine, which first saw the light of day in 1911, was signed on 31 May by Wilhelm II in his own hand with the soaring flourishes, and sealed with the imperial seal.

This Law had blossomed into three main headings and twenty-eight clauses, which foresaw everything that simply was and might be, how many votes Alsace-Lorraine should bring to the Bundesrat and when such votes should be invalid, namely when by the addition of these votes the presiding vote would obtain a majority for itself. The Law presented the Kaiser as the actual repository of state power, he could appoint a governor at the head of the Territory who would reside in Strassburg and exercise every competence of territorial rule. And so in 1911 he chose his former adjutant-general, general in the entourage of the II. Uhlan Guard Regiment, Graf von Wedel from Oldenburg, veteran of the wars of '64, '66, '70-71. The old warhorse saw no more of the most recent war, of course, as death had carried him off, so the disaster could fall on the shoulders of Herr von Dallwitz. A certain Zorn von Bulach ruled under him as Secretary of State, a Strassburger with a big wide moustache. He also exercised the duties of Castellan of the restored castle of Hohkönigsburg.

Two Chambers were created to form a Territorial Assembly, the First Chamber for the great of the land, the Second for the common people. The "great" were the bishops of Strassburg and Metz, presidents of the Superior Consistories of the Churches of the Augsburg Confession, presidents of the Synodal Board of the Reformed Church, presidents of the Territorial Supreme Court. The law considerately allowed also for a representative each from the University of Strassburg, the city's Chamber of Commerce, the Agriculture Council, the Israelite Consistory; even the working class was permitted to send three representatives.

In the First Chamber, representing the city of Strassburg, sat its clever and zealous professional mayor Schwander, legally trained man from Colmar. Also showing up, nominated by the Kaiser, were a certain Graf Arnim from Potsdam, who now lived near Metz; noble proprietors of estates; factory owners; commercial counsellors, the Suffragan Bishop of Strassburg, who like the State Secretary was a Zorn von Bulow. Careful attention was given to religious balance in the selection of the nobles: nineteen were professed Catholics, one an Old Catholic, one Israelite. Alsace-Lorraine was able to provide twenty-three gentlemen, seventeen more provided an admixture of Old Germany. And they themselves were pretty old: none under forty, four over seventy, and ten between sixty and seventy. Among the oldest was the famous teacher of Criminal Law, Laband, who was near his venerable eightieth.

Now, the Second Chamber presented a different picture. It was constituted by universal direct suffrage and a secret ballot, and housed the young ravens, the have-nots, to whose squawks the First Chamber was meant to close its ears. These gentlemen, in order to raise the volume of their squawks, banded together in parties, and elected as their president one Ricklin, doctor of emergency medicine and resident physician from Dammerskirch, a very amiable gentleman accustomed professionally to dealing with excitable people. Under him in the Chamber sat sixty demanding men, including a restaurateur, a cabinet-maker, a miner, together with the inevitable lawyers, editors, and brickyard owners. Timid professors sought in vain to pour onto them the oil of considered reflection, social democrats brandished the clenched fist bequeathed from antiquity, but remained genial colleagues and friends of social order. Several priests swished black robes and offered super cleverness, but there were few takers; even so, they could be sure of their power in these parts.

The great Law of 1911 did not prevent the Alsatian deputy Haegy rising to his feet in the Reichstag in October of this year of 1918 to declare: "The war situation has brought matters rapidly to a head. In the Reich, and among my people. It required a sombre situation such as we now find ourselves in. Today, at last, it has become clear that a break must be made with a system that has been adhered to with obstinate tenacity for forty-five years. If I may characterise this system in one phrase, it is foreign occupation on the soil of our land."

Armed with a pince-nez, next to rise was the unruffled president of the second Alsatian chamber, doctor of emergency medicine Ricklin: "Be under no illusions," he said in the same amiable tone he adopted when addressing his delegates in Strassburg and his patients, "allow yourselves no false notions. Nothing will come of it. We, at least, have the duty of conscience to speak the whole truth to the German people. Harbour no false hopes in respect of Alsace-Lorraine. Our electors tasked us even before this war to attain for Alsace-Lorraine at least the status of autonomous federal state within the Reich. Matters have progressed far beyond that. Our mandate has been overtaken by events." No one could have spoken more plainly.

★

The acting Commander in Chief of the XV. German Army Corps had resided in Strassburg as if all-powerful, as if for all time secure in his position.

His Excellency the Commander held court at 11 Brandgasse along with his chief of staff (a major-general) and an adjutant (a captain of the Landwehr). Located there were Department 1a and its sub-departments dealing with army organisation, troop deployment, new formations, training, crop damage, with marches and billeting.

Sub-department 2 was responsible for Withdrawal Under Threat. It had been busy recently planning march routes, protecting railways, demobilisations. The two officers at its head did what they could. Linked to it was Dept 1b, headed by a major in charge of four sub-departments. These considered such gloomy matters as semi-invalids, military police and protection forces, coded communications, interpreters. They turned also to matters of horses, convalescent homes, convalescent companies, to military bands and consignments of timber, to entrenching tools for the troops, to munitions, flags and standards. And that was just Dept 1. What could possibly be left over for a Dept 2 or even Dept 3?

But the department numbers extended to 8, and even there you're not done. Dept 2 busied itself with formalities. It issued marriage permits to officers and rehabilitated felons, processed petitions to the throne and commendations for award of the Iron Cross. A special section was formed to deal with Iron Crosses for the severely wounded, and for exchange prisoners. Endless lists were drawn up: of officers sent back from the field; of available generals and staff officers; of officers in military hospitals and on home leave. Dept 1a monitored sick and wounded officers, for this too was necessary. Honour courts, His Excellency's personal affairs, officer suicides, and similar discreet matters were not neglected.

An important building shrouded in squeals of pain and hopeful outcries was Brandgasse 2, which housed Dept 2a, the Complaints Department. Here an office comprising two heads, a first lieutenant, four lieutenants and an all-powerful staff sergeant had set itself up, and toiled away day and night. On matters of life and death. Countless cases came their way, "the woe of all Mankind", a love of peace, a love of thousands for life, clung to Brandgasse 2. Every appeal was handled with benign or less benign intent, a bitter on-its-own-merits. Deferments of not yet inducted conscripts, dismissals, deferments, grants of leave to already inducted conscripts. What passionate letters with patently spurious grounds arrived up here. How many covert conversations took place, or were attempted to no avail.

There were animals, too, in the army. This justified Dept 4d. Now our lovely equine stock will be managed.

Counter-intelligence, Dept 1d at Brandgasse 11. This maintained contacts with many other departments. The discreetest of communications had to be discovered. There was intelligence about espionage, sabotage, about surveillance, about military intelligence, prisoners of war, about all other matters of high or low politics abroad, surveillance of railways, pigeon post, unexplained fires, about leave taken abroad, about the release of explosives.

Transport of corpses, war graves, ceremonies for warriors, and traffic regulation were undertaken by Dept 6, the composition of army formations was supervised by Dept 7, through which too the delivery of parcels and goods to field armies and to the homeland were coordinated. See the building at number 9 Kleber Place, how quiet and harmless it stands now, still waters run deep, on its third floor the General Headquarters had ensconced its War Economy Department. And what did this do? It liaised with the civil authorities, took part in discussions, especially with the price control office in Strassburg; it monitored the nutritional status of the civilian population, but from its own resources the third floor was unable to contribute to any improvement. All the more diligently did it monitor the specialist press, maintain a register of persons convicted of raising prices beyond the permitted highest price – not, of course, so that they could be recommended to Dept 2 for an Iron Cross – and every month it sent a report to the War Ministry. But in no way did this Department show particular malice. There were even those who asserted that this location, like others, attracted people who, while eligible for conscription, were emotionally unable to face the prospect of soldiering, and to the vagaries of the front preferred a stable and well-paid posting in the rear.

Let us now mention the Welfare Department, located in Post-strasse and represented by a first lieutenant, a captain, three lieutenants, and last but not least three chief medical officers. This department delved into the sad business of providing for bereaved dependents in the lower classes, also for lump sum payments to pensioners, for spa cures, for civilian provisions. It did much, achieved much, but had no authority over events, hence much remained in the realm of promises.

To gain a full picture of the extent of the Acting General Headquarters of the XV. Army Corps, we must turn from Dept GO in Apfel-strasse, from Dept K (Classification Commission), and make our way to the most malign Section 3, which occupied the entire basement of Sternwart-strasse 11 and was composed of jurists who addressed one another in the third person as Chief Martial Law Counsellor, Martial Law Counsellor, Chief Martial

Citizens and Soldiers

Law Secretary, but this only when an interrogation was in progress. Here was the abode of terror, where everything of a horrible and life-threatening character congregated. These gentlemen provided a president or an assessor for the Main Court Martial. On a sober stomach they busied themselves with various criminal prosecutions, for example under §9b BGB. They dug deeply into denaturalisations, desertions from active service, espionage, decided on protective custody and all kinds of other evil. It would not be accurate to call them vicious bloodhounds or bulldogs. They were military law incarnate, clotted to gall.

We may report on Kleberstaden 12, where a Privy War Council had free rein without exactly braiding earthly bodies with heavenly roses. Its role was to pay military units, compensate for damage to crops, educate the children of soldiers, and in general hand out money for useful purposes, albeit sparingly. Let us praise this Privy War Council, and reveal the number of its department: 4a.

On we go to Hohenlohe-strasse 26. Here was ensconced a Physician General who along with a Chief Medical Officer and a Chief Staff Pharmacist did everything that a combat medical officer could do with regard to supervision and management, beginning with the training of combat medical teams, the very foundation of emergency medical services; with medical services for the troops, on which they kept a close watch; with the equipping of health services at the frontline and for the troops – including accommodation for the mentally ill (we encountered an example of this category earlier in our story); up to canine auxiliaries for digging out and retrieving poor wounded men in the field.

The Protestant Chief Military Pastor – how could he be excluded from such a humanity-encompassing structure! He's a Privy Consistorial Counsellor. The Catholic Chief

346

Military Pastor alongside him is merely a prelate. Totally invisible is the Jewish Chief Military Pastor, there is none such, not in the form of Chief Pastor, Assistant Pastor or even synagogue helper.

Lastly, the office of this Commander in Chief over all mankind thought it necessary to set up at Manteuffel-strasse 49. The workings of this office of war extended into infinity: here, three Sections busied themselves with very remote matters; the point of this official body can only have been to demonstrate that nothing, absolutely nothing, would escape the eye of the rulers. Here they came up with astronomical statistics on the workforce in factories and mines, behind the bustling personnel were rows of filing cabinets, and these cabinets had to be filled. There were discussions on the use of convicted prisoners, on support for school leavers, they controlled sacks, jute and bast fibre, cleared and set up factories, steered the removal of motors and drive belts, they turned their attention to roofing felt and cement in the homeland, enquired and investigated into the locations of heavy workers and the heaviest workers, read specialist journals, released reports and surveys.

There was within the realm of the Commander in Chief even a solitary female, an unmarried lady. And as she wandered the vastness of corridors, they discovered how she might be kept busy. For there were women too in the homeland. And with the slaughter of the males, their relative numbers kept increasing. And so the solitary lady was assigned soft and semi-erudite matters. For the sake of completeness the lady took a seat at Manteuffel-strasse 49. When asked what she did, she would frown and breathe mystical words: "Social welfare, female counselling."

Defeated Germany. No nation can enjoy greater happiness than in pursuit of its inclination towards enlargement. Chewing and digesting are no longer sufficient for the individual. A nation no longer sprouts sturdy limbs if it can't create for itself majestic figures and images by which it can grow.

Arrogant and thoughtless, the German Reich set out to face its utmost test. Into the battle it cast people and resources, young and old, produce of fields and mines, discoveries of laboratories. It was sure of winning the laurel crown, but had, without realising, cast its soul into the decisive struggle.

The old giant, rump and limbs twitching yet, had, it seems, suffered a broken skull.

★

To wait for 22nd November, the day when the French would enter Strassburg, seemed to the Alsatians too long. Already on the 14th, just three days after the Armistice, there was rejoicing in Mulhouse. A delightful sight met the eyes that evening. The chain of Vosges hills appeared illuminated from the summits down into the valleys in the sweetest conjunction of colours the whole world could offer at this moment: blue, white and red. Rockets soared, first greetings from the fraternal French over there.

In the week before 22nd November local socialists, like many others, trod lightly. Rumours circulated that press articles had been drafted, in which they would deliver a mighty parting kick not just to the German Reich but to German socialism too. (But, people welcomed the red flag on the cathedral! No, that was a concession to the times, the red flag just appeared, who wouldn't greet an old friend passing through!)

Herr Pierotes, mayor and socialist, toiled tirelessly and very cleverly to this end. He spoke with a Strassburg bank director and a representative of the automobile trade. Both offered their services: they would sound out the French directly. For what purpose? Not to bring to Strassburg the same magical lights that the fraternal French had poured across the Vosges hills. They were thinking of the much-touted trains said to be standing ready at Nancy packed with grain and wine, and planned to open the mouths of Strassburg not just in an Ah! of solidarity, but in a grateful bite and swallow. The bank director and the automobile man felt very wary of ambush as they approached Markirch, where barracks were on fire and German troops trudged down from the hills; maybe they were a bit too hasty, turning up at a wake when the patient was still alive. But then they came upon huge holes in the road and whole battalions of French riflemen on foot, and their doubts were allayed. They continued through St Dié. News spread like wildfire: Strassburgers are here. This pleased them. They suspected that two weeks later nary a cock would bother to crow when Strassburgers appeared, so they were happy to skim today's cream. And when they presented themselves in Bruyères to the Divisional Commander of X. Army Corps, they were invited to supper. They were all in high spirits, the officers because of the Strassburgers' joy, the Strassburgers because of the officers' joy, and also because they were drawing nearer to the streams of milk and honey in Nancy. Kitted out with new tyres, petrol and oil so they could actually reach Nancy, they drove via Épinal, and in Nancy spoke with the Prefect, Mirman, whom we shall meet a few days from now as Civil Commissioner in Metz. The bank director and the automobile man could be content: fifty thousand kilograms of coffee were already on their way to Strassburg.

And as for grain and wine, a few days later, on Sunday, little ones and babes born during the war in Strassburg experienced a true miracle. In the same way that canine creatures were gradually domesticated as dogs – probably they were once wolves, and fetched their prey from forests, now they lie in the barren lap of some ancient female, eat moistened bread, the tail docked, and every few years a different breed appears because the tastes of old ladies change, but the lapdog still knows it's a dog – just so had children been persuaded that what they were eating was bread, and they believed it was bread. It had indeed emerged from the baker's oven, as children could ascertain for themselves when they went hand in hand with their parents. But what happened in the depths of the baker's shop and in the ovens remained hidden from view. And so the erroneous idea arose that what they were eating really was bread. They realised the truth no more than did a sick person who buys pills for gout from a quack, and has nothing but little balls of ordure. Bakers baked bread, and put into it anything that came to hand and was recommended by their guild and by high authorities to whom nothing human, or inhuman, was alien.

For it was wartime. And when copper kettles disappeared, and doorbells, and baking pans, casseroles, tin bowls, fruit boilers, and money transformed itself from gold, to copper with brass, and finally to paper, then cheese, butter, sausage meat, bread could not hold the line. What advantage, so said the war-waging power, should the contents of a pickling kettle enjoy over the kettle itself? Had not human beings – of whom it possessed millions and who settled their affairs and paid their taxes – been transformed and simplified to the status of warriors in trenches, shirkers on the staff, and heroes back home? And so cheeses still had a smell, but of what, none could say for sure. The sausage contained meat – but not even that was certain. For oxen and calves fled from military authorities, they vanished as if with wings from the human realm, and no one knows where amid the terrors of war they ended up.

But in the manner of its composition, bread resembled the Garden of Eden. Every creeping thing and every creature, all things that do crawl and fly above and beneath the earth, and all things that are found upon the earth, be it swaying grass, be it the bark of trees, be it vegetable, shoe leather, fragments of glass, be it shirt buttons, sticking plaster, railway tickets, all came together in a simple loaf, so that later a learned man in Germany said (he published a book on the topic): Let not the memory of this bread be allowed to fade, for it was one of the most remarkable discoveries of modern times.

It was in fact bread, and as such could be sold and eaten with minimal damage to the digestive organs, but at the same time was a museum in view of the number and variety of articles assembled in it from nature, art and technology, and at the same time a percussion instrument given its hardness, and at the same time a first-class nutritive medium for moulds of all kinds, and at the same time a steam engine actually inside the guts of the human, where after the shortest interval it produced steam and fog and gas in such quantities that, had the war continued much longer, the notion would have arisen of installing people who had eaten this bread into idle factories, thus alleviating the coal shortage.

So what a miracle it was for children, that Sunday before the entry of the French troops, when their mothers sat down in front of them, attracted them with a "tsh tsh tsh" and held out something light brown, gold-blond, fragrant, and when you broke it open it was yellowish-white, and they were meant to eat it! What is it? – The children amended their understanding: it's bread! So much had a bank director and a representative of the automobile trade achieved.

SPRUCING UP, AND DISAPPEARING

Just as light delicate mists fell ever and again on the city, resembling the mists of the new capital, Paris, so now one delirious rush after another swept over Strassburg as it busied itself soberly and gladly with its many dear little tasks and made itself ready to give the liberators a festive welcome. The city scrubbed and spruced itself up, as much as its current poverty allowed. Already it looked sweetly and wonderfully new.

Outside the Palace of Justice, where the Workers' and Soldiers' Council met, around midday on this Wednesday the 20th a wretched huddle of people assembled. Field kitchens steamed as usual on the ground floor, the few people standing there – none merely gawking, none agitated – waited patiently for their bowl of soup. It was the same hour when over in the old Reich, in Berlin that sinister churning megalopolis, the huge mourning procession was just setting out from Tempelhof Field. Only a week ago the hundred and eighty revolutionary sailors had marched in behind their red flag along Finkmatt Quay, soldiers had barred the entrance with rifles at the ready (among those turned away, as we know, were the Pastor of our little Alsatian town, and the First Lieutenant's Widow). Now the last remnants of the revolution hunkered in the courtroom and exchanged consoling words. A good dozen had a need to make haste across the border; they must be over the Rhine Bridge by noon tomorrow, any later and they'll be taken prisoner.

In a sadly meek appeal they prayed for good weather. "The years of war," they asserted, "have brought thoughts of revolution to fullest ripeness, even among those who have never bothered their heads with politics. The first duty is to maintain peace and order. Social democracy, which called forth this movement and which at this moment holds power in its hands, requires that every comrade cooperate in building the new order. Without peace and order we face dissolution and death by famine. Keep your distance from disturbances. Arrogate no rights to yourselves. Do not stay outdoors unnecessarily. Children and young people should not play with fireworks, every bang alarms the people." They were raised well, the revolutionaries who wrote this. The townspeople read it with interest and satisfaction, so no one intends to stir us up. At three o'clock that afternoon the red flag was brought down without fuss from the cathedral spire. Around the same time, unnoticed, a delegation of senior French police officers slipped into Strassburg, to assess the security situation.

Final session of the Soldiers' Council under Sergeant Rebholz, that tall grave man. He delivered a report summing up the ten days of his revolutionary government, thanked the National Council, announced that mail was being delivered via Switzerland, and confirmed for the tenth time, albeit swearing those present (mostly Alsatians) to absolute dogged secrecy, that the French delegation had promised they would keep the current civil power in office. He stared around in his old way, looking for acclaim, almost begging the now deserted hall that had so recently been filled with turmoil and was now vigorously turning itself back into a court of law and pronouncing sentence on Rebholz: even he, who wanted so badly to remain, had to leave. He stayed stubbornly in his seat. Someone from the National Council thanked him and all the others, wished the German Republic good luck all round, the seed of the Internationale has been planted in people's hearts. What need for more fine words.

Now some spoke up who would soon be disappearing. The Alsatians kept quiet. But all had the same thought: What did we achieve? The red flag on the cathedral has already been taken down, hardly anyone came to our meetings, we took on security duties: a shabby outcome. They pledged to one another in that huge hall to defend the revolution, it's the brotherhood of all mankind, we're good people, time's short, the room must be cleared by 2 p.m. for a thorough cleaning. And one member in particular urged punctuality – a carpenter from Strassburg, who had to repair benches damaged during the revolutionary élan.

Remainers consoled leavers. They swore: yes, the revolutionary seed of the Internationale will germinate in Alsatian hearts. In all probability they had no such confidence, but this was a time for vows, and you had to do something to remember it by. And anyway, large numbers had skipped this final session.

Some soldiers expressed a fear of being assaulted as they marched off. So representatives of the civil defence nobly undertook to escort the troops as far as the Rhine. A captain was present, he shouted that he'd be the last German soldier to quit Alsace, no problem.

Once again some Old Germans spoke up: their revolution, they boldly announced, is now just about to let rip. And so every man jack of them will cross the Rhine with a glad heart. To the Alsatians, whose mouths dropped open, they held out a picture of their future task: to make Alsace-Lorraine a bridge between France and Germany, across which the international revolution will march. And now came three huzzahs for the long life of the revolution.

Finally a resolution was read out: "It was not possible in Alsace-Lorraine to secure the initial successes of the revolution. But no power can force us to renounce our international efforts." (An early draft mentioned "continuing the revolution", but the Alsatians rejected it, they won't be left to carry the can, they want no replay of the Paris Commune.) Then the Soldiers' Council appealed to deputies, workers and peasants to form up under the banner of International Socialism. A Reich German roared: "That's what they said before the war." Another picked up his cap and left: "If that's historical materialism, then it too must be swept away one day." Glowering Rebholz waved his arms over the speaker's podium: "Onward to struggle and victory!"

A much reduced number of Alsatians betook themselves to a nearby brasserie, having decided they would all go over to the Workers' Council. A doctrinaire person, a young teacher who had never joined a party, burst out, once the door was shut, that it was all a cowardly compromise, and he now demanded, here in the brasserie, that they make a better job of it in the Workers' Council. Over the next week they did gather a few times for secret meetings, but attendance dwindled every time.

Finally the teacher sat there with just one person, namely the one who paid for his glass of cider, namely himself. For a whole hour they sat silent in the thoroughly revolutionary but otherwise peaceful wooden-tabled room.

And neither hide nor hair was seen of them again.

★

All this while, Seaman Thomas was tramping down the misty Rhine valley in the company of Bottrowski from Neukölln. Both wore grey-green military greatcoats. As the French marched into Metz, there they were too. Nothing marked them out, Thomas spoke unimpeachable

Alsatian German, and Bottrowski kept to the background. Both enjoyed getting to know Metz. They couldn't tear themselves from this land. They had no idea why.

As the last German troops pulled out from Metz between silent sullen crowds lining the road beneath a leaden sky, Thomas said to his comrade: "I know what makes them tick. With us down there in Strassburg it'd be different, they'd whistle and make a racket. These Lorrainers are plodders."

Bottrowski trotted alongside, his mouth frozen shut. All he said was what he'd been saying as they tramped: "But how will we make it through?" Thomas had grown chattier along the way: "I'm waiting for the day when Alsatians realise what revolution and socialism are. So first we have to push the German revolution along a bit. I spoke with Peirotes, and his friends were there too. He roared at me and laughed, he said, our revolution consists of chasing out the Prussians, and that's being taken care of for us by the French, and they've done the same for you lot, and all you've done is yield one small step. Bottrowski, the man was right. But we'll take it further. For us, revolution means more than yielding one small step to the Prussians. And then he said he wouldn't like to be in our shoes when the Prussians make a comeback and the French let them go at it. For afterwards they'll all just be a bunch of capitalists, and one hand washes the other."

"Why doesn't he tell himself that?"

"Because he's Majority Socialist, all he does is make speeches. For the rest he just chews on bones the capitalists throw him. He'd go to war again tomorrow if the capitalists told him to."

"How will we make it through?" Bottrowski sighed.

Thomas: "When we were in China once, we went ashore at Shanghai. They were executing people, said they were pirates, ten of them. A right massacre. All with hands tied behind the back, and up behind each head a pole with writing, telling what he'd done, Chinese. And then all in one spot, kneeling down. We wondered: how will they do it, shooting, hanging or what. They had no rifles, only drawn sabres, big and curved, I've got one of them back in Wilhelmshaven. And you should have seen it, Bottrowski, how those pirates, they all looked the same, staring boldly into the world. Each of them said something, must have been juicy, you can imagine, and then not a word more – and off comes the bonce."

Bottrowski, puzzled, asked: "Where was this?" Thomas: "Shanghai. Six, eight years ago." Thomas often told such tales, never followed up with a handy practical moral. Thomas: "The question is: should we let the people play out their fate so blindly, the Alsatians?

Bottrowski: "We can't run around like this for ever, they'll be asking for our papers."

"Then they'll put us in a cell. Won't be so bad. That kind of case takes ages. Before it comes to trial, I know my Alsatians, they'll already have realised what their French are up to. 'Cos you should never come down hard on an Alsatian. In the course of centuries they've grown over-sensitive, prissy as an old maid. It's true. We want to be left in peace. And they won't let us. And if it comes to trial, then ..."

Bottrowski: "Then you'll be like Liebknecht or Rosa, a big deal. Thomas, us revolutionaries must be idealists. But you're too much of one. They'll put you away before it comes to court."

Thomas: "I've thought about that. But if there are ten or twenty of us Alsatians together sitting there protesting against the occupation? You still have no clue about us. The French will take it very badly."

Citizens and Soldiers

"But what do you want, Thomas? If you think you can be more effective here?"

Thomas rubbed his stubbled face and gazed ahead, reflecting: "Once a shipmate, same age as me, caught a rat on board. First he kept her tied up, and then he built a cage. But a rat's not a mouse, a rat's clever. In time, though, she grew tamer, only towards him of course. He got her to a point where he tied a string to one of her legs and she hopped along at his side. And as long as he was there keeping an eye on her, she never ran off. And I'll tell you what he did once, he was from Sélestat, I'd like to know what's become of him. He takes a coil of thick ship's cable up on deck, a good long piece, ties it good and high and paints it with tar. He leaves a spot in the middle clear. He sets the rat down in the middle, he called her Coco because she loved coconuts, we were anchored off Togo at the time. She sat there frozen, couldn't jump out, she was five metres above the deck, she could estimate, and there's tar all around. So she tries it with the tar and gets stuck. He had to pull her free and clean her up with benzene. She didn't like that, and she kept it in mind. She never went near the tar again. She sat up there, sometimes she'd hang down by her tail, then rappel herself back up. All he ever did was feed her. Of course she always tried to jump onto his hand. It was an amazing trick, feeding her from above and from the sides."

After five minutes of silence had elapsed, Bottrowski asked: "So why'd he do it?"

Thomas: "He always had such notions" (laughing proudly down at his comrade). "You really think when I'm in a hole I'll never come out!" But then he sighed: "I'd like to try it with all that lot in Strassburg, just not the Social Democrats. They're the sticking point. They're my tar." He came to a halt, sought to marshal a thought, made big exploratory gestures in the air: "Bottrowski, they are our misfortune. They're the buffer between us and the people. Worse than the bourgeoisie, they are. And that's why I'm leaving Alsace."

Bottrowski, brightly: "So, on to Germany!"

They were at a street corner, tall Thomas leaning on a lamppost: "That would be best, Bottrowski. I shall head for Wilhelmshaven."

★

Boldly, now that it had all turned out so happily, the socialist press made fun of "Wilhelm the Sissy". The way it crowed was nothing short of heroic. Once he promised to lead his people to wonderful times. Now began the darkest most pressing hour, when he was to account for all his sins, but he knew no other care than to bring his own person to safety. In every pose he strode tall, for as long as the imperial cloak flapped at his shoulders. Otto the Child, Ludwig the Sheep: now Wilhelm the Sissy! And editors, who knew that Peirotes planned to pass harsh judgement on the lukewarm and the undecided in the party, found courage to state unambiguously: "As Social Democrats, which we have always been and shall always remain, we take leave of the great fraternal party that has proved such a model for the world! It is not our fault that such leave-taking comes so easily. We maintain: a man's word is his bond! Our convictions and principles allow of no such capacity for metamorphosis as we, to our great disappointment, have been forced to witness in German social democracy."

(They will soon witness even greater miracles in the "model fraternal party".)

Citizens and Soldiers

★

Meanwhile the lovely city was decked out ever more gaily with garlands, flowers, flags and banners. Truly, here military occupation held no fears. Strangers never found such a welcome. So delightful, every alley wide or narrow, Stone Alley, Blue Cloud Alley, Long Alley, Spear Alley, White Tower Street, Oberlin Street. Old French inscriptions and business signs made an appearance seemingly out of nowhere, as if they had spent the past fifty years dreaming: they were small, pale and faded. Ugly black varnish was peeled away.

And in storerooms of the municipal architect's office, a ghostly knocking and bumping began. Windows were flung open, dust billowed, searches were made in old chests. Street signs from the time before 1870 had been secreted away in loving hopefulness. Young people took in hand what had been laid away by the old, the dead. They read Rue Vauban, Manège, Daguerre, Magenta.

And the Imperial Palace ceased to be the imperial palace and became a Rhine Castle. Kaiser-Wilhelm-strasse was changed to Freedom Street, Kaiser-Friedrich-strasse to Peace Street, and Falkenhausen-strasse to Mainz Street.

And everywhere in the ancient city a burst of painting, re-painting, and charming makeup.

★

The Reception Committee that had formed in all secrecy as early as 23rd October invited more than a thousand young women to appear at the Aubette on 18th November; these were to form an honour guard in traditional costume as the French marched in. They filled the huge salon and the staircase with laughter and hubbub. And as they hushed for a few minutes to receive instructions, a French plane with an enormous cockade swooped low over Kleber Place; the fliers, clearly visible to onlookers, waved a huge banner. Who would stop the girls rushing to the windows; they stormed onto the square and waved and cheered and shouted "Bienvenu!"

And one well-respected citizen, Fritz Kieffer, whom the Prussians had banished to Kassel and Thuringia for three and a half years (in Kassel he got to know Peirotes and a dozen other companions in sorrow at the Café Polter) – he couldn't bear to stay at home when he heard that troops would march in via Molsheimerstrasse and along Slaughterhouse Quay. For this Alsatian patriot remembered well 28th September 1870, when the unhappy Strassburg garrison, decimated, came out through the gates along White Tower Street, the National Thoroughfare, to surrender to the foe. Kieffer drove to Obernai, where General Gouraud, commander of the IV. Army, had occupied the property of Baron von Hell. He was received by the general attended by his staff officers. The man from Strassburg burst into tears at this first sight of the liberators, and the general too was overcome with emotion. Then Kieffer explained his concern, the general delegated the matter to his chief of staff for resolution. And soon the man from Strassburg was overjoyed to hear that his wish would be granted. The triumphant shame-erasing entry of the French Army would trace the same route that had endured the fateful decampment of 1870.

A reprobate gang of Strassburgers felt an urge, on the day before the French would arrive, to achieve something decisive and radical, something that would not be overshadowed by anything done by others. They waited for night to fall. And then, when the city became quieter, they took charge of a great length of rope and dragged it, together with a few hand tools, several men together (civilians, soldiers, sailors) off through the town on an adventure. Anyone curious to know what they meant to do with the rope and the tools had to join in, for better or worse,. And soon hundreds followed behind the rope, the ship's cable, borne on the shoulders of four men in the midst of the throng. A few at the front sang the Marseillaise, others, whose French was not so far advanced, were content just to bawl. They crossed Theatre Bridge onto the wide open space before the sombre Imperial Palace. They halted at the Kaiser Monument. They surrounded it singing and yelling. Here was their goal. It had already been encased in wooden boards in anticipation of coming events; but these were easily torn down.

The monument stood exposed. A couple of men jumped onto the pedestal, and now the role of the ship's cable became clear: it was wound three times around the bronze torso of the Kaiser figure, and then, when the men jumped down and a big circular space was cleared, a regular tug o' war began with the active and inciting participation of the assembled crowd. Their heave ho! echoed rhythmically across the square. A tremor above, a yielding, a visible swaying, now a general yell of heave ho!, a shout, and with a cracking sound the bronze figure leaned forward and crashed splintering onto the cobbles. Such cheers, such tumult. And now the hand tools leapt into action, deployed according to a well conceived plan. Groups of three or four squatted on the smashed figure, chiselled, hammered, bent. The bronze head came off with a grinding screech. Their work was done. They wound the rope around Wilhelm I's bronze head and dragged it clanking and bouncing to the statue of their Alsatian General Kleber. With huzzahs they laid the head of the Prussian conqueror at the feet of the hero of the great

Revolution. Sailors clambered onto the plinth, waved flags and made speeches.

Even this was not enough. They had other targets in mind. At the main post office three statues of the Kaiser gazed haughtily down, high over the front entrance. They wanted to get at them, but how. They called out the fire brigade, who were to place ladders at their disposal. The firemen came along, ringing merrily, and would gladly have joined in the business – next day they showed themselves with their blaring brass music to be good Alsatians and no friends of oppression. But they could offer their ladders only in case of fire, this was in their blood, and they could not be persuaded. They negotiated at length, and laughed along with the shock troops. But at last they rang the bell vigorously, the crowd cleared a path, and away they drove.

SNIPPETS FROM THE DAILY NEWS, BERLIN

In Berlin, in the Reichstag building, a congress took place of German poets, writers, artists. It should not be said, where all is in flux, that the Intellect stands aloof.

They had been held down, nay treated with contempt, by the military government. They tiptoed forth from their nooks, nay, dared a handspring as their entry to public life. Among them were clear-headed well-trained men, brave and disciplined, who knew what they wanted and who applied the brakes. But it all headed unstoppably out onto the old high seas of World Improvement where sirens sang, where Scylla and Charybdis waited to smash them to pieces, and where a goddess lurked, a demon, in order to make fools of clever men.

They took over a large room. On the door they stuck a sign with the inscription: Congress of Intellectual Workers. From there they issued mighty pronouncements.

President Wilson's Fourteen Points they cast playfully into the shadows. They demanded, as every man had to at that time, the freeing of workers from the capitalist system, and also (though without explanation) personal freedom. They wanted the best, the absolute never to be outdone best, to the bafflement of their clever heads. Every progressive programme was plundered, starting with the Bible. They demanded social justice, but resisted radical methods which might lead to anarchy; supported the League of Nations, the Parliament of Nations, a compulsory arbitration court, social ownership of land and soil, confiscation of assets above a certain level. All this they demanded, and because they were merely intellectual workers they felt no need to go into the usual details, or even how to implement any of it. That was for politics and the parties, which to be sure they either buried deep in land and soil, or attacked from all sides at once. To leave no stone unturned and consummate the re-creation of the world just now in train, they proposed Unity Schools, professors to be elected by students, cleansing of the press from nationalist and capitalist corruption.

It all proceeded with enormous vigour.

With poets, there can be no lack of fun and idealism. But how many were actually serious? They had the use of several typewriters and even, since the second week of the revolution, of typewriter girls. These young ladies were content to sit there, because in the offices where they usually sat they could hardly finish their sandwich for all the pestering. But among these intellectuals, the poets, the artists, it was a veritable idyll. They had feared that with so many writers they'd be dictated to all day long. Instead, the men smoked, shouted, and used the telephone. And now and then some would use a pause in the discussion to say hello to the typists, where do you usually work, where are you from, etc., and some were nice without it coming to a serious pursuit, because, as is the rule in smaller offices, someone always came along to interrupt, and the typewriter girls had the habit of keeping one gentleman to step out with and another for office hours. To keep the young ladies busy, now and then some man would bring along a manuscript, poems, a manifesto, these were actually more in the nature of a declaration of love and a competition for the favours of the ladies. And at last, thank God, a pencilled note would turn up in the middle of an appeal for the self-redemption of mankind, with a little date and the address of a bar in Kleine Wilhelmstrasse. Thus did the lady acquire her stepping-out gentleman. The artists in question no longer turned up at the congress sessions. In ignorance of the real reason, they were castigated as renegades. They only reappeared when new young ladies were posted to the typing pool.

The intellectuals, workers of the mind, poets and artists, debated endlessly. They quarrelled, first because they couldn't stand one another personally, secondly because they couldn't stand artists as a category. Doubts arose as to the possibility of spreading true ideals and a genuine culture among Germans. They soon all had a feeling that if it went on like this in the Reichstag building, the revolution could not possibly be sustained. That would mean a dreadful dereliction by the Mind that had been called to the rescue, and there would be no one left to protect the German nation from chaos.

It was Wednesday 20th November, the day when the Fallen for the revolution were buried, a misty grey day of early darkness, when in the evening beneath glaring electric lights a manifesto was read out, composed by a member of the congress. The manifesto declared:

"A monstrous sin has been inflicted on Humanity.

(*Irrefutable!*) The civilian world was turned into a military camp and a field of slaughter. Millions of the best sons of every nation lie in their graves. The fallen, fraternally united, are at peace, and silent. (*Kitsch.*) For us, too, the armed struggle has ceased, but not the struggle for our nation's survival or demise, this nation that in a future age of justice will appear in all its glory. (*Hail to Thee in Victor's Crown.*)

"We creators, we architects and musicians, we men and women (*we knights and heroes, babes in the crib, oldies with a walking stick*), we who are first and foremost human beings and in our souls entirely German, do not doubt: our nation, our land will endure and will not be defeated. (*For faith makes one blessèd, and can move mountains*) We have realised with a shudder that Mind is intangible. (*This fustian should have been struck out. No, let's be honest, the eternal bawling can't be held back. Who's bawling? Please don't start that again*) But Love is fruitful and creative (*Don't dare say "generative"*) and streams out only from a true heart. Let us therefore not only share bread with our brethren returning from the front, let us also greet them with our true heart. (*They'll reject it with handwringing. This is idle sophistry. Whom do you think to make blessèd with this. We're not here to make people blessèd, we're not the government. So better say nothing at all*) With a clear and dreadful logic, one might say, human plans have been replaced by divine. (*I don't understand a word of this. Please be patient, sir, you'll soon detect a train of thought*) But although it is so, and although every word appears fragile faced with the severity of the transformation so caused, the visionary can still perceive what has at the same time fought its way through in a new form: the ancient, powerful particular essence of the Germans, unscathed. (*Hail to Thee in Victor's Crown! Please, enough's enough*) And whoever lives shall – in the not too distant future, of this we are certain – see German soil flourish as never before. *(Of this we are certain, oh sure! Rhetoric. For the love of God, we can't even supply bread. So you really should stop supplying slogans. We encourage, that's our function. Tripe)* For a thousand years the German nation has experienced nothing that can compare in significance with the events of the past few days. Whoever understands this feels the incomparable power. *(I hadn't noticed. So why are you sitting here? Leave that to me)* Even the new government will have to take note of us, where they find our activity to be propitious. *(Crawl then! So what do you want to do? Show the 'Scheidemen" what a revolution is. Why don't you talk in Fraktur to the treacherous pack? Silence! We're not a political assembly. So what are we then?)* Let none of us hesitate to do all he can from the bottom of his heart in the welfare service of peace. *(I can't listen to this! It's awful! I'm leaving the congress. We shall take a vote)*"

After fist-shaking exchanges of insults, the manifesto was endorsed by a barely visible majority which opponents at once rejected as an artefact of chance. It ended with a lengthy debate on procedural rules and statutes; proposals for amending the statutes continued late into the night.

As it grew late, towards midnight, and the session continued with only a few still in attendance, there appeared in the overheated room among the disordered chairs the dramatist Stauffer, an elderly amiable gentleman, small, with a soft dark moustache. Stauffer had been spotted now and then at the congress, always keeping silent. He wrote novellas and well-received plays, mostly set in the Middle Ages, some allegorical, finely chiselled works in rhyme. He was very retiring. Now he sat down next to a tall young lyricist, a lively man with a big dark woolly head, one of those new poets of humanity. They chatted. Head against the windowsill, the very elegant Stauffer, who already inclined to a certain stoutness, listened with mild weariness to the silver-tongued poet, a true apostle of novelties. As he listened he became invigorated. He followed attentively, anxiously even, the words that flowed so effortlessly from the lips of the man opposite. Clearly he was learning something. The tall hymnodist was complimenting his older colleague for having taken the trouble to descend from his lofty belvedere. "Spoken without the least irony. I am a true admirer of yours. I have paid close attention to all your writings."

Stauffer: "You say lofty belvedere. You mean ivory tower." He thanked the younger man for the proffered cigarette. "Of course, what else can you mean. And you're not far wrong, in some respects. I feel it myself."

"And that's why you're especially welcome here."

With a great cry of joy and a hearty laugh, a sturdy athletic man approached from the front, much younger than the quiet dramatist. His face was flushed, his light brown hair hung untidily over forehead and ears, his little eyes looked out with a cunning shrewdness. It was the much-read and very active novelist Wilhelm Morgen. "What! Stauffer in the lion's den?" And he actually hugged the shy visitor, who had stood up with an embarrassed smile. Morgen gushed: "A stroke of genius, your coming here. Stauffer, what if we were all to stand in the corner sulking and not taking part! Wonderful, wonderful. Do you come here often?"

Stauffer replied bashfully that he had turned up a couple of times. Morgen threw up his hands in horror: "And you never made contact with us, and never put your name on the attendance list, and never came forward to the committee table where you'd have been welcomed with open arms?"

And in a quiet but furious voice he related, one arm

on the lyricist's shoulder, the other on Stauffer, how things had gone with him and how he'd come through. Had he not been typecast as a conservative, a patriot? "And I make no apology. We've all made mistakes. And I still have certain old predilections. A man can't change just like that. But for that very reason, full speed ahead! Don't keep to the sidelines. People need us."

"Quite right!" the lyricist applauded.

Morgen: "I began as a monarchist. How many of us did not. Does it make sense to be a monarchist today? Play a Cinderella role, like the Carlists in Spain, or the supporters of Mary Stuart in England? Ridiculous, ridiculous. Go along with it, that's the watchword, and the right one, honestly."

"Exactly what I think," the tall lyricist added, tapping Morgen on the arm. "Naturally, I had no need to change course first." Morgen crowed with delight. He let go of them both: "That's why you are also our flag-bearers, our flame, the pillar of fire in the desert, no anti-Semitic allusion intended. For you ought to know, Stauffer, what he wrote recently, I know it by heart: 'Arouse thyself, man from the masses. Come away from the doltish, the desiccated. Abandon the sad heaps, leave the past behind. Come to me, brother!'" The lyricist gave a smug smile. "You've remembered it perfectly. It begins: 'I see thee that mournest in thy lonely room.'"

Stocky Morgen suddenly offered Stauffer his short firm hand in a sober and businesslike manner: "Anyway, Stauffer, it was a splendid idea for you to come here." He had noticed that a vote was being taken up front, and dashed off.

The young lyricist gave a knowing nod at his back: "That man went with one bound from monarchist to confirmed democrat."

Stauffer: "A whirlwind. Such vigour."

The lyricist: "Of course there are opportunists too."

They stood silently, side by side. The lyricist waited for the famous visitor to make some kind of statement. Then he forced a smile, excused himself and left. Stauffer bowed politely. He gazed across rows of empty chairs to the front, where a small crowd was arguing. He drew back the curtain, looked out onto the dark Tiergarten.

No one noticed him leave.

*

If a day is the hen that hatches the next day, then all you can say of the kind of hens that showed themselves one after the other in Germany during November 1918 is that they were surprising, outbidding one another with their curious notions, but what they were not was a pleasant philanthropic breed of hens.

What, for example, should one think of the growing habit in Berlin at that time of shooting people by mistake?

In Gabelsberger-strasse in the far east of Berlin lived a man by the name of Bernhard Broikowski. He had a brother in law, Brass, who during those revolutionary days moved in excitable circles, opposed by other circles excitable for other reasons. He also had numerous personal adversaries from previous lines of work. This hotheaded fellow was held responsible by other hotheaded fellows for everything that failed to transpire according to their wishes. In consequence they desired to take action against him. He got wind of it, and changed his location. But staying put in the old location and living his peaceful and unsuspecting life in Gabelsberger-strasse was the furniture-maker and craftsman Bernhard Broikowski. He read his *Morning Post* and was glad the revolution hadn't strayed down his street. He worked at a factory making cheap furniture for buy-now-pay-later shops. Now and then, let's admit it up front, he suffered pangs of conscience. In the depths of his soul (only his wife knew of this) he feared an act of revenge from customers of his firm. For what was made in the factory for precious money, albeit on the instalment plan – how shoddy the timber was that they used – how superficially they polished – how frugal they were with glue: it all screamed to Heaven for retribution. He, the foreman, feared an assault for example from the direction of one of the young newly-married couples under whose bottoms the chair seat broke, or from a larger lady who fell backwards off her chair and damaged her coccyx (chairs built for buy-now-pay-later prices), and from old bachelors who bought a single storage box to hold their books, their mementos, their clothes, and who by subjecting the sensitive furniture to vigorous movement encountered a shattering natural event that tumbled glasses, books, trousers and shirts all in a heap and gave them, personally, a shock. "Our furniture requires handling with especial care," said the firm's brochure, "I.R.V. instalment-plan timber is fine and delicate, I.R.V. instalment-plan glue and I.R.V. instalment-plan furniture are top-of-the-line products that have no competitors. I.R.V. instalment-plan bedsteads, storage boxes, chairs, tables are the choice of the discerning modern man," but no such turns of phrases could wash the conscience clean.

Early in the morning of 21st November a detachment of ten armed men appeared in the courtyard of the tenement building in Gabelsberger-strasse. The dragged the old foreman from his bed and asked him if by chance his name was Bernhard Broikowski. He admitted it. He also admitted, when to his bemusement they demanded to know, that he belonged to the party of traitors (at the moment this was the Social Democrats), that he was in fact treasurer of dues collected in Gabelsberger-strasse and had been for the last fifteen years, and pointed out quite readily that the collection box held 32.50 Mark. At this point he had to get dressed. Jacket, trousers and slippers were OK by the armed men.

His wife, seeing the rifles and her husband in the middle, had no good feeling. She ran to the third floor, where dwelled a district functionary of the party, a close friend of her husband. He came down with feigned bravado, questioned the squad's leader, threatened to make a protest, but as the men whispered among themselves and cast dirty looks his way he slipped out and down to the ground floor, then up stairs to the attic where he could gain access to the neighbouring roof (a route he'd planned out long before in case of emergency). He sat up there, heart thumping, glad to have escaped, on a low pile of briquettes in an open attic space, noticed there were mice and wondered if people might have provisions tucked away up here, maybe I can help myself some time. Then a salvo cracked from below, followed by a shrill female scream, and in his fear he stayed rooted to the spot for two whole hours. When he met the concierge on the stairs sweeping – the man shrank back from him – he made enquiries and learned that old Broikowski had been shot. "Why?" A shrug, keep sweeping.

The squad had confused Broikowski for his brother in law Brass. The mistake came to light the very same day, because the man they'd shot, namely the targeted brother in law, who heard about the assault, was seen going about unharmed; and he dropped a note to the effect that they could get knotted, and he invited them to perform other indecent procedures on him. Anyway, dead is dead, goes for the foreman too, and not even the investigation that was initiated could do a thing about it.

He himself now sat far from earthly cares, from revolution and war, and from his factory as well, up there in Heaven (as a pious Catholic he had a claim on Heaven) and from there looked down on the further progress of the German revolution, especially in his local area. He sat smugly on his cloud and judged: "Really I got away lightly. For if it had come out in the end about the thin glue and the crate-boards for solid oak beds, they wouldn't have sent me up here." And so as not to imperil his status, he kept mum and mixed inconspicuously with the hordes of the heavenly host.

MARSHAL FOCH

This 21st November, rolling in on the heels of the 20th, 19th, 18th, in no way repudiated its dreadful antecedents. To see this, there was no need to go back to Adam and Eve and the Fall, it was enough to flick briefly through some still-damp pages of newsprint.

The German armies were defeated. Then a munitions train exploded at Hamont in Belgium. It seems trivial. But those who experienced it never forgot, and many lost their lives to it. The railway station and the entire surrounding area where the train had come to a temporary halt was blown to smithereens. At the same station (O dreadful interweavings of Fate) three hospital trains were waiting to proceed, filled with sick and convalescent patients, sufferings and newly-budding hopes. Young nurses wandered in this garden of humanity. They intended to travel via Holland. The three trains burst into flame. Eighteen wounded on the trains burned to death. In the town of Hamont, entire houses collapsed under the hail of grenades, Dutch and German soldiers and civilians were laid low. This happened on 21st November, the Armistice was agreed on the 11th, but Time did not allow the roots of sorrow to wither, war still came sweating out from the world's pores.

Then again, following behind the VI. and XVII. Armies, which crossed the Rhine at Bingen, there came more armies fulfilling what was agreed and imposed on 11th November. Between Düsseldorf and Bingen the V. Army appeared. General von Einem approached Koblenz with the III. Army. Sixt von Arnim was all ready to appear on the Rhine with his IV. Army, as was Herr von der Marwitz with his V.

The V. Army of Herr von der Marwitz had not in the least frittered away its time. At the start, in August 1914, it had comprised parts of the V. and VI. Reserve Corps, together with Foot Artillery Regiment no. 12 and Pioneer Regiment no. 20, lots of strong fellows, healthy, they were men, they breathed, ate, drank, they could hit, push, shoot, run, climb. They were severely harassed by the enemy when they were hurled in late August at the murderous fortress of Verdun. Then they absorbed the V. Army Corps, the V. Reserve Corps, the II. Territorial Division, the XXXIII. Reserve Division, lots of strong men, not all still young, all breathing, eating, drinking, muscles fit for combat, cunning creatures. Because there was nothing doing here, and the situation was changing elsewhere, over the course of months they were hurled this way and that, and thousands died. We find them in the summer of 1916 at the battles around Fleury, at the stop-gap redoubt of Thiaumont, the years rolled on, again they stand before insatiable Verdun, and fight for Hill 304. Finally they had to take the common fate on their shoulders and slip away with the enemy hard on their heels, out of Champagne and all the land down to the Maas. And that's the V. Army, which by 21st November has managed to make it to the Rhine between Düsseldorf and Bingen.

The III. Army was led in by General von Einem. Who, after four and a half years, could possibly recognise in this army the regiments that in August 1914 fought the battle of Dinant, intervened with the II. Army in the battles before the fortress of Namur, and took part in the great drive forward into France. There they were formed of the XII. Army and Reserve Corps, the XXIII. and XXXIII. Infantry Divisions, the XIX. Army Corps, Rifle Battalion no. 11. After the great battles of the war of movement, this Army settled into the static battles of Champagne; its name now comprised the VI. and VIII. Army Corps, the VIII. Reserve Corps, the XIX. Army Corps, the V. Cavalry Division, the I. Bavarian Territorial Brigade. And when this Army turns up in 1918 at the battle of Vouziers, in October, it has many components, but the components were not large, the XXVI. Army Corps, the I. Guards Infantry Division, the I. Bavarian Infantry Division, the XLII. Infantry Division, the LXXVI. Reserve Division, the CXIII., CVC., CIC., CCII., CCIII., CCXLII. Infantry Divisions, along with parts of the XVII. and CCXIII. Infantry Divisions. They fight on the Aisne and the Aire. When the hour strikes they find themselves alongside other armies in defensive actions outside Antwerp, on the Maas line.

Behind them, every day brought the Allies closer to the frontiers of the Reich, hitherto defended with such vigour. The Allies ensnared them with their might, their fury. They said: "We came past Givet, where we freed eight thousand Allied PoWs. We occupied Neufchâteau-Etalle. By midday the French had occupied Neuf-brisach and Hüningen. We entered Metz at half past one, our I., IV. and X. Armies with Marshal Pétain at the head, six hundred aeroplanes flew over the city. Pétain took the salute at the march-past by troops on the esplanade beneath the statue of Marshal Ney."

The Académie française decided to award the estate of the Marquis de Vogüé to victorious Marshal Foch, and the estate of Emile Faguet to the President of the final triumph, Clemenceau.

*

Because they found the conditions imposed by the Armistice intolerable – and only during the withdrawal did you realise what was happening to you and that you'd lost the war, and that the other lot were well placed to press a sword to your throat – two members of the Armistice Commission protested in great detail and with calm crafty faces: they were named Erzberger and von Winterfeldt, both Germans, of course, one a former member of the Reichstag, now Secretary of State of a state that had no frontiers, no feet and no head, the other, general of an army in which all knew the past, fewer knew the present, and none knew the future.

This is what they argued: "According to the decision of Foch, Armistice conditions such as have never before in history been imposed are to remain effective. A modern army of three million men with a complex technical apparatus must be withdrawn by forced marches at an unfavourable time of year over badly ruined roads and hills, and must then cross the Rhine in good order."

At this point in the protest document Marshal Foch, sitting in a salon at his headquarters in a heavy grey jacket, pressed a small button of bone; an adjutant appeared, and then the colonel presented himself.

"Sit down," the Marshal said. On the other side of his

wide desk was a simple chair with a plaited-straw seat. To call the whole place a salon was simply a mark of respect to its occupant. "Light up your pipe," the Marshal suggested, "there's nothing of significance. Or are you busy at the moment?"

The colonel, as he tried to light his pipe with a mechanical lighter, smiled: "Business arrives at noon with the post. Diplomats are just now assembling in Paris."

"How many will there be, in your estimation?"

"Like grains of sand on the beach."

"That's all right then. Of course that lot can do nothing. – But your lighter's not working." The colonel was struggling red-faced to make his little petrol lighter work; he mumbled: "American patent, a colleague on the Commission gave it to me." The colonel clicked, growled, snuffled at the mechanism.

Foch, at last: "You know my predilection for infantry. The individual soldier should be well trained. In an emergency one has nothing; petrol won't burn, wet ground impedes tanks, so they remain stuck in mud, airmen have problems with meteorology. But war must be waged."

The colonel rose to his feet and asked to be excused for a little moment, which Foch granted with a smile. Two minutes later he was back, rubbing his right arm and right leg as he sat down. Foch commented wisely: "Ah, now it's alight."

"Yes," the Colonel growled, "but a proper safety match would seem like a gift from Heaven."

"How did you manage it? Your right sleeve is singed."

"We have some German flamethrowers outside. The Pioneers use them as cigarette lighters. I came too close."

Foch, shaking his head: "You might have bought it."

The colonel, puffing away: "We should hand the flamethrowers back. This point in the conditions should be amended."

Citizens and Soldiers

Foch bent over his desk, put on his pince-nez and hunted through his papers. "We've landed ourselves in a pickle with this so-called Armistice Commission. The Germans, it seems, want to secure something they showed little enough of during the war, namely tardiness. For them the whole problem consists of: how can I put pressure on myself. Here's a protest from Messrs Erzberger and Winterfeldt, the latter's a general. Grateful to know my colleague's reaction. They say they can't take the army back across the Rhine according to the prescribed timetable, because the roads are so bad, the hills, the weather, they can't guarantee complete good order during the withdrawal. So, my colonel, I sit here with this bumph and ponder. Something doesn't seem right, either in my head, or on their part."

The colonel, having so narrowly escaped death, puffed silently away, clearly his superior would give no hints.

Foch: "I would like you to attend the next session of this so-called Commission, and ask the Germans if they have read the conditions they signed on the eleventh. Is there one word about good order during the withdrawal?"

The colonel: "Absolutely not, and why should there be."

"My view exactly. How could this general sign his name to such nonsense, that the German army, meaning the defeated enemy, should be led back in good order. All we have stipulated is the deadline by which specific areas must be cleared, and the weapons that are to be handed over. Everything else is his own affair."

The colonel: "Say he fails to lead his troops back in good order and so misses some deadline or fails to adhere to the weapons handover schedule, it's not our headache. We'll sort it all out soon enough."

Foch: "Listen to this: 'There should be an appeal

to the impartial judgement of every experienced line officer or member of the general staff as to whether such deadlines lie in the realm of the possible. Is it to be assumed that the Allied Supreme Command intend that during the Armistice an army should be totally dissolved and annihilated, one which honourably stood fast for fifty months against a superior adversary, and whose front at the cessation of hostilities had not been breached.'"

The colonel put his pipe on the desk, his mouth open: "Excellency, they really wrote that?"

Foch let his hand fall slack on the page. "Literally. Honourably stood fast for fifty months against a superior adversary, the front at the cessation of hostilities had not been breached. One asks why then did they give up the war, why was their Ludendorff for months demanding an immediate ceasefire, why two weeks ago did they accept supposedly monstrous conditions that have never before in history been imposed."

The colonel nodded sadly: "It was right not to make this sort of armistice earlier. It's an act of clemency to an enemy who throughout the war showed not the slightest trace of clemency. We shall pay for this clemency. They're incapable of understanding clemency. It will in time, as we see now, be shown to have been a wasted effort."

Foch: "They lie, these Germans. In the midst of defeat they try to lie away their defeat. I promise you, colonel: after reading this I shall do everything in my power during the implementation of the Armistice and the subsequent peace negotiations to open the eyes of the Germans to their defeat. The battle of the Marne, Ludendorff's failed spring offensive, the unsuccessful breakthrough at Amiens, their last fling, will be drummed into them. And yet ..." Foch slowly shook his head and read the protest once more: "and yet there's something here I do not and cannot

Citizens and Soldiers

understand. A general signs such an appeal, in which the question is raised in all seriousness whether, yes or no, we intend the dissolution or annihilation of the German army. What, I ask myself, is the German general thinking of? How and where has he been waging war? Is it possible, is it conceivable, that a general, a military man, accuses the adversary of wishing to dissolve and annihilate the enemy army?"

The Colonel shrugged: "Hypocrisy."

Foch: "To our faces! To other soldiers!"

"It's for internal use within Germany."

Foch: "Submitted officially to me. They complain (it's already the pinnacle of shamelessness) that forced marches may cause soldiers to succumb to exhaustion and be left lying at the roadside, or (listen to this!) be taken prisoner shortly before they reach the homeland."

The colonel shook his head.

Foch clenched his fist. "It's shameless. It's so obvious. They pretend they don't know that in Belgium and northern France they billeted themselves on helpless civilians. In their offensives, without twitching a whisker, they deployed and sacrificed tens of thousands of their own people, and now pretend to make a song and dance about some falling by the wayside during a forced march, or ending up in prison. What do they mean by this effrontery? To escape the consequences of defeat. What? Can it be anything else? They don't shy away from whining like slaves. Next will come all the drivel about peace, reconciliation, justice, that President Wilson of Princeton University has landed us with."

The colonel: "That's Germans for you. I know them from my time at the embassy. Nobility at the top hard as glass, servants of the king, the working masses amenable, sentimental, not averse to brutality, middle class well trained and cowardly to the point of crawling."

Foch tapped his foot impatiently: "That won't clear the matter up. The way they fought the war was for the most part clever, even though they had no ideas and in the end toiled like Asiatics, only with the biggest masses of men and materiel. Right up to the Armistice they showed themselves brutal, but militarily comprehensible. Now" (again he struck the paper) "they've lost the plot. Sound like Wilson." Foch bit his lip: "I fear the Americans will cause us no small inconvenience."

Colonel: "The generals who lost the war are groping for tactics that will bring civilians to the fore, as in a street demonstration where women and children are allowed to go first."

Foch: "That seems to me to be the main point of their whole so-called revolution."

Colonel: "Without a doubt."

Foch: "Otherwise they could have overcome the revolution with three or four reliable divisions. But they don't want to. Firstly, they feel the shock of defeat in their bones, secondly it suits their book. The generals want to shuffle off responsibility, and steal victory from us."

Colonel: "That won't be so easy, as long as Your Excellency has a word to say."

Foch, after a pause: "This ... wasn't actually addressed to me, but to Wilson." He flings the paper aside and stares coldly ahead: "No reply."

Colonel (stands): "Our peace negotiators will soon unveil what's behind the curtain."

Foch: "I know what's behind the curtain, from my time at Versailles. The business with the thirty-nine divisions that were going to achieve everything in March, and then St Quentin was left with no reserves just so the Englishman Marshal Haig would attract no blame. Now

Citizens and Soldiers

the Americans are at it. I shall soon be seventy, colonel, and I can tell you, they will pay attention to wailing and gnashing of teeth and acknowledge the 'human rights' of German generals. They presented me in March with a lost battle, and I won it back. The war is not over. France has not won. To hell with coalition wars."

THE FORESTER WATCHES THE FRENCH MARCH IN

The Forester, relative of our old knock-kneed general, senior man at the garrison in the little town, was still in Strassburg.

He wrote to his wife: "My own true girl, circumstances finally make it possible for me to pen a letter to you." (This was not strictly correct; our depressed Forester was, like many others, powerfully carried away by the mighty emotions of these days, and he really did like the taste of cider.) "My friend, Sepp Kundt, will cross the Rhine today, though we exchanged oaths that we would only take that final step together. But he can't bear to see what's happening, and I think of what you said, my true girl: stay in Strassburg till you know for sure if we have really and truly lost everything and if it's all up with us, or the opposite. Today is 24th November 1918, a holy Sunday, and tomorrow Kundt will cross the Rhine into our old Germany that you and I love so well, as is our holy duty and all the more so in such a grave plight, but it was in Alsace that we found a position and respect and our daily bread.

"In the two weeks since I last wrote, I have not once been back to my forests. The first time all the roads were blocked by returning German troops, the railway was still operating and I sometimes stood glumly beside our train but, my dear Rike, there were so many familiar faces on it I feared betrayal and so would rather stay on in Strassburg. What abominations were carried out up to the 21st of this month by people wearing the Kaiser's uniform I shall recount to you when I see you. They planted the red socialist flag on the cathedral, and behaved in all kinds of swinish ways. Respectable Reich German citizens I got to know told me quite openly: if those are Germans and the Germans do nothing to counter them, then the French will have to come. Which alas I couldn't contradict. In their hatred they have torn down every statue of the Kaiser and just left the empty plinths standing, and the things they write on them my dismayed mouth cannot allow to pass my lips. Some people have bought up all the livestock in the country villages and slaughtered it in contravention of the prevailing decrees. They were peasants whose minds have been poisoned by the notion, oh the Frenchies will soon be here and then the livestock will be worth nothing. So the livestock was slaughtered. But who stuffed themselves with meat afterwards? Do you think, my dear Friederike, did even a mutton bone, a little slice of veal, ever reach the likes of us? Gracious me no! It was snatched from us by deceit, even when we were willing to pay. Where did it all go? To the hoarders and black marketeers. Same with milk and potatoes. Our Alsace has never experienced anything like it. Dear old uncle has taken me along a few times to meet with our officers passing through here, dressed in civvies and poor as church mice. I myself helped a few, they were so desperate and barely out of childhood, and I've chatted to lots of them, because you entrusted me to do everything I can to enable us to return to our lovely house in the forest where our two precious gifts were born and we experienced so much joy. But that is all over now, my poor true girl. You have already taken that difficult step and are back in our old beloved homeland. I am unable for sorrow to tear myself away yet, and so have already suffered much grief from the French occupation. For we are already under French occupation, Friederike! I don't know if your newspapers are reporting on it, or if the red socialists where you are even allow newspapers to be printed, or if our enlightened Fatherland is to drown in lies and deceit.

"Let me apprise you of the actual truth. We here in Strassburg are French! My pen, dear Friederike, is loath to write this, but it is so. And how our dear city must become French, despite the frontier being so near. If only I were back there and could give the liars and the Frogs a good one on the head with my bullwhip. But I no longer dare to travel by train. Last night, when I thought of you, in my dreams I gave our duplicitous landlord at the Golden Crown and the chap at the post office, once my closest pals who then declared themselves to be Frogs, as I shall tell you about later, both a stab in the neck with my hunting knife. May God the Almighty and Righteous drive home this blow so sincerely aimed.

"Friday, the day before yesterday, is when it happened, with the big march-in. The previous day, early in the morning, they had sent security troops on ahead. They came in from the south, by the Schirmecker Gate, as General Gouraud did the next day. But although lots of men came in there wasn't much to see. They were three battalions of an aerial brigade. To welcome them, the Firemen's Band, who as you know are much loved in Strassburg, put on a big show, so very early on Thursday morning there was a tremendous drumming and blaring in every street. I was on my feet almost the whole day, to observe the shame of our former compatriots. And if my heart will break for grief over our lost forests, then it has

THE FORESTER WATCHES THE FRENCH MARCH IN

every right to do so. What I saw and felt, dear Friederike, I shall never forget as long as I live. I rose early on Friday along with Konrad Witz, son of our wood-turner. I was lodging most unfortunately in Giesshaus Lane by the Officers' Casino, where an officer I used to know had a room, I'd taken over his room and Konrad slept on the sofa. For Konrad is a young recruit, everything he has is in Alsace, he didn't follow his parents to Germany, and like me doesn't know if he's coming or going. So now, to our misfortune, a couple of Frog cavalrymen are billeted in the house, and the landlady would prefer to rent the room to French cavalry than to stray Germans, though she's a good Alsatian woman, clean and straightforward, but the French franc rings more nicely than our brass. So we had to leave and are without a roof over our heads. We left our belongings in the cellar. It was clear frosty weather, with ice cracking in the puddles. The sun showed itself around nine. Alsatian peasants were pouring in along every street and lane, this time not to plunder our undefended military warehouses or make an outrageous profit, but to see who's in charge here now. And I fervently hope they'll be dealt with more harshly than they ever were by us, alas. Indeed, dear Friederike, I confess that the cruellest people I came across during the war, through all those years of war, were peasants (with a few exceptions), they buried and hid away bacon and eggs and flour and charged city folk extortionate prices. They have the deaths of many poor people on their conscience. They came riding in along every street, acting all grand and important with their brass buttons and white caps, and the stupid city people thought it great fun. But if ever there is a divine judgement in our lifetime, the Lord must have been delighted to have all these liars and hypocrites and wicked profiteers all in one spot as the French marched in, and He would make them all go crazy so all the stolen silver flies out of their pockets. And even the starving came in from outside the city, grown-ups and children, but rich people too. And now I won't shy, my dear Friederike, from telling you what abominations I saw yesterday with my own eyes. I was walking down Meisen Lane with young Konrad, it was eleven o'clock, not quite so noisy, we were looking for a quiet spot because we were so upset, and then we heard a racket and what did we see? A group of well-dressed people, several quite elderly, with fat stomachs, some were Jews, around a dozen altogether. They were proceeding arm in arm down the lane. They took up the whole street, so we two had to step into a doorway, they kept singing and shouting Vive la France, vive la France. Konrad says they also shouted Vive le beefsteak. I imagined what I would do if (what I don't think will happen) I was to encounter one of them with no one else around, I'd deal with him in such a manner that you'd be able to tip the whole fellow into a soup tureen.

"These good little people planned to inflict indignities on the statue of Father Rhine in Theatre Place. As the song says: *They shall ne'er have him, our German Rhine so free, e'en if like greedy ravens, they caw so raucously*. But the good Father was already behind a wooden casing in the shape of a pyramid, because General Gouraud is to pass by here tomorrow, and so they leave old Father Rhine in peace behind his fence.

"Peasants and townspeople, big and small, men and women, were clustered like fieldfares early on Friday on every rooftop, on lampposts, up in trees, and they covered the ground like sheep all herded together, and they had an enormous supply of little flags, blue white red, my heart stopped when I saw them, Friederike, my fists clenched at every blue white red ribbon in a buttonhole or on a

The Forester watches the French march in

hat, to think that something so shameful could occur on German soil. At Schirmecker Gate, two locomotives stood on the railway bridge, they were going to use them as a podium. Big lads squatted on the smokestacks, and these snotnoses who were taught in our schools and for whose schooling we had to lay out every year such and such an amount, they were leaning over the bridge railings and crowing 'Vive la France! Give the Swabs what for!' So deep, Rike, is human treachery, and we must keep a tight grip on our heart that it may not break. They announced that at nine o'clock as the troops begin to march in, all the bells will set up a mighty pealing. But there we played a fine trick on them. When nine o'clock came and the bells were supposed to start ringing out, all we heard were two or three little tinkles in the distance, and no others would join in, pull as they might. For the bells were all gone, we melted them down during the war, and they served us well in battles against the French.

"The march was led in by General Gouraud. His right arm is missing. They say he lost it in the Dardanelles when he was flung six metres by one of our grenades, losing the arm and breaking both legs. Despite the severity of his wounds, they say this general resumed active service three years later, turning up to face our General von Einem in Champagne. He's a tall slim man, formerly African. He has gleaming eyes and a proud face. Whatever you might say of the French, they do have brave officers.

"Behind the general came the Chasseurs d'Afrique, the 1st Foreign Legion Regiment. You will surely ask, my dear wife, why the French chose to place their Foreign Legion at the head of the march-in. You will understand at once, but you'll have a hard time not choking on it immediately. So, why did they put the Foreign Legion in the lead? Because this 1st Regiment – attend and be

Citizens and Soldiers

amazed! – is full of Alsace-Lorrainers! Full of German compatriots, who stood against us in the war! These traitors fought against their own Fatherland, which to me is the most shameful of crimes, second only to a sin against one's parents. When I saw them, my eyes started from my head! It took a horrible effort to control myself when everyone cheered them. Behind them came artillery and infantry, all in sky-blue uniforms. Big canon as well. They showed the famous 75 mm gun, which to me looked like nothing special. They must have posed a challenge to our side with their long flat-trajectory gun, and a gun called the 10 cm Rimailho Field Howitzer. And there were mule wagons carrying crates, this was the mountain artillery. There was no end to the din: Vivat France, down with Germany.

"So we decided not to wait until all the Strassburg clubs had paraded before us, attesting to their perfidy before the whole world: Harmonia, Stella, Argentina. We quickly headed alongside the procession across White Tower Bridge, then to the old Wine Market and Iron Man Square. The head of the column was just riding around Kleber Place. And at the statue of Kleber they had erected an enormous pole, and they were hoisting their lovely new flag with a blare of trumpets, every part of the procession had its own brass band drumming and blaring with all their might. Then we crossed the Broglie and watched a big parade and review of troops till after midday, freezing despite the crowds. But I thought: better a frostbitten toe than not watching this and not being able to write to you about it.

"We stood on Kaiser Square. Forlorn, undefended, filling our hearts with sorrow, there before our eyes was the magnificent Kaiser Palace. It stood there like a prisoner, but they could not strip it of its dignity. Regardless of all the blaring fanfares and all the brightly coloured uniforms marching past, young Konrad Witz and I gazed only at the palace and asked in the silence of our hearts to be forgiven for our presence at such a parade. Then over the Theatre Bridge came the Fire Brigade with its band, and the new mayor, a socialist of course, he wore a tricolour around his waist and is called 'le Maire'. Good luck to him. They had erected a stage on the square, with officers and guests sitting and standing up there. And at last the main parade approached over Theatre Bridge. General Gouraud steered his horse towards the stage, whereupon the march-past began. The people around us all growled out every marching tune the military bands played, Sambre et Meuse, the Marseillaise, Chant du depart. No comment necessary. Maringer is the new High Commissioner named by the French to head the civil administration. And when the soldiers were through with the march-past, a pair of very posh Red Cross ladies from Strassburg society joined this new Herr Maringer on the stage and presented him with a historic flag. But I don't know why it's historic. At this a loud cheer erupted. But the high point didn't come until the commander gave the signal for the bugles to play Trooping the Colour. All hats came off, the fanfare played, flags were lowered, and – our hearts stopped – the tricolour was raised high over the Kaiser Palace. Dear Friederike, for both of us it was a dreadful moment. We too had our caps in our hands, we didn't look around, but we were both weeping into our caps.

"People say of this day which is so unforgettable even for me that Gouraud, the general, was taken off to the mayor's hall on Broglie where they had a feast. A lady is said to have presented him with a bouquet on behalf of all the women of Strassburg. He replied: Apart from my wedding, this is the happiest day of my life.

"Friederike, it's enough to make you howl and scream.

Citizens and Soldiers

Such a disaster has befallen us German men. For the whole world has taken against us, and because a single opponent could not fell Siegfried, ten came along, with Negroes and Americans, and struck him down. Let them find no joy in their Hagen-blow.

"The bad man who offered himself to the French as mayor flattered the foreigners in the Town Hall and buttered them up no end: an outworn and odious regime has long terrorised Alsace-Lorraine, forty-eight years of slavery are now over. You can read it here in the newspapers. There are even some French papers already. And the new High Commissioner made a reply and spoke of 'Mother France'. In the evening the soldiers had free beer.

"This letter that has turned out so long, my own true wife, I meant to give to Kundt today, but he's not leaving till tomorrow, I don't know why. And now I must pass on some sad news. Our mutual friend, young Konrad Witz, who was with me all day yesterday and slept on my sofa, has joined the Foreign Legion. Please let his parents know! A colonial regiment marched in, you could see Negroes in it. After yesterday's grand parade, Konrad became very quiet. I told him that when Kundt leaves he must go with him across the Rhine, it's too dangerous here. He looked at me and at once turned grumpy and asked what he was supposed to do over there. Then he bumped into some friends from Vendenheim who were in the Legion, and early today the penny dropped, they must have talked him into it, and now he's a Foreign Legionnaire. And he says he won't be one for long, for though his parents are Reich Germans he was born in Alsace and will become a real French citizen. This put me in a rage and I congratulated him and he replied, just as furious, that he would not go across to Germany to take part in their stupid revolution. And he wouldn't give in, and if he hadn't made himself scarce I would have knocked the renegade to the ground.

"I shall give the letter to Kundt now, he has just appeared. Greet him nicely."

THE PROCURATOR SEEKS HIS SON

The Hotel Paris on the evening of Gouraud's entry was nothing short of a masterpiece of illumination. Patriotic processions formed up heading for the former Kaiser Square, where Wilhelm's statue had been toppled. A scruffy old man sat in the dark on Gutenberg Square and kept declaring: "I knew they would come today." Telegraph operator Wolter appeared on the square, in tall thigh boots. Before the war he'd put the entire Strassburg garrison on alert with a fake Kaiser telegram, in vain they'd stood for hours with all their officers expecting the Supreme War Leader. It was Wolter's little carnival joke, the whole of Alsace shed tears of laughter, but Wolters ended up in the asylum. Now he has been fetched out, enjoys his long-denied freedom and distributes leaflets, the hero of 1913.

★

The Procurator from the little town we know so well had been summoned to a meeting next morning to the Foreign Legionnaires. He was on tenterhooks, everyone strolling the beloved streets wondered what the coming days would bring. But what he hoped for surpassed all other hopes. He had stayed behind in Strassburg for three days already.

In his breast pocket the old gentleman kept the last photographs of his son, his two letters from Hartmannsweilerkopf, various replies from missing persons offices, a portfolio of his fears and hopes. This black tattered portfolio had lain on his wife's bedpost in 1916 as she faded. Towards the end, every few hours she had taken it in her hand without opening it. Her death-sweat soaked into the leather. As all of Strassburg rejoiced, it occurred to him: why should he too not have his joy. Though erect he was very old, and emotionally no longer very lively. Just one question rose up in him: what induced Fate to seek me out for such heavy burdens? As he wandered the streets and lanes – he had arrived even before the security forces – he noticed little signs, little portents. I am an ancient Roman, he flattered himself, and tried to suppress his fears. The decisive hours of his life, it seemed to him, were now approaching. On the Wednesday night he had lain sleepless apart from odd half-hours of dozing. His wife had been a pious Catholic, he himself had lost contact with his faith, at bottom a result of constant friction with prelates. Now, on the first night when the shallow dozing lifted from him, each time his searching thoughts turned to the great Helper and took cover, still ashamed and combative, behind his wife, and he beseeched behind the dead woman's back for succour in her name, for the granting of this plea, this unique request.

Next day he began his pilgrimage through the former offices of the High Command, he knew them well, but look, almost every door is closed, in a few rooms people sit, minor officials, some from the Soldiers' Council, they shrug at his approach and almost ridicule him. He knew this expedition was superfluous, it was only to bring closer the day of the missing son and avoid falling once again into fear or final certainty. In the streets he saw excited people, indifferent faces, none with a glance for a sad withdrawn man turned almost to ice. Why did he look for his son? To avoid turning completely to ice? He kept this question in mind. No; it's not about me, I'd be able to sleep well, I'm old enough. But when I look back on my life, and this happy, sweet young man, to think he could have been taken from me, that too, this good, dear – no, not for me, I should not like to think this young life was snuffed out and was unable to live on, finding no place on this great Earth. He was so full of joy, grown up now for sure; he consoled us, wrote to his mother every week, he was her child and mine, our darling only child.

The Procurator, a lean lawyerly figure with sparse grey side-whiskers took up position on the morning of the 21st at Schirmecker Gate, a blue white red ribbon in his buttonhole, and waited. He said he was watching out for his son; they made space for him. Then they saw him walk silently away once the procession had passed. "But you won't find him like that," his neighbours consoled. He thanked them quietly: "I know. They won't be here till tomorrow."

His hopes lay with the Foreign Legion.

On the 22nd he encountered the same people at Schirmecker Gate; soon it was known far and wide: an Alsatian here is looking for his son. He pulled photos from his pocket, kindly men and women studied them, and now here were the first riders. In the front row, before the eyes of all these people who knew his fate and felt that it was theirs too, he stood and gazed.

The Foreign Legion. And – he saw him.

He shouted René, René, the cracked voice of an old man who always quietly spoken. He was on horseback. Gone past already. Waving and tears all around him. No one asked: "Was it really him?" All along the roadside the rumour spread: an Alsatian, an old man, has found his missing son among the troops.

Paramedics led him away from the crowd. A hundred

new lines had appeared in his wrinkled parchment-grey face; he told them: "It was my son, with the Foreign Legion." They calmed him, brought him to an ambulance, he announced he would go right away to the barracks; they were cautious how they spoke to him, said it might be better to wait till noon, the men are only now reporting in, would he like someone to go with him, and so on. He agreed to have a paramedic with him, who would take him to the hotel and then fetch him away to the barracks at two o'clock.

Now the two men entered the barracks, the troops were only just returning from the parade; they couldn't find the colonel's room or office. To the paramedic's surprise, the Procurator remained patient. When they both turned up again at five, they found they were by no means the only ones looking for son or brother or father in the regiment. The adjutant ran desperately up and down the corridor between all the worried men and women, calling out in French: "But my dear people, we are not the entire Foreign Legion. You must be patient, you must write, to the office." And he named an office, but no one wanted to write, no one wanted to know about some old office, all they wanted was their son, father, brother back again.

Towards six the regimental corporal emerged from a room with the colonel. In his hand was a list of the names being sought. In fact four are in this regiment, we have checked names and data carefully against the lists, whether other relevant persons are there is another matter. In any case, these four names will be summoned to the office at once, and the relatives should hold themselves ready. As for the others, they were not with the regiment, at least not with this particular regiment of the Foreign Legion.

Very few were satisfied with this pronouncement. The Procurator's son had not been named. A dozen or so were importunate enough that the colonel called them in one by one. And when he spoke with the Procurator, and heard the description of the son, with specific data, the colonel grew doubtful and invited the Procurator and one other man to return to the barracks next morning, when two companies would be on parade. For the Procurator insisted he had quite certainly identified his son among the mounted troops of the 1ˢᵗ Company.

"But why in all this time has he not made contact with you, sir?" asked the colonel.

This was the question the Procurator himself could never evade. Now all he said was: "Thank you, colonel, it is enough for me that he is here."

The business was not so simple for the colonel. The colonial troops were not like others. There were for sure many Alsatians and Lorrainers among them who had simply moved across to avoid serving the hated Boche; but on the normal strength of the unit there were also plenty of dubious, albeit brave, men who wanted nothing to do with their family, and whose papers (as was quite obvious but best not looked into) were not in order. They had no right, and it was not in their interest, to confront these with their more or less ruined civil existence. Nevertheless the case of the Procurator seemed impeccable, there might be something to it. The dignified person of the father, too, caused the colonel to take the case to heart.

Next morning the two companies were on parade. After the usual announcements and inspections, they were informed that two Alsatian fathers searching for their sons would be escorted by the corporal along the ranks. Grins of curiosity spread among the men. The younger of the two fathers was led along, a sprightly fellow in a black suit, carrying a knobby walking stick and gazing sternly out from beneath a black beribboned slouch hat. He thought

Citizens and Soldiers

he was inspecting the troops, in fact they were giving him the once-over: "Would you like him? How much is he worth, how much will he give, I'll put my hand up."

Then, while he was still at it, the second father, the Procurator, started off, obviously a legal person, one not to be joked about.

When he had passed down three ranks, a disturbance became evident. Whispers flew, it was hard to keep formation: "He's got him." "Who is it?" A rifle clattered to the ground, the next soldier picked it up. Father and son held each other tight, not moving. The men to left and right and the accompanying NCO looked away and at the ground. Several lowered their head and wiped their eyes with the back of a hand.

Then the Procurator, while the other father continued his search, was escorted to the colonel's office. His face was a burning red, sagging. He stepped along beside the NCO and seemed not to know that he was walking, or where to. Only when the colonel held a hand out to him in the office and shook his vigorously and he had to make a reply did a few words come out and he pulled himself together. Then he bore himself with courtesy, thanked the colonel and thought he need not detain the colonel much longer, ended by expressing thanks for the particular kindness of his son's superior officer in granting him an afternoon's leave in the city.

Back in his hotel room, the old man paced up and down. He told no one what had befallen him. He couldn't believe he was in this world. He was confused, took off his jacket and put it on, his boots off and back on. At last he lay down on the still unmade bed and quickly fell asleep until clocks struck one in the afternoon. A loud knock at the door, he called out a fierce "Enter", and his son stepped over the threshold, in uniform, and begged his pardon.

They were together until six in the evening. To evade the stream of curious, congratulating, joyful people, many of them weeping, they escaped to the big Piccadilly Café where they were able to converse amid the bustle for a good long hour. What the Procurator heard from his son differed little from what fathers in every land at that time were hearing from their sons. They spoke in low and seemingly impassive tones, faces turned to the white marble tabletop. The son explained his silence: he had been afraid his father would find him a burden.

Love and joy in the father's heart, love and joy in the son's.

The war was over, mother dead, for four years they'd had no news. But despite all the love: it was an angel of vengeance that sat across from the old Procurator. They discussed family matters. They were no longer simply son and father.

FRAU ANNY SCHARREL

Around the time when French troops under General Gouraud came marching in through Schirmecker Gate, in foggy Paris people were gathering at the venerable monument to the City of Strassburg on Place de la Concorde. War President Poincaré spoke:

"We could never pass by this monument without feeling the secret pain of our defeat, and without sensing an accusation against our passivity. We waited in silence for Righteousness to awaken. Germany, which believed it had shattered Righteousness to smithereens, and meant to deliver the final dagger-thrust, has now aroused it from its slumber. The war that was declared on us freed us from the oppression in which we found ourselves following our defeat. On 4th August 1914 we swore a formal oath never to lay down our arms until Alsace-Lorraine is restored. We have suffered the most tormenting shifts between hope and despair. The nation has fearlessly and without complaint sacrificed the blood of its young.

"Nothing broke the nation's will, the energy is rewarded, Alsace-Lorraine is again French.

"Germany has been shameless enough to turn to us to protect its armies from the population. Thus has it been forced to repudiate itself in the crudest manner. What emotions for those who for fifty years awaited this day of glory. To justify the return of Alsace-Lorraine to France, our centuries of shared glory and the heavy years of war that we have suffered together are sufficient.

"Righteousness would face a severe challenge, if the restoration to freedom of the violated peoples were to be made dependent on a new referendum."

*

Sitting alone in the big low prosperous-looking room at an enormous table – three gas flames hissing ovehead in tall frosted-glass cylinders, table covered by a big heavy red plush cloth – this is Frau Anny Scharrel, owner of this house on Hoher Steg. Down below the streets are loud with life on this day of the march-in, music booms and blares unceasingly from the nearby Café Westminster, which has transformed itself overnight into the Café de la Paix. No longer heard are the Über Alles and the Herz am Rhein, instead the anthems of every Allied nation, and every fifteen minutes the Marseillaise obtruding between waltzes and jazz music like an out-of-breath swimmer who submerges himself for a short time and then has to lift his head out of the water, and snort.

An air of exotic beauty still hung about Frau Scharrel,

even now. Her father had been a Catholic mill-owner in Lorraine, she married a wealthy spinning-factory owner from Colmar, but he had died already before the war. The family was decidedly French, Anny's father had served in 1870-71 as captain of a mobile Guards corps in Haut Rhin. Southern blood flowed visibly in the veins of Frau Scharrel. She sat in a narrow red armchair with her elbows on the chair arms, hands clasped as if taking her pulse. On the table, around the red alabaster vase, were heaped piles of papers, letters, cards, folders. She stared absently ahead, sadly. Again the Marseillaise, women's voices singing. She went to a window, made sure it was closed, sat down again. Complete silence in the big room with the French mirror over the fireplace.

She wore her chestnut-brown hair combed high, parted in the middle, waves of hair lay heavy over each ear. Simple silver ear-hoops emerged, nudged the yellow silk scarf tucked loosely around her neck. The grave face was full, complexion a little dark. In her distracted state the eyes, black and prominent, flicked gently left and right. The full lips below had a sulky air. Her hands parted, shuffled once again among the papers.

The doorbell rang. The door was opened. It was Hilde. She had come to visit this relative of her former friend Bernhard. You madman, she thought, you make yourself invisible, you think I shall come anyway. I will not come. But ... she went to Frau Scharrel's where, as such a young thing before the war, she had come to know Bernhard. Her heart pounded as she stood at the door of the room, opened to her by the maid, and peered into the familiar space. And there's his aunt, unchanged with her old high-piled coiffure, she rises with a smile and approaches in a black clinging dress fastened under the breast with a big gold buckle. Such gorgeous lace wings over each shoulder. She's in mourning for her fallen eldest, yet so elegant – mourning that with a tender gesture apologises for intruding. They embraced and kissed; sat down side by side. As she spoke and listened, Frau Scharrel placed the soft loose black fabric at her arms over the papers on the table.

"In the meantime, Franz-Maria is dead," Frau Anny said, playing with a sheet of paper. Hilde noticed she wore no mourning-ring, only a great big pearl.

"What is all this?"

"Papers they sent me afterwards. Things kept in his briefcase."

"You tried your best to get him released, Anny?"

"Tried! I blew up every bomb I had. He wasn't clever, he spoke as he thought, I told him when he came home on leave that one must be more cunning than a snake, all the more so with these adversaries, the Prussians. He promised me hand on heart he would do nothing to cause me concern. He was proud."

"What's this?" Hilde asked. It was a little book.

"Little Roger was given it at school when he moved up a class. I sent it to Franz-Maria, to amuse him." She smiled at Hilde, and offered her the book. *Fritz the Airman*.

Hilde skimmed a few lines: "By a great blessing, Fritz healed completely. Father's wounds were light, but Fritz lay for several weeks in the military hospital with a high fever. But he was young, and he recovered. Becoming whole again so soon, he merited a letter from the Kaiser. It said: 'Because of your great bravery and because of your many victories, I promote you to Lieutenant!' Do you not think this was a good medicine? A poor locksmith's lad had become an officer. And I believe that he also received the Service Medal, the Pour le mérite. I at least shall grant him this. Will you, my lads?"

Frau Anny watched Hilde as she read: "It will have amused him, don't you think?" She ruffled in the pile of papers and picked out a military travel pass third class, not valid on express or fast trains, on the reverse: To Infantryman Scharrel, on recovering his health. A theatre ticket, Union Theatre, in the right hand corner it said: Stay calm during an air raid, do not collect coats from the cloakroom, in case of danger guests may shelter in the cellar of the building. The programme was *Good morning, Herr Fischer*, together with *A complete woman* and *The man who said Goodness me*! Frau Anny told how she'd laughed at the time, they'd taken little Roger along and he was terrified of air raids. His paybook goes up to the middle of May. A ration coupon for a ready-made nightshirt, a 5% War Loan certificate. Her own work, in typescript: "Petition by widow Anny Scharrel in Strassburg regarding transfer of her son. I most humbly request the High Command to allow me to renew my petition to grant to my son Franz-Maria on account of my own serious illness – I believe the attached attests to the validity of my petition, my husband ..." (pooh, how contemptible these junior officers are). Frau Anny showed Hilde a press report, extra edition of the *Strassburger Post*: "We have learned that at four o'clock this afternoon the order was given for the total mobilisation of French armed forces. By Imperial decree the Reichstag will convene on 4th August. Price 5 Pfennig." At the bottom the younger brother had written in a clean schoolboy hand: "Sunday 2nd August 1914: the General Commanding in Strassburg is von Deimling, the Mayor of Strassburg is Dr Schwander, the High Commissioner of Alsace-Lorraine is von Dallwitz. The Kaiser of Germany is: Wilhelm II, the Kaiserin of Germany is Auguste Victoria. The Emperor of Austria: Joseph II. The President of France: Poincaré. The King of

England: George. The King of Serbia: Peter. The Tsar of Russia: Nicholas."

A small crumpled sheet of green paper ("I forwarded that to him in the field myself!") Despatch. Berlin, 12 December 1916: "Soldiers! With the scent of victory gained through your bravery, I and the rulers of our loyal Central Powers have made an offer of peace to the enemy. Whether the goal of this action will be achieved is as yet undecided. Meanwhile, with God's help you shall continue to resist and strike at the enemy. Supreme Headquarters. Wilhelm. To the German Army." Underneath: "If despite this offer the struggle must continue, the Central Powers are determined to bring it to a victorious conclusion, but formally repudiate any responsibility."

Hilde: "He would have been glad to see this. If only they had agreed to it."

"You mean he might still be alive."

Frau Anny rested her head on her hand. "It's happened. If you were to ask him now and he appeared as a ghost (sometimes I imagine him here in this room, he sits just over there), I know what my Franz-Maria would say. He'd reject any such question out of hand. Could he do anything better with his life than destroy tyranny – tyranny was his word – that's what he used to ask me. He had to endure much, in his unit."

A line of blank picture postcards from the Association for Infant Care that she had bought from a collector; on the face a motto: "We bow down to God because he is so great, and to the Infant because it is so small." (He never used any of these cards, if I know him, he found such nonsense amusing.) One picture showed a young mother with an infant in her arms, an eagle overhead: "The German Eagle spreads his protecting pinions over you all, German mothers and children!" Frau Anny, fire in her eyes: "They lie. They have shattered us."

And then there were the bundled piles of letters. Frau Anny laid both arms across them like a black cloud: "So here we all are, fathers, mothers, children, and when we hear the military marches and the Marseillaise we think: what use is that to us now. Gone is gone. It tears the heart when they sing and blare away. But, whether we will or no, whether we feel guilty or no, we are the survivors."

"God, Anny," Hilde breathed, staring at the calm, even placid woman. See those wonderful lace wings on her shoulders, how delicately the lipstick has traced the lips.

"I'm sure you never thought you were coming to a house of mourning, Hilde. What do you think those out there, the statesmen, will do with those who died, and whose death enables them to hatch their plans? I already see them, everywhere, in Strassburg, all over Alsace-Lorraine, in every village, in the main square close by the Post Office busy erecting a monument, a hero, a warrior, he's falling, holding a flag. Then there'll be an unveiling ceremony, speeches will be made, the minister will play his part. And then I'm supposed to think of Franz-Maria. Statesmen draw their consequences from the war, we draw ours. But weeping is not a consequence."

"Then what is the consequence, Anny?"

Frau Anny lay back in her armchair with a mildly mocking expression. "I will not be robbed of my inheritance. I shall take up my inheritance. I – and not some intriguer, deputy, minister. For example, Prussian judges took from me and my late husband the right to my Lorraine properties, it was an unjust trial. I have instructed that my claim be reasserted. You think me common? That I'm acting like a petty shopkeeper who exults in the French victory because he can chase all the other drapers out of town? Let's just do it! Let's be common."

The maid knocked, and placed a covered tea-trolley next to the mistress of the house's armchair. Frau Anny poured for her guest in silence, dismissed the maid with a nod. As they bit into their biscuit she kept an attentive eye on her guest, who was pensively trickling sugar from her spoon into the cup. Hilde was thinking of reservists in the East where she had been with a Red Cross group, Vilnius wasn't it, such jolly men, all having tremendous fun, one had a chicken farm, another had built a pigsty. "We're making ready for a long war," they laughed, with their big beards they already looked Russian, all they objected to was the many immunisations, they asked if they'd be immunised next against hunger and thirst.

"You're engaged, Hilde, or married?"

"Why?"

"You seem so. More mature."

"I wasn't such a baby chick then."

"Still."

"One lives through so much, Anny. War is no child's play."

"Once you had a crush on my nephew, my so-called nephew Bernhard. I haven't seen him in a long while. What's happened to him."

"I don't know." Hilde laughed.

"Why do you laugh?"

"Because you live closer to him than I do. We were out in Ukraine, so far away."

"And you didn't write to one another?"

Hilde sipped at her little cup. "Bernhard and I? No."

Frau Anny fiddled with her left earring. "You've matured. Perhaps you're mature enough to be annexed by France?" Hilde glanced at her. Frau Anny was smiling into her cup, such a barbed, mocking, maddening smile.

"You're a complete Alsatian, Lotte from Goethe's *Werther*, or Gretchen from *Faust*. You were born in Strassburg, but your family comes from Sesenheim. That man from Frankfurt am Main, Goethe, came over the Rhine to us, he didn't make babies, not even with his Lotte, and so he brought into the world an entire generation of Gretchens, Lottes, peopled Alsace with them and let them all go to seed right up until yesterday. You're one of them. Not me, I come from Lorraine. But I too had to take a bite of your apple, living here as I do." She put her cup down, shifted closer to Hilde. The piles of paper on the big table lay silent and forlorn beneath the white hissing gas lamps like some jagged hollow moon crater, and who knows how those once burned, glowed and blossomed.

Hilde sat hunched on the little wicker stool. Frau Anny laid both delicate hands on Hilde's knees and gazed up to her lips, her eyes: "They've made this land so ... stupid. Wherever they go they make people clumsy, fat and stupid. They spread the mentality of sheep. Am I right? Clean streets, punctual post, and this. I don't even like their Heinrich Heine, though he was Jewish and was said to oppose them, but the 'Lorelei', 'She was like a flower' - syrup, syrup."

Hilde: "And what was her love like?" (Lieutenant Becker in his chair, we said goodbye, my breasts, such a magical hour.)

"So I'm Penelope, awaiting her husband who has been in the Trojan War?"

"I never thought of you like that."

"You should have. I've spent painfully long years getting over it. Or the Indian widow mounting the funeral pyre. All that was nearer to me than the truth. You know the German midday meal, a thick hot slab of meat, twenty potatoes, each one this big. Sit down to a French déjeuner. It starts with an hors d'oeuvre, three, four, five items accompanied by a Pernod. Then comes the fish course, followed by a slice of meat or chicken, vegetables, salad, and then cheese, many kinds of cheese, you can choose, fruit, dessert, cognac; wine throughout the meal, white or red depending what they have, finishing with coffee and a cigarette. One déjeuner. That's German love and French love. But they're by no means 'heavenly love' and 'earthly love'."

"So what are they?"

"Hah, German ineptitude. From a German all you get, let me try not to be indecent, is at best a bellyful. A Frenchman bestirs and involves you totally."

"It's all in your dreams, Anny."

Hilde understood none of this. Anny, with the little dimple in the round full chin, seemed to her more delightful than ever, but from the corners of her mouth such sorrowful little lines tracked downwards.

Before Anny could reply, the bell in the corridor rang. Both stood up. The maid appeared in the doorway to announce two young ladies. "Show them to the sitting room, please," Anny said. They went across.

As soon as the guests were in, Anny closed the door. They seemed cut from a photograph entitled "The two sisters of Herr X" or "The daughters of Madame Y". They approached Frau Scharrel slowly, smiling. Shiny black hair, combed tight with a centre parting, covered the ears. They were of a small build, stocky without being dumpy. And as soon as they were through the door – they had to enter one behind the other – they came side by side again and linked arms. There was a slight flush on the round clear faces. What emphasised their identicality was less the exact same costumes, the same heavy black shawl with the ornate fringe, rather the identical gestures, the mild attentive intelligent open gaze from big brown-black eyes beneath strong severe brows. Unusual, the eyebrows, they lay like furry caterpillars and at any moment might show signs of a quite different and unexpected life. The rather long, finely chiselled nose was not prominent. In this they resembled Frau Anny; her face inclined like theirs to broadness. The younger sister's mouth, as she approached, pouted for a kiss.

They stood there in long loose afternoon frocks that revealed not a trace of breasts, hips and legs, and offered a cheek for Anny to kiss. For all that they concealed the rest of the body – a convent of fabric, meant as an invitation to rape – the frocks were cut away a little at the throat. Into this space pendants dangled on a fine gold necklace. Once they came free of Anny they once again linked arms, and were introduced: nieces of Frau Scharrel, Bernhard's second cousins. They stood on the carpet in the circle of yellow satin covered armchairs, chatted and observed one another, the young ladies were so happy they'd be able to visit Paris this winter, it was so unexpected, such a surprise that it's now become possible. The young ladies let their clever gaze rest attentively on Hilde, they had not met before, they were from Lorrainean Metz, while Hilde was Alsace society.

A curate was shown in, a slim elderly gentleman with a sharp active face, pince-nez on his nose, you could see the professor in him, a clever talker always ready for a debate, he too Lorrainer by birth who had studied at the episcopal Gymnasium in Montigny, later in Rome and Paris. They sat in a circle. Hilde looked on bemused, she let herself go, related her war adventures.

As the two sisters– there was something softly catlike about them – made ready to leave (maybe we'll meet again in Paris), and everyone stood up, the older of the two adjusted her shawl, having cast a little pious glance at her sister, and asked with elegant sangfroid, whether it's all still on for Sunday, yes? "And will Bernhard be there?"

Frau Anny, resisting the temptation to look back at Hilde, put an arm over the older sister's shoulder as she saw them out: "I hope that young man will have the grace to remember older ladies too."

Hilde remained seated beside the curate, as if held at swordpoint. Bernhard had visited his aunt, and she'd kept quiet about it. Why? What's going on? When Anny came slowly back in and sat down, she seemed distracted, avoided eye contact with Hilde. The priest had a lot on his mind, and was happy to sit between the two ladies.

He praised the splendid behaviour of the Alsatian populace, who with a few trivial exceptions had not allowed themselves to be drawn into acts of revenge; of course the sensible way in which the so-called Soldiers' and Workers' Councils of the Germans had confined themselves to practicalities made peaceful developments easier. "But then," he clapped his hands together, "the Protestants. One cannot accuse the Catholic Church of harbouring sympathy for people who commit stupid acts like placing a red flag on the cathedral. A prank by young boobies. Still, they could have dropped the idea. But Protestants, professors, men in official positions, trying to bring a dissonant tone to the pacific and joyful celebrations of these past days! So foolish! Where, I wonder, would they be if the Reds had not been so afraid of the French but had been able to take their revolutionary programme as far as they wanted. What would become of their churches and schools. And instead of being grateful to the new upholders of state power, some even plonk themselves down and protest about the evangelical service to be held in celebration of the entry of the French, to welcome

Marshal Pétain."

Anny seemed to have found herself again. "But our Church takes a different stance towards France."

The priest removed his pince-nez, and smiled: "I wasn't sure if I should nod or shake my head. You mean the old powerful Catholicism of the French. But they had a Revolution in France too. In the Germany of old, the Catholics had no bed of roses, but then along came Bismarck to do battle against us, and never, so he said, would he go to Canossa as once a German emperor did, but he had to in the end. Our Church is not surprised by events such as those happening around us now, she has for everything, in official parlance, a *precedent case*, should it be necessary. But is it necessary? Think how we as Catholics stand in relation to our respective Fatherlands in which we dwell in accordance with Nature. The Church gives preference to no state. She doesn't exult when some state is victorious, she grieves when one is defeated, she takes sides in no war, and no state is her state, because it is said: My kingdom is not of this world. She grieves over every war. She rejoices when hostilities end. Her task is always to strive to minimise and bring an end to hostilities. Her domain is Love."

Now Anny was playing with her lace wings, and suddenly Hilde felt the questioning satiny gaze alight on her. Anny said: "Before your reverence arrived, I was having a long conversation with my friend Hilde about Alsace. We have to think how to modernise the Alsatians. To me they are too German. Even my good Hilde. She admitted to me: her model is Werther's Lotte. Every night before she goes to sleep she opens the window and looks up at the heavens and sings: "I don't know what it could mean, or why I am so sad…' or "Once a boy a rosebud spied…'."

"Anny," Hilde pleaded. Priest: "It must delight the

neighbours."

But Anny was on the scent, and pursued it. "We women rejoice that refined France is taking over and the Church goes along with it. For we know they walk hand in hand."

The priest gave a complacent smile, and was all ears.

"For there's something about the Germans, linked to their primal-forest nature, which is in direct contradiction to the French, and to the Church as well. It reveals itself in the Germans, primal-forest-wise, in so many respects. You will permit me to think as a woman of that renowned German 'sensibility' and the ghastly way it makes itself known in German declarations of love."

The priest, amused: "You seem to be launching a veritable campaign against German love, now we have the Armistice. Madam, this we do not want! We prefer not to involve ourselves either in politics or in love."

"Oh, but you involve yourselves very much in love."

"On one particular point. We desire a place in love for divine laws as well."

Anny, opening her right hand: "But I think so too. If I may speak a little coarsely: where German love falls, there grows ... no, not that, no, I was about to say, there grass no longer grows; what I mean is, there *only* grass grows." The curate became uneasy. He said nothing. A confession, in disguise. Was this thin ice, something interesting?

Anny, not quitting the scent: "For a woman (and as a widow I can say this) it is important to know: to what extent does the man see in us only the fleshly human, the woman, Eve."

"Absolutely right. The Church concerns herself intensively with this question. Of course she provides only basic principles. It is up to the married couple, especially the woman, to take care of the practical aspects."

Anny was mollified. Having achieved this result she

turned to Hilde, her face young and happy: "So you see, Hilde, what it's all about: the degree of rapprochement. One should not lose the initiative. Withdrawing, attracting, rejecting: we women determine the degree of magnetism by our deliberation."

The priest chuckled: "You're turning it into an essay on physics and coquetterie."

Anny: "And on the education of the male."

Hilde was disoriented. She grew ever more deeply disturbed. What is this? A relapse into old times? As she left she noticed a slender walking pole in the umbrella stand in the corridor. She recognised it; the handle was a fire-breathing dragon in ivory. It was Bernhard's. He had left it here. Her heart faltered.

At last she gained the street, furious that she had allowed herself to be persuaded to make this visit, on the trail of Bernhard, as if she would ever find anything other than poison.

She stood outside the Café Westminster, with its new sign, Café de la Paix. A crowd was listening to the music and ignoring the cold as the bright light streamed over them. This is what he has made of her, that even now she must stand like this, distraught, shattered, he who never lets her be. But why has she gone through the whole war, why has she come here, and she had freed herself from him, from the man who has used this entire terrible time to continue his wicked ways.

And now he has Anny.

And those two smooth mamselles, the sisters who want to go to Paris? The whole long war and the deaths of millions of good men were not enough to slay that beast.

I left here in 1914. I toiled day and night. I lay ill. I came back ill to Alsace, did more nursing. The sick, the dying blew in upon me like a cold draught through a gap in the door. It never stopped. They collapsed at our feet, refugees, women and children. The little hospital, Richard the airman, Maus, Becker, all, all of it. And after four years of such a life, such horrors, self-sacrifice, sacrifice, devotion, it's all back where it was. Nothing has changed. God has seen none of it. All of it ... must once more fall on me.

She went back home, thinking: So Anny betrayed her husband whom she idolised, and her son was killed, and she's false enough to ask if Bernhard ever wrote to me.

In bed she wept in shame and rage. By morning she had decided to go across to Germany. But something held her back. She would not make it so easy for them.

What if I still love him, still cling to him as horribly as before, shall I let myself be torn to bits and tear him to bits and let him humiliate me and be unable to escape? That murderer. What did he make of my youth. Did I still have a Self?

And she laid herself on the rack of the four days until Sunday, when she would meet him again.

She went daily to the cathedral. She stood outside, asked: did the war change nothing? She went in, and grew calmer.

And when she came out and stood on the square, she sighed again and asked herself in wonderment: of what stuff did God make us?

OF DEEP AND DANGEROUS GERMANY

Maurice Barrès arrived in Strassburg overflowing with impressions of Metz. He stayed with a young lawyer, Kössel, who had visited him shortly before the war in Paris, in Neuilly. Kössel, an admirer of Barrès' style, had even then invited him to be his guest, if his path ever led him back to Charmes, his childhood home south of Nancy, and would like to see friends old and new in Strasbourg. But Barrès, the old Hellenist, had gone travelling in his beloved south, to the Orient, until alarm bells began to ring out over Europe after Sarajevo. Barrès, returning to France, saw the excitement, the enthusiasm and the tears at the start of the war, the abyss gaping beneath the thin ground of bourgeois existence, lived through the fearful days and the evacuation of Paris at the end of August, beginning of September. But he did not leave the city which had suddenly become a small town; how he felt himself ageing. Now, fifty months later, here he was in Strasbourg. The lawyer welcomed him, proud as a boy at this visit by a holy man. That evening at dinner, the young couple had invited the proprietor of a Lorraine newspaper, an elderly bald man who had come with Barrès from Metz to witness Marshal Pétain's entry. After the meal they sat in the very roomy and cosy library, which was also the lawyer's music room, on the corner sofa with their coffee.

"One feels just like a couple of newly-weds," Barrès said again as he lowered himself to the sofa, "arms full of flowers, everyone laughing, waving." The small young very blond wife told what she had seen today in the streets. It was delirium, a tumult. Barrès said: "A sea of joy."

"Young Alsatian girls were kissing French officers. Strasbourg never saw so much kissing."

The bald man from Lorraine, grave, with a pointed beard, screwed his thoughtful eyes even smaller: "There are other things. We've had difficult days. As you've heard, Barrès. There are girls – I can give you their names – who swore to take the veil if God should ever let Alsace fall to the French again."

Barrès waved it off: "I know." He was tall and slender in stature; his face was unusual, long and sallow with a hooked nose, a thick dark melancholy moustache. You could see why people saw Gypsy blood. But his origins were on the Moselle, and on his mother's side from the Auvergne. His black hair stuck to his head in a thin layer. "Let us be glad and thankful. The days of the evil overlords are past. It will be long before they have a chance to be evil again."

He looked into his coffee cup, made a little gesture with the flat of his hand. "Let me tell you something. Listen to what I experienced on Wednesday, this Wednesday just past, in Metz. I accompanied the prefect, Mirman from Nancy, who has been appointed civil governor in Metz for the Republic. At nine in the morning we left our hotel to go to the governor's palace, which is now once again the seat of a French prefect. The gate still sports the old Napoleonic eagle. On the steps the former employees and officials were drawn up as a glum honour guard. We saw correct but somewhat worried men. They knew to bow very low before their new masters. We had to pass through a dozen rooms and eventually reached the salon. The windows had no glass. Some of our officers and officials were waiting there for us. Mirman ordered that the German ex-governor, who was still in the building, should be told that his immediate presence was awaited at the requested audience. What, my dear friends, did I imagine after these fifty months of war, after the enormous battles, the devastation and burning, after the whole indescribable process by which the world was set in motion and by which it almost went down in flames? What did I think, who would appear now? I thought: the one now coming, this high-ranking personality of the enemy power, representative of the Kaiser at a significant juncture, he will approach glowering, maybe maintain silence. He will find it hard to open his mouth. We shall now and then retreat before his angry gaze so filled with grief and hatred. We shall see the bitter expression of the defeated, deprived of his sword, hands bound behind his back." He paused, fiddled with the pearl pin in his wide black tie, a hint of a smile at his lips and eyes:

"One of our younger literati once described the entrance of a famous but no longer young actress in the role of Athalia, how she was set down on the stage in a golden litter beneath a baldachin, how she rose from it. God, everyone gasped, so she can still stand! She moves, she can still walk! She opens her mouth, she can still talk! Tumultuous applause, a total success."

The listeners chuckled.

"So, there we are, sitting. And in comes, not someone struck by lightning, but a tall dried-up gentleman with spectacles, a man of around sixty, he makes a formal greeting left and right, and sits down at the table opposite Mirman. Now you should know that at the entry of our troops into Metz, a French staff officer, as provided by law, informed the German governor in the citadel that his post was abolished, whereupon General Maudhy Mirman installed himself in the building, and Mirman, as he entered his office, did something self-explanatory, even officially required: he had the portrait of the Kaiser that still hung on the wall removed by French soldiers. This action upset the remarkable baron, and he complained to French officers about improprieties, provocations. Now, with the Kaiser's ex-governor sitting opposite him, Mirman began by describing this incident. He remarked in a temperate tone that one could hardly speak of provocations and improprieties. The only point is this: that you, sir, left behind a picture in a house that is no longer yours. The baron kept silent. He lifted his chin high in the air, his face was very pale. He was quite unable to respond in an equally simple and temperate way. Quite unexpectedly he made a bow in the manner of a pocket-knife snapping shut. In bureaucratic speak, this meant: Noted.

"Mirman continued. He maintained his calm benevolent tone. It was to the credit of the former governor, he said, that, in contrast to the usages of other Germans, he had ameliorated certain tensions between the local population and the German military. This was one reason why he had felt it appropriate to grant the baron an audience. He offered to take measures to ease his departure. Whereupon the baron made the same jerking gesture, and now something fantastical occurred. You will not believe me, but I report what I myself heard and saw.

"Maybe I had indulged in too much romanticism as we waited for him, when, instead of a pensioned privy counsellor, I had expected a Vercingetorix face to face with Caesar. For what follows I claim no poetic licence. Imagine: the baron suddenly begins to speak, vigorously, indeed he actually comes alive. What has aroused him to life? His family, family cares. They should be allowed to remain in government buildings. He requested this. He recounted to Mirman in great detail all the difficulties that would arise if he and his family were forced to move to a hotel. You will scarcely believe it possible, the day after our occupation of Metz, he, the governor. We exchanged glances, Mirman gave an evasive reply. But now the no longer diffident gentleman really went to town; he proposed to vacate all the offices leaving just a few rooms for himself and his family, please please, just this! A lamentable, horrible scene. We couldn't believe our ears. I assure you, my dear friends, we were stunned. We asked ourselves: What is this, is it really just stupid private egoism, a naïve, I'd like to say insolent egoism, that he dares at such a moment calmly to expose himself? Or is it a cunning trick? Does he believe

OF DEEP AND DANGEROUS GERMANY

that while we may have an Armistice, afterwards it will turn out differently? Mirman became icy cold. He replied: a choice must be made as to who shall reside in a hotel: the commissioner appointed by the French Republic, or the baron, who no longer represents anything in this city. And does he need workmen to help with his packing. The audience was over."

Everyone was astonished. The hostess said: "It won't have been a trick. He's a type, Molière's miser Harpagon. The old man wants no disturbance to his orderly life."

The lawyer nodded, smiling: "And in wartime."

The bald Lorrainer said he had observed the same in Germans he had encountered during the war. On his own the fellow's small and ordinary. Many who instil fear in their official position turn out to be utter dopes. But command, official position, makes him fearsome. "The baron, the ex-governor, stands there suddenly without his corset, and now you see him."

Barrès was dissatisfied, he stepped nervously to the round marble table. "So you accept the thesis that the Germans are actually good people, and that only the Hohenzollerns, the generals, the general staff have made them what they proved themselves to be during the war."

"One need not take it so far." The editor applied the brakes, fearing a rising storm – but it had already broken. Barrès had a nonchalant, reserved way of speaking. Now he laid both hands on the satin lapels of his black frock-coat: "They don't take it so far, you believe. But where is the limit? Do you not realise that such expressions lead to a dangerously slippery slope? There!" With a little turn to the right and one little reach to his side – remarkable, such obviously prepared sureness – he pulled a leather-bound volume from the shelf: "Romain Rolland, Jean-Christophe Krafft and the superiority of the German race. As taught

Citizens and Soldiers

at the Sorbonne after 1870. He sang Germany's praises. And now the war, the horrors, Miss Cavell, Dinant, the torpedoing of the *Lusitania*. These perfect Germans! The experiment, do you not see it? Those well-meaning professors, how they befogged the world. Rolland is proven wrong by the war. His entire oeuvre has gone bankrupt. What we have experienced is the unmasking of the philosophy of the conqueror. Romain Rolland – France rejects him, as it rejected Caillaux, Malvy and Almereyda. Whither can he flee, to elude the verdict that has been pronounced on him!"

The Lorrainer took a sip of coffee and said soothingly: "D'accord. As for Romain Rolland, we all heard the news from Vienna at the outbreak of war, that the city had banned all French plays from its theatres, but soon they were playing Romain Rolland. Conclusion: to them he is no Frenchman. And he never protested to Vienna."

Barrès, with a slight nod to the host, replaced the book on the shelf. The hostess looked away, her face burned, she'd been persuaded to place the book within reach of where Barrès now stood. To hide her embarrassment she offered the gentlemen cigarettes, smoked one herself. Barrès, who had noticed nothing amiss, was still deep in thought. He thanked her softly, eyelids lowered, he does not smoke, he must be content to inhale the pleasant smoke of the others' cigarettes. And as he pursued his train of thought, the young lawyer scrutinised the grim earth-coloured face that seemed so cold and immobile, like Pascal's death mask. Someone had said: he is a Prometheus, who has become his own eagle.

Barrès: "They mean to make the Kaiser their scapegoat. You can understand why, it's not a bad notion. Some Englishmen are playing along, I don't know why. A mischievous notion. The dishonesty is patent. The Kaiser's actions were endorsed by all Germans. They kept silent, fought, manufactured munitions, until there was no longer any point. It is especially important in Alsace-Lorraine to make this crystal clear in the light of all that is now coming, the cleansing of the region, the great sieve. This was not a Hohenzollern war, but a war of all Germany. With a few exceptions, who don't count. The whole of Germany went along, provided accomplices. Now that the time has come to settle accounts, they revile him. They vie with one another in their rage against the dynasties. No, I say, no, three times no! With blood on their hands and deceit in their faces, every German is the image of a Hohenzollern."

He laid this out with cold assurance. They saw him and knew him, the tireless man who since the war's beginning had, year in year out, four and five times a week under a relentless compulsion, fired off his articles for the *Echo de Paris*, urging, assailing, domineering, denouncing – and always the same two words: France and Victory. The young lawyer once visited a Hellenist at Neuilly: now how he's changed, how he throws himself into the War, his whole being burns about the War, but it has consumed him as well. How gaunt he is. He looks as if he won't long survive the triumph.

The hostess overcame her discomfort the longer she observed him. A feminine desire to mollify arose in her. She said her husband had obtained a French newspaper for her, this was already some while back, from the beginning of the month, the time before the Armistice. And in it she had read of a grand celebratory assembly at the Sorbonne in honour of Alsace-Lorraine (Barrès gave a confirmatory nod), presided over by a State Secretary from the War Ministry. (Barrès: State Under-secretary Jeanneny.) "I beg your pardon. And besides Charles Andler, whom we know, and others, you spoke as well. We were very glad to see this, because we are always glad to come across your name. You could not believe, Monsieur Barrès, how books bring people together, and how you too bring my husband and me together." (Long surprised gaze of unwonted tenderness from Barrès over the two young people.) "And then you spoke of Alsace, and our dialect. This made us unspeakably happy."

Barrès: "I know Alsace, madame. It has a wonderfully refined, hearty and humorous dialect. We alas were educated only in High German, so we miss many nuances of this unspoiled language. There is no reason to blend it with High German. To do so would only demonstrate its dependence, the political dependence of Alsace on Germany. As I said at the Sorbonne, and you read about it, the Alsace dialect will fit well with our Provençal, Basque, Breton, Flemish. We are faced, slowly, with a kind of decentralisation. What do you think of that, my friend?"

He turned to the editor, who raised both hands: "Don't pour too many blessings on us. First we want to be left to savour France again at our leisure. That's the only wish of us all."

Barrès: "So much the better."

"You don't mean to swallow us up hair and hide, all at once. And anyway you know, Monsieur Barrès, that you're in the Strasbourg that gave France its national anthem?"

Barrès, animated: "Does he have a memorial here, a plaque, Rouget de Lisle?"

The hostess laughed: "Where is this leading to, Monsieur Barrès?"

He drew out his notebook: "I shall make a note."

The hostess, with a playful bow: "Aha, the parliamentary deputy."

"I was alas unable to serve France in the trenches,

madame. But I strive wherever I can, without jostling a neighbour, to make myself useful."

The lawyer: "Since we're talking of autonomy, are you two gentlemen aware of the curious manoeuvre à la Lenin they tried to play on us last week? Ah! I'm glad. Now I can take my little revenge, just a little bit, for the fantastic story Monsieur Barrès brought us from Metz."

The editor from Lorraine: "A Leninist manoeuvre?" (He stared wide-eyed at the host.) "Last week, in Strasbourg?"

The proud host laid his head back: "You mean your journalists missed it? Well, you know it in outline, of course. But permit me my revenge. Monsieur Barrès. You recall that business in 1917, when Ludendorff, instead of destroying the Russian front with canon, stuck Lenin and his associates in the famous sealed train in Switzerland and let it travel across Germany. The attempt succeeded, so much so that an encore was called for. They tried it on us. Word of honour, Director, please hear me out. Berlin tried it first in the usual way, grant us autonomy Prussian style, that business with Schwander and Hauss, shocking, the way they sang the song of democracy to us back then. They were convinced a referendum in Alsace-Lorraine would show eighty percent in favour of Germany."

The editor laughed his deep complacent laugh: "And why not? I was convinced it would succeed, with appropriate support from doctored voter lists, maybe they'd have ordered people to come across the Rhine."

The lawyer: "Our golden man Peirotes and his counterpart in Metz, Jung, were supposed to play along. Instead they queered the Berliners' pitch. But they were a long way from giving up. They were all too keen to maintain their protecting little hand over Alsace-Lorraine. Comes the revolution. You can't deny their tenacity and guile. They set revolution in play. And now the Lenin tour. In Wilhelmshaven they gather two hundred sailors from Alsace-Lorraine fresh from the wellspring of the revolution, pack them aboard a cosy special train, and send them on down here with a huge red flag."

Barrès: "When was this?" The lawyer, to his wife: "When did they come? You were down by the station when they arrived."

"It was Mamma's birthday, the fourteenth."

Barrès: "This 14th November?"

"Yes, not ten days ago. The whole drama actually played out very swiftly, it became a wholly Alsatian story. So the sailors arrived all eager and wanted to declare the Republic of Alsace-Lorraine without further ado, as they'd been tasked. Anyway we suspected something of the sort, at least an impulse, a mutual understanding, and our sailors, as honourable men, at once promptly acquitted themselves of their task. But now, as in the business with Schwander and Hauss, our Peirotes intervened – he really deserves a monument – and declared: that won't do. You have to know with what assurance Peirotes can declare that something *won't do*. Why won't it do, and how. No, what won't do, won't do, the situation now is like this. Basta. They caught on quickly. Their rebellion didn't last long. The revolutionaries believed him when he said it *won't do*. They were Alsatians with an Alsatian."

Barrès, smiling: "Clever revolutionaries. They should be tracked down and given a medal."

The mood was cheerful as could be. Barrès leaned back comfortably in his seat: "Alsace-Lorraine should become an international republic within the national framework of Germany."

Loud laughter. Barrès: "Among ourselves, I consider the entire revolution a deceptive ploy. If it wasn't concocted by the generals, it is certainly very convenient for them. These fellows, you can be sure, will over the next few months on no account be robbed of their revolution."

More laughter. But not from Barrès. No, he gestured with his hand, inviting attention: "The revolution suits them down to the ground. Just think: neither the Hohenzollerns nor the Supreme General Staff sent a representative to the Armistice negotiations. A General Winterfeldt came, the main spokesman was the Reichstag deputy Erzberger. The plan, the line is clear: to brush off responsibility, absolve themselves of the consequences. Then they can use brave Herr Erzberger as a punching-bag. The summit, the Supreme Headquarters, soars silent above the clouds."

They pondered this. The host spoke quietly: "We noticed something strange at the time. At the start the commanding general here offered serious resistance to the Soldiers' Councils, which is quite understandable. We heard of long conferences. Suddenly, an order from above: give way."

Barrès: "There you have it. The plan, the line."

The lawyer: "Indisputably. On the other hand, not everything goes as one might wish. Eight days ago a Division marches in with music blaring, all ranks displaying badges, not one red armband. The next day: revolt. It was elementary."

Barrès, attentive: "I agree. So you think it had something to do with the revolution?"

"Maître Barrès, the generals and the government make use of them to deflect from the demands that are coming. But they won't find them so easy to deal with."

Barrès brought his surprised face directly into the light of the electric table lamp: "There are real revolutionaries among the Germans? No joking, please."

The lawyer, in earnest: "There are."

"And what do they want?"

"Peace. I don't know. Respite, bread, no officers."

Barrès: "Moscow?"

"Playing along. I often heard World Revolution in the Workers' Council. They want to abolish militarism and capitalism."

Barrès sat back with a shrug of the shoulders: "Slogans. I know the slogans. They mean to declare insolvency, so there'll be nothing to pay."

The lawyer and his wife exchanged a brief glance. She leaned forward with her left arm on her knee supporting her head, listening intently. Yesterday, learning that Barrès would be in Alsace, she had spoken of him as such a socialist-eating ogre; the day before the murder of Jaurès he had used words in the Chamber that could be construed as instigating the assassination, but after the assassination he visited the house of his martyred adversary and shook hands with the daughter and the socialist Blum, who was also present – so, notwithstanding, an upright man, a character.

Barrès cast a veiled look at the hostess: "I seem hard to you, madame? I do. I see it. I would ask you to consider something in my favour. We represent a great, proud, downtrodden people. Our weakness was used in 1870 to defeat us and wrest these provinces from the motherland. And then we were attacked again by this same adversary. He thought we were still as decadent, in the same state of weakness, as in 1870. We did have fits of weakness during the war. Our blood flowed in rivers. The adversary was overwhelming, more than that, cruel, merciless, without pity for weak or strong. He had eyes only on victory. He tore open our sacred soil in order to implant himself in it. But this soil engendered Joan of Arc. A demonic terror preceded the enemy. Towns, villages, churches lay in ashes.

He must have victory! One and a half million of our best men had to sacrifice themselves to bring him to a halt. No longer was it a war by France, England, America. Christian, Catholic, Protestant, Jew, teachers, priests, all brought their spirit into the war. They made it Christian, Protestant, Catholic, Jewish. They turned it into a war of religion. I, madame, remained what I always was: a small voice in the struggle. But if you regard this struggle, which has wound down but is not yet over, in such a light, you will pardon my use of this or that expression. Do not call me hard. Call me devout."

She had grown pale, and whispered: "I do beg your pardon. I didn't mean to make you angry." Tears rose in her eyes, he leaned forward and kissed her hand.

"It is I who should beg pardon, madame, for uttering such grave words in your lovely library, and while we are at coffee."

The bald Lorrainer stood up with a sigh: "Great days, my friends. Which have an obverse for our sort, namely that they allow us no rest. Alas, alas, I must take my leave."

Barrès too stood up with alacrity: "You're going outside? I shall join you. I want to see, hear, taste. Ah, dear friends, how happy I am."

And he shook hands with them all, one after the other, with an intimacy they never would have expected from this reserved man.

★

When lawyer Kössel and his wife stood alone in the music room and looked across to the empty corner sofa, she put her arms around him, clung to him: "I feel sad."

He stroked her gently. "I understand."

She: "I'd have liked to keep him. So liked to keep him

as he used to be. There are writers who disappoint when you meet them. Not he. He terrifies."

She sat down on the sofa. Grumpily, with a movement like Barrès', she pulled out the Rolland volume and opened it. Then, in great agitation, she pressed her head to her husband's shoulder. And as he felt for her hand and they kept silent – she with eyes tight shut and lips pressed together – a rapid conversation flitted through her head: How actually, Monsieur Barrès, did you come by your enormous anger against Germany? – I saw their brutality already as a child, in the war of 1870. – Has your anger not abated in the meantime? You've studied German writings, philosophy, poetry, music. You've met decent Germans. – There are worthy Germans. I never heard their voices during the war. – That tells us nothing. War is a tyrant. It suppresses speech. – The mask has fallen. They have exposed themselves. With this war they have befouled themselves before all ethical humanity. – Who? How? In what way? Did their troops not fight according to the rules of strategy? Mozart and Beethoven, Dürer: do they now count for nothing? – Don't mention strategy to me. Things happened that ...

Suddenly she lifted her head from her husband's shoulder. He watched her attentively from the side. No, I won't listen to him. What he says is lies and deceit. He is a big repellent brain. They should never have sent him here from Paris.

*

Barrès and the Lorrainer strode along the streets in search of sensations. They had their money's worth. An excitement that mounted day by day to a state of tumult had taken hold of the city. Few could bear to stay indoors.

Until deep into the night they paraded around singing and making a din, locals in civvies, demobbed Alsatians in army greatcoats and civilian hats.

In the cold and darkness of the main street people now thronged together and formed a procession. A military band at the head, a big torchlit parade set off from Kleber Place, accompanied by loud cheers. And there they were, flanked left and right by torchbearers: the musicians. The drum major in the lead with the whirling baton and huge moustache, the drums and fifes, bugles, cornets, and behind them, crash, crash, cymbals and thumping kettledrums. It unleashed such tremendous enthusiasm, and they all loved it so, this uproar in the city that had come alive as if at a wedding, they so loved the drums and the fifes, the trumpets and bugles, the tambourines and drums, and those, those who banged and blew them, trumpeters, fifers, drummers, tambourine men, so much that as they returned through the wild carnival streets they never made it back to barracks.

The first to be dragged from the procession were the tambourine men. Girls took them by the arm and off they went. They carved a little slice of wedding cake for themselves. The drum major with the waving whiskers and beaming smile was next. The band marched on without him. Lightning struck the buglers. The trumpeters were abducted and carried off into the heavens by eagles with female hair shrieking in delight. The fifers, where are they? Vanished, the first, the second, the whole rank. The tempest enveloped the drummers, who had hoped to escape. And finally, the kettledrums with their thundering challenge. But the drum and the man behind it could not evade Fate. They were the last lappet of the flag that the masses swung. Once again he boomed, and then his hands were no longer free, somebody else grabbed the drumstick, the

Citizens and Soldiers

drum was pulled off him.

That night they never made it back to barracks. History does not relate how much time they were granted to dream it off in the police cells.

★

But behind unlit windows, Old Germans sat in their houses. There were some sixty thousand of them, a big number for the city of Strassburg. They were not allowed a voice, no one wanted to hear what they were going through. They were frightened, hid away. Would they be hunted down, like wild game.

Read what they write about us, who we are. That's what we have become. – Yes, and it's true. Now our eyes are opened. How we've been lied to. By those over there. They've ruined us. – If only we'd known. If only we hadn't gone along. If only we'd defended ourselves. – If only, if only. How? And now it's too late. We've been beaten. – Are we bad just because we've been beaten? Worse than the others? If others have committed crimes, must we pay for them? – Yes, and three times yes. The sins of the fathers shall be visited on the children unto the third and fourth generation. – It's not true. It cannot be true.

★

The voice of Barrès. The remorseless voice of Barrès: "The hour we waited for is here. I raise a prayer of thanks to the dead of 1914-1918, to the dead of 1870, 1815, 1814.

"Germany's feudal façade has collapsed. Revealed behind it is a nation of seventy million, burning to resume its life and regain its former predominance.

"They do not feel they are defeated. Every German

says: they are not defeated. They threaten with the Bolshevist bacillus. They try to dupe us with their misery and the Bolshevist peril. But the German people detest Bolshevism. We know it. This so disciplined country they understand only as industrial hierarchy, as the domination of the economy by the state. We understand, completely! We reject this new mix of pleading and threats. What does it mean? Wilhelm and his cronies give us to understand that they are prepared to bury us, like Samson and the Philistines, beneath the rubble of civilisation. Ah! The house of France, which in the noontime of their success they were unable to destroy, shall withstand even their defeat.

"The German façade has collapsed. The seventy million are revealed, a Company Limited betrayed by its Board of Directors. They want to evade their responsibility by striking down the Board of Directors.

"No! For five whole years I cried out every day: Have trust! Hope! Now I call out: Be careful, mistrustful, on your guard.

"The German is no democrat. The Devil's stronghold has fallen, the Devil remains. They have great qualities. Their great qualities could not hold firm against success. For reasons as clear as day, they degenerated to a belief that they could rule the world. Now, amid defeat, the horror stares them in the face.

"For the next twenty years their country will have no capacity to do us harm. But in twenty years it will again arouse itself.

"See how they beg today! Today! Tomorrow they will thirst again to fall on us. Prussian imperialism, the whole world's foe, must be subjected to the implacable law of justice. The German nation, awakened from its evil dream, must be liberated from it.

"I stand on the Rhine, look out over the Rhine: everywhere relics of ancient Roman life, centuries of advance and defence of our civilisation into the Rhine valley. Our thanks to those who strove here, our gratitude, and the firm resolution to continue and complete their task.

"Before the war we demanded three years of military service, heavy artillery, munitions. We demand of the Peace Treaty clauses that will arm us and secure us.

"So that we do not have to pray for another Miracle of the Marne, we must prepare the natural defensive line of the Rhine. For two thousand years Galloromans and Germans have fought over the Rhine's left bank. Every generation senses anew the need to possess it.

"Faced with a bloc of eighty million Germans invisibly uniting, forty million French men and women will live in a constant state of utmost peril. We want to come together with our ten million Belgian and Walloon brothers in arms, and bind the populations of the Palatinate, of Trier and Cologne, to our cause. The roots of these populations must form a dense mesh that creates a strong dyke, from the height of which a free people can keep watch on a deep and dangerous Germany below."

STRASSBURG, I MUST LEAVE THEE

Amid processions, flags and music, Jakob, the solemn unprepossessing druggist from our little town, made his way along Hoher Steg. His runny nose was evident, but not his euphoria. For Hanna, a tasty sight in her chic fur coat, was walking at his side. She wore high shiny boots, and pinned to her chest was the little bouquet of violets Jakob had presented to her at Gutenberg Square. There the violets sat, not as the song says *with humble brow, demure and good*, but, in Jakob's eyes, proud and strong. He still wasn't exactly sure why they were actually in Strassburg, but he had suspicions.

With a great deal of effort they made it through to Broglie Square. The crowd's excitement was mounting, there were so many people they had to push their way along the walls of buildings. Hanna stopped outside the former Officers' Casino. A doubled picket of sky-blue uniforms with steel helmet and bayonet stood at the entrance. No need for lengthy enquiries about her lover: he's not here and no one knows anything. But she lingered close to the entrance and observed the comings and goings of officers and orderlies. He must have gone in there. He sometimes mentioned the Casino to her. What was the point of standing and looking, she was freezing, Jakob was beside her. They left. She had no idea where to go, a dog that has lost the scent. So she took her Jakob by the arm and let him lead her out of the crowd. Every eating place was full. They wandered around until one o'clock, then found places in a warm restaurant by the railway station, where they ate and sat a long while. Then they were once again outside the Mairie, pulled along by an enormous throng. The Fireman's Brass Band was playing. Cheers when *Hans im Schnakeloch* struck up. Everyone sang along, Hanna squeezed up to Jakob, she stood there like a guilty person, didn't sing, he knew what was going on inside her. At the end a man roared out of the crowd up to the balcony: "Now us has all that us wants." Thunderous applause.

As they drank coffee at the Piccadilly around three o'clock, people nearby laughed as they told how the comedian Haniel was fooling around at Kehl Bridge. The Swab compelled to go across down he had to a T. Hanna looked at Jakob, whispered: "I want to go across."

They rode out on the tram, down Schwarzwald Street,

past the Commissariat and the vast complex of fortress and esplanade, barracks, to Kehl Gate. A broad prospect opened up, docks and industrial buildings. More and more people were streaming along. The tram conductor grinned: "All heading for the bridge, Haniel's there."

They approached the Rhine. Rolling levels with withered grasses, few trees. Whoops and shouts already from afar, that swelled at intervals.

How glorious it had been, the entry of troops along Hoher Steg and into the city, officers riding along flag-decked streets through a storm of jubilant cheers, cavalry flourishing sabres, sombre infantry in steel helmets, greatcoats fastened back over the knees, the thump of heavy boots, rumble of canon, droning aircraft overhead.

Here was old River Rhine, wide and smooth. Two strong bridges linked the banks, it wasn't far to cross. But now you couldn't see the entrance to the pedestrian bridge. The whole access road was besieged by a mass of humanity that as it neared the bridge became a single black clump. With difficulty a narrow lane was held free to allow access. A few people were moving through. These were Old Germans, expelled, heading to Kehl on foot.

Hanna pushed forward. She made it to the ruckus at the start of the open lane. A regular folk festival was in progress, lots of children and youths, hawkers going around with French flags and cockades, which occasionally were flung after one of the expelled, onto the luggage or even onto the bridge, and then the little flag went drifting down the Rhine. Confectionery, hot sausages were on offer. Leaflets and pictures were distributed. One particular leaflet became attached to the expelled, in the way many plants hook their seeds onto passing men and beasts so that they can be carried onward. The leaflet was printed in French and German, and had a black border of mourning:

"Announcement of death and last testament of Wilhelm of Hohenzollern, called Wilhelm II, Kaiser of Germany"; he was also called "bloodletter and former Kaiser of all the German states". In several places the "testament" aroused laughter as it was read out. Even the children listened eagerly, and when the signal was given for laughter they shouted and jumped, that was their role.

What were they laughing at? Here's what it said:

"From my legacy I bequeath to my family the shame of my glorious past together with responsibility for all my crimes. To my comrade Hindenburg, all the nails he caused to be hammered for my benefit. To Ludendorff, my big wooden sword" (How the children howled). "He may use it to scare away sparrows (*hurrah*). As General, I offer to the entire Fire Brigade of the capital all my numerous uniforms on condition that they must be worn during Fasching. To my confederates, a straitjacket with a certificate signed with a tiger's claw in recognition of their excellent work in support of the King of Prussia. To naturalists, the right to list me under the most bloodthirsty creatures of every species. Given at Potsdam with no other regrets than the lost throne and the veneration of a stupid mob. – Wilhelm, currently on the run."

The expellees entered the narrow lane.

Many had believed they could hide away, or rely on victor's clemency. But even if the victor showed clemency, their own neighbours did not. So here they were on the move, day after day since the first entry of the troops, and every day more. For vengeance sniffed out ever more of them. Envy, malice had free play, a rampant plague of denunciations. You can vent your feelings on the friend of yesterday. You can effortlessly inherit all he has. It was mob rule, it demeaned the population. People clung to lampposts and leafless trees to scream mockery at the emigrants.

Citizens and Soldiers

A population is a marvel to behold. It can be jubilant, rejoicing at its liberation. It can show itself for centuries obstinate in resisting serfdom. But it can also rise up like a sea that once lay calm in its bed and fructified the land with its breath, it can overspill its banks and in a hurricane hurl debris and devastation across that same land that once it fructified.

They had to make themselves ready between dawn and midday. Just as the beaten army on its retreat had to leave behind everything that could not be carried, and carried swiftly, so the expelled had to leave behind all their fixed property regardless of its extent and composition, and were allowed to take away only what they could carry in a bundle, a case, a sack. Which was not to exceed a given weight.

There goes a professor. Pursued by the crowd's mocking laughter. Why? The old man carried nothing but five umbrellas and a little briefcase. What else he should take he had no idea. Others stumbled slowly along with wife and children. Everyone had some baggage, the men often in sacks. At some points the crowd fell silent. No one knew who this one was. Not everyone left on foot, some took the train and were dealt with on the other bridge.

Across the flowing waters, on the Kehl side, a small silent crowd waited to receive them, peering as they approached. Nurses provided first aid services. This was the spot past which fugitive Lieutenant Heiberg had been shoved by the throng not two weeks before. He came harried from the rear, the concert of whistles no longer reached his ears, he was across, on German soil, he became faint and lay in a barracks among many others, all around him groans, children screaming, women weeping.

The revolution, a bequest of the war, sat now in the form of soldiers and civilians with red armbands at wooden tables, checked papers, issued some, steered the expelled onwards. Day after day the barracks were the stage for outbreaks of despair, and for every kind of grief down to a speechless feeling of annihilation. Some gazed cheerfully about and sighed with relief that now they were on home ground. But there were also well-dressed men and women, no doubt officials, teachers, who stepped into the emergency barracks, observed the conditions, joined the queue of those waiting to have their papers stamped.

There, see that lot sitting in civvies and army greatcoats, with red cockades and armbands, it's all their fault. Grave, calm, even friendly and sympathetic, these simple men at their task.

With the same hatred, thirst for vengeance, grimness with which the educated and well-dressed back there had glared at the howling mob and had to suffer their scorn, they observed these calm men to whom they must present papers. The Soldiers' Council men scribbled and stamped, heads lowered. They were not well practised at writing. The ladies and gentlemen as they waited looked down at them with hatred. Their hatred of these was greater than their hatred of the mob back there. Their hatred was unbridled. They looked down on the Soldiers' Council men like wolves about to bite the neck of a sleeping lamb.

Hanna managed to press back through the crowd, she pushed on down to the riverbank, Jakob following. She wandered slowly along the narrow riverside path, dense with people. Some trained binoculars on the opposite bank to see how the expelled were being received and directed, watching in curiosity, sensation-seeking as at a circus, filled with malicious glee as the ones over there vanished silent and bowed into the barracks with the red flags.

By a leafless clump of bankside vegetation, Hanna pulled her fur collar tighter, she stared at the long yellow strip of sand in the middle of the river, awoke from a dream and said in a toneless voice to Jakob: "Let's go."

With what yearning towards those vanishing over there, torn from her.

HERE ENDS VOLUME 1 OF
NOVEMBER 1918: A GERMAN REVOLUTION

ADDENDA

The following episodes, cut from John E Woods' 1983 English translation of Volume 2: *A People Betrayed*, mostly pursue the fates of characters introduced in Volume 1. Two other cuts – a digest of American history from the *Mayflower* to Woodrow Wilson; and a novella-length storyline centred on the writer Stauffer – are not included here.

Some of the storylines in the Addenda are pursued, in part, in the Woods translation – in particular those concerning Hilde-Bernhard and Anny Scharrel. The omitted passages presented here may therefore seem somewhat disjointed. They are nevertheless offered so that keen readers of Döblin with access to the Woods volumes may at last find the full text of *November 1918*.

> A Returnee
> [APB p. 31]
>
> Maurice Barrès
> [APB pp. 202 and 271]
>
> Obscure goings-on in Cologne
> [APB pp. 204 and 245]
>
> The Pharmacist
> [APB p. 226]
>
> The Pastor
> [APB p. 234]
>
> Anny Scharrel
> [APB p. 516]

A RETURNEE

An elderly Procurator from the little town where First Lieutenant Becker and Lieutenant Maus had spent the final days of their time in hospital had waited all through the War for his missing son, who, like so many other Alsatian lads, was rumoured to have gone over to the French. When troops led by General Gouraud entered the city, the Procurator was standing near Schirmecker Gate and – saw his son.

Several days have passed since Gouraud's entry. And so the Procurator, blessed with this joy, felt no temptation to monitor closely all the weighty orders, decrees, revocations to which the city of Strasbourg had become subject, nor the varying extent to which they were put into effect. Instead he invited his son to pay a visit to his little paternal town, and the son's colonel granted him two days' leave. And so off we go with the two of them to that little forest-girt place, leaving the charming misty city of Strasbourg to its lanes, alleys, squares, to its flower and vegetable markets, to its covered arcades, to its suburbs of Königshofen, Kronenburg, Schiltigheim, Ungemach, Ruprechtsau, to the meandering Ill and the River Rhine, on the justified assumption that anyone with the right means can peruse those decrees at leisure.

Rumours of the lost-and-found son had spread through the little town. So when they arrived – Procurator in his familiar civilian grey, son in the uniform of the liberating army – a crowd already thronged the bleak station forecourt. A delegation from the Provisional Town Council stood freezing on the platform. Two young ladies wrapped for winter, surrounded by many older ladies, presented huge bouquets together with a few barely intelligible words – to the Procurator for his steadfastness, and to the son for his valour.

A lovely festive procession formed up that took in the entire assembled crowd, at its head dear little schoolchildren who kept being elbowed aside, then policemen clearing a path into town for the reunited couple (it was only a three minute walk). Behind the two heroes came the red-nosed delegation, the mummified maids of honour, the Red Cross ladies and the simple masses later depicted as The Public, who were in fact various unemployed persons.

Numerous gaunt dogs joined in, to the surprise of the heroic son treading again the soil of his native place. These had once belonged to private families, some to officers' families, or were barracks hounds uncared for since the withdrawal on Wednesday 13th November. The private owners had kicked the creatures out on the grounds they could no longer be fed. "Take up your staff, and be off into the world," said these owners male and female, often tearful. "We ourselves have no food; you're old enough to stand on your own feet." A vigorous struggle ensued between owner and outcast. The dog didn't understand, it knew nothing of coupons for fat, bread and meat, there was a howling outside the house, the familiar front door that, to its bafflement, remained shut. At last it realised: they don't want me. And when they now joined in the procession, it was because they had spotted their former owner in the crowd and meant to reclaim him, walk alongside, just like the father with his lost son.

When it reached the Procurator's house, the procession dispersed. There were several cheers for the returnee and the French army, then everyone fled from the cold. Hard-hearted ladies and gentlemen were beset by barking leaping tail-wagging pets. The chronicler is in the happy position of being able to confirm that, on this morning, many a despondent private dog was restored to its old home, partly borne along by the general joyful mood,

Citizens and Soldiers

and partly on the consideration that now, surely, those promised trains would arrive, bringing wine and grain.

*

The dear little old town in which we now find ourselves is, in terms of age, no second best to radiant Strasbourg. Here even Frankish and Saxon emperors had held court within the walls, and hunted in the gloomy forests. Later the town was unable to rise higher than the production of hops. No one knows why. In one respect, it's true, this was a blessing for the town: since it made no effort to activate its ancient legal title to welcome the German emperor within its walls, it was spared the pain of the dethronement and the tumult of revolution as experienced by the citizens of Berlin.

Among the crowd that forms this guard of honour we notice a lone lanky invalid. He has a sticking plaster over his left temple, and a thick dressing over his mouth, as if he's just had a tooth out. We press a hand to our brow and think back. This man, standing so anonymously in the crowd, is already known to those who experienced here the week of revolution. Slowly a scene with a stool emerges, he climbs on, they see the small crowd watching him make a speech in a narrow street, in his hands is a newspaper, he reads from the *Strassberger Post:* "Shreds". That was on 11th November. They see him in another scene: he pushes through a mighty throng, it's Revolution Day in the market square, an old Prussian general struts alone along the sidewalk, no one salutes him. The lanky man is the local Pharmacist, he's made his way to the speakers' platform with its red flag flying, and he orates, and orates. Oh dear, several asked themselves at the time, will this end well, will he be able to answer later for all those words that come pouring from his capacious mouth?

Here we have the answer. When the revolting German soldiers departed Alsace, he received a blow to the left temple. A second blow, an uppercut to the region of the left upper jaw, rendered him for some time incapable of speech. This occurred on the day the French security troops entered Strasbourg, Thursday 21st November. The human eye can discern no link between the two events. The blows were foretold in a letter on Wednesday 13th November, the day the German regiments withdrew. The following Wednesday, the 20th, when in Berlin the revolutionary Fallen were being ceremoniously laid to rest, he was favoured with a letter addressed to "Pharmacist So-and-so, purveyor of filth, revolutionary". Again he was advised of mutilations to his limbs. The police showed a curious lack of interest, in either the letters or himself. Nervously he observed a shift in the public mood. On Thursday 21st November, as he was opening the shop, it happened. He was assaulted in the pharmacy. He was grateful to the assailants for their choice of location, where bandages and his little Druggist colleague were on hand. So here he is in the crowd, bearing no grudge, and hoping for good weather.

★

The elderly Procurator is sitting with his son in his big old-fashioned dwelling. The office is closed today. The Chief Clerk has not foregone the chance, when he hears the apartment door closing, to emerge from the file room into the corridor dressed in his frock coat and, touched with emotion, to hold out his hand to the son whom he knew as a little boy. Then he took his leave.

In the living room the son stands, steel helmet in hand,

before the flower-wreathed picture of his mother between the wall clock and the sideboard. He doesn't move. Behind him the father, head bowed. A sob can be heard in the doorway. It's the old housekeeper.

Then the son makes a decision, places his helmet on a chair, the housekeeper enters, takes the helmet, the son speaks kindly to the loudly weeping woman, who has covered her face with her blue apron. He unfastens his belt, takes it off with all the attachments, unbuttons the jacket, asks where his green loden jacket is. "It's all there," the father nods. The housekeeper brings the jacket, they sit facing one another in the bay window, which in summer is green and shady. The son in a thick fleece jacket and puttees and military boots, he's still the soldier. He asks after former teachers, the father waves a dismissive hand: "Across the Rhine."

""Who actually is still here? Zittel's gone, and the headmaster, that old Caesar enthusiast who made, or intended to make, excavations in Alesia, where Vercingetorix fought."

The father is frankly amazed: "You can remember this – after Gallipoli, after Syria, after the Somme?"

"Yes, just imagine," the son smiles, with an ironic twinkle. (How, for goodness sake, do the people here actually envisage Syria or Constantinople and Gallipoli? Why actually should we let them gobble us up whole?)

"But the war, this Hell you had to go through."

The son, at ease: "There were nice days too. Some good memories, wonderful amusing things. Could all have been worse. But I for one shan't let my war memories be stolen from me by patriotic hogwash. None of us will be up there on a granite plinth. No sir. I see great times coming, father, for stonemasons and sculptors. And medals will rain down. With thanks from the Fatherland.

The Fatherland so highly venerated thanks those who are worthy of even more veneration: us, so long as we're alive, and those who are no longer around. You wait, father, they'll prate like blazes over every little chap and peasant lad – as long as they're dead. As for us who are still alive, I foresee something else. But I suspect we'll make our voices heard."

The Procurator nervously stroked his white moustache, murmured: "Interesting views."

As the housekeeper spread the white tablecloth, she looked across at the bay window, the father, the son. Her face quivered with emotion in every little wrinkle. The son noticed her tender gaze, called her over, they exchanged greetings without formality.

The father: "There are such curious fates. You know the cabinet-maker Jund, the young fellow who built the bookcase, your library? He was a solid chap. You got on well with him."

"Of course, Jund. Where is he?"

"Never came back. Not yet, anyway."

"With the Prussians?"

"Nothing at all is known. We thought he might be with the Foreign Legion, but no Jund has turned up so far. His wife is on tenterhooks, not knowing if he'll come or not. But not what you're thinking. Across the road from her there's a tinsmith, a sharp fellow, did well for himself in the war, he hitched up with her, and now he's bought up all kinds of property left by the Reich Germans, and the two of them are doing well. And Frau Jund is wondering if her husband will come back. Not exactly looking forward to it."

The son stared into the distance, head propped on his hand. The Procurator was puzzled but happy to see him deeply serious.

The son: "So that's how it is here. We too shall wait. We shall settle scores. Even if Jund never comes back, we are back. Don't believe, father, that everything will go on as before."

Barbara set out wine on the table. She had smartened herself up and called happily across to the bay window: "Counsellor! M. René!" She was substituting for the mother.

A LITTLE MISCELLANY, ALL KINDS OF EVENTS
There's no sign of peace in Trier, to the dismay of a visitor. People in Cologne get up, telephone, and lie down to sleep. Meanwhile they busy themselves with things they can make nothing of.

MAURICE BARRÈS IN TRIER

Maurice Barrès, the French writer, attached himself to the Americans, who reached Trier on 1st December.

His dream was that all land to the west of the Rhine which now belonged to the Germans should be attached once again to the culture of his own country. He researched like a diver who descends to the bottom of the sea and there discovers a shipwreck, on the hunt for clues to ancient attachments. He yearned for any sign of Celto-Romanic life.

So on a cold December morning he is standing in the street of this German diocesan town. No sullen grumbling crowds as in Metz, gazing on as the hated occupiers march away, nor the delirious joy of Strasburg. Alienation, emptiness, danger. Field kitchens rumbling one behind the other, regimental music, a few youngsters.

He sat uneasily in one of the few open restaurants for a meal with a journalist, a bald Lorrainer who had latched on to him. He tapped him on the arm: "So, you were right." The Lorrainer: "I hope I still know my Germans. You thought they'd feel liberated, like the Alsatians and us Lorrainers. Whatever were you thinking! Here they're honest to goodness Germans, however many Roman remains are uncovered from Augusta Treverorum."

Barrès: "The fact is, they all feel they must keep their voices down. So what do you make of it, for God's sake? Orders from above? Or is it genuine?"

The Lorrainer was surprised: "Genuine! And the most natural thing in the world. The Germans grieve at their liberation."

"Then I was right: they did identify with the Kaiser, the army, the war."

"Totally. You didn't believe it?"

Barrès, glancing at the waiter: "Does the fellow understand what we're saying? Please!" He gave a start, then continued quietly, eyes on the empty plate: "Are they poisoning us?"

The Lorrainer patted his hand and laughed: "You're a writer. Everything makes such an impression on you."

"But the consequences," Barrès glared at him, "what consequences do you draw from it? Where is it heading? We need this region. If we don't hold the Rhine frontier, we are lost. And with these people …"

The Lorrainer rubbed his bald skull. He sighed: "You're staying here today, maybe tomorrow too, keep your ears open, ask. I'll help you. It's all a matter of time. If France were to govern the Rhineland for a century, peacefully, then a transformation would be possible. I said: peacefully. For in war these people would set on France from the rear. A century or so."

Barrès: "Good. And is it thought possible that after this victory we cannot hold this region peacefully for a century?"

The Lorrainer regarded him gravely, head lowered: "Since I've spent my entire life under German rule, I can tell you: no. Hold, yes, but peacefully, no. You've spoken often of the probability of a reborn Germany. However you twist and turn: you can never live in peace with a defeated people – unless you absorb them all. And never, never – I can tell you this, Monsieur Barrès, with complete certainty, based on lifelong experience – never will Germany's defeated class, the Kaiser's family, the generals, the officers, the Pan-German league, abandon their thirst for revenge."

The waiter filled the soup bowl. They waited till he had gone. Barrès, huskily: "So? Then we must get rid of that class." The Lorrainer dipped the ladle into the hot tomato soup: "That's what the revolutionaries want – but you don't like that lot either."

"I have no faith in them. My dear friend, today you're quite horrific, you bring me to despair. What kind of perspectives are these."

"We have learned from the war. The first thing is, know your enemy's strengths. You must look facts in the eye."

Barrès played with his spoon, wiped the serviette around the plate: "Inconceivable, how the entire great German army marches in such a spirit back to its homeland. What will they get up to. We must remain dreadfully armed."

The Lorrainer began to eat: "Why think so far ahead. Much may turn out differently. Developments in Germany. Who has any idea."

Barrès: "I hope they will be weakened for a time by this revolution."

"There, that's also a perspective. And now let's eat."

★

Maurice Barrès is Depressed

During these days a young couple from Strasbourg, the Kössels, were staying in Paris, French at last. They had an old love for Paris, and now an understandable desire to take their new status for a stroll in France's centre and discover who they really were.

In Paris they found a sombre and strangely mixed mood: no rejoicing, no real excitement or relief, doubts and anxieties about the progress of the Peace Talks, and inexpressible sorrow for all the losses. Political antagonisms buried during the war now came into the open.

The young Kössels sought our Barrès. He had visited them, his loyal admirers, a short while before in Strassburg.

Barrès was working up lectures on the Celto-Roman Spirit and its spread along the Rhine. When they arrived he greeted them with the greatest cordiality. But his temples were now hollow, his mouth slack. "I am drained," he confessed, "I write this, but I'm playing the ostrich."

They were struck by his dejection.

"Have you looked around Paris, spoken to people, who, what do you hear, great joy, hopes, what? Well now, they have reason to rejoice."

Frau Kössel: "Why do you not?" The human weakness of this sparkling beloved spirit distressed her.

Barrès: "You know that Edmond Rostand has died. He was at the Armistice talks here in Paris. As Clemenceau drove up he climbed onto the car's footplate. That's how he got in. A few days later he was gone. He died as he wished. They found a poem on him. Listen: 'I wish only to see victory. Ask me not: what next? Next I wish for black night, a sleep beneath cypresses. Then I have nothing more to hope for, and nothing more to suffer. Vanquished, I could not have gone on living. As victor – I can die.'"

After a silence, Barrès added: "That was Rostand.

Blessed be his memory. Who could match him."

He rifled silently through the pile of manuscripts in front of him and drew out two sheets of newspaper stapled together. "Someone sent me this. Articles from the *Daily News* and the *Star*. You could do worse than read them. What are they about? An English military critic, formerly a general, Sir Maurice, expresses himself on the victory. He takes us by the ears, this gentleman, he really does. You see, if it was only the usual English carping about us, we could brush the matter aside with all the rest. But this is more, it concerns victory itself. Whether the Allies and Foch actually achieved victory. You are surprised. That's how far we have come."

Kössel: "I don't understand. Who is this Sir Maurice?"

"Not just anybody. He's well in with Lloyd George. During the War he was Director of Military Operations in the War Office, was then dismissed, I don't know why. He informs us bluntly that the German Army was not beaten by Foch, it simply fell apart. Almost by itself, from internal causes. The German Army, he says, was on the day of the Armistice no way inferior to the Allies in either numbers or other military aspects. But German discipline, their slave morality, could not withstand the test. 'The discipline of free men overcame the discipline of slaves', he says, word for word. And here, underlined by me – one moment, I shall translate: 'An army cannot fight without a nation behind it. Since the courage of the German nation had been thoroughly worn down, army and navy both collapsed.'"

Kössel: "For God's sake, what is he driving at?"

Barrès cast a long slow look over him: "Dear friend! I hope he does not know. It would surpass all imagination if it turns out he does know. He robs Foch and all the Allies of their wonderful victory. He negates (heed me now) he negates our very own victory. The Germans collapsed for a reason quite independent of us. Nothing to do with the Foch offensive of 18th July, with Ludendorff's black 8th August and so on. The German Army remained undefeated."

Resignedly he shoved the sheets back under his pile of manuscripts. "What more could the Germans want? It's actually an invitation to the Germans to start up again at a favourable moment. We need not expect a war of revenge, as I had feared, but a continuation, after a period, of this same war, once the hinterland has been cleansed. Our defeat is already certain."

Frau Kössel looked back and forth between Barrès and her husband: "You exaggerate, Monsieur Barrès. Admit it. That is not the actual point of the article."

Barrès bowed: "I am afraid, dear lady."

Kössel rubbed his brow: "No preliminary peace treaty has yet been concluded. We don't even know the terms of the peace treaty. This article must serve a certain political stance. You said Lloyd George is there behind this Maurice."

"Close by, at any rate." Barrès smiled, now visibly more relaxed and cheerful. His young guests saw the warrior awaken: "But why do I talk of this to you, my friends? You must think me a hysteric. We've won a victory. Not, thank God, on paper, but in reality, at the hands of Marshal Foch. Apart from which – your presence here is proof."

Frau Kössel said: "The Allies won, and we shall remain French. Of this I am certain."

Kössel smiled, Barrès kissed her hand: "Charmed, Madame."

"Ah," he sighed, "these Germans are like Grimm's Hans in Luck. Everything falls in place to favour them. They have caused us so much suffering. Then on our side appears this President Wilson and hands over his Fourteen

Points. They are his conditions; they have to be accepted. Now they almost treat them as their own peace conditions, held out to us. Then following on their defeat, on their palpable and obvious military catastrophe, they have a revolt, and look, they blare out that it was revolution that ended the war and denied them their victory."

Frau Kössel: "But please, Monsieur Barrès, nobody in Germany or elsewhere could believe such a thing."

Barrès stiffened his easy posture and spoke as softly as he always did when deadly serious: "Not believe it? The Germans won't believe it? Not believe that their Hindenburg and Ludendorff remain undefeated? Madame, they have not deviated for one second from this belief, and they will grow ever stronger in their belief."

Kössel: "But let's leave them to it. We have the actual victory."

Barrès frowned, doodled with the pencil and said quietly: "Right. Like I myself, you have the notion that to every victor belongs a vanquished. But a guilty person must first be condemned. He must admit his deed. Or the evidence must force him to it."

Kössel: "Well, that's what they're doing."

Barrès cut him off with a weary gesture: "Let's drop it. First came Wilson with his lovely ideal very difficult demands, and now the other allies, the English, to make our lives easier after this bitter war that has laid waste to our land. Oh, our wonderful Marshal Foch. How I grieve for him."

And then Barrès laughed a hearty youthful laugh: "A strange folk, these English. Even during the war their generals never believed they had won. You had to take them by the nose. Now they cannot forgive Foch for winning in 1918, because their thesis was that victory would not come until 1919, with the entry of millions of

Americans. So I would like to make a concrete proposal: let's hold back our joy, await for the entry of those armies, and then we shall win, really, pitilessly, without mercy and with no possibility of misunderstanding."

They turned to personal matters. Frau Kössel's delicacy and tenderness towards Barrès, now restored to cheerfulness, delighted her husband.

★

Obscure Goings-on in Cologne on the Rhine

In Cologne on the Rhine, on Monday 2nd December 1918, some elderly men rose from their beds grumpy and still sleepy, made a slow morose business of pulling on socks, yawned, changed the shirt, tugged warm Long Johns over the shins, and felt for trousers. In order to fasten the braces they sat down again, and yawned a while longer lethargically on the edge of the bed. Then they made a decision, and washed and combed with much snorting and wheezing. Then they had breakfast, and set about their usual work.

By midday they were more cheerful, lunch tasted good (two found fault, but ate nonetheless) and two ate without reservation. It all slid down nicely, and warmed them a little, so the inevitable happened and they soon sank into a snooze.

The snooze had to be a short one, for they had much to do, and did it. Now and then one of the four telephoned the other three, who paid careful attention one after the other to what he said, and were in complete agreement. Later on two of them abruptly took leave of their wives. The other two were bachelors, and glad to have sorted out their evening.

Around eight o'clock– they'd been awake now for twelve hours, if you discount the one-hour lunchtime snooze – the four of them were sat together in the modest simple lodging of one of the bachelors. They still wore the socks they'd pulled on that morning. In one case these had sagged and now overhung the edge of the boot, but he hadn't noticed. Two had fastened the socks with tight rubber bands. They were elderly men, and knew nothing of the newer garters that would pour in from the West in massive quantities in the coming years. The fourth man was plump, and each sock clung fast to a sturdy leg, as long as it was new. Later of course they would loosen and sag. His socks were still holding up well, as the nervous man (it was his apartment) ascertained by means of several discreet glances.

They conversed long and seriously, as was their way and as befitted this late hour when in fact they felt themselves at their perkiest. They drank the tea of which the nervous man poured a continuous supply. He had nothing else to offer. None of the men smoked, out of respect for the host's apartment.

Two hours passed, towards the end of which they began slowly to breathe again – something of which they became gradually aware. At the same time they felt warmth in the arms and legs, heaviness in the head, a painful pressure in the hindquarters that had already been too long burdened. None of it bothered them. But the conversation was clearly drawing to a close. Before the eyes of all four, like a magic emblem, stood a bed and a quiet bedroom.

One after the other they stood up, stretched legs. Then they were near the door, and went.

Back home they opened the door quietly, removed hat and coat, and sat on the edge of the bed to remove

[THE PHARMACIST]

outer clothing. They went out once more to attend to the call of nature, then slumped on the bed.

Underpants and socks were next. The man whose socks sagged was glad they came off at once. The two with the rubber-band garters were relieved when these were removed, they looked at the welts on the legs and tugged at the bands to make them bigger. The plump man did as he had done since childhood: massaged one leg with the other to roll the socks down. When it went smoothly he was happy. At the same time it was a sign he should change socks.

All four pulled on a nightshirt, settled under the blankets and endeavoured, breathing deeply, contented, to fall asleep.

Lots of images floated through their heads, from the day, the departed day, until they knew no more of themselves and in their sleep, their dreams, went changeable ways that troubled them not at all, some deep, some high, and sometimes conversations happened.

The conversations in the apartment of the nervous bachelor had covered schooling, measures planned by the government, etc.

*

[THE PHARMACIST]

... Overhead the tall wounded Pharmacist and his wife sat on the sofa with their arms around one another, drinking coffee. She comforted him, and allowed herself some tricks she had never dared before, to which he reacted with indignation. She dipped a rusk into his coffee and made him snap for it. The game made her tremendously happy. It was a child's game she used to play with her younger sisters when she was meant to be feeding them, but tormented them instead. Because the child had always to snap higher, she called it the "fish game".

She practised this on her tall husband. She enjoyed it enormously, and it was a condition of his being accepted back into her good graces. He went along with it. He was back, but into what graces. How he had to snap, sitting beside her on the sofa, after the bait she held now left, now right, before his mouth. She unwound her arm and held the bait higher over him. She laughed, ran away. He caught her in the middle of the room, there ensued an excited romp that she would not allow to get out of hand. She ordered "Enough", put on the spectacles that bobbed on a string and signified Housewife. Then they drank more coffee and eyed one another, he exhausted, lurking, on the offensive, she in a defensive trench, behind the barbed wire entanglement of a conversation about housekeeping.
...

*

A Westphalian snuffles around in Berlin

While our jaunty General was still sitting in the Major's office and working there – meaning, showing off his general's uniform – he was not a little astonished, but certainly little pleased, to receive another refugee from the Alsatian garrison town that he'd once ruled over: the former garrison Pastor. The jaunty General absolutely did not relish being greeted by anyone as his companion in sorrow. But the clerical gentleman was truly delighted. He almost flung his arms around the General, and when this proved not possible, instant patriotic tears too drew no reaction. In due course he could no longer fail to notice the old man's complete indifference, and he addressed him with a few consoling words.

The General's face darkened, he retreated behind a desk and asked: "What's business do you have here, you? Aren't you from Westphalia? Taking a little look around the capital? Widows' soirées and so on. Left the wife at home?" In earlier times the General would never have directed such questions at a pastor, now it was just the way he was.

The Pastor came to attention: "I intend, General, and this is the purpose of my visit, to place myself at your disposal. When the ship is sinking, all hands must come on deck."

"Sinking, that's good," the General laughed, "now that we're all of us drowned already. Sir, have you not noticed?"

The Westphalian now realised the difficulty of the case. He had come here as if called. He unleashed his whole armoury of clerical tricks with remarks now grave, now reproachful, now admonishing. This had the effect of causing the General, from his position behind the desk, to regard him with some amusement. Before it became clear to the Westphalian that he had, so to speak, brought the house down, the Major stepped in, the General was happy to hand his visitor over, and the scene changed.

Major and Pastor engaged in a lengthy round of pensive handshaking. A wide-ranging discussion followed. Yes, the Pastor wished to place himself fully and totally at their disposal. But he just said this. It wasn't full and total. For the private interests of the clerical visitor were also entangled in the matter. These concerned the furniture he'd left behind in the garrison town, and now he was stuck in Westphalia and had no way to retrieve it.

The furniture, and how he could retrieve it and his books, had in the last few weeks become an *idée fixe*. His wife scolded him, in a manner scarcely tolerable even for one of Christian patience, for not having noticed in time that it was all over and so he hadn't gone looking for a furniture van and a week earlier there were lots of vans to be had or he could at least have brought the silver and the jewellery boxes and the jewellery with him.

Oh, the Pastor felt his guilt, and to the extent possible poured oil on the billows of the raging wifely soul. He had at that time, more's the pity, spent the last days before the collapse in a state of mindless melancholy, and only when it was too late and he emerged from it did he confide his dire need to a First Lieutenant's Widow. But then all the talk and general hullaballoo around them completely drove the furniture problem from his mind. In the panic he'd given no thought to silver and jewellery. The widowed female had suggested that his only duty (the Pastor's wife being long since back in Westphalia) was as her protector. And so he'd gone with her to Strassburg. But he daren't divulge this to his wife, and why, when you're already a sinner, should you cause another already suffering creature even more suffering by confessing another sin. And he'd sat drinking with the Widow in the Aubette, then let her lead him astray to a music café across Kleber Place, and danced with her. Yes, all true and hard to believe: in those days of darkest calamity, with the Fatherland lost and his furniture now booty for the enemy, he'd gone dancing in Strassburg with a saucy First Lieutenant's Widow, in a public venue.

Now he was in Berlin. He did not, as he had feared, relive any of his nefarious exploits in Strassburg, and the name Strassburg was now synonymous with Den of Iniquity. He had come to Berlin firstly in order to evade for a few weeks the enfilading domestic fire, and secondly to check out the possibility that in Berlin, the centre of events, he might perhaps find a way to retrieve his possessions. There must be someone in Berlin who would know how to travel through neutral foreign territory and make contact with the janitor couple in the small town to whom, before he left, he had entrusted the apartment.

His wife, unencumbered by legal niceties, berated him for placing unreliable janitor people at the head of the household. For she considered them unreliable, and alas had good reason. For the couple had already discovered the pastor's wife's jewellery hidden in the sideboard under a pile of serviettes, and at the moment the only piece of any value, a necklace, was gracing the neck of the mother of a liquor dealer in Schiltigheim, to whom it had been offered at a favourable price.

Being so poor, the Pastor accepted an invitation from an unmarried colleague and friend from student days to stay with him in the east of the city. There the Pastor lived in a grey monotonous wilderness of tenements, afflicted with something like fear and seasickness. He looked for open receptive faces, but encountered only grim denizens of the big city, and his own project made no progress. But he could not make up his mind to go home.

He did receive one happy piece of news from the colleague he was staying with. In the parish there dwelled an elderly lady very active in Christian welfare, a Frau Becker, whose son had been in action and was now back home seriously wounded. And if I'm not mistaken, the Pastor thought, this Frau Becker's son lay latterly in that Alsatian military hospital and was transported back here. How happy the Pastor was. He had only the haziest memory of this badly wounded officer, had seen him only once or twice early on, had never managed to speak to him. But now he really wanted to head over and see Frederick Becker. He had to postpone the visit: Becker's mother, whom he was able to contact quite quickly, proved very reluctant. She wanted to spare her son this visit, and said that Frederick was still too ill.

BRINGERS OF ORDER
Some men in Cologne discreetly threaten that the Rhineland will renounce.
A general in Kassel also thinks of threatening, but will first sleep on it.

THE MEN IN COLOGNE HAVE COME THIS FAR

The men in Cologne had come this far.

Each had, in his own way, stuffed socks into boots, braces were in place, waistcoats sat buttoned, and watch chains with their trinkets dangled. Each had to check that the tie was neatly knotted, and the general appearance – not pretty, but that was of no consequence these days - was grave, ponderous, as the situation demanded.

Once again they placed feet in boots, bent to tie laces. There. Makes the face red, brings colour to the cheeks. Nicely shaved? So-so, it'll do. Nothing to be done about hairs in the ears.

And now, for God's sake, to arms! On with coat, hat, umbrella. It must and shall happen.

Two climb with wife and big children – for youth too must be in attendance – into the tram, which conveys them with the desired despatch to their destination. The third man lives close by the destination. So he goes on foot, conscious of his superiority, slows down later, collar turned up, two streets to his goal. He has no need to drum up courage. He is certain of the outcome.

The men met as agreed downstairs in the brightly lit building with the restaurant business. A mean little room was reserved for them, containing six chairs and a coat stand. They were pleased to find themselves all here, to shake hands even before removing their coats. They kept coats on, because the room was unheated. Whether upstairs was heated would, they all agreed, be confirmed later.

Yes, they had reached this point, thanks to their own efforts and the dauntless spirit of sacrifice demanded by the times, which, having hauled November along day by day like a coal dray, now sidled unwearied up to December, which had already arrived at its fourth evening. The three men acknowledged this with great appreciation, and felt themselves well served.

They moved about full of confidence in the mean little space that for today was called the Committee Room. They were aware of sensations to which normally they paid no attention – under the shoulders, in the legs, the back. They had a constant feeling that the tie was slipping.

There was noise outside of people arriving, chatter, laughter, shouts. Cars drove up.

"Lots of people," a voice spoke into the room, "must be hundreds."

Two of them beamed. The third stood by the coat stand trying to write on his knee. The other two, doing nothing but freeze and stamp their feet, took pity and handed him a fountain pen and a briefcase to lean on. He accepted these. In doing so he opined that it was dratted dark for writing; but there was nothing they could do about it and it wasn't their fault. They regarded with bemusement the tiny gas flame that seemed about to go out at any moment. One said: "They're economising."

The other whispered: "It'll do, for a Committee Room."

The third man was under no obligation to accept their prompting to write, but he considered it a point of honour, and wrote.

Now came the mighty clang of a bell. The three men exchanged looks. They debated hastily whether to leave coats and hats here, but decided to go up first and take them off there.

On the stair they heard from youngsters that upstairs was heated. They dithered. Then the youngsters helped them off with their coats, which were carried back downstairs.

The three men – slightly dazzled, timid, ingratiating, ill at ease – stepped into the room. They were greeted with loud cheers and applause. The room was indeed heated.

Five more grave gentlemen were already sitting at the committee table. Handshakes were exchanged. Now the men could sit. It had happened. No more twinges in the legs, under the shoulder. They simply sat, waited, and were there.

As one of the five gentlemen made a speech, roaring, waving his arms, the three men felt more at ease, and were occupied with staring ahead, moving the head from side to side, which was easy enough to do but offered no new perspectives.

But then gradually the tie regained its function, and fingers made their familiar way to the throat to tug and twitch. They stared straight ahead.

Then it was their turn, and each man said something.

One after the other, beneath a massive wave of handclapping, they sank back onto the chair and kept quite still. They just sweated.

It was the crisis, this outbreak of sweating. They were on the mend, were saved.

As they wiped their faces they regarded one another. They hadn't imagined it like this. Now they felt thoroughly at ease. They spotted their relations and youngsters in the hall. And suddenly it was all over.

Down there everyone stood up with lots of shouting.

The podium was stormed, and they had to respond to questions. Shoulders were clapped, congratulations offered. It was amazing, honestly. They'd never intended this.

Only the man with the slip of paper was in a tizzy and declared as they went down the stairs: it went exactly as he'd intended. They were happy to go along with that.

The resolution the man with the slip of paper had read out was a protest against Berlin's plans for schools, and mumbled something about the Rhineland renouncing.

Then, back in the Committee Room, all felt in their backsides the after-effects of sitting on rough wicker chairs. One limped and complained of pins and needles in his leg. All three, as they stood with coats and hats out in the street breathing fresh night air, said: "Thank God."

And having had their fill, they all betook themselves off home as quickly as possible and crawled into bed. All those who had attended the meeting did likewise.

★

[PARIS – FEARS AND SINS]
...
[WARRIORS, COMPLAINING PHYSICIANS, AND MERRY WIDOWS]
...

ANNY AND RENÉ SEEK MUTUAL CONSOLATION
Around this time lonely Frau Scharrel lay sighing in her lovely Paris apartment. She felt impelled to visit Bernhard's grave in the cemetery. She prayed. Then back to bed to recover, in order to succumb once more to her sweet lascivious thoughts.

Her two nieces have clearly benefitted from their stay in Paris. The twins dream of returning soon, and Frau

Scharrel suspects that they both experienced more than they have let on. Yes, I know, it's youth, the body in bloom, but I'm no longer blooming.

She thought often of Hilde, with mixed emotions. She knew nothing of Becker, she assumed Hilde had extricated herself from the snares of the obsolete affair with Bernhard and would now enjoy new and lovely experiences in Berlin. How she envied Hilde – and hated her. Bernhard had already become Anny's property, he had suited her taste, and what's more, how nice, he was a relative. Hilde had broken in on her placid joy, stolen Bernhard away – and was the real cause of Bernhard's death. Hilde had once again dragged the now gentle and pliable Bernhard away, and then callously thrown him aside. And now she had run away to Berlin.

The curate, her confessor, helps her and admonishes her. She keeps busy with her legal cases and waits for Life to cast new shiny shells and colourful stones onto the beach. To discuss one of her cases, the old Procurator from the little not so distant town turns up at Frau Scharrel's. His kindly manner and good cheer does her good. He is jovial, and for good reason, and when they come to speak of personal matters recounts quite naturally the miracle of his son's reappearance. Tears spring to her eyes as she hears this, she recalls her fallen elder son, and another who has been torn away. The old Procurator notices the tears, he knows her history, and when he next visits he brings her the unexpected pleasure of his son's company – the young man is stationed here with his unit. Frau Scharrel invites René to tea that afternoon.

She is amazed, as was the Procurator, at the young warrior's earnestness. Ah, how different they are returning than when they set off. There'll be a new world once they're all back. Let's hope it won't be too wild.

Anny and René seek mutual consolation

We know the tastefully furnished rooms of this apartment. We watched Hilde looking for Bernhard again after fifty-five months apart. Young René sits in his uniform by the black marble fireplace under the mirror. There's a porcelain vase on the mantelpiece, it's painted, muscular men from antiquity throw balls to one another.

Frau Scharrel has a full dark-complexioned face. It's narrower than it was four weeks ago. Her chestnut hair is combed high, parted in the middle, a few grey hairs can be seen in the waves, she knows they add to her attraction and makes no effort at concealment. A yellow silk scarf is draped loosely at her throat. She sits in a red armchair next to the little tea-trolley with its teapot and cups, and on the lower shelf little cakes and cigarettes. She has a sturdy bust, the black dress clings, a white lace collar lies on her shoulders.

René crosses his legs in their black leather spats. He's unfamiliar with ths kind of situation, taking tea on his own with an elegant society lady. He was too young for such things when he went off to war. She asks about his home town, and how he managed to return. And when the heart is full, the mouth runs over, and so he tells her, staring before him – she studies the sleek dark-blond skull as he keeps his head down – he tells of the business with the tinsmith Jund. There was a man who deserted the town with him and never came back; he's his Doppelganger. – Why Doppelganger?

Now René comes out with his secret, of which his people back home know nothing. Well, back in August 1914, when he went to the other side, he too left behind someone with a dress and long hair. He thought of her all through the war, but of course had no way to write to her. She was the daughter of a German schoolteacher.

"And?"

Citizens and Soldiers

"Her father's gone across the Rhine, taking her with him. But she left a letter for me with a girlfriend, in case I should ever come back – she brought me the letter just last week. She writes: greetings, wishes me all the best, but of course she's going off with her father. And she's engaged to a teacher, a war-wounded man she got to know."

"Hm."

"Frau Scharrel, don't think I'm unhappy about it. For who knows how we might have got on after four and a half years."

Frau Scharrel: "After four years, especially years like these, everything looks so changed."

René: "Anyway, about the tinsmith Jund. I knew the stationery shop owner Kauss in our town very well. The husband has still not returned, up to this day. His wife let Jund make advances to her, and at first I was terribly enraged because the woman couldn't wait and was to some extent assuming his death. I actually thought of intervening, on behalf of my friend."

Frau Scharrel, inwardly amused, arms spread wide on the arms of the chair, said: "Well, what happened?"

"I confronted them right away, as soon as I came back and wasn't aware how things stood. I gave the wife a piece of my mind. She cried so much it almost frightened me. She thought her husband must have sent me, he must be following hard behind, and I let her go on thinking that. There must have been loads of howling and teeth-chattering in the days that followed. Well, then the letter from my former girl friend was brought to me, and because I had no one to talk to about it, and I was in such a state, I went to Frau Kauss to take out my anger on her. She was just the same, literally went out of her mind when she saw me. She thought her husband would be back next day, and was in total despair, and I was to stand by her and she showed me her little child to soften me up."

"A little child? Whose was it?"

"Her husband's, Kauss, who else?"

Frau Scharel shrugged: "How old is it?"

"It was lying in the cot."

Frau Scharrel: "Maybe it was very small?"

"Yes, very small, a baby. Ha, I never thought. You think the baby is tinsmith Jund's?"

"That's exactly why the woman showed you the child. She wanted you to take pity on her because of the child."

René, astonished at himself, shook his head: "It never dawned on me. But even so I didn't do anything to her."

"And because your own flame is away and no longer your concern, you spared this woman."

The soldier sat there, grave, half boy, half man, thinking how to answer. "I thought, there's enough misery in the world already, my own mother passed away while I was gone, I really don't want to add to it."

They sat and smoked cigarettes in silence. Frau Scharrel felt truly grateful for the dispensation this young man brought into her home, scaring away the evil spirits that still disported themselves there. If only he's not soon redeployed elsewhere.

They began to chat. He had lots to tell about the Foreign Legion. She heard about Spaniards who served in the Legion during the War. There were over ten thousand of them, famous people, among them students and writers. René told how he had stood in a trench on the Somme next to Pujulà I Vallès, a writer. He spoke of Pere Ferrès-Costa, another Catalan, who brought a whole unit of Catalans to the Front, they were at Amiens and Arras, and in 1915, during the advance, many Spaniards were left lying, Ferrès-Costa among them.

René felt in his breast pocket and pulled a crumpled

scrap of paper from his wallet. It was the beginning of a madrigal written by Costa, a song to Santa Catarina. René read the first lines: "*Si gosava, Catarina, us faria una canço, mes ja se que ma complanta no us agradaria, no.*"

René had learned a little Spanish, and loved the Catalan spirit of freedom. He hummed a tune they had sung later, at Verdun: "You shall not pass, and if you were pass through it would be to a heap of ashes. *No pasaren.* They earned lots of medals. One regiment got seven Palms and a Légion d'honneur."

Smooth and beardless, with not a wrinkle, was René's tanned face. Little pouty lines ran down from the corners of the lower lip. The chin was soft, but the young man had a defiant way of tossing back his head and jutting the chin; she thought: it's still soft. But his hands, strangely, were very strong and bony. And as he spoke of medals in the IV. Army, his voice echoed the steely roar of the trenches, and his eyes took on an unexpectedly chilly glint.

She said: "We had a soldiers' and workers' council here."

"Pah," he said, "they were copying the Russians. We shall rid the world of war." Again he jutted his weak chin. She was worried that if he were suddenly to ball his fists and bang them on the table, the teapot would fall off. René concluded: "Wilson will soon be in France. We'll see from there what's to happen next."

She looked into her cup, stirred the tea. "You young people – are you also a little religious?"

He answered gravely: "People have duties now. When I think of those poor Spaniards who fought alongside us, I'm ashamed to own anything and sit here drinking tea with you. Truly, if we leave things as they were in the world, we'd be common tricksters."

He felt at ease. Who was this woman? His mother,

his girl friend? She found him childish and delightful in his dispassion. To establish how religious he was, she came to mention a marvellous story told by people here concerning the Chief Rabbi of Lyon, Abraham Bloch. He was a man over fifty, serving with the frontline troops. In battle a soldier beside him was hit. The rabbi held out a crucifix to the man, who was Catholic, and as he did so he himself was brought down by a bullet.

Curiously, all René said was: "Bloch? I had a friend in Gebweiler, a famous footballer, who was called Bloch."

She nodded: "You knew him?"

"Why, what became of him? I saw him briefly once, afterwards, but might be mistaken."

Frau Scharrel: "His forename was David, from Gebweiler?"

"What happened to him? Fallen?"

She glanced to the side: "Firing squad."

"What?!"

"He was a daredevil."

René, breathless: "He stood with us."

"He had himself flown in behind German lines, to gather intelligence."

"They caught him?"

"My gardener told me. It was months ago. My gardener knew the young man."

As René sat and his face twitched (she was watching him) a plan developed in her. She had lost her son. What would it be like to draw this young man to her? Put him in the dead boy's place. I could be his auntie, his godmother.

When darkness fell they went out and watched a play. It was a comedy.

★★★

NOTES

page

7 The essay is translated at https://brooklynrail.org/2019/03/fiction/On-Cannibalism

11 Only two reviews: Reprinted in the valuable collection by Ingrid Schuster and Ingrid Bode *Alfred Döblin im Spiegel der zeitgenössischen Kritik* (AD reflected in contemporary criticism), Francke 1973.

54 Bordeaux: where in 1871 Léon Gambetta rejected the surrender by the Paris Government of National Defence.

64 Wilhelm **Sollmann** (1881-1951): SPD politician; along with Konrad Adenauer helped suppress revolutionary disorder in Cologne. Albert **Schulte** (1877-1952): SPD head of the Worms Workers' and Soldiers' Council.

68 'O Germany...' '...raging storm': from patriotic song *O Deutschland hoch in Ehren* composed in 1858 by Englishman Henry Hugh Pierson.

87 Paul **Göhre** (1864-1928): SPD, State Undersecretary for War in 1918. Heinrich **Schëuch** (1864-1946): Prussian War Minister from October 1918 to New Year 1919, a rare high-ranking Alsatian in the German military.

117 'must leave': from an early 19th century folksong, the basis of Elvis Presley's "Wooden Heart".

118 'O Strassburg': from an 18th century anti-war folksong.

118 'holy flame': from *Heil Dir im Siegerkranz*, the national anthem of first Prussia and then the German Reich.

120 KRA: Kriegsrohstoffabteilung (War Raw Materials Department).

122 cobbler's globe: glass globe filled with water, used in pre-electric times to focus diffuse sunlight in a dimly-lit workshop.

133	Friedrich Rückert (1788-1866): Poet, linguist, Orientalist, popular for anti-Napoleonic writings.
134	Prince **Max** (1867-1929): cousin of the Kaiser; Chancellor 3 October to 9 November 1918. Friedrich von **Payer** (1847-1931): Parliamentarian, vice-chancellor November 1917 to October 1918. Georg von **Hertling** (1843-1919): Chancellor 1 November 1917 to 30 September 1918.
135	Fr. Lehne, pseudonym of Helene Butenschön (1874-1957), prolific writer of formula fiction.
140	'What do the trumpets...': jolly jingoistic military march, words by Ernst Moritz Arndt (1813) to the tune *Frisch auf, ihr Tiroler, wir müssen ins Feld* (Up, up, Tirolers, we must go to the wars).
142	'No there's a limit...': Schiller: *William Tell*, Act 2 scene 2.
160	Old Fritz: Friedrich Althoff (1839-1908), influential in Prussian cultural and university politics, and in Germanising of the annexed territories of Alsace-Lorraine.
164	Kaufhaus... Küfer...: These two lanes are now once again Rue de la Douane and Rue des Tonneliers.
183	'Ah how could...': 18th century folksong popularised by published scores in the 19th century.
185	Johannes Tauler (~1300 – 1361): Dominican theologian and mystic in Strassburg.
189	Army Det. A: formed in September 1914 after the Battle of the Marne from scattered remnants of reserve divisions. It was headquartered in Strassburg.
190	'Forlorn forlorn am I': maudlin late 19th century folk song from Carinthia.
191	Jean-Baptiste Kléber (1753-1800): Strassburg-born general in the French revolutionary army.
203	Jacques Peirotes (1869-1935): elected (by universal franchise, a rare feature in the German Reich) to the

Second Chamber of the Regional Assembly in 1911, and to the Reichstag in 1912.

206 Alvin Köbis, Max Reichpietsch: young sailors hung for their part in the summer 1917 naval mutiny.

208 Antigone: Tr. R. C. Jebb 1893.

212 love-death motif: see the bilingual libretto at www.murashev.com.

220 Tauroggen: In December 1812, Prussian General Yorck signed a convention with Russian General von Diebitsch in this border town (= Torege in Lithuania), whereby Prussian forces would detach from Napoleon's armies. Before news of Napoleon's disaster at Moscow arrived, the nervous Kaiser had wanted Yorck arrested.

235 Naumburg: railway junction between Weimar and Leipzig, SW of Berlin.

241 thin transparent brew: 'Bliemchenkaffee'. Saxon coffee culture was famous since the late 17th century. Saxon dialect had many terms for the thin brew necessitated by hard times, through which you could see the flowery base of the cup.

249 'For You, O Democracy', in *Leaves of Grass*.

285 'That's how we live...': North German folk song popular in World War I: "Brandy at morn, beer at midday, nights with a lass we frolic away". Sung to the Dessauer March.

290 hurdy-gurdy man: In the absence of state aid for war wounded, many became itinerant hurdy-gurdy men. Arno Holz wrote a poem which ends: "Between the shiny organ pipes, / painted bloodily on porcelain, / my battle-scenes do the begging. / Even children show no interest! / The snow on my nose is melting. / My peg-leg hurts." (*Phantasus*, 1916 ed, VII/11. Tr. CDG.)

291 Sergei Sazonov, Russian Foreign Minister 1910-16.

297	Mephistopheles: *Faust* lines 1990-92, tr. Walter Arndt.
308	Brutus **Molkenbuhr** (1881-1959): soldier, advocate of the Soldiers' and Workers' Councils; Hermann **Müller** (1876-1931): Social Democrat politician; Hugo **Haase** (1863-1919): pacifist, co-founded the USPD (Independent socialists) in 1917.
312	Emil **Barth** (1879-1941): significant figure in the revolution about whom little is known. Luise **Zietz** (1865-1933): co-founded the USPD.
328	Wilhelm Solf (1862-1936): current State Secretary in the Foreign Office.
333	Barrès (1862-1923): nationalist writer and politician; argued strongly for return of Alsace-Lorraine.
337	Guy de Cassagnac (1882-1914): writer.
338	Gerbéviller, Nomény: French villages destroyed by German troops in August 1914, with civilian massacres.
339	Friedrich von Bernhardi (1849-1930): Prussian general, in 1912 wrote *Germany and the Next War*.
340	wars: Prussia's successive victories over Denmark, Austria and France. Karl von **Wedel** (b.1842) was Statthalter in Strassburg 1907 - 1914. (He actually lived until December 1919.) Johann von **Dallwitz** (1855-1919) was Statthalter from 1914 to 18 October 1918.
344	'woe of all mankind': Goethe's *Faust* I, line 4406.
346	§9b BGB: This section of the Civil Code dealt with the place of residence of a soldier.
349	Markich: Sainte Marie aux Mines, west of Sélestat.
360	**Vauban**: 17th C military engineer. **Daguerre** invented the daguerreotype. **Magenta**: in 1859 France beat Austria. **Falkenhausen** (1821-89): Prussian general during the 1870 war.
367	Scheidermen: pun on Philipp Scheidemann, who on 9 November declared the German Republic.

367	Fraktur: Germanic typeface 𝔉𝔯𝔞𝔨𝔱𝔲𝔯.
377	Hamant: Some 1500 people, mostly German soldiers, were killed in the disaster.
386	beefsteak: the English.
386	'They shall ne'er': 1st verse of *Die Wacht am Rhein*.
389	*Le regiment du Sambre et Meuse*: composed following the 1871 defeat. *Chant du depart:* revolutionary song revived during WW1.
392	Hartmannsweilerkopf: A hilltop (Vieil Armand) NW of Mulhouse, much fought over in WW1.
401	*Guten Morgen, Herr Fischer!* 19th century operetta in one act. No reference found to *Eine vollkommene Frau*. *Der Schockschwerenöter*: 1918 silent film by David Oliver, who acquired Union Theatres in 1915, and in 1917, with Ludendorff's backing, helped found UFA. (In UK exile in 1940 he helped A. Korda found Denham Studios.)
405	Sesenheim: Goethe fell in love with the Pastor's daughter Friederike Brion, making the village north of Strassburg a place of pilgrimage for his devotees.
405	'like a flower…': Heine's returning lover prays that his beloved remain forever so pure and fair.
409	In 1076, excommunicated King Heinrich IV had to humble himself before the Pope at Canossa.
409	'I don't know…'; 'Once a boy…': from Heine's *Lorelei*, and Goethe's song of rejected love addressed to Friederike Brion.
415	*Athalie*: Racine's last tragedy, made into an oratorio by Handel.
418	Krafft is the central figure in Rolland's ten-volume novel.
418	Dinant: On 14 August 1914, German troops massacred 674 civilians in this Belgian town.

418	Joseph **Caillaux** (1863-1944): as prime minister 1911-12 held secret meetings with the German government. Louis **Malvy** (1875-1949): wartime Interior Minister. After the war, sentenced with Caillaux to 5 years exile. M **Almereyda** (1883-1917): anti-militarist accused of being a German agent. Father of film director Jean Vigo.
420	Charles Andler (1866-1933): Strassburg-born French Germanist scholar.
421	Rudolf **Schwander** (1868-1950): Alsace-born mayor of Strassburg from 1906, in October 1918 named Imperial Commissioner for the Reich Territory. Karl **Hauss** (1871-1925): Strassburg-born state secretary in the Ministry for Alsace-Lorraine.
424	Jean Jaurès (1859-31 July 1914): anti-war socialist leader, assassinated as he was about to form an alliance with Caillaux.
431	*Hans im Schnakeloch*: Comic Alsatian folk song, on the lines of a pig in clover who has everything he wants.
433	As a fund-raising ploy, people paid to hammer a nail into a propaganda pole.
443	'Jund': When he wrote this scene, some time after completing Volume 1, Döblin mistakenly named him the cabinet-maker, while earlier Jund was the cuckolding tinsmith. Cf. page 465.
448	Sir Frederick Maurice (1871-1951) was sacked for publicly accusing Lloyd George of misleading Parliament.
465	Jund: cf. page 443.
465	**Pujulà** (1877-1962): Catalan writer and fervent Esperantist. **Ferrès-Costa** (1888-1915).